The Welfare of the Dead

The Welfare of the Dead

by

Lee Jackson

WILLIAM HEINEMANN: LONDON

Published in the United Kingdom in 2005 by William Heinemann

1 3 5 7 9 10 8 6 4 2

Copyright ©Lee Jackson 2005

William Heinemann
The Random House Group Limited
20 Vauxhall Bridge Road, London, SW1V 2SA

Random House Australia (Pty) Limited
20 Alfred Street, Milsons Point, Sydney, New South Wales 2061, Australia

Random House New Zealand Limited
18 Poland Road, Glenfield
Auckland 10, New Zealand

Random House (Pty) Limited
Endulini, 5a Jubilee Road, Parktown, 2193, South Africa

The Random House Group Limited Reg. No. 954009
www.randomhouse.co.uk

A CIP catalogue record for this book is available from the British Library

Papers used by Random House are natural, recyclable products made from
wood grown in sustainable forests. The manufacturing processes conform
to the environmental regulations of the country of origin

Typeset in Sabon by SX Composing DTP, Rayleigh, Essex
Printed and bound in the United Kingdom by
Mackays of Chatham Plc, Chatham, Kent

ISBN 0 434 01248 3

PROLOGUE

I DESCENDED FROM the dome of St. Paul's, back down
the iron staircase. I found the view utterly dispiriting.
There was nothing to be seen from the Gallery but fog:
even the spires of the City churches were mere pin-
pricks in a billowing sea of brown filth. I can hardly
now recall why I went up there at all. It was, I suspect,
a ridiculous attempt to calm my nerves. Indeed, the
only thing I remember is the iron-work of the staircase
itself. As I followed the spiralling steps, I had a peculiar
fancy that I was caught in the coiled springs of some
giant clock. I wondered, was it possible that both I and
my fellow sight-seers, travelling up and down in weary
groups of two and three, were ourselves simply parti-
cles of dust, the dirt in the ancient, rusting mechanism?
It seemed rather fitting.

Then the bells chimed four o'clock. I stopped upon
the stairs to gather my thoughts. I must have looked
somewhat distracted, since a solitary woman, who was
ascending up to the Gallery, gave me a queer look. She
was a woman of middling years and wore a capacious
old-fashioned crinoline. She merely looked away when
I nodded back to her.

Dust to dust, I thought.

I stepped aside, leaning against the railing to let her
proceed. Of course, there was still very little space

between us. Her skirts rustled over my feet as she passed and her face flushed crimson. But she pulled up her skirts a little higher, all the same, to allow me a quick glimpse of her stockinged ankle. What do you think of that? A woman of her age and station baiting such a trap; it quite turned my stomach.

I see. Yes, we have little time. Pray, forgive me.

I made my way down to the nave, and tipped the attendant a ha'penny, much to his annoyance. Doubtless I had the look of a half-crown about me. Then I quit the place by the southern door, and stepped outside. It was far worse than up above: the fog had rendered everything dark and muddied. Believe me, if a man tells you a London fog is a romantic affair, he is a liar. Indeed, I felt as if I had wandered into a different element, in which it would have been just as natural to swim or fly, as to walk. I wrapped my scarf about my mouth, though it did little to remove the stink in the air.

'Sir?' said a voice by my side.

I peered about me, to find a little girl, a sweet-faced creature, a deceptively angelic countenance, perhaps thirteen years old. She sat upon the ancient steps in the dirt, her rust-coloured skirts spread out around her, a bunch of wilting violets and dried blooms in her lap. She reached down and held one up to me.

'Penny a flower, sir? Nice violet?'

I have a weakness for a pretty face, I admit. Please, do not blush. But she had the voice of a typical cockney street-child, quite belying her looks. Now, how did she speak? I cannot put it any better than *flaar* and *vi-let*, as if her lips were too slipshod and lazy to express anything more than a syllable or two at a time. Indeed, I do recall I noticed her mouth in particular; her lips were chapped and dry, fissured by the winter air.

'I do not want your flowers,' I said, pushing her hand aside; but I dropped a penny in her lap, all the same.

I carried on down the steps into St. Paul's Churchyard and then directly across the road, down Godliman Street. I knew the route well enough, even in the fog. In no time I stood in the courtyard, opposite the entrance to Knight's Hotel.

Now, it was a modest place; not what you might imagine, if you read the papers. An old stucco-clad town-house, pristine and decent as to its exterior, most likely the home of some prosperous merchant in the days of the Prince Regent. A whited sepulchre, mind you, like so much of our great metropolis.

I steeled myself and went inside – for the door was left open for visitors – and addressed myself to the owner. He was a large, round-faced swarthy fellow, whom, at the time, I took for a Jew. I found him seated behind a large mahogany writing desk, in the front parlour.

'May I help you?' he said, standing.

'Mr. Brown?'

'At your pleasure, sir.'

'I hope I have not called at an inconvenient time.'

'Not at all, Mr. . . .'

'Smith. An acquaintance mentioned your establishment to me,' I replied.

'I see.' He said, nodding, but eyeing me cautiously. 'An acquaintance.'

'I should like a room.'

'A room?'

'If you please? I would very much like room fourteen. Is it vacant?'

'Fourteen? Oh, sir, that is one of our best. That will be a difficult matter . . .'

'How much?' I asked.

'A half-sovereign, my dear sir. No more than an hour.'

'Here.'

I handed him the coin; I had it ready. He looked at both sides, admiring the gold. It was, I do recall, rather tarnished. I half expected him to bite it.

'It is legal tender, I assure you. '

The wretched man chuckled to himself, and pocketed it. 'I mean no harm; please, I mean no harm,' he said, opening a drawer in the desk, and retrieving a key, which he handed to me. I noticed that he had dirty, stubby little fingers, his nails quite gnarled and unpared. 'You will find it on the first floor, up the stairs, to the left.'

I took the key and thanked him. He did not smile, as such, but there was a curt insolence about him, something in his manner. I do not have much time for such specimens of continental manhood, I confess.

No matter.

I turned about and ascended the stairs. The landing was lit by an ornate, gilded gaselier, five descending circles of spurting flames, an abbreviated *Inferno*. It shed light upon the small brass numbers attached to the lintel above each door. In consequence, I found the door, fourteen, with no difficulty. I knocked and walked in.

It had the appearance of a makeshift, rather ill-kept *seraglio*, for which I was quite unprepared. Indeed, it was as if some poor relation of the great Haroun al-Raschid had decamped from Bagdad to the City of London in some distant decade, and speculated upon a job lot of velvet drapes. For there was no inch of the wall not smothered in crimson cloth, hung at jaunty angles from the picture rail, the ceiling, from every conceivable corner. And upon the bed lay a pile of Arab cushions, heaped into a veritable mountain. And, as if it were the most natural thing in the world,

4

leaning back upon the cushions, lay a fair-haired young woman. She did not seem at all surprised by my arrival. I placed my hat down upon the dresser that stood by the door.

'You were expecting me?' I asked.

She smiled, and gestured to the ceiling above the door. There hung a small, wired bell; a neat arrangement – merely the servants' bell in reverse. Doubtless the proprietor had rung it, upon exchange of the key.

'I see,' I said.

She made no reply. I removed my collar and tie, and placed them both by the hat.

'Are you mute?' I said.

'I speak when I'm spoken to, darling.'

Flaar. Daar-lin. How remarkable, I thought to myself, that this flower should have bloomed in the sound of Bow Bells. A Bow *belle*! But she was a beauty, dressed in a night-gown of fine white silk, that clung to her body as she reclined upon the bed. Her arms were bare and milk-white, her hands dainty and graceful; her smile as sweet as any I have ever seen. An awful shame.

And then?

Why, I locked the door.

PART ONE

CHAPTER ONE

IN THE CHILL, fog-bound air of a November evening, a carriage descends the slope of Pentonville Hill, its twin lamps gleaming in the mist. It is a small, black brougham, a very ordinary conveyance, with a ruddy-faced coachman in the driver's seat and two passengers within. Upon the outside, the coachman shivers in his great-coat, even as he flicks the reins and mutters words of encouragement to his horse; inside, the two passengers, a young man of twenty-five years or so, and a woman some ten or fifteen years older, appear just as uncomfortable. They sit in silence, side by side, rugs draped over their legs. The man rubs his hands together, in a vain effort to fend off the cold. The woman, meanwhile, keeps her arms close to her body; her hands are concealed deep within a rabbit-fur muff.

'An awful night, Mr. Langley,' says the woman at length, as their carriage pulls past King's Cross station. Her breath is visible in the cold air. 'Can you make out the time?'

'I believe,' says the young man, peering towards the clock-tower of the station, 'it is just past the hour. Although I cannot be utterly certain.'

Richard Langley looks apologetically at his travelling companion. Mrs. Melissa Woodrow is an attractive woman, her face plump but not fat, her eyes a deep hazel, complemented by the autumnal colours of her clothing. Even under several layers of clothing and a heavy dolman mantle, she visibly shudders, unaccustomed to venturing out in such temperatures.

'You should have stayed at home, ma'am.'

'That,' she replies emphatically, 'would never do. What would Miss Krout make of us, if neither my husband nor myself were to greet her?'

Langley nods and looks out of the window. The carriage rattles on, and he can just make out the Gothic grandeur of the Midland Grand Hotel.

'It is awfully cold, though, is it not?' he says, breaking the silence between them. 'Even for the season.'

'It was good of you to accompany me, Mr. Langley, really it was. I was so glad you happened to call.'

'I will catch the train home from Euston Square. It is no matter. It saves me the expense of a cab.'

'Still. I really cannot imagine where my husband might have got to, truly. And now we are late for the train.'

'The trains are never on time, ma'am. Not in this weather.'

'Yes,' she replies, 'I suppose that is true.'

The brougham turns right, cutting across the Euston Road, and round the gas-lit perimeter of Euston Square. It is a peculiar place in the fog, the great Doric columns of the monumental Euston Arch half-visible, resembling the portico to some lofty Peloponnesian temple, transplanted into the heart of the metropolis. The driver directs the brougham through the gates, and pulls to a halt upon the asphalt fore-court. Patting the horse's flank, he gets down from his seat and taps on the carriage window. Mrs. Woodrow pushes down the glass.

'Pardon me, ma'am,' says the driver, 'but I can't get down to the platforms; it's blocked solid. I think the train's in already.'

Mrs. Woodrow peers out of her window. The approach to the platforms is crowded with a line of vehicles, not least an endless parade of cabs, both hansoms and clarences. Around them, black-suited, peak-capped porters tend to all forms of luggage, with heavy suitcases and hat-boxes flying hither and thither. The cab-men themselves, meanwhile, seem to sit back in their seats, above the hurly-burly, watching the procedure with great disinterest. They certainly pay no heed to the third-class passengers who appear in straggling groups, dragging cases, small children and other encumbrances, searching for a cheaper means of transport. There is little hope for them: only a shifting wall of fog and not an omnibus in sight.

'Oh! It is no use,' exclaims Mrs. Woodrow, 'I shall have to go and look for her.'

'Please, ma'am, you will catch your death,' replies her companion. 'Allow me.'

'Are you sure, Mr. Langley? I do have a photograph of her, if you are sure you do not mind?'

'Positively, ma'am.'

'You are too good, Mr. Langley. I will make sure my husband hears of this. Now, one moment—'

Mrs. Woodrow breaks off from speaking, producing a russet-coloured plush reticule from under her coat, and delving inside it. After a few seconds of confusion, she pulls out a small photograph and hands it to Langley.

'I am sure I will only be a minute or two, ma'am,' he says, peeling off the rugs from his legs, and opening the carriage door.

Richard Langley walks to the station building, colliding with several confused ladies and gentlemen who seem quite unaccustomed to the opacity of a 'London particular'. At length, finding the entrance, he proceeds through to the Great Hall, which serves both as the station's concourse and waiting-room. Here, at least, the atmosphere is a little more transparent. In part, it is the gas-lamps that project above and below the first-floor balcony; in part, it is the sheer size of the hall, an airy chamber some sixty feet in height, and twice as long. It is, moreover, light enough for him to look at the photograph entrusted to him by Mrs. Woodrow. It shows a bright-eyed young woman of about twenty-one years, with light-coloured hair, tightly chignoned, standing in her day-dress before a forest clearing, albeit one of the painted-canvas variety. He takes a look around the hall, but cannot see any likely girl. He proceeds, therefore, to the platforms and asks advice from a guard. He is informed that the Liverpool train has already arrived. Worse, it is plainly almost empty, except for an elderly couple engaged in a heated debate about the cost of porterage.

Langley returns to the Great Hall where, after several minutes of fruitless searching, he sees a woman, surrounded by a dozen or more bags and cases, standing by the marble statue of Stephenson that dominates the far end of the chamber. He takes another look at the photograph, and walks over to her.

'Miss Krout?'

She smiles a brief, nervous smile. 'Yes. I was expecting . . . I am sorry, but you are not Mr. Woodrow?'

'Ah, no. My name is Langley. Mr. Woodrow is detained elsewhere, I am afraid. But your cousin has a brougham waiting outside.'

'Does she? Oh, how good of her!'

'I fear your luggage will have to go separately. Can you wait, while I find a porter?'

'Of course,' she replies. 'You must excuse me, I should have arranged something myself.'

'No need,' says Langley, looking round the hall for an attendant. 'I confess, I thought I had missed you.'

'I do beg your pardon,' she says earnestly.

Langley smiles. 'No, no. We are late – do not apologise. I imagine you are exhausted, Miss Krout. It is a long way from Liverpool.'

'Even further from Boston, sir.'

'Indeed! Well, you are safe and sound now, rest assured. I expect you are looking forward to seeing London?'

'Yes, sir. Truly, I—'

'Ah, hang on, here's our chap. Boy – over here!'

The 'boy' who takes charge of the despatch of Annabel Krout's luggage is barely three or four years younger than Richard Langley. Nonetheless, he does not object to the description, and the business in hand is soon dealt with. In consequence, it does not take long for Langley to guide Miss Krout back outside to her cousin's waiting carriage. A few polite words are exchanged, and he cordially takes leave of the two women.

As for Mrs. Woodrow and her cousin, the cold night air forbids the customary ecstasy of greetings and exchange of affectionate familial bulletins, until they are both ensconced inside the brougham and wrapped in several layers of blankets. As the vehicle begins its slow ascent of Pentonville Hill, however, a litany of American relatives 'send their love', via the medium of Annabel Krout. In turn, Mrs. Woodrow replies with a host of family members 'dying to meet' Miss Krout, a veritable hospital ward-full of aunts, uncles, first, second and third cousins upon the brink of metaphorical extinction, scattered throughout the kingdom. It is only as they approach the Angel at Islington, the famous public house barely visible in the enshrouding darkness, that the conversation turns to other things.

'I trust the journey was not too awful?' says Mrs. Woodrow. 'Now, Mr. Langley said he found you all alone? Did I hear right? I do not know how things are done in Boston, my dear, but that is rather foolhardy for a young lady. I thought you had a chaperon, a friend of your dear father's?'

'Yes, ma'am, indeed, Mr. Johannsen and his wife; but I told them there was no need to wait on me, once we were off the train. They have rented rooms in a place called Bayswater, I think – is that far?'

'Not too far, my dear. Perhaps we may call on them in a day or two, if you think that would be agreeable. But please, do call me Melissa, won't you? We are flesh and blood, after all.'

'Yes, ma'am . . . Melissa,' replies Miss Krout.

'Good. Now, I only hope Jasper has returned home – we were delayed by waiting for him. You will have to forgive my husband, Annabel, he is so devoted to the business that he sometimes forgets all social ties. He is an awful beast, and I will tell him so when I see him.'

'Please, not on my account, cousin,' replies Miss Krout, anxiety in her voice. 'I would not want to start off on a bad foot.'

'Oh, Annabel, he will adore you, I am sure. Ah, now here we are at last.'

The brougham turns left, into Duncan Terrace, a narrow street just off the City Road, flanked on one side by lofty Georgian houses, and on the other by neatly kept public gardens protected by iron railings.

The coachman pulls to a stop and, once a man-servant appears by the side of the vehicle, the two women are swiftly ushered into the hall of the Woodrows' home. Coats are hung upon the coat-stand, the blankets taken away and despatched to some secret location. Mrs. Woodrow, meanwhile, acquires a few items of evening post, left waiting for her upon a side-table.

'Come up to the drawing-room, my dear,' says Mrs. Woodrow. 'You may as well see us at our best.'

The drawing-room, upon the first floor, boasts a roaring fire and a pair of comfortable armchairs arranged before it.

'Mr. Woodrow is still not home, Jervis?' asks Melissa Woodrow, addressing the man-servant who awaits instruction by the door.

'No, ma'am.'

She sighs with exasperation, placing the envelopes upon the mantel, and extending her hands towards the fire, rubbing them vigorously. 'He has sent no message?'

'No, ma'am.'

'Very well. Ask Mrs. Figgis to make some tea and toast, if you will. We'll take them here.'

'Very good, ma'am.'

Mrs. Woodrow watches the butler depart, and turns her attention to her guest.

'Jasper will be home soon, my dear, I am sure; then we can eat properly. Do sit down. And I expect your luggage will arrive shortly. But the cab-men are a law unto themselves, you may take it from me. They should know Duncan Terrace, mind you. It is a thoroughly respectable road.'

'It is much the same in Boston, with the cabs, ma'am.'

'"Melissa", my dear, please. Will you forgive me if I open these?' she says, gesturing at the pile of envelopes. 'It is just that Jasper likes everything to be dealt with immediately. He can be very particular in some things, when it suits him.'

'Of course,' replies Miss Krout.

'I know it is awfully rude of me, Annabel dear. I won't be a moment.'

Annabel Krout looks idly around the room as her cousin takes the envelopes to a small writing desk against the far wall, and slices into them with a paper-knife. It is a pleasant parlour, with a marble fireplace, and a great gilt-edged mirror hung above the mantel-piece. The furniture is a little gloomy perhaps, all dark mahogany and walnut, a little old-fashioned. But it is a comfortable, well-upholstered sort of room. There is even, Annabel notes with some satisfaction, a piano-forte. But as she looks about her, she happens to notice a peculiar frown upon her cousin's face as she opens her post or, at least, one particular item. Indeed, if she were more familiar with Melissa Woodrow, Annabel Krout would express some polite concern about the contents of the letter in question; but it is too early in their acquaintance for such confidences. Instead, she waits patiently while Mrs. Woodrow replaces it in the envelope, and continues with the remainder.

'Annabel, I think I might go and change,' says Mrs. Woodrow, once her task is done. 'I do believe these clothes positively trap the fog. Would you mind awfully?'

'Why, not at all.'

'The tea will not be a moment – do begin without me.'

Annabel denies that she would ever dream of doing such a thing; more exhausting smiles and pleasantries are exchanged, until she is left alone in the room. She sits still for a moment or two, and then gets up, idly running her hands upon the keys of the piano, taking care not to depress them. Looking at the pictures upon the wall, a number of prints of famous personages and painted rural scenes, she passes by the writing desk in the corner. The post is still lying there, and she recognises the small manila envelope that so perturbed her cousin.

It is perhaps indicative of a certain strain of Annabel Krout's character that she cannot resist snatching it up and opening it. The contents, however, surprise her considerably, both in their brevity and sentiment:

YOUR HUSBAND IS A FRAUD

It is so distracting, that she visibly jumps when the door opens behind her.

Fortunately, it is only the maid-servant, with a tray of tea and buttered toast.

CHAPTER TWO

A SOLITARY HANSOM CAB travels at speed along the Victoria Embankment. Of the two men inside, one is engaged in giving a rather voluble monologue, attempting to gain the attention of the other.

'And so, the man's in bed somewhere, laid up, sir, you see? And the doctor, he says, "I think you might drop a line, and have your wife come up." Because his wife's somewhere else, at home, I suppose. And the gent in bed, he says, "Oh, Doctor, you're always for such extreme measures!" Prime, isn't it, sir?'

The look upon the face of Inspector Decimus Webb, as he listens to his sergeant's verbal re-creation of his favourite cartoon from the week's *Punch*, says otherwise.

'I mean to say, you do get it, don't you, sir?'

Webb nods his rather jowly face, solemnly and slowly, in a manner that he hopes is calculated to prevent another word being spoken upon the matter. He takes his pipe from his coat pocket, and begins to fill it with tobacco. He has enough time to light it, before the silence is broken once more.

'And there was this other—' continues Sergeant Bartleby.

'Tell me,' says Webb, judiciously interrupting, as he begins to fill the cab with a pungent cloud of Latakia, 'what precisely the message said.'

'The message, sir?'

'The telegram. The reason we are progressing so precipitously towards Ludgate Hill.'

'I have it here, sir,' replies the sergeant, a little abashed. He reaches into his pocket.

'Just read it to me, if you please,' says Webb.

' "Knight's Hotel, Knight's Court, Godliman Street. Murder. Please come. I seek your advice. Hanson, City of London Police." Not much one can make of that, is there, sir? Must be a bad business, mind, to call us. The City boys like to keep things to themselves.'

'Indeed. They are fortunate we keep late hours at Scotland Yard. You know this Hanson fellow, Sergeant?'

'No, sir.'

'You know the hotel, by any chance, Sergeant?'

'Can't say as I do, sir.'

'Well, then it is a curious request. Let us reflect upon it.'

'Sir, there isn't exactly much to—'

'In silence, Sergeant. I think best in silence.'

Sergeant Bartleby opens his mouth to speak, but one glance at Webb is sufficient for him to close it again. Webb, in turn, takes another satisfying draw of smoke. If he thinks upon anything, it is that his tobacco-pouch is rather empty and that he must soon pay a visit to his tobacconist.

Webb's reverie is interrupted after a few minutes, as the cab turns off the great sweep of the Victoria Embankment, up New Bridge Street, then a sharp right into the narrow lanes that nestle in the shadow of St. Paul's. The great cathedral is, however, quite invisible in the fog; it is only when the driver of the hansom raises the trap in the roof, through which he communicates with his passengers, that the latter can be quite certain they have arrived at their destination.

Knight's Court itself is a remarkably quiet square, protected on all sides by tall buildings, shielded from the noise of the great thoroughfares around the cathedral. It is not so wretched a place as many London courts, and the houses that surround it, though divided into rented rooms, look smart enough to be the homes of decent working men. But one building, slightly grander than the rest, is marked out by the presence of a solitary police constable upon its doorstep. Webb and Bartleby follow his directions, and, in short order, find themselves in the hall of Knight's Hotel. They are greeted by Inspector Hanson, of the City of London force. At thirty-five years of age, he is a younger man than Webb, by twenty years or so.

'Hanson's the name, sir, Detective Inspector. A pleasure to make your acquaintance, if I may say so.'

'Likewise, Inspector. This is Sergeant Bartleby,' replies Webb, in an off-hand fashion, not even allowing a pause for the two men to shake hands. 'But perhaps, Inspector, you could begin by explaining why you called us here. I need hardly remind you that St. Paul's is not our jurisdiction, murder or not.'

Hanson frowns. 'Well, it's murder all right. I'm sure of that much. I telegraphed, sir, because, well, firstly I've been an admirer of your work for some time, since the Railway Murder, as it happens.'

'You are too kind,' replies Webb with a dismissive wave of his hand, although his naturally glum-looking face brightens considerably.

'Second, because I've a feeling in my gut about this.'

'In your gut, Inspector?' asks Webb, a teasing hint of sarcasm in his voice.

'I think it may be the start of something. And I thought Scotland Yard might care to hear about it sooner rather than later. Here,' he says, moving towards the door, 'come and have a gander, eh?'

Webb agrees, and the two policemen follow the Inspector up the stairs.

'You know what this place is, I take it?' asks Hanson as they come up to the landing.

'A hotel?' says Bartleby.

'No, Sergeant, not quite. It's more what they call a "house of accommodation".'

'A knocking-shop?' replies the sergeant. 'Well, I've seen worse.'

'It has quite a reputation, so they tell me. Attracts a slightly better class of—'

'Gentleman?' interposes Webb.

'I was going to say girl, but it amounts to the same. Ah, now here we are. Number fourteen,' says Hanson, waving aside another constable standing guard. 'Shall we? I assume you aren't of a nervous disposition, as they say, Inspector? Or you, Sergeant?'

Webb nods. Bartleby looks slightly less confident, but assents all the same. The inspector opens the door.

Webb surveys the room. It is lit by the dull gleam of a pair of oil-lamps, in dim contrast to the strong gas-light of the hall. There is a dresser, a wardrobe, a chair, a couple of cabinets; but in each case the wood is poor quality, old and chipped, the surfaces dusty with disuse; even the cheval-glass, which stands in a corner, has a crack in it. The principal item of furniture, however, is a large, wrought-iron bed that stands in the centre. In contrast to the shabby fixtures and fittings, the bed's mattress is wrapped in fine white linen and the sheets neatly pressed; the covers of the pillows and cushions, heaped against the curlicued iron-work of the head-board, are made of silk; the rug beneath it bears a finely woven, intricate oriental pattern.

The only thing out of place is the corpse of a girl, no more than eighteen years of age.

She lies prone on her back, atop the sheets, her head arched back over a pillow. It is not a neat death, for, from a gash deep in her breast, blood has seeped into the silk of her night-gown, colouring the fabric dark red, congealing around the curve of her stomach; and upon either side of her, the sheets are blotted with the faint, rusted impression of her body.

'Tell me,' says Webb, his voice quite dispassionate, 'when was she found?'

'At about seven o'clock,' replies Hanson. 'The, ah, proprietor, a Mr. Brown, became suspicious about how long a particular man had been up here.'

'How long was that?'

'Two hours or so. Brown found that the door was locked from the inside. He had to use his master key, so he tells us, at least. When he finally opened the door, the man had vanished – we can only assume through the window – and Brown found the girl, dead.'

'He went directly to the police?'

Hanson smiles wrily. 'Hard to say. I am sure he cleared out all the other girls and their gentlemen friends from the place. He denies that part, of course. Nor does he know the name of the man, so he says.'

'Do you believe him?'

'I don't know. For one thing "Brown" is just the name he goes by; he's a Greek, as it happens. Let's say I reserve my judgment,' replies Hanson.

Webb walks over to the window; it overlooks an alley by the side of the hotel. 'It is a considerable drop from here, if someone jumped. Not impossible, mind you. What do you make of it, Bartleby? You are very quiet.'

'I was thinking she was a fine-looking girl, sir, that's all,' replies the sergeant, looking at the girl's face.

'It would be a forgivable lapse if she were ugly,

would it? I asked for your professional opinion, man, not your sentiments.'

Bartleby straightens his stance.

'It's a knife wound, sir, that much is clear. Deep and all; it'd need a strong arm – a man's work, I'd be certain of that. Fairly precise too; no messing about with this one.'

'How so?'

'Straight through the heart, sir, between the ribs.'

'Anything else?'

'There's not much blood. I mean, there is, but it's not splashed about, not so much as you'd expect. And the sheets aren't much disturbed either.'

'I noticed that too,' remarks Hanson. 'Hardly a struggle.'

'Probably killed her stone dead. A blade through the heart – I suppose she would be hardly likely to wrestle with him,' continues Bartleby.

'No, I suppose not,' replies Webb. He frowns and turns to address Inspector Hanson. 'This is all very intriguing, but I am sure you'll forgive me if I don't understand why this regrettable business is a matter for the Yard.'

'Because I am afraid there's more to it, Inspector,' replies Hanson. And, without another word, he peels back the drapes from the nearby wall, to reveal a connecting door, half-open, to the next room. He beckons Webb and Bartleby to follow him.

It is a smaller, plainer, wall-papered room, a little narrower than room fourteen, but large enough to contain a similar run-down assemblage of furniture. It too boasts a smart iron bed-stead, with clean sheets and linen, only this one is unmarked by blood. But, in the lamp-light, there is something on the bed that causes both Bartleby and Webb to stop in their tracks. It is the body of a second woman, dark-haired, of a similar age to the first; she lies quite still, her body stretched out, though clad in a day-dress, its copper-coloured silk hardly creased.

'Another?' asks Bartleby, a note of disbelief in his voice.

'Indeed,' replies Inspector Hanson, 'although not quite the same. We will have to wait for the doctor, but I would hazard she was smothered.'

'How do you know?' asks Webb, approaching the body.

'There are small haemorrhages around her mouth and eyes. I have seen it before. And the pillow beside her; there is a good deal of rouge smudged upon the cover. I think he used it to cover her face.'

'Two of them,' says Bartleby. 'That is why you called us?'

'Indeed,' says Hanson. 'I can make out no good motive, you see. Or, at least, not one I would like to countenance.'

'I don't understand, Inspector,' replies Webb. 'Surely it was some argument? A dispute over money perhaps? Such things happen.'

Hanson nods. 'But, you see, I found this in the second girl's hand. Our man placed it there, I think.'

Hanson reaches inside his jacket pocket and retrieves a scrap of paper. He hands it to Webb, who walks over to the nearest lamp and peers at the hand-written note.

'"He uncovers deep things out of darkness, And brings the shadow of death to light." Biblical, is it not?'

'Job, I think, sir,' says Bartleby.

'How peculiar,' says Webb, not heeding the sergeant. 'You fear you have a religious fanatic on your hands, Inspector?'

Hanson frowns.

'It rather appears that way.'

CHAPTER THREE

Annabel Krout pulls back the moreen curtains of her new bedroom and looks outside, into the dark street below. A light breeze is stirring the fog in Duncan Terrace. It sends dead leaves rustling through the public gardens, and, all along the road opposite, the gas-lamps appear to flicker in sequence, as if at the passing of some unseen presence. There is, she thinks, something unusual in the distance; odd lights and movement that she cannot quite make out. She turns round to address the maid-servant who is unpacking her clothing, engaged in the delicate process of laying out her dresses in the ottoman beside her bed. The maid is a plump young woman, some twenty-five or -six years old. She silently scolds herself that she cannot remember the girl's name.

'I'm sorry,' she says at last, shyly, 'you must forgive me, but I don't recall your—'

'Jacobs, Miss.'

Of course, she thinks to herself. Not Annie, Mary or Sarah – the surname is the thing.

'Jacobs, tell me, what is that?'

'Miss?' says the maid, looking up from her task. Annabel beckons her over to the window.

'There, past those houses.'

'Oh, I see, Miss. That's the canal, and there's a

tunnel just there,' she says, pointing, 'with boats coming through it pretty regular. It runs right under these houses. It's the lights off the barges, and the water. Looks queer with the fog, don't it?'

'Ah, I see. Thank you.'

Jacobs nods. 'Begging your pardon, Miss, but you're from America?'

Annabel Krout smiles at the observation. 'Yes, I am. From Boston.'

'Well, you'd hardly know it, Miss,' says the maid, in a confidential, sympathetic tone.

'Thank you!' replies Annabel, amused.

'What's it like over there, Miss?'

'Well, this time of year, it is a little colder than here, I should say. But the air is better. We have fogs, but we don't get fog like this.'

'Oh, I shouldn't like it colder,' the maid replies, placing the last dress in the ottoman, 'begging your pardon.'

'You were born in London?' asks Annabel Krout.

'Yes, Miss, just down the City Road here. Not half a mile away.'

'Well, you must tell me about your family sometime, and where you grew up.'

'Oh, I don't know about that, Miss,' replies the maid.

Annabel blushes, feeling she has overstepped some invisible boundary of familiarity.

'I'm sorry, I didn't mean to pry. I can finish here, if you like. I mean to say, that's fine, Jacobs. You go on.'

'Miss?'

'I'll do the rest myself. That should do for now.'

'Thank you, Miss.'

Annabel Krout watches the maid depart, with a peculiar sense she has somehow embarrassed them both. Her remaining cases sit idle by the side of her

26

bed, but she does not quite have the enthusiasm to open them. She consoles herself with the thought that it is a pleasant room. The walls are papered a light shade of green, with a pattern of trailing leaves; a brass half-tester bed, draped with rich pink-striped chintz, dominates the centre and, against one wall, is the otto-man, a chair and a writing desk. Upon the opposite side, by the door, sits a japanned toilette table and marble-topped wash-stand. All in all, she decides, her new room is much better than her bedroom at home.

A noise downstairs distracts her from her thoughts. She walks from her room and descends to the first-floor landing. Annabel watches as the front door is opened by the butler, Jervis, and a man enters the hall. The new arrival is more than fifty years of age, his hair black, with flecks of grey, slicked back from his forehead, with side-whiskers and a closely clipped moustache. It is an angular, handsome profile. Moreover, there is a certain imperiousness to the man's manner, in the way he presents his hat and gloves to the butler, that instantly marks him as the master of the house, even before the appearance of his wife.

'Woodrow!'

'My dear?' replies Jasper Woodrow.

'Where on earth have you been?'

'A matter of business,' says Woodrow hurriedly. 'You know I cannot keep regular hours like some petty clerk.'

'But, Woodrow, did you forget Miss Krout? I had to go and collect her myself, you know. Why, if Mr. Langley had not accompanied me, I don't know what I should have done.'

'Langley? What has he to do with Miss Krout? I hardly—'

Jasper Woodrow falls silent as, looking up by chance, he catches sight of Annabel upon the first-floor landing. Annabel herself colours visibly for the second time in as many minutes; and, although it is an irrational idea, she cannot shake from her mind the thought that she has somehow been caught eavesdropping.

'Annabel,' says Mrs. Woodrow, 'do come down.'

'I am sorry,' she says, 'I did not mean to . . .'

'Did not mean to what, my dear? Do come down and let me introduce you.'

Annabel descends the stairs, and smiles nervously at Jasper Woodrow. He smiles back, but it is as polite and business-like a smile as she has ever seen.

'Woodrow, this is my cousin Annabel. Annabel, this is my thoughtless beast of a husband.'

Mrs. Woodrow utters the words with good humour. Nonetheless, the man in question interposes, 'Really, Melissa, a bit strong.'

'My darling, you kept Annabel waiting in the cold at that awful station,' says Mrs. Woodrow, 'she might have froze.'

'Really,' interjects Annabel, a trifle weakly, 'I really was not cold at all.'

'We even delayed dinner,' continues Mrs. Woodrow, 'although Mrs. Figgis was not best pleased.'

'But we have just eaten,' adds Annabel, attempting something conciliatory.

'We could wait no longer,' says Mrs. Woodrow, reaching out to her husband. 'Let Jervis have your coat, and we will see what Mrs. Figgis can manage. You must make amends.'

'Don't fuss, woman,' says Jasper Woodrow, brushing her hands aside. He checks himself, however, as if suddenly conscious of how brusque his words may sound. 'You'll forgive me, Miss Krout, I have had a long day, and I must go and change. Have you met Lucinda?'

'It is hardly the hour for that, my dear,' says Mrs. Woodrow, chiding him.

'No, I suppose not. I will be in the study – have something sent up, I don't much care what.'

'You are not coming down?' asks Mrs. Woodrow. 'I thought we might have a nice talk and teach Annabel whist; she tells me she does not know it. Can you believe that? We might play single dummy, at least.'

Jasper Woodrow emphatically shakes his head. 'I will be in the study. Have something sent up.'

His wife frowns, but assents. 'I'll see what Mrs. Figgis can do.'

'Good. Good night, Miss Krout.'

With a bow, Mr. Woodrow ascends the stairs. There is a distinct muttering under his breath, which both Mrs. Woodrow and her cousin can hear quite clearly.

'Damn Mrs. Figgis.'

Once Mr. Woodrow is out of earshot, however, his wife takes her cousin to one side. 'He is out of sorts, my dear. You must forgive him, for my sake.'

'Please, cousin, there is nothing to forgive,' says Annabel Krout.

'I swear,' continues Mrs. Woodrow, 'I wish I knew what it was. But he is such a dear man, you know. You will see, my dear.'

———

Jasper Woodrow closes the door to his study, and slowly locks it from the inside. There is a blazing fire awaiting him in the hearth, as is the household custom on a winter's evening. Under his arm is a clean shirt, taken from his wardrobe; he puts it down upon the leather armchair, before the fireplace. He then takes off his coat, and jacket, and removes his collar and cuffs. Finally, he takes off his shirt, and places it upon the floor, quickly changing into the new one.

The old shirt is soaked through with sweat; and upon one side the material is stained a dark blood-black.

Woodrow begins to tear at it with his hands, his movements frenzied and nervous, throwing the scraps of cloth upon the fire.

CHAPTER FOUR

IN ROOM THIRTEEN of Knight's Hotel, Sergeant Bartleby holds up an oil-lamp close by the bed, as Decimus Webb examines the second body, teasing back the sleeves of the girl's dress.

'There is some recent bruising on the upper arm, here,' says Webb. 'I rather fancy she was held down.'

'That doesn't mean much in a place like this, I should say,' says Bartleby. Webb looks at him askance.

'If you'll allow me to make an observation, sir,' adds the sergeant.

'Do we have their names?' continues Webb, regardless.

'Betsy Carter,' replies Hanson, nodding in the direction of the first room, 'and Annie Finch. That's what Brown told us, and one of our lads recognised them both, in a professional capacity. He says they've been gay girls, around hereabouts, ever since he's known them; three years or more.'

Webb smiles a thin smile. 'A professional capacity? *His* profession, I trust, Inspector.'

Hanson shrugs. 'I did not ask. So tell me, what is your opinion? There are curious circumstances here, are there not?'

'Such as?'

'Very well. Firstly, the murderer – what is his motive?'

'A religious mania,' says Bartleby.

'That is quite possible,' says Hanson. 'Indeed, that may be the only conclusion – I have no better idea. But, even so, it is a curious place to come, is it not, if one had a mind to do away with such a woman? To put oneself in a locked room, and with a man downstairs, liable to recognise you?'

'No interruptions,' suggests the sergeant.

'But leaving Brown as a witness.'

'Perhaps,' says Webb. 'Please, continue.'

'Next – why the pair of them? Why not three? Four? The whole hotel?'

'He knew he would be discovered,' suggests the sergeant. 'This second girl here was alone – the others might have had men with them.'

'Yes, Sergeant,' interjects Webb, 'but how did he know that? Did he kill the first one then listen at the door? Was he merely fortunate that he found her by herself? Or was it she who found him?'

'Sir?'

'Did she hear a scream, a peculiar noise? Open the door and . . . well, he had no choice but to silence her.'

'That might explain it, sir,' replies Bartleby.

'That occurred to me,' says Hanson. 'It would explain the two deaths, in part. But it does not quite make sense – and this is my third point – why use a pillow? It is odd, is it not? If he has the strength and inclination to stab the first one? I should think that blade came back out easy enough. It's a clean wound, and the man is strong, like you said. Why not use it again?'

'If you'll forgive me saying so, sir,' says Bartleby, 'maybe you're looking for reason and logic where there's none to be found. The man had some petty argument with the girl; he kills her. The other disturbs him. He does for her too. The pillow's to stop her shouting out, first thing that comes to hand. It might be that simple.'

'But The Book of Job, Sergeant?' replies Hanson. 'That implies a degree of premeditation, I think? I should still like to hear the inspector's thoughts upon the matter.'

Webb steps back from the dead girl, and motions Bartleby to return the lamp to the nearby dresser. He opens the door of the small cabinet beside the bed, peers inside, and closes it again.

'Which window was it he got out by?' he asks, at length.

Hanson frowns, glancing at the sash-window behind his interlocutor. 'We don't know as yet. The windows were unlocked but closed, in this room and next door; they're both quite loose, don't stay up if you lift them. We won't be able to see much in the alley until the morning, either; I've had a good look myself with a bull's-eye. I couldn't see a damn thing.'

'And the door between the rooms? Was it locked?'

'No. Brown says the key for it was lost, years ago.'

Webb sighs. 'Well, I can give you no answers, Inspector. But I think you have missed one thing, at least.'

Hanson raises his eyebrows. 'Really?'

'The brandy.'

'Brandy? What brandy?'

'Exactly. Have you looked in the cabinet, in Miss Carter's room, next door?'

Hanson nods. 'There are some tumblers, a bottle of gin and a decanter of brandy. Both about half-full, I'd say.'

'But in this room, in Miss Finch's little cabinet, there

are identical tumblers, the same bottle of gin but, I think you will find, no brandy.'

'What of it?'

'Come here, Inspector, have a closer look.'

Hanson walks over to the cabinet, and Webb opens the door, a trifle theatrically, like a conjuror revealing a small but satisfying card-trick. The dusty interior of the cabinet, only half-visible in the dim light, contains a trio of dirty glasses, a bottle of Thwaite's Superior Cream Gin, and nothing else.

'There, Inspector, do you see it now?' asks Webb, tracing a small circle on the floor of the cabinet with his finger. 'Look.'

Webb holds his finger up to the light.

'An absence of dust,' replies Hanson.

'A decanter-sized absence, to be precise,' says Webb. 'I'll warrant that you'll find the gin and brandy standard issue in this rather liberal establishment. But here the brandy appears to be missing. Perhaps you could check that for us, Sergeant?'

'Sir?'

Webb gives the sergeant a sharp look. 'Whether there are decanters of brandy in each room?'

'Ah, very good, sir.'

Bartleby departs, leaving the two detectives alone in the room.

'You have an acute eye, Inspector,' says Hanson.

'Well, perhaps,' says Webb. 'Still, I think I have seen all there is to see. I will think upon this business, you may be sure of that. And if there is anything the Yard can do to assist in the meantime, do not hesitate to let me know.'

'Thank you. But you have not told me what you make of this missing decanter. What inference do you draw from it?'

'I think,' says Webb, choosing his words carefully,

'the murderer wished to remove or conceal it. And it seems likely it was the contents, and not the bottle per se, that he wished to keep to himself.'

'What? Do you think the brandy was drugged? Poisoned? Why?'

Webb shrugs. 'It is too early to say, is it not? If it was my decision, I would make sure the doctors examine the contents of little Miss Finch's stomach with particular thoroughness. And the other girl, too.'

'We will do that, naturally.'

'Well, at present, then, there is nothing more to be said.'

'Unless you would care to see Mr. Brown before you leave? We have him downstairs.'

'Ah, the good Mr. Brown. A Greek, you said? Our fair city attracts all sorts, does it not? Still, we might learn something from Mr. Brown, I suppose.'

———

Vasilis Brown stands up as Webb and Hanson enter the parlour. The constable by his side makes a move to push the large man back to his seat, but Inspector Hanson motions the policeman to be still.

'Inspector,' says Brown, walking up and attempting to clasp Hanson's hands in supplication, 'please, release me, I beg of you. I cannot remain here a moment longer; this place is cursed.'

'You will remain here, Mr. Brown, as long as you are needed. This is Inspector Webb of Scotland Yard.'

Webb nods.

'Why?' says the Greek. 'What is this? Another policeman? What do you want from me? I tell you everything, sir. There is nothing more to tell.'

'You are a long way from home, Mr. "Brown",' says Webb.

'What are you saying? That is a crime?'

35

'What is your name, your real name?'

'Ionnidou. But the English, they do not understand it. I change it to "Brown". No harm. I have nothing to hide.'

'But a great deal of harm has been done this evening, has it not?'

'I called the policemen! Me! Now I am here, like the common criminal! It is not my fault. I beg you, sir,' he says, turning to Hanson, 'please, let me go, eh? I do not wish to stay under this roof.'

'We know what you are, Mr. Brown,' continues Webb. 'Tell me, why did you become suspicious? Why did you go up to the room?'

'I told them already. You want me to tell you again?'

'Please.'

The Greek sighs. 'The man, he stays for long while, two hours. The man, he is still up there. I think, maybe there is something wrong here. That is all.'

'You bill them by the hour, I understand?'

'I rent rooms by the hour. That is all.'

Webb smiles. 'If you say so. Well, I am done here. I wish you a good night, Mr. Brown.'

Vasilis Brown looks on in confusion as the two policemen turn and leave the room. Outside, in the hall, before they can begin to converse amongst themselves, they come upon Sergeant Bartleby.

'You were right, sir,' says the sergeant. 'Same decanters in every room. All the ones I checked, leastways.'

Webb nods, and allows himself a hint of a satisfied smile.

'We will look into that,' says Hanson. 'So, Inspector, was Brown as you expected?'

'I don't know,' replies Webb. 'I would not trust his sort an inch, but is he a murderer? Anything is possible, I suppose – one should never rely on instinct. Do you intend to arrest him?'

'I would prefer to let him dangle for now, keep a close eye on him, watch his movements.'

'A wise course of action,' replies Webb, putting on his hat. 'Well, good night, Inspector Hanson. It has been a pleasure. Keep us informed of your progress. I am sorry I could not be of much help.'

'The pleasure was all mine, sir.'

———

Webb and Bartleby sit once more in a cab, leaving behind the great cathedral, and the confines of Godliman Street. The former seems more inclined to conversation than previously, his features more animated.

'You were gone a long time, Sergeant?'

'I spoke to a couple of the constables, sir. I had a word with the one who knew the girls.'

'And?'

'He said they weren't best pals or anything. In fact, he'd heard they had a falling out over some gentleman friend.'

Webb laughs. 'A gentleman friend?'

'No, sir, I mean a particular fellow, a sweetheart, not one of their callers.'

'Does he have a name?'

'The man didn't know the details, sir. Said he would ask around. They were both regulars in the local publics. Did a good trade at Knight's; always had a good deal of ready money.'

'Hmm. Doubtless your constable will tell Hanson if he finds anything. It is not really our business. Still, intriguing.'

'And that was a stroke, sir, noticing that decanter. Something queer in it, you think?'

'You do not need to butter me up, Sergeant. But, yes, they will find something, I am certain. I just do not know what or why.'

'And who was it for, sir? I mean to say, if he knifed one and smothered the other, what was the point of that? Or,' says Bartleby, struck by a sudden thought, 'did they try to poison him? He discovered it. Turned nasty.'

Webb ponders the idea but shakes his head. 'Why remove the decanter? You let your enthusiasm run away with you, Sergeant. Think it through.'

Bartleby shakes his head in defeat. Webb, however, continues. 'But I know which of the two it was for, brandy, poison or whatever; or, at least, I think so.'

'Sir?'

'In the first room, Sergeant, I looked in the cabinet. The brandy was there, but there was also a tacky circle on the wood, a stain, matching the outline of the base of the decanter. They must have spilt some liquor down the neck when they poured it, and it had stuck to the bottom of the glass, and then left its mark. I have the same problem with my tea-pot at home.'

'I don't follow you, sir.'

'No, well, I have not finished. The stain was almost a perfect circle, but it was not quite beneath the decanter; it was an inch or so to the right; they over-lapped slightly. Nothing remarkable in that, of course. But I lifted the base of the decanter itself and it was not remotely damp, except where it overlapped the stain.'

'You mean it was not the same decanter as left the stain?'

'Precisely. I'll warrant it was from the second room. Miss Finch's room. Now, why should that be?'

'The man moved it, from one room to another?'

Webb nods. 'To conceal the fact the original had

38

been taken. A clumsy attempt, mind you. But it shows our Miss Carter was his intended victim. It shows us that whatever took place in room fourteen is the key; anything else is incidental. And, I suspect, that our man was not a complete madman.'

'Did you mention this to Inspector Hanson?' asks the sergeant.

Webb looks out of the window, as the cab speeds along Fleet Street.

'It is only a theory, Sergeant. And it is not our case.'

'And it is the City force, sir,' says the sergeant knowingly.

'It is not a matter for Scotland Yard, that is all,' replies Webb in a curt tone.

The sergeant assents, albeit raising his eyebrows.

'Although I suspect it will be,' mutters Webb, under his breath.

CHAPTER FIVE

'GOOD MORNING, MISS. I've got the fire going.'

Annabel Krout opens her eyes, uncertain as to her location, or the owner of the peculiar voice addressing her. It takes a few seconds for her to recall that she is in London, England, in her cousin's house, and that the voice in question belongs to the maid-servant to whom she spoke the day before. She sits up awkwardly in bed.

'I'm sorry, Miss,' says the maid-servant. 'You did say to wake you for breakfast? Shall I open the curtains?'

Annabel nods and smiles weakly. 'Yes, I did. Thank you.'

'It's a beautiful morning, Miss.'

'The fog has cleared then?'

'Clear as a bell,' says the maid. 'I've left you a basin of hot here, Miss.'

'Thank you, Jacobs,' says Annabel, looking at the steaming bowl of water upon the wash-stand. 'What time is it?'

'Almost eight o'clock. Is there anything else, Miss?'

'No, I do not think so. Thank you.'

'Very good, Miss.'

Jacobs walks briskly on to the landing, closing the door behind her. Annabel waits until the maid has left, then gets up and walks to the window. She looks almost unsteady; perhaps she needlessly anticipates the pitch and yaw to which two weeks upon a steam-ship have accustomed her. Peering through the glass, she is struck by the odd dendritic patterns of minute black crystals left upon the surface, a legacy of the fog. Beyond that, outside, there is a frost on the ground in the gardens below, and she can now see the canal across the way. The slumped figures of several labourers are engaged in heavy labour, with ropes and crates, atop a long barge.

She shivers and looks for her dressing-gown, and a suitable dress.

———

'Annabel, my dear, did you sleep well? Do take a seat. How was the bed?'

'Fine, thank you, cousin.'

Melissa Woodrow smiles, and gently taps her husband's hand, who sits at the breakfast table, his head invisible behind a copy of the day's *Times*. He lowers the paper and looks up; his eyes are slightly bloodshot.

'Ah, Miss Krout,' he says, repeating the question, 'slept well?'

Annabel nods. 'I did indeed, sir. A great improvement upon my berth on the *Alathea*.'

'I am glad,' he replies tersely, without much enthusiasm. He returns his gaze to the newspaper, as if reluctant to meet her glance.

'I have never sailed myself,' says Mrs. Woodrow. 'I understand one needs a strong constitution, Annabel? Is that the case? Were many people bad on the trip?'

'Bad? Well, I suppose I made a few pleasant acquaintances . . .'

Mrs. Woodrow laughs, and smiles politely. 'No, no,

my dear – you misconstrue me. I mean in ill-health. *Mal de mer.*'

'Oh, I'm so sorry,' replies her cousin. 'Yes, a good number. We would not put it that way, in Boston.'

'Well, really, you must accustom yourself to our way of speaking, dear,' continues Mrs. Woodrow. 'Mustn't she, Woodrow? "When in Rome . . ." isn't that what they say?'

Mr. Woodrow nods, rather stiffly.

'Ah,' continues Mrs. Woodrow as Jacobs appears, bearing a tray of bacon and eggs, 'now I trust you like a good meal to begin the day? A girl your age should eat well; but I can ask Mrs. Figgis to make up something else, if it's not to your liking.'

'No, really, that's fine, cousin. Eggs are a favourite of mine.'

Mrs. Woodrow smiles, but an awkward silence ensues, as both women begin eating, and Mr. Woodrow continues his determined perusal of the newspaper. A plate of cold-cuts follows, together with bread and anchovy paste. Mr. Woodrow makes a series of desultory forays into the meat with his fork, hardly eating anything. At length, he pushes his plate to one side, takes a swig of tea, and stands up.

'You must excuse me, Miss Krout, but I have business to attend to. I'll have to leave shortly.'

'Of course,' replies Annabel.

'Now, do not allow my wife to exhaust you on your first day – she has a mania for "sights".'

'I have nothing of the sort,' protests Mrs. Woodrow.

'I expect we will have an opportunity to talk this evening,' continues Woodrow, even as he passes his house-guest and leaves the room.

Annabel turns to bid him goodbye but finds herself addressing the empty doorway. She turns back to face her cousin, whose features betray a certain displeasure with her husband's abrupt manner. Nonetheless, Mrs. Woodrow immediately forces them into a more benign arrangement.

'Do ignore Woodrow; he is awfully busy. He means nothing by it, my dear. Now, what shall we do today? We must see something, I think – when one is fortunate enough to enjoy the advantages of travel, one must see something.'

'Whatever you suggest, cousin, though I should most like to see the Crystal Palace, and St. Paul's, and the Abbey . . .'

'Yes, yes, naturally, my dear. I am just thinking what might be for the best today, to begin with. Perhaps, first, I should introduce you to Lucinda – I had thought we might take her on a little outing.'

'Yes, I have been looking forward to meeting her,' says Annabel, brightly. 'Your letters have painted such a lovely picture. And that photograph you sent Momma and Poppa was so pretty.'

Melissa Woodrow smiles, a glow of maternal pride suffusing her cheeks.

⸺

The Woodrows' nursery is located on the third floor of the house, above Annabel's room, overlooking the street. The room itself is a light and airy space, which commands a good view of the terrace's rooftops, and the canal opposite. The walls are plain and white-washed, the floor carpeted with a mat of dark felt. The only substantial items of furniture are a bed, a small table and chairs, a dresser and a wicker toy-hamper, the lid of which is rather poorly secured, so that the bow of a brightly painted wooden ark projects from the top.

The room's solitary inhabitant is a little girl, about six years old. She sits on a small stool in the corner, in front of a miniature wooden desk, engaged in the contemplation of a book. Dark-haired, like her parents, she bears a rather earnest expression. As Mrs. Woodrow and her cousin enter, she looks up at the two adults expectantly. Mrs. Woodrow meets her daughter's gaze with a smile, but bustles over to the hamper, straightening the toys.

'I do wish, Lucinda, you might keep things in better order,' she says, fastening it shut.

'Sorry, Mama,' says the little girl. She puts the book to one side, a railway alphabet, open at 'T is for Tunnel'. Her mother bends down and strokes her face.

'This, Lucy, is your cousin Annabel, from America. Do you remember I said that she was coming to visit us?'

Lucy nods.

'What do you say to Annabel?'

'Pleased to meet you,' says the little girl, after a pause for thought.

Annabel Krout smiles. 'Likewise,' she replies, crouching down to Lucy's level. 'You are every bit as pretty as your picture. I hope you and I will become the best of friends.'

Before the girl can reply, however, a voice interrupts from the landing, behind the two visitors.

'Good morning, Lucinda.'

It is the voice of Mr. Woodrow, dressed for the outdoors, in his large black great-coat, holding a walking stick and hat.

'Good morning, Papa,' replies Lucy, sitting up straight.

'I see you have met my daughter, Miss Krout,' says Woodrow. 'What do you make of her? I am inclined to think that she needs bringing out of herself. My wife is against the idea of a governess, although I do not see why.'

44

'I find her charming, sir,' replies Annabel.

'Yes, well. It is hard to judge on first meeting, I suppose.' He seems to pause for a moment, as if on the verge of saying something more about her. Instead, however, he merely continues with, 'Have you made plans, Melissa?'

'Nothing as yet, my dear,' replies Mrs. Woodrow.

'Really? Well, I have told Jervis to have the carriage ready for ten sharp – I thought that would suit. But I am late already.'

'I will speak to Jervis, my dear,' replies Mrs. Woodrow. 'Don't let us detain you.'

Mr. Woodrow nods farewell once again, and departs. The sound of his boots echo on the stairs. Mrs. Woodrow waits until he is out of ear-shot before she speaks.

'He so wants the best for her,' she says at last, patting her daughter on the head, 'but, to tell the truth, I am so loath to give her routine over to a perfect stranger. She is a sensitive child. Do you think me foolish?'

'Not at all. I am sure it is very natural in a mother,' replies Annabel.

Melissa Woodrow smiles, and gently touches her cousin's arm. 'I am glad you agree, my dear. But, I should say, best not to discuss the matter in front of Woodrow. He detests arguments. Now, young lady,' she says, addressing the little girl, 'we are planning an excursion. Where should you like to go today?'

'Today, Mama?'

'Yes, today.'

The girl looks pensive, twisting a lock of her dark curly hair about her finger.

'The Zoo!'

Melissa Woodrow smiles. 'It is always the Zoological Gardens! But I can recommend them,

Annabel – we can take the brougham and have a pleasant stroll round the park?'

'I should be delighted.'

'Excellent. Do you have a day-dress, my dear?'

'Well, the one I am wearing,' says Annabel, unconsciously looking down at her clothing, a mauve dress of a rather plain design.

'Oh, I do not think that will do, my dear. We do not follow the American fashions here, you know. I will see if I can find you something from my wardrobe; and I just bought a delightful new cloud from Whiteley's – that might be just the thing. It is still so cold. I am sure Jacobs will have an idea – she is quite the last word on such matters, although you would not know to look at her!'

'Really, cousin, there is no need to—'

'My dear, there is every need. You cannot be seen in Regent's Park with nothing from this season . . . Well, anyway, do talk to Lucinda while I go and have a look.'

Melissa Woodrow hurries back to her dressing-room, calling for her maid, ignoring the slight look of annoyance on Annabel Krout's face. Annabel, however, does not protest any further, beyond a quiet sigh of resignation. Conscious that her little cousin is watching her, she bends down over the child's desk.

'How old are you, Lucy?'

'Nearly seven.'

'That is grown up, isn't it? Have you been to the Zoo before?'

'Yes,' says the little girl, a slight note of childish contempt in her voice, as if insulted by the suggestion that she might want for such an experience.

'With your Momma, I mean, Mama and Papa?'

'Papa doesn't go anywhere.'

'No, well he is a busy man. I suppose he must go to

46

work, to earn a living, to keep you and your Mama happy.'

The little girl frowns. 'I wish *he* was happy,' she says.

'Isn't he?' asks Annabel, puzzled.

Lucy Woodrow shakes her head, very firmly.

'Why, dear?' persists Annabel. 'What do you mean?'

The sound of Mrs. Woodrow's voice, calling Annabel Krout from down the hall, interrupts the conversation.

The little girl returns to looking at her alphabet.

'I like the Zoo,' she says.

CHAPTER SIX

'THAT,' SAYS LUCY Woodrow, pointing emphatically at the large animal approaching step by step, 'is an Indian elephant. Because it has small ears.'

'For an elephant,' suggests Annabel Krout.

The little girl looks up at her cousin, unsure if she is being teased. 'Yes,' she replies at last, with considerable seriousness, 'for an elephant.'

The grey beast lumbers slowly along the tree-lined path towards them. Annabel and Lucy, together with Mrs. Woodrow, stand to one side. Led by a peak-hatted keeper, the animal bears a load of half a dozen passengers, also visitors to the Zoological Gardens. All of them, a man, woman and four children, are balanced precariously upon a wooden knifeboard seat, roped to its back.

'It's a miracle they don't fall,' says Annabel.

The keeper, over-hearing the comment, politely raises his whip, held firmly in one hand, to touch his cap.

'Don't you fret, Miss,' he says. 'Safe as a regular omnibus, if you care for a ride?'

'She cares for no such thing,' replies Mrs. Woodrow, ushering her cousin along.

'"Safe as a regular omnibus" indeed,' says Mrs. Woodrow, once the man and his charges have passed by. 'Let me tell you, my dear, that is no great recommendation.'

'But can't we have a ride, Mama?' says Lucy, tugging her mother's skirt.

'Don't do that, dear,' replies Mrs. Woodrow, grabbing her daughter's hand. 'You will tear it. And, no, we cannot have a ride. I have told you before, it would not suit my constitution. Have some thought for your mother's feelings.'

The little girl's face darkens considerably, but she says nothing. Her mother looks sharply at her.

'Lucinda, I swear, you quite exasperate me at times,' says Mrs. Woodrow. 'She is playing up,' she continues, *sotto voce*, to Annabel, 'because we are in company.'

'Please,' replies the little girl, elongating the word enormously.

'I could take her, Melissa,' offers Annabel, looking back at the elephant.

'My dear, your dress would not survive it. Think of the bustle.'

Annabel Krout looks down at the borrowed bottle-green polonaise she is wearing under her cape, and does not seem overly distraught at the possibility. Nonetheless, she does not argue.

'I suppose, before we go, if you are a good girl, we might see the hippopotamus,' says Mrs. Woodrow, addressing Lucy in a conciliatory tone. The little girl, in turn, gives a rather grudging nod.

'Is he your favourite?' asks Annabel, as they walk on.

Lucy shrugs.

'Do you know,' Mrs. Woodrow asks her daughter, 'that I can remember when they first brought the hippo over to the Zoo, when I was a little girl, not much older than you are now?'

'No,' says the little girl; but her voice has a hint of curiosity in it.

49

'Yes. It caused quite a stir. They even wrote songs about it.'

Lucy furrows her brow. 'How did they go?'

'Now that I cannot quite recall, my dear,' replies Mrs. Woodrow. 'Perhaps I will see if I still have the music when we get home. Ah, and here we are.'

Before them is a barred enclosure, surrounded by an additional set of iron railings, over which the various lookers-on lean. By far the majority are children, and Lucy Woodrow's face is illuminated with pleasure as she pushes it against the metal, and sees the recumbent, corpulent body of the hippopotamus, glistening with moisture, stretched by the side of his pool. Its eyes are closed and the curves of its scooped mouth peculiarly suggestive of a certain degree of smug contentment.

'He is rather an ugly brute to be your favourite, Lucy dear,' says Mrs. Woodrow. 'For my part, I much prefer the lions.'

'I like him,' replies the little girl.

Mrs. Woodrow pats her daughter's head. Turning to her cousin, she whispers, 'He reminds me of Woodrow after his Sunday luncheon.'

Annabel Krout, in turn, laughs, albeit rather nervously. It is, she cannot help but think, an intimate analogy that does not chime with her limited experience of her host and his humours. 'He certainly looks well cared for,' she replies at last.

'Oh, I should think so. I expect it is quite delightful for him to receive such attention, and have as much food as he likes and so on. Well, come on, Lucy, we have seen your favourite. We may go back now. We can go through the park.'

'But Mama!' pleads the little girl.

'No "buts", my dear. Come.'

There is some argument. Lucinda Woodrow resists the injunctions of her parent in the most solemn and determined manner imaginable, until a mixture of threats and gentle coaxing finally persuade her to abandon her place by the railings. Once this is achieved, it is a more simple matter for them to make their way to the entrance to the Zoological Gardens, and out into the neatly kept paths of Regent's Park.

'What did you make of the Zoo, my dear?' asks Mrs. Woodrow of her cousin, as they stroll towards the Inner Circle of the park, where numerous carriages are parked.

'Oh, very pleasant – I have never seen quite so many different animals.'

'And what about you, Lucinda?'

'I like the hippo.'

'Yes, well, that is not in doubt, although I am not quite sure why you should do so to such a degree.'

Mrs. Woodrow pauses, as she notices a figure walking briskly along a nearby path that intersects with theirs.

'Why, would you believe it? It is Mr. Langley,' she says, nodding in his direction.

'But he has not noticed us,' replies Annabel, waving. 'Mr. Langley, over here!'

'Really, Annabel,' says Mrs. Woodrow in an urgent whisper, 'you ought not make quite such a display. People are staring.'

Annabel looks suitably chastened, but her apology is cut short as Richard Langley raises his hat, and changes his course. In a moment, he stands before them.

'Mrs. Woodrow, Miss Krout, how delightful to see you. I trust you are both well. Have you recovered from the train, Miss Krout?'

'I think so,' she replies.

'And I hope your baggage found its way to Duncan Terrace?'

'Yes, it has, thank you,' replies Annabel. It strikes her that she should say something more, but she struggles to find suitable words.

'Mrs. Woodrow is showing you the sights of London, no doubt?'

'Oh yes,' she replies, eagerly, 'the park is so charming.'

'And what brings you here, Mr. Langley?' asks Mrs. Woodrow.

'I live in St. John's Wood, if you recall, ma'am; it is not far. I regularly walk this way into town, if the weather permits. I am hoping to see your husband, as it happens, as we could not meet yesterday.'

'I am sure you will find him at his office,' replies Mrs. Woodrow. 'I would offer you our brougham, but there is barely space for two of us, let alone Lucy and yourself.'

'Lucy?'

'Why, yes, you've met Lucy, have you not? We have come from the Zoological . . .'

Mrs. Woodrow's sentence trails off as she looks around for her daughter, who is nowhere to be seen.

———

Lucy Woodrow walks back through the gates to the Zoo, behind a large woman and two little boys, a year or so younger than herself, in matching blue and white sailor-suits.

She tries to recall where to find the elephants. Then she sees one in the distance, and runs towards it. It is not hard to catch up; the elephants plod ever so slowly, and she has never seen the keepers use their whips. She walks behind the great animal, watching its tail twitch now and then, its great feet crunching footprints into the gravel. She waves to a girl seated on top of the animal, and the girl waves back.

'She cannot have gone far, ma'am,' says Richard Langley.

Mrs. Woodrow looks anxiously about her. 'No, no, I am sure. We must be calm, my dear,' she says, grasping her cousin's arm, though Annabel herself seems more composed. 'No, she cannot have gone far. Lucy!'

Both Richard Langley and Annabel Krout join in and shout the little girl's name; but there is no reply, nor any sign of her in the wide, grassy expanse of the park. A few strollers and passers-by turn their heads, but that is all.

'What is she wearing?' asks Langley.

'A little white frock, very plain,' says Mrs. Woodrow, not looking at her interlocutor, then hurriedly adding, 'I mean to say, she is wearing that, but she has her shawl, and winter coat on top, and a beret.'

'They're a reddish brown,' says Annabel.

'Cremorne brown,' adds Mrs. Woodrow, a particular that Annabel cannot help but think is unnecessary.

'Would she have gone back to the Zoo?' suggests Annabel.

'She might,' says Mrs. Woodrow, as tears well up in her eyes. 'Oh dear! Mr. Langley, you must forgive me, it's merely . . . oh, you must help us look for her! She might be anywhere!'

'Of course I'll help, ma'am,' says Langley, 'but I suggest the best thing for you to do is to wait here, in case she returns or someone brings her back to where she left you. I will run back to the Zoo and inquire at the gate, and have the keepers look for her. And if either of us sees a policeman, then I suggest we enlist his assistance.'

'A policeman?' exclaims Mrs. Woodrow breath-lessly, giving every appearance of being on the brink of fainting.

'I am sure she is fine, ma'am,' he says. 'I only meant as a precaution.'

Lucy Woodrow climbs up the wooden steps to the platform beside the elephant, then clambers a little unsteadily on to the seat, her feet slipping on the carpet laid upon its back.

'She's not with us,' exclaims the boy next to her.

'My mama's over there,' she says in reply, without pointing to any particular direction. 'She doesn't like elephants.'

'Here,' says a keeper, bending over, and pulling a leather strap tight across her waist. 'That's it. Are you ready?'

Lucy nods. Her fellow passengers add their assent, and the seat suddenly bumps, as the elephant begins its circuit of the Zoo.

But it is not as Lucy Woodrow had imagined. For she finds the seat rather uncomfortable and the strap chafes against her stomach, even though she hangs on ever so tightly.

Bump, bump.

Moreover, the people below do not look half so diminished as Lucy had expected. And she has no-one to whom she might wave.

Bump, bump.

The disappointment is such that it is all she can do to prevent herself from crying.

Bump, bump, bump.

At last, the creature stops. She returns to the platform, with a helping hand from a keeper, and runs directly back down the steps.

Then another hand grips her arm; a man's hand.
'Are you lost?'

~

'Oh, Mr. Langley, thank goodness! You found her!'

Richard Langley strolls towards Mrs. Woodrow and Annabel Krout, holding the hand of Lucy Woodrow, who trots along beside him, rather red-faced, though it is hard to say whether with shame or simple breathlessness. Mrs. Woodrow, her face ashen, hurries directly towards them, and hugs her daughter to her side.

'You stupid, naughty girl,' she exclaims, then bursts into tears. Lucy obliges by doing likewise. It is a moment or two before either can relent.

'Mr. Langley,' says Mrs. Woodrow at last, retrieving a handkerchief from her bag, and drying her eyes, 'you must forgive me. I am quite overcome. How can I repay you?'

'Anyone would have found her, ma'am; she was quite safe,' says Langley. 'I believe she took a ride on an elephant.'

'Well, this is the last time we visit the Zoo, young lady,' exclaims Mrs. Woodrow, at which Lucy begins to cry once more. Her mother, however, deliberately ignores the outburst.

'Perhaps,' she continues, 'you might come to dinner one evening? Our Mrs. Figgis is really a delightful cook.'

Mr. Langley smiles. 'I would be most happy to, ma'am, but I fear I had better conclude my arrangements with your husband first; I would not wish to impose upon his hospitality before we have settled matters.'

'Well, I will talk to him about it,' replies Mrs. Woodrow, smiling.

'Perhaps I can escort you to your carriage?' he replies.

Mrs. Woodrow assents and, with Lucy still rather tearful, they begin to walk back towards the Inner Circle.

'You are in the same business as Mr. Woodrow, Mr. Langley?' asks Annabel, as they approach the brougham.

'Well, I am an architect by training, Miss Krout. I met Mr. Woodrow in my professional capacity – I am designing his new premises.'

'But Mr. Langley is also considering investing in the business,' adds Mrs. Woodrow. 'Isn't that right, sir?'

'Indeed, ma'am. I have some money to invest and Mr. Woodrow has suggested a partnership. It is just a matter of agreeing the terms; but these things can take some time. A partnership should not be entered into lightly, by either party.'

For a moment, Annabel Krout fancies that Richard Langley's gaze lingers upon her as he speaks. Then, he steps to one side, politely ushering both women out through the park gate and onto the road.

'Well,' says Langley, as they come to the waiting brougham, with the coachman perched upon the driver's seat, 'here we are again.'

'I am so grateful we met, sir,' says Mrs. Woodrow. 'I don't know what I might have done if—'

'Please, ma'am, you have thanked me already. I bid you both goodbye; and you, young lady,' he says, leaning down towards Lucy, 'should be more considerate to your mama.'

Lucy says nothing as her mother and Annabel Krout say their goodbyes. Langley, in turn, doffs his hat and departs, continuing his walk at the same brisk pace as when they met him.

'Such a charming young man,' exclaims Mrs. Woodrow.

'Yes, he is,' replies Annabel.

'Phelps,' says Mrs. Woodrow, turning to address the coachman, 'do come and open the door, if you please.'

'Sorry, ma'am,' replies the coachman, jumping down from his box-seat, 'I was just keeping an eye on the horse.'

'I don't care what you were just doing, please pay attention. I have had a trying day already.'

'Sorry, ma'am.'

Annabel looks at the driver's seat; she notices a newspaper, hastily pushed under the cushion. There is only a little of the text visible, but she cannot help but shudder when she reads it:

Dreadful Murder of Two Young Women.

CHAPTER SEVEN

JASPER WOODROW'S BUSINESS premises are situated
upon the busy thoroughfare of High Holborn, within
a substantial building, in the classical style, a short
walk from New Oxford Street. The property is
unmistakable, since the building itself is topped with a
tower of letters, sculpted in iron, that project above the
roof, spelling out the words 'Woodrow's General
Mourning Warehouse'. Further announcements are
liberally painted upon the brick-work, promising
'Mourning for Families, In Correct Taste', 'Court and
Family Mourning', and from the cornice itself hangs
the proud motto 'Every Article of the Very Best
Description'. Each sign, moreover, has its own gas-
lights, which can be illuminated at nightfall or at the
slightest hint of fog. In short, no expense has been
spared to advertise the propriety, variety and suit-
ability of the wares within; thus it is a business that, to
all appearances, thrives.

Jasper Woodrow himself, however, sits in his office,
looking rather vacantly into space. Before him, laid
upon his burgundy leather-topped desk, is a portfolio
of papers, tied with string, bearing the words
'Woodrow's : Reports & Accounts, 1873'.

He places the bundle to one side, and looks at the
nearby clock. It is a favourite of his, chosen by his wife,

an ornate ormolu time-piece, whose enamelled dial is supported by a forest of golden metal, crafted into minuscule flowers and garlands of leaves.

One o'clock.

He reaches out and moves his bronze ink-stand, positioning it a little to the left.

One o'clock still.

The fire in the nearby hearth crackles noisily, the flames finding some impurity in the coal.

Woodrow pushes back his chair and gets up. Taking a brass poker from its stand, he stokes the fire. There is something comforting in the blaze, in the rising heat, that holds his attention for a few minutes, until he hears a knock at the door. He seems to find it difficult to place the sound's significance.

Another knock.

'Sir?' says a voice from outside the door.

'Yes,' replies Woodrow at last, 'come in.'

A clerk, a grey-haired man in his forties, enters the office, timidly pushing open the door. He looks first at the desk, then to his employer, standing by the fire-place.

'Well, what is it?'

'Mr. Langley is in the office, sir. He wonders if you might spare him a moment.'

'Langley?' say Woodrow, as if not recognising the name.

'Yes, sir. Langley.'

'But I have a luncheon appointment. I am about to go out.'

'Shall I ask him to call again, sir?'

Woodrow looks into the fire; the clerk fiddles nervously with the hem of his waistcoat.

'No, damn it, have him come in.'

The clerk nods, and swiftly departs. A few seconds later, there is a second knock at the door, and Richard

Langley enters the room, carrying his hat and coat. 'Good afternoon,' he says, offering his hand.

'Good afternoon, sir,' says Woodrow.

'I hope I have not called at an inconvenient time.'

Woodrow takes a deep breath before turning to address his visitor, straightening his posture. It is not unlike a swimmer coming up for air.

'No,' says Woodrow, with a rather forced smile. 'But I regret I have a prior appointment.'

'Well, my apologies, sir. I will be brief. I just thought that I should advise you that I have heard back from my solicitor. I am to see him this afternoon.'

'I see,' says Woodrow, nodding. 'Yes, excellent.'

'Forgive me, sir,' continues Langley, 'I hope I am not too blunt, but you seem a little distracted. I expected . . . well, I confess, I rather thought you might be glad of the news.'

Jasper Woodrow looks back at his visitor, almost as if noticing him for the first time. The question, however, seems to jolt him back to life.

'No, your frankness does you credit. It is just . . . I am due to dine at the Rainbow in ten minutes, and I do not care to be late. Perhaps we might meet tomorrow. Mr. Prentice, whom you just spoke to, attends to my diary.'

'Well, one moment, did you say the Rainbow? I am going that way myself. Might I walk with you?'

'Of course,' replies Woodrow, rather mechanically. 'I suppose you may join us for lunch if you wish – though it is really a matter of business, not pleasure.'

'I should be delighted.'

'It will be quite dull,' continues Woodrow.

'I have no objection to that,' says Langley, cordially. 'It may, at least, give us an opportunity to talk about the design upon the way? I have an idea concerning the tiling upon the façade and some other matters. It must be a week since we last spoke?'

'Now, I recall very little of that evening,' says Woodrow, gesturing towards the door, his spirits seeming to rise a little. 'A fellow can have too much brandy, eh? Still, we must do it again, Langley, once our arrangements are settled. A man should always drink to a bargain, eh?'

'I look forward to it,' replies Langley.

The ante-chamber to Jasper Woodrow's office, into which both men adjourn, is a small room, where two clerks sit at high desks against opposite walls, their backs to each other, like a pair of living book-ends. Both turn around and listen intently as their employer utters a few words relating to his plans for the remainder of the day. Only when Woodrow has retrieved his coat, and left with his visitor, do they return to silent contemplation of the papers laid out before them.

Woodrow, meanwhile, leads his companion through the precincts of his offices, in which a further dozen men are occupied with invoices, accounts, receipts and all the paper paraphernalia of business.

'It is quickest through the shop,' he says, taking Langley through a door that leads on to the first-floor show-room of Woodrow's General Mourning Warehouse. It is a large room, furnished in sombre shades of red and brown, with a rich Kidderminster carpet, and walls panelled in dark polished wood. A series of walnut tables and comfortable chairs and sofas are placed at intervals across the floor, and around the walls are drawers and cabinets, marked in a Gothic gold-leaf lettering: 'Bonnets', 'Mantles', 'Shawls', 'Capes' and 'Gloves'. In turn, beside each cabinet are long mirrors, kept spotlessly clean. And, beside the mirrors stand the Warehouse's shop-girls, who attend to the demands of customers. Indeed, there is a constant to and fro of these women, as they move between their lady clients, seated at the tables, and the stores of mourning costumery. Mantles beaded with jet are swapped for widows' caps trimmed with black lace, merino cloaks for fur-lined capes; some are modelled by the girls themselves, some laid upon tables. And everything is done with the least noise, so that the only constant is the rustle of silk, as the girls fetch and carry, hither and thither. The atmosphere resembles less that of a retail establishment than that of a private chapel, with each shop-girl performing some unique sacrament for her client.

'I am always impressed by the quality of your staff, sir,' remarks Langley in a whisper, as the two men descend the carpeted stairs to the ground floor.

'All well-trained and rigorously selected,' replies Woodrow. 'That is half the secret of running a decent establishment, of any kind.'

The ground floor of Woodrow's is principally devoted to dresses and materials: merinos, velvets and satin lie upon counters; jewellery has a separate corner; black-bordered stationery another. Woodrow and Langley, walking together towards the entrance, receive a nod from the doorman, and proceed into High Holborn.

'You say "of any kind", sir. Were you not always in the mourning business?' asks Langley.

'The mourning house was my wife's family's; but I have always been in business,' replies Woodrow, as they turn right, down Drury Lane. 'You must forgive me taking you down this wretched street, I hope. I believe it is the quickest way.'

'Of course.'

⸺

'Ah,' says Langley, at length, as the two men cross the Strand, by St. Mary's Church, and proceed towards

Fleet Street, 'I neglected to mention that I chanced upon your wife and her cousin this morning, in Regent's Park.'

'Indeed?'

'I believe they had been to the Zoo.'

'I should not be surprised – they had Lucinda with them?'

'That would be your little girl? Yes, they did,' says Langley. If he contemplates mentioning Lucy's truancy, he decides against it.

'The child has a fascination for the place. Quite unhealthy.'

'Really?'

Woodrow frowns. 'And I understand you accompanied my wife to Euston station last night, to meet Miss Krout?'

'I had hoped to find you at home, sir – you said I might call, if I was near by? And Mrs. Woodrow seemed a little distressed. I thought I might be of assistance, under the circumstances.'

'No, I am in your debt, Langley. I would not have heard the end of it, had you not been there. Tell me, what did you make of Miss Krout?'

'A charming girl, I should say.'

'So should I. She is an heiress too; did you know that? The father made a fortune, invested in railroads; now he owns a biscuit factory or some such.'

'Biscuits?'

'Hard to credit it, I know. A pretty little mouse, isn't she? A man could do much worse. I'd marry her myself if I were twenty years younger.'

'Mrs. Woodrow might object.'

'That she might, Langley, that she might. I expect she's after some young buck, anyhow, eh?'

'I'm sure I couldn't say,' says Langley.

'Ah, here we are,' says Woodrow, as they approach their destination.

'After you, sir.'

Langley follows Woodrow inside the Rainbow Tavern. The building itself lies on the south of Fleet Street, a few paces from the ancient archway of Temple Bar. It is an old musty place, with the outward appearance of an ancient, timbered public house, and a dark gas-lit interior that might even be considered more sombre than Mr. Woodrow's Mourning Warehouse. In truth, though blessed with an ancient pedigree, the Rainbow has been built and rebuilt, again and again, such that no-one can recall exactly where the old coffee-house that first bore the name precisely stood. But it has retained a patina of age and is every bit an antique City dining-room, down to the heavy mahogany tables, at which lawyers and *hommes d'affaires* address themselves to equally ponderous saddles of mutton and sirloins of beef. It is to one such table that Mr. Woodrow directs his steps. Already seated there is a thin man in his sixties, in an aged dark frock coat and silk suit of matching colour, sipping from a glass of port. Most remarkable, given his age, is the colour of his hair – as black as pitch – and his moustache, neatly trimmed, shares the same distinction. Both are so uniform as to suggest the application of dye.

'Mr. Siddons,' says Woodrow, as the man gets up to greet him, 'how pleasant to see you again.'

'You echo my sentiments. You could not have put it more precisely.'

'And may I introduce an acquaintance of mine, Mr. Langley. I expect I have mentioned him to you. He has a mind to dine with us, if you do not object.'

Langley offers his hand, which is shaken firmly.

'Of course! Please, gentlemen,' says Siddons, 'take a

seat. I trust you are well, sir? Mrs. Woodrow? Your family? Are they well?'

'They are as well as can be expected,' says Woodrow, rather dourly. 'As for myself, the business keeps me very busy.'

'It does you credit, sir,' replies Siddons. 'And, I dare say, it keeps you active, eh? A man without a trade is a man with purpose, without vigour. That has always been my watchword. People say to me, "Siddons, you must retire; quit London." I say, "Never" – sooner cut my own throat.'

'Indeed,' says Woodrow.

'And you, sir, I am pleased to make your acquaintance,' says the older man, addressing Langley. 'Remind me, what is your profession?'

'I am an architect, sir.'

'Mr. Langley is designing our new establishment,' adds Woodrow, beckoning over a white-aproned waiter. 'You care for ale, Langley? Or would you prefer porter?'

'Porter, thank you.'

The waiter nods and hurries away.

'Yes, it will be quite impressive,' continues Woodrow. 'I have a place in mind, upon Oxford Street. Five storeys. Separate floor for jewellery.'

'Of course! Langley – yes, I recall. It sounds excellent, sir,' says Siddons, raising his glass to Woodrow. 'It is a pleasure to see you prosper, I can assure you.'

'One does one's best,' replies Woodrow.

Siddons nods, smiling beneficently, but says nothing, merely raising his port to his lips.

'And your business, sir?' asks Langley, turning to the old man. 'Are you in the mourning trade too?'

'After a fashion, my good fellow,' says Siddons, 'after a fashion.'

'Mr. Siddons,' says Woodrow, by way of explanation, 'is in the undertaking line.'

'Please, sir, I beg you!' exclaims Siddons. 'You make it sound like I am a dealer in tea. I would prefer to say, if we must say anything upon the matter, that I minister to the dead. Discretion is the thing, eh?'

'Indeed. A difficult business, I should imagine,' says Langley.

'I do not complain, sir, I do not complain, but you are not wrong. Ah, here are your drinks. And here is my steak! What do you say to that, Mr. Langley? Are you partial to *filet de boeuf*?'

'It looks excellent.'

'I recommend it – please, do order something. Yes, as I was saying, it is a trying business, especially for a man of sentiment; and there are so many details to take care of. And the mutes, sir! I would not recommend you ever deal with mutes – drunkards to a man.'

The old man downs another gulp of his port, before slicing fiercely into his steak.

'We warn the bereaved, sir,' continues Siddons, 'but they will force wine and liquor on them. Like pouring water on a drowning man, it is. "Traditional".'

The old man takes another slice of meat, red and rare, and warms to his theme.

'Yes, the business takes its toll, I'll give you that. I had a terrible time of it only this very morning. Arrangements for a pair of young girls, taken in their prime. Laid them out myself. I was quite overcome, sir.'

'I can imagine it would be awfully distressing,' says Langley.

'It was, sir. Quite. Waived a crape hatband for the chief mourner. Gratis. Couldn't bring myself to add it to the bill. Two and six I'll never see again.'

'Two girls, you say?' says Jasper Woodrow, with a peculiar urgency.

66

'Pretty little things. Drowned, playing by a lake. But what a place to play, eh? Still, referred the mother to your delivery people – wouldn't leave the house till after the funeral.'

'Quite right,' says Woodrow hurriedly, 'only proper.'

Mr. Siddons nods, piercing a potato upon the end of his fork. Jasper Woodrow, meanwhile, takes out his handkerchief and wipes his brow.

CHAPTER EIGHT

'ANOTHER MYSTERY, EH, SIR?'

Webb nods.

'Must be the week for it, eh, after that business yesterday? "A very delicate matter," it says. Signed "Mr. S. Pellegrin, General Manager".'

Webb nods again.

'Can't say as I know Stoke Newington too well, sir. How about you?'

Webb shrugs. 'Well enough.'

'Now, south of the river, that's another matter. Lambeth, sir, now that was my old patch.'

'Really?'

'Know every alley like the back of my hand, sir.'

Decimus Webb nods, a rather dejected look upon his face. It may relate to the fact that, for the second time in as many days, he is trapped in a cab with Sergeant Bartleby. Worse, that he has forgotten his pipe.

'How about you, sir? Know Lambeth at all?'

Webb sighs. 'I make do, Sergeant.'

'I expect you do, sir. Now, take the Lower Marsh, say, there's a thieves' kitchen, if ever there was. I could tell you a thing or two about the goings on there, sir, things that would make your hair curl.'

Webb raises his eyebrows, touching his own slightly balding head rather self-consciously.

'So to speak, sir,' continues the sergeant, coughing.

Before Webb can reply, the cab pulls to a halt, stopping upon a cobbled fore-court.

'At last,' mutters Webb under his breath.

The driver of the hansom opens the trap and leans down to address them.

'Abney Park, gents. That'll be two bob.'

Webb and Bartleby lean forward to swing open the cab doors, and step out on to the paving. The latter pays the cabman two shillings, whilst the former surveys their destination: the tall wrought-iron gates of Abney Park Cemetery, Stoke Newington.

Webb looks down the long gravel drive beyond the entrance, then back to the gate-posts, Egyptian in style, the fashion of an earlier decade. The twin stone lodges that guard the path likewise evoke the land of the Nile, decorated with painted stone hieroglyphs. And, beside the left-hand building, nervously tapping his foot, waits a man, about fifty years old, with a sallow moustachioed face, dressed in a smart, black great-coat and a tall hat, wrapped about with a neat band of black crape. He looks rather expectantly towards the policemen. Webb walks through the open side-gate, and goes over to him.

'Mr. Pellegrin?' asks Webb.

'Yes?'

'Inspector Webb, sir, at your service. This,' he says, motioning towards the approaching Bartleby, 'is my sergeant. Your letter was passed on to me to deal with. You received our telegram, I take it?'

'Yes,' replies Mr. Pellegrin. He seems, however, more preoccupied with looking out on to the road.

'You were expecting someone else, sir?' asks Webb.

'No, no. Well, not until three o'clock, at least.'

'Three o'clock?'

'Local gentleman. Consumption.'

'A funeral?'

'Yes, of course,' replies Mr. Pellegrin. 'Please,' he says, rather urgently, 'come inside.'

Mr. Samuel Pellegrin, General Manager of the Abney Park Cemetery, leads the two policeman into the nearby lodge. The interior contains two sparsely furnished rooms for the reception of visitors; the one farthest from the door is a small office, with a desk and a trio of chairs. Pellegrin ushers Webb and Bartleby within and motions them to sit down. As he seats himself, he tidies the desk, moving several sheets of paper to one side, and closing a trade catalogue of masonry, that lies open upon a page marked 'Ten guineas and above'.

'I am sorry, Inspector,' says Mr. Pellegrin once he is settled, 'forgive me if I am rather abrupt. This business is an awful strain on my nerves. I am very grateful for your prompt attention. But, really, I am not sure how to begin – it is such a delicate matter.'

'Well, your letter was somewhat mysterious, sir,' replies Webb. 'You mentioned a theft of some kind? That would be a matter for your local constable. No need to write to the Yard in such strong terms, surely?'

Mr. Pellegrin shakes his head emphatically. 'No, sir, not the local man. Word would get round every house from here to the river in next to no time. I suppose I am fortunate you are not in uniform – if anyone were to see the police . . .'

'We generally keep to plain clothes at the Yard, sir.'

'Good, good. But I need your word, Inspector, that this will go no further. Discretion is vital in our business.'

'And mine,' replies Webb, though there is a degree of impatience in his tone. 'You have my word, sir. Perhaps if you can begin by telling us what was stolen?'

Mr. Pellegrin looks nervously at the two policemen; noticing the door of the office has been left slightly ajar, he quickly gets up to go and close it. Once he has sat down again, he bites his lip before he addresses Webb.

'A body, Inspector.'

Samuel Pellegrin leads the two policemen along the winding path that curves round the back wall of the cemetery, at the rear of the chapel.

'Any famous names here, sir?' asks the sergeant.

'In the cemetery?' says Pellegrin. He seems visibly cheered by the opportunity to talk. 'There is the Watts' memorial. And Mr. Braidwood, the fireman, of course, the far side of the chapel – you recall the Tooley Street fire? That was a fine day – the whole city lined the route – or that's how it seemed; quite affecting.'

'I can imagine, sir.'

'Ellen Warwick, of course,' continues Pellegrin, as if going through some memorised roll-call of the dead. 'Also a large turn-out, if I recollect correctly. Not long after I started here.'

'Who?' asks Bartleby.

'She was . . . ah, now, here we are, gentlemen. I am just grateful it was here, and not somewhere more in the open.'

The area in question, to which Mr. Pellegrin points, lies against the grey stone wall of the cemetery, in its farthest north-westerly corner. Shaded by an old cedar, the cold ground supports nothing so substantial as the stone angels and monumental urns that mark the cemetery's more prosperous burials. Rather, it is only broken by a scattering of makeshift-looking wooden crosses, none of which are quite perpendicular or particularly well-crafted, so that they appear to rise from the earth like the shoots of some peculiar withered shrub. In front of one cross, however, a series of planks have been laid out, which partially conceal an open grave. Bartleby leans down and looks at the cross, upon which the inscription 'J. S. Munday, 1848' is painted in small black letters, though the paint is considerably weathered and faded.

'Tell me again how you discovered the, ah, theft?' asks Webb. 'You said, did you not, that you think the grave was opened and then filled in again?'

'There is no question, Inspector,' replies Pellegrin. 'It was Greggs, one of our gardeners, who spotted it. He noticed the earth had been disturbed.'

'Very observant of him?'

'It is his job – he knows the grounds well enough. He thought at first it was an animal.'

'And what caused Mr. Greggs to change his opinion?'

'He could see it was the whole plot – I mean that it was a very particular area. Then he turned over some of the earth and found the nails.'

'From the coffin?'

'All in one spot, or thereabouts, where the fellow had left them. It was obvious the grave had been interfered with, so I told him to open it.'

'And you found?'

'It was empty. The lid had been replaced, rather inexpertly, upon the top. Please, take a look – I took care not to damage anything myself.'

Pellegrin bends down and, motioning for the assistance of Bartleby, slides away the planks covering the grave, revealing the dark long-buried wood of the lid, splintered in several places.

'It is not very deep,' says Webb. 'Three feet at most?'

Pellegrin nods. 'The ground in this corner is not so

good, Inspector. I believe the roots are a hindrance. It is, in part, why we reserve it for paupers and other unfortunates.'

'But the coffin is quite substantial, is it not? Too substantial for a parish burial?'

Pellegrin shrugs. 'I should say so. But it was not a normal parish affair. It was a case of *felo-de-se*. Suicide. It seems the family made some provision for a decent coffin.'

'Really? That is interesting. You do not know the details, I suppose?' asks Webb.

'That is not really our business, Inspector. We place a mark against our register for all such burials, but no more.'

'No, I suppose not. May I see your records, all the same?'

'Of course – we have them in the chapel – but they will tell you nothing more, I am afraid. They merely confirm the name and year.'

'Nevertheless, I should like to see it,' continues Webb. 'And I should like to speak to the gardeners, diggers . . . all your men.'

'That may take some time to arrange. We have business at three.'

'Still, if you please, Mr. Pellegrin,' replies Webb. 'Whoever you can muster – we must speak to all of them, whether now or later.'

'But, Inspector, why should someone take a body like this, and after so many years? To break in at night and do such a thing?'

'It must have been at night?'

'Nothing like this could happen during the day, Inspector. They would be noticed.'

'Perhaps there was more than a body, sir?' suggests Bartleby. 'Something buried with him, maybe. A family heirloom, that sort of thing.'

'Perhaps,' replies Webb, bending down and looking closely at the coffin lid. He stands up abruptly. 'In any case, Sergeant, I will go with Mr. Pellegrin and talk to his men. You stay here and see what you can find.'

Bartleby nods, but as Webb turns away, he stops and looks back at the sergeant.

'Well, what are you waiting for, man?'

'Sir?'

'Get down there and examine the blasted thing.'

Bartleby looks into the grave. 'Down there, sir?'

'If you have any other suggestions, Sergeant, I am happy to listen to them.'

Bartleby takes a deep breath. 'No, sir, can't say as I do.'

———

The two policemen stand to one side, hats in hand, as the three o'clock funeral procession rattles down the drive towards Abney Park's chapel. At its head are the mutes, a pair of stately, bearded men in middle age, bearing long crape-encrusted wands and black sashes about their chests. Then the four coach-horses drawing the glass hearse, their harnesses wrapped in black velvet, their heads plumed with black feathers. Finally the mourners, a dozen gentlemen in solemn mourning, arm-bands and hat-bands in black silk. Mr. Pellegrin brings up the rear, head bowed, hands clasped in contemplation. And yet he steals a nervous look at Webb and Bartleby as he walks past. Webb waits until he is out of earshot before speaking.

'Nothing in the grave, I take it?'

'No, sir,' mutters Bartleby, 'not much except dirt. Though I'd say the coffin was well lined. There was a good deal of cambric. Probably very fine in its day.'

Webb nods. 'Pellegrin thinks he may be able to find

74

the manufacturer through his catalogues – he will let us know.'

'How about the men, the diggers, sir?'

'Hmm. Neither the gardeners nor diggers had much to say for themselves. Except to confess that they hadn't cast an eye over that plot for a month or more. Mr. Pellegrin was quite aggrieved about it.'

'You don't think it was one of them, sir?'

'Maybe; but they would conceal it a trifle better, would they not?'

'Why take a body at all? I mean, sir, let's be blunt – it'd just be the bones, wouldn't it? I'm blowed if I understand it.'

'I don't know, Sergeant,' says Webb pensively. 'They bury the suicides at midnight – did you know that?'

'I knew it was after dark, sir, yes.'

'And here, someone comes at night, twenty-five years later, and digs one up.'

'Maybe they wanted to give him a decent burial.'

Webb shakes his head. 'A queer way of going about it.'

'Folk are very concerned with the welfare of their dead, sir.'

Webb looks at the now distant cortège, approaching the tall spire of the chapel and frowns.

'So are we, Sergeant.'

INTERLUDE

THAT EVENING? LET me see. The fog had cleared and so I took a walk through the streets. To begin with, I had no particular purpose in mind. I merely needed time to think and I found myself on Drury Lane.

I expect you do not know it?

You have heard of the theatre? No. Even the theatre of that name is a couple of hundred yards shy of the road itself; and with good reason. It is an awful street by night, the haunt of beer-soaked Irish and the lowest sort of unfortunate, with a ginnery upon every corner to sustain them. They are the rougher sort of public house, too, with large advertisements for Cream Gin upon the door, and blazing naked jets of gas that spit fire into the street. I expect the landlords despair of decent lamps, even if they might afford them, since they are so easily broken.

In any case, it was there, as I walked along and watched the drunks and the whores, that it struck me. It is a simple truth that is never acknowledged: a man may do exactly as he likes, in this life at least, as long as he is not *caught*. You see, all that day, I had had nagging fears of the police, of the prison cell, nay, even the gallows. But there was no detective at my door, nor policeman dogging my steps, nor was there likely to be. A man requires only a little good fortune, courage and intelligence, and he cannot be caught.

Very well. Then I shall stick to the facts of the matter.

In short, I walked without stopping until Drury Lane gave way to Holborn, and, quite by chance, I turned eastwards and suddenly came upon the crowded pavement outside the Holborn Casino.

Yes, indeed, the dance-hall.

I knew of its ill fame, of course: a magnet for fast young men and loose women eager for their company. And, indeed, that night, there was no doubting the wretched place's popularity with a certain class of 'gentleman'. For a seemingly endless row of beetle-black hansoms and clarences lined both sides of the street, whilst unacquainted men and women trotted gaily in, or stumbled drunkenly out, in bunches of two and three. In fact, it was a scene of utter dissipation.

Then it came to me, what I must do.

The police? Oh yes; they were there, to 'keep the peace'. Two of them. But my theory was quite correct. They had their minds fixed upon pickpockets and carriage-sneaks – I was quite safe. I strolled in with a few young gentlemen in evening dress, accompanying a party of ladies in satin gowns and an excess of frills and feathers. An attendant relieved us of our hats, another of our coats. Then we went down a half-dozen steps into the hall.

What do I recall about the Casino? A good deal of gold leaf and marble. I could make out the band in the gallery, a dozen or more strong, striking up a merry polka; but I could barely see the floor for dancers. The women wore high-heeled boots, the men patent leathers, and both made a riotous noise as they spun this way and that in the large hall.

The clientele? Ah. The men affected pristine kid gloves and jewelled tie-pins, but I should say they were

77

largely the middling sort, clerks and the like, that seek out such fast entertainments. There were only a handful of true gentlemen, who had quit their clubs and homes for a night on the 'spree'. They mostly hung back by the tables, smoking cigars, talking amongst themselves.

The women? I could see that many were *demimondaines*; they made no secret of it. Others, I found harder to place. Some were most likely shop-girls, who had already gone wrong, in thought if not in deed. A few were the daughters of tradesmen, perhaps; the sisters and cousins of the young men and their friends, who dragged them this way and that across the dance-floor.

You think so? I do not know. I suppose it is possible that some of them retained their virtue; that they had come in ignorance of the place's reputation. But I rather doubt it.

What then? Why, I saw her; I had been strolling around the balcony above the hall. A pretty thing. Dark-brown hair and deep hazel eyes, lace around her neck, and a gold locket that danced about as she danced. She was a graceful creature, though quite free with her favours; it was not long before I saw her kissing some pimple-faced shop-boy upon the cheek. Then, to my good fortune, her hair became loose and she had to withdraw and spend a minute or two fixing up the pins in her chignon. It was clear she was by herself; there was no beau, nor a particular table to which she retired. I went down and stood near by as the M.C. called up parties for the next set. Then, as we danced, I asked her her name, and if she cared to take a drink with me, so that we might talk.

What? Oh, I believe it was 'Kate', or 'Kath' or some such.

I have found it does not take much to win such a

woman's confidence, not one of that sort; in this case, a glass of champagne was quite sufficient. And I told her she had beautiful eyes; it is always best to say something of that nature. In any case, she was mine, if I wished it; we had but to agree a price. You see how easily virtue is bought and sold in this wretched city? But then the band struck up some wretched Prussian waltz, and she averred it was her favourite song, and 'didn't I want another dance?'

I had the knife. I might have done it there, in that booth under the stairs. No-one would have noticed. But I bided my time and said I would see her again.

Really? The family said she was not loose? Yes, I do recall that; I thought it odd at the time. I mean to say, why was she there at all?

CHAPTER NINE

ANNABEL KROUT SITS at the desk in her bedroom, her dressing-gown wrapped tightly around her. Having lit the brass oil-lamp that sits near by, she takes a note-book, pen, ink and blotting paper from the desk drawer. She opens the book and it is not long before the left-hand page is full of dense lines of neat handwriting, her words sloping strongly to the right, written in haste, as if eager to escape the confines of the page. Indeed, it is five or ten minutes before she stops, pausing for thought, touching the top of her lip with the tip of her pen.

A knock at the door interrupts her reverie. Before Annabel can contemplate uttering the words 'come in', Melissa Woodrow lets herself into the room. Like Annabel, Mrs. Woodrow is still in her night clothes, though her dressing-gown, white silk embroidered with a lotus pattern of oriental flowers, is perhaps a little more striking than her cousin's somewhat plainer article.

'Good morning, my dear,' says Mrs. Woodrow. 'I saw your lamp . . .'

'Oh!' exclaims Annabel. 'Did I disturb you? I am so sorry. I tried to keep the light dim.'

'Now, my dear, don't be so silly – we are not a penitentiary! I just wanted to make sure you were all right. Couldn't you sleep?'

80

'No, I mean yes, I slept fine, thank you. I just thought I might write my journal, before breakfast.'

Mrs. Woodrow smiles indulgently. 'Oh, your journal? Why, I quite forgot. Your mother told me about your writing – you had some little thing published, didn't you?'

'Oh, that was nothing, cousin, really,' replies Annabel.

'No, tell me, what was the magazine?'

'The *New England Monthly Bazaar*,' replies Annabel, rather shyly.

'Well, true, we don't take that here, but it was published all the same – how nice for you. You must tell Woodrow you are a "lady journalist", it will quite thrill him, I am sure. You aren't writing about us, I hope!'

Annabel Krout blushes, unconsciously placing a hand over the pages of the book, smudging the ink.

'No, just our visit to the Zoological Gardens,' she replies.

'Good! I cannot imagine what the *New England Monthly Bazaar* would make of us!'

Annabel smiles politely.

'Well,' continues Mrs. Woodrow, 'I will see you at breakfast, and we can make our plans for the day. I am sorry I retired so early last night – Lucinda quite exhausts me at times.'

'Mr. Woodrow was so late home, too.'

'Yes, I'm afraid he was. Oh, now that is some news . . . I made a suggestion, and Woodrow has taken my advice, and we are to have a little dinner party. We can introduce you to all our friends! And I have told him he must invite Mr. Langley – he is such an agreeable gentleman – so there will at least be someone whom you know.'

'Oh, really? That is very thoughtful of you,' replies Annabel.

'As long as you promise not to put us all in your

little book,' replies Mrs. Woodrow. 'Now, will I see you at breakfast?'

Annabel answers in the positive, and Mrs. Woodrow takes her leave, closing the door behind her. As soon as it is shut, Annabel turns hurriedly to her notebook, applying a sheet of blotting paper to the smudged ink. Her hands, however, are worse than the page. She goes to the wash-basin, and tries to remove the ink from her fingers, doing as best she can with the previous night's cold water and soap. It proves difficult and, resolving to wait for the morning's supply of hot water to complete the job, she tuts to herself, and dries her hands with a towel.

Outside, beyond Duncan Terrace, the trundling sound of morning traffic on the City Road can be heard in the distance. She walks over to the window. Pulling her gown close around her neck, she teases back the curtains, and peers into the gas-lit street below. It is not yet dawn, and the sky is itself an inky blue-black, hinting at daylight. Looking out along the street, on the opposite side of the road, she can make out a man, short and stocky in build, wearing a thick winter coat.

He stops and stares up at her; it is not merely a glance, but a long inquisitive stare. Instinctively, she draws the curtains shut, but then she cannot resist opening them a inch or so, and peering through the gap.

The man in the street, however, has already moved on.

━━━

Breakfast with the Woodrows passes much as the day before. The same bacon, the same eggs, and the same supplementary cold cuts of ham and pork, elegantly laid out upon a silver platter. In fact, it strikes Annabel

Krout that the cold meat on offer is precisely the same, to the very last scrap of fat. But if she wonders about this coincidence of household economy, she is too polite to mention it to her cousin.

Mr. Woodrow, in turn, retains the same taciturn manner, removing his gaze from the newspaper once to inquire on Annabel's health, and a second time as to whether the Zoological Gardens were pleasant. He gives no great impression of listening to either reply; he merely nods at suitable intervals. Mrs. Woodrow, on the other hand, supplies any silence with what amounts to a litany of possibilities for travel and exploration in the great metropolis. If Annabel herself expresses a slight preference, it is again to see either of the grand churches, the Abbey or St. Paul's. She finds it moderately surprising, therefore, that her cousin assures her that she 'must' first see Regent Street. And she cannot help but think that, given Melissa Woodrow's elaborate descriptions of the quality and elegance of millinery and haberdashery on display in said thoroughfare, there is a certain degree of self-interest in Mrs. Woodrow's eagerness to parade her cousin along the 'finest street in London'. Moreover, Annabel suspects that, conjoined with the exhortation that she herself must acquire 'a hat suitable to this season', there also is something of a hat-shaped yearning in her cousin's heart.

Nonetheless, she agrees graciously enough to the proposal, and so finds herself, an hour after breakfast, sitting in the Woodrows' brougham, together with Melissa Woodrow, as it speeds down Pentonville Hill, towards King's Cross station. Annabel peers eagerly through the vehicle's windows, looking for landmarks she might recall from the previous day. Even though their carriage goes at a fast trot, she soon recognises the distinctive domed bell-tower of St. James's church,

Pentonville, as they hasten down the hill. Likewise, the sooty terraces of two- and three-storey shops and houses that line the lower reaches of the road, their rows of chimney pots, puffing smoke into the clear winter sky. The houses, however, rather offend Annabel's conception of the great city; they seem far too small and packed close together. They appear so cramped and confined that she silently wonders if, each night, they do not impatiently nudge one against the other, and thus quietly descend the slope by a few inches.

She puts her disappointment with the homes of Pentonville to the back of her mind. For the great shed of St. Pancras station comes into full view, looming above the King's Cross rooftops, like the beached, upturned hull of some enormous abandoned ship. As they draw closer to the station, and the Gothic extravagance of the Midland Grand Hotel, Annabel presses her face against the window of the brougham. But the window seems determined to make itself disagreeable, rattling with every bump in the road and clattering noisily in its frame. Annabel, therefore, reluctantly sits back in her seat, much to the relief of her cousin who talks ominously of 'catching a chill'.

'But it's such a beautiful day,' exclaims Annabel, regardless. 'It's so bright – I wasn't sure you got such days here, after that terrible fog.'

'Yes, my dear, but it will change just as quickly. And think of the wind – you must keep yourself warm. Your dear mother would never forgive me if I sent you home ill.'

Annabel reluctantly agrees, making a somewhat token rearrangement of her scarf. And, as Mrs. Woodrow enters into a discourse upon the dangers of the English climate, her American cousin quietly takes in the sights of the Euston Road. From the monumental Greek females adorning St. Pancras Church, to the discreet stone steps leading to Euston Square's subterranean station, Annabel Krout finds something of interest on every corner. And if, as the brougham turns south, Gower Street's tedious terraces offer little excitement, there is some satisfaction in the transitory glimpses of everyday life: a woman waving her umbrella frantically at a passing Brompton omnibus, failing to catch its driver's attention; a boy, in the distinctive red coat and blue cap of the Shoeblack Brigade, who sits mournfully against a lamp-post.

Annabel contemplates writing an article for the *New England Monthly Bazaar* entitled 'London Street Scenes'.

Melissa Woodrow gently taps her on the arm, as their carriage turns on to New Oxford Street.

'There is the Warehouse, my dear, just down there. We might pay a visit on the way back.'

Annabel cranes her neck to see Woodrow's General Mourning Warehouse, but the building is far too distant, and the brougham far too quick, for her to make out anything whatsoever.

'Ah,' says Mrs. Woodrow, 'now we are almost there. Oxford Street. We won't stop here, mind.'

'There are so many stores, though,' replies Annabel.

'Shops. Yes, but they are generally, well, not what one might call "select",' says Mrs. Woodrow, wrinkling her nose slightly, as if noticing an unwelcome aroma.

'I see,' says Annabel.

Indeed, there is some truth in Mrs. Woodrow's comment, even to Annabel's untrained eye. For every three-storey 'Warehouse' and 'Establishment', with a fine name painted in black upon the ground-floor cornice, or spelt in curlicues of iron-work, or etched in gold onto pristine plate glass, there is a shoddier, smaller relation not too far distant. For every giant of commerce proudly proclaiming its wares, from the seller of feather beds to the grandest Gentleman's Outfitter, there is a dustier, bullion-glass window, behind which hides a crumpled Wholesale Stationer, or mildewed Wine Vaults. And every few hundred yards squats a public house, none of which resembles the fine timbered coaching inns and friendly taverns that form Annabel Krout's impression of a proper English drinking-place. Thus, if Mrs. Woodrow does not think much of Oxford Street, her cousin is content to agree with her.

As they near Oxford Circus, progress in the brougham becomes rather slow. Mrs. Woodrow tuts at the snaking queue of omnibuses that prevents the vehicle making headway. Annabel, for her part, passes the time making a mental note of the different colour liveries and place names of the buses passing by on the other side, the faces of the passengers and the nimble conductors, who seem able to balance themselves precariously upon the iron step at the rear of their bus, at the slightest notice.

In fact, it is some ten or fifteen minutes before the Woodrows' brougham can finally turn into Regent Street, drawing to a halt outside King and Sheath, Linen Drapers.

'Of course, the eastern side of Regent Street is the fashionable side,' says Mrs. Woodrow, as she leads her cousin from the interior of Barrett's, Milliners. 'It is *the* place to be seen.'

'Why is that?' asks Annabel, stepping out onto the busy pavement. 'The other looks just as grand.'

'Loungers, my dear. The west side attracts the worse

sort of gentleman, if that is the word. They say it is the shade it gets in the summer.'

Annabel looks at the objectionable western side of the street. The classical façades of the shops are as tall as those of the east; the columns and entablature as pronounced; the plate-glass as transparent. She can, moreover, see no evidence of the worst or best sort of gentleman. There is simply a multitude of men and women, and a few children, some strolling, some pausing in front of shop windows. And what luxurious windows! Within one, elegant shawls sit draped over tilted display tables; in another rows of lace-fringed bonnets hang upon pegs; in the next, moiré and brocaded surah silk, ready to be fashioned into costumes by a talented dress-maker. Next a music-shop, in which colourful lithograph covers are presented like fans. Then a confectioner's, with cakes and bon-bons and jellies, glistening in the light, framed by frosted barley-sugar. In fact, the only difference Annabel can make out between east and west, as she strolls beside her cousin, is that the eastern flag-stones attract larger carriages, parked by the kerb.

These, she is discreetly informed by Mrs. Woodrow, are Mayfair coaches, stately landaus that rarely trespass beyond the confines of the West End. Twice the size of a humble brougham, she notices that several bear a crest, emblazoned on to the carriage door. One even boasts a strong-calved footman, who, to all appearances, does nothing but perch at the rear of the vehicle, staring sternly into the middle distance. Any pedestrian activity is carried out by shopmen and women, who scurry between their business and the waiting carriages, arms laden with goods. A nod or smile from within the confines of the coach, and they return happy; a shake of the head, and they return crushed, muttering the words 'carriage-trade' bitterly under their breath. In either case, the comings and goings quite fascinate her. Mrs. Woodrow, in turn, slows her walking pace to a crawl, casting cautious glances into the interior of each vehicle.

'You never know who you might see, my dear,' she whispers, confidingly to her cousin. 'Now, where shall we go next? Allison's, I think.'

Annabel smiles, but her outward good humour conceals an awkward hour and a half already spent in three milliners, at none of which a hat has been purchased. The prospect of immediately repeating the experience, watching her cousin vacillate between various grades of fabric and lace, does not fill her with enthusiasm.

'May we not get something to eat, cousin?' she suggests placidly.

'Why yes, my dear, why didn't you say if you were hungry? I know a delightful little confectioner's in the Quadrant.'

❧

It transpires that there is a bonnet-maker's and a milliner's upon Mrs. Woodrow's route to Cooke and Stephenson, Quality Confectioners. In consequence, it is still a good hour before the two women repair to said establishment. Two hats have, at least, been purchased in the meantime, and delivery to Duncan Terrace arranged.

The interior of Cooke and Stephenson proves to be a welcome oasis of calm, beside the bustling street. It contains a dozen or more small tables, topped by lace cloths; these, in turn, face a long mahogany counter upon which sweetmeats and cakes are proudly displayed. Behind the counter, the wood panels along the walls are inlaid with mirrors, above each of which a small gas-light flickers. Meanwhile, two or three women sit at each table, chatting quietly, as a pina-fored waitress ferries tea and coffee, and all manner of sugared eatables, about the room.

It takes a moment for a space to be found; but, at last, Annabel and her cousin are placed in a window seat, facing the traffic as it trundles down to Piccadilly Circus. Once an order for tea and scones is placed, however, Mrs. Woodrow delicately excuses herself to 'rearrange her hair', leaving her cousin to watch the world outside.

Annabel, for her part, is content to enjoy a few moments of solitude. She tries her best to store the details of Regent Street in her mind, the better to record them later: the men and women in smart morning dress, the dirt upon their boots; the sandwich-board man, weary in appearance, whose signboards proclaim 'Westley's Restorative Mixture' and a dozen illegible testimonials to its efficacy. Then a crossing-sweep, who rushes by, a Hindoo boy by the look of him, whose face so intrigues her that she is half tempted to run after him, as he scurries along the street, pestering likely prospects for a penny. So engrossed does she become in the minutiae of the scene, as if in some panorama presented for her enter-tainment, that she does not notice the man standing beside her, until he leans down to address her. He is a fat, round-faced man, with a dark Mediterranean complexion, hidden only a little by the lapels of his coat, pulled tight up about his neck.

'Miss Woodrow, I presume?' he says, making Annabel jump with surprise.

'No, I'm sorry,' she replies, uncertain quite how to frame a polite reply to the stranger. 'I am a friend of the family.'

'Ah, I see, I am sorry to give you any trouble.'

'No, you haven't. If you wait a moment—'

But before Annabel can finish the sentence, the man has turned and left. She watches him in astonishment, as he walks briskly through the door, brushing past a woman coming in, and then across the street, disappearing into the crowd.

She stands up to see if she can still see him, further along the road, when Melissa Woodrow reappears at her side.

'What's wrong, my dear?'

'A man just came in here and asked if I was "Miss Woodrow", then just rushed out.'

'Really? How odd – did he leave his card?'

Annabel shakes her head. 'No – he was very peculiar. I think he might have been an Italian or—'

'A foreigner? My dear, the man was trying to proposition you – and I thought this was a respectable place!'

The nearest waitress scowls at Mrs. Woodrow's highly audible exclamation.

'But how did he know your name?' continues Annabel.

'I should imagine he was walking behind us, overheard us talking. They have terrible cunning, my dear. You have had a lucky escape.'

'Yes,' mutters Annabel, looking over to where the man disappeared from view, a distracted look upon her face. It suddenly occurs to her that she has seen him before.

It takes her a moment to recall, then it comes to her. It is the face of the man from earlier in the day; the man who stood outside the Woodrows' home in Duncan Terrace, looking up at her window.

CHAPTER TEN

It is late afternoon when Sergeant Bartleby jogs
up the narrow winding stairs that lead to Decimus
Webb's office. The room is one of several belonging to
the Detective Branch, situated above the old arched
gateway that guards the cobbles of Great Scotland
Yard. Cramped, ill-ventilated, with the distinct smell
of horse dung from the yard outside, it is little used by
its tenant. Today, however, with nothing to occupy his
time but reading several long-winded reports and
pursuing a detailed claim for the sum of £2 10s.,
travelling expenses, Inspector Webb is to be found *in
situ*.

Bartleby takes a breath and knocks on the open
door, cautiously stepping over several crates full of
books and papers that partially block the entrance.
Webb looks up from his work, and beckons him to sit
down – but it is no easy task for the sergeant. The
office interior, dimly lit by a pair of gas-lamps, its walls
decorated with ageing yellow flock, contains obstacles
for the unwary pedestrian, similar to those on the
landing. In fact, the accumulated detritus of several
years of investigations are laid out upon the floor, with
papery traces of old murders, abductions and frauds
scattered around Webb's desk.

The arrangement is not entirely Webb's fault. It is

common knowledge that the search for a new, spacious, more reputable headquarters for the Detective Branch has long been a talking point and a challenge for the Police Commissioners. Nonetheless, as Bartleby sits waiting for his superior to finish writing, he wonders if he ought to suggest the purchase of some drawers for filing. He is about to say something, when Webb speaks up.

'Well, what is it?' asks the inspector, at last, putting down his pen.

'Nothing much, sir,' replies Bartleby, instantly repenting of the putative drawers. 'A letter from Inspector Hanson, and a telegram from Mr. Pellegrin, Abney Park.'

'I remember the fellow's location, Sergeant – well, what does it say?'

'Which, sir?'

Webb sighs. 'Begin with Hanson.'

'Ah, well, in short, sir,' says Bartleby with a slight smile, 'it appears they've lost Mr. Brown. They had a watch on his lodgings but he . . . ah, here it is,' he says, pulling out the letter in question, 'he "evaded the constable on duty" and he asks us to notify the divisions. Wouldn't think it, would you, sir? Big fellow like that. Hard to miss him, I would have thought.'

'Yes, yes. In any case, have you arranged it?'

'Telegraphed all the particulars to the divisions, and put a note in next week's Bulletin,' replies Bartleby.

'Good. Well, we can keep an eye out for him. Poor Hanson. What does Mr. Pellegrin have to say for himself?'

Bartleby retrieves the telegram. 'Ah yes, well, turns out he found the undertaker that made the coffin, like you asked – Siddons & Sons, Salisbury Square, Fleet Street.'

'Siddons? Ah yes, I know the name.'

'You think they might have a record?'

'Well, I do not suppose they buried that many J.S. Mundays in Abney Park in 1848, do you, Sergeant? At the very least we might inquire.'

'I suppose so, sir.'

'Well then,' says Webb, looking back down at his papers, 'what are you waiting for?'

'I'll be off, sir,' says Bartleby.

⁓

Sergeant Bartleby strolls briskly out of Scotland Yard, past the Clarence public house, and on to Whitehall. It is almost dusk and a cold evening. Although at first inclined to walk, the approach of a chocolate-coloured 'Westminster' omnibus, bound for the Bank, persuades him to take a seat inside. It is a choice he regrets, however, since a crowd pile in at Charing Cross. They include a large matron with a hatbox and mysterious wicker-basket, from which emit occasional yaps and barks; a junior office boy, dressed suitably for the part, with a workaday tweed suit and a super-abundance of hair-oil; and a trio of infant boys, given to climbing, together with a harassed female, most likely a servant, since she is too young to be their mother. Pushed into a corner, the sergeant idly wonders if a uniformed officer would receive the same treatment.

The bus, nonetheless, travels swiftly along the Strand. It only slows when it has passed St. Clement's. For, as it approaches the narrow arch of Temple Bar, a brief altercation with the owner of a waggon serves to distract the driver. Once this is resolved, the vehicle does not stop until Bartleby alights, a little past Bolt Court, where the conductor offers a gracious 'mind yer feet'. Thence it is a short walk to Salisbury Square, on the opposite side of the street, through a narrow alley.

The square itself is no match for the regular London square, such as Trafalgar or Bedford, being both considerably smaller and irregular in appearance, an accidental void between opposing buildings. It boasts a hotel, a couple of printers, and, upon the western side, the public façade of Siddons & Sons, identifiable both by its name in tasteful gold leaf, and a window displaying a draped urn, carved from marble, illuminated by a half-dozen small jets of gas. It is to this establishment that Sergeant Bartleby turns his steps.

The interior of Siddons & Sons, or at least the antechamber in which visitors are received, before visiting the show-rooms, proves to be as plain as the exterior. Dimly lit, it contains merely a trio of uncomfortable-looking chairs, and a sombre-looking black-suited employee seated at a small desk, atop of which sits a single vase of dried flowers. The only lively touch is the small fire crackling in the hearth, though it gives out little heat, and, above, upon the mantel, the room's solitary nod to ornamentation: a small Parian statuette of a girl, dressed in Roman attire, her head bowed, a piece marked 'Maidenhood', in small chiselled lettering.

Bartleby briskly introduces himself. He relishes using the words 'of Scotland Yard', and they have the desired effect. For he is swiftly ushered through an unobtrusive side-door, along a corridor, and, after a few hushed words of consultation, into the presence of Joshua Siddons, proprietor.

The room of Mr. Siddons is a little brighter than those reserved for his visitors. In addition to the lights on each wall, his desk supports two lamps, capped by shades of delicately etched glass; moreover, his fireplace blazes fiercely, and is wide enough for two persons to stand or sit in front of it. The chair upon which he sits, and the one to which he directs Bartleby, are well-padded. It is, in short, more like the study of a comfortable bachelor.

'So, my dear sir,' says the undertaker, before Bartleby is settled, 'this is a sad day. A loss. A great loss. But, if it is not presumptuous of me to say it, you have chosen the right establishment.'

'Sir?'

'I mean to say, Sergeant, a loss for the Metropolitan Police is a loss for the metropolis; there can be no doubt of it. And, rest assured, it will be not so much a job of work for my men, sir, as a welcome duty. A duty, I dare say, Siddons and Sons are best equipped to perform.'

'No, sir, you don't quite—'

'Come, come,' says Siddons, talking over the sergeant's protestations, 'I know, my dear fellow. The Commissioner is not made of money; we can discuss a small discount when the time comes. The first matter, I should say, is the coffin . . . I assume the deceased had no family. Married to the "force", eh?'

'No, sir, please – I am not here to arrange a funeral.'

'Not here to arrange a funeral? My dear fellow, I am at a loss.'

'A police matter, sir. I think your man must have misunderstood me. We rather hoped you might be able to assist us.'

Siddons looks surprised. He takes out his black-bordered handkerchief, and rubs his nose.

'I see. You must forgive me, Sergeant. I believe I have caught a slight cold. But how on earth can I assist Scotland Yard? Oh, pray, my good man, say it is not an exhumation! They are so contrary to the spirit of our profession.'

'Well,' replies Bartleby, 'it is rather too late for that, sir.'

'Too late?'

'To be blunt, sir, a body was stolen recently from Abney Park Cemetery, dug up. The manager, Mr. Pellegrin, has asked us to look into it.'

'Good Lord – yes, I know Pellegrin – but why on earth should anyone do such a thing in this day and age? And how do you imagine I can help you?'

'He said it was one of your coffins, sir.'

'Really?' replies Siddons. 'Well, then I am sure it was. Pellegrin knows his business.'

'Then might you have some record of the deceased? At the moment, we merely have the name and year.'

'Records? I might find you the man's profession, I should think,' replies the undertaker, pensively. 'We take note of that, and we may have the next of kin – but Pellegrin should have all this, else who pays for maintenance of the plot?'

'That is the thing, sir. The chap was a suicide – though he had some money to be buried, looking at the coffin.'

'How odd. What was it? What type?'

'The coffin?' says Bartleby, taking out his note-book, 'I have it here. Ah, yes, a "Patent Inconsolable" in rosewood, cambric-lined.'

'Three and six. Your man was not an utter pauper, at least, Sergeant. Well, you had best tell me the name – I will have someone look into it.'

'J.S. Munday, sir. And the year was 1848.'

Mr. Siddons laughs, a rather nervous impulsive laugh, that quite unsettles the studied sobriety of his thin face.

'Forgive me, Sergeant,' he says, 'you are chaffing me, surely? This a prank of some kind?'

'Not at all, sir,' says Bartleby, perplexed.

'But surely Mr. Pellegrin would recall,' says Siddons, ruminating, 'although, I suppose it is a few years before his time. Good Lord. Well, what is promised us in

Isaiah, Sergeant?' continues the undertaker with a slight smile. '"The earth shall cast out the dead", is it not?'

'I think we can assume it wasn't the hand of God, sir. Perhaps you had better tell me what you know?'

'You need only go back to the newspapers for that year, Sergeant.'

'And what should I look out for, sir?'

'Eloi Chapel, Sergeant. Let me tell you about Eloi Chapel . . .'

———

Inspector Webb puts down the last of his reading material, just as Bartleby enters his office.

'You might knock, Sergeant,' says Webb.

'Sorry, sir.'

'Well, you've found something, I can tell from your eager expression. It reminds me of a dog with a bone. Out with it, if you must.'

'The grave, sir, Siddons knew it straightaway.'

'Really? How so?'

'He said the man was notorious in the undertaking trade, sir. Jeremy Sayers Munday. Hung himself. I hadn't heard of him myself, but perhaps you have – he was the man behind the Eloi Chapel Company.'

'I recall the name of the chapel – a scandal of some kind?' says Webb.

'Apparently. It was an old church they fixed up in the forties and cleared the vaults for burials. Siddons said they held services for six thousand dead before they closed it down in forty-eight.'

'Ah yes,' says Webb with a smirk, 'but, in fact, it only held a few hundred? Yes, I remember it well – it caused quite a commotion at the time.'

'They only found out when they caught them dumping bodies, burying them with quicklime. Mr. Siddons couldn't quite recall the place – Hackney

Marsh, he thought. I can look back through the papers, if you like.'

'I should say you'd better,' replies Webb. 'Well, at least now we can find the gentleman's family, inform them of their, ah, loss. Did Siddons have any note of the next of kin?'

'He said he would have to dig around for it, sir, if you'll forgive the expression. Wasn't sure he would, given the unfortunate circumstances. Even if he does, I don't suppose the family'll be too glad to hear about it.'

'No. Still, ironic, is it not? That someone should exhume Mr. J.S. Munday, when he couldn't bring himself to bury most of his customers?'

'Mr. Siddons said much the same, sir – quite tickled him.'

———

Joshua Siddons looks thoughtfully at the leather-bound ledger that sits upon his writing desk. The leather itself is a light brown, the cover embossed with a geometric pattern, the spine rather care-worn but with the date '1848' visible in gold letters. Siddons opens the book, leafing through the pages until he comes to a particular point. He pauses for a moment, as if lost in thought, then tears the page out, creasing it into a ball, and turning to throw it upon the fire.

He returns his gaze to the damaged book and, after a few moments more, begins to methodically tear out the remaining pages.

CHAPTER ELEVEN

'THAT CHILD IS determined to thwart me!' exclaims Melissa Woodrow, returning to the downstairs parlour of Duncan Terrace. Annabel Krout, who sits upon the sofa, reading the latest issue of the *Leisure Hour*, looks up. 'A whole bag of sugared almonds,' continues Mrs. Woodrow, 'and she barely said "thank you"! She was so sullen, I'd half a mind to take them back.'

'Oh,' replies Annabel, 'perhaps she is just a little tired?'

'A little terror would be more accurate,' replies Mrs. Woodrow, sitting down. 'Lucinda can just be so stubborn when she has a mind to be – she has it from her father's side – and she is quite determined to sulk.'

'Because we did not take her to Regent Street today?'

'Precisely,' replies Mrs. Woodrow.

'May I say something, Melissa?'

'Of course.'

'Well, it really is not my place, but I can't help wonder if she would improve with more company of her own age? Does she have many play-mates?'

'Annabel, my dear,' replies Mrs. Woodrow, putting her hand lightly on her cousin's arm, 'I know you mean well, but she has such a delicate constitution, and, besides, she has Jacobs and myself here. In any case, we could hardly have taken her out after yesterday's little adventure. She must learn her lesson . . .'

Mrs. Woodrow pauses, at the sound from the hall. 'Ah, that will be Jasper! Best not to say anything about Lucinda's little mood, dear. It will only make him cross.'

Annabel agrees, putting down her magazine, as the front door slams shut. The voice of Jasper Woodrow can be heard, calling for his manservant, to assist in the removal of his coat and procure him a 'refresher'. When he finally enters the parlour, Annabel notes the latter article to consist of a large glass of brandy.

'Good evening,' says Woodrow, nodding rather uneasily to his house-guest, then to his wife. 'Terrible night. Awful chill in the air. Thought I'd come home at a decent hour, my dear.'

'Well, thank heavens,' says Mrs. Woodrow, gesturing towards the glass, 'but isn't it a little early for that? Whatever will Annabel think?'

'I am sure Miss Krout, though of Boston, is not a Puritan, Melissa,' says Woodrow, though he gives no opportunity for Annabel to reply one way or another, for which, in fact, she is rather grateful. 'And, besides, I believe we have something to celebrate.'

'Really?'

'Saw Langley again. His man's happy with the deed – only wants signing. Junior partner.'

'Why, that is excellent news,' remarks Mrs. Woodrow. 'Mr. Langley is such an affable young man.'

'Is he? Well, he's a wealthy one, according to his bankers,' says Woodrow.

'Really, my dear!' exclaims Mrs. Woodrow.

'Forgive me, Miss Krout, if I speak too bluntly,' says Woodrow. 'My wife is quite right.'

'Not at all,' replies Annabel.

'A man of business will be blunt, you'll find – it becomes a habit. I expect your father is much the same.'

'I couldn't say, sir,' replies Annabel. 'He doesn't talk much of his business affairs at home.'

'Quite right,' replies Woodrow, taking a nervous sip of brandy. 'Quite right.'

'Well,' says Mrs. Woodrow, cheerily, 'I shall go and have Mrs. Figgis prepare dinner. Something special – Lord knows what we have in the larder, mind.'

Her husband, however, shakes his head. 'Ah, no. Not tonight.'

'Not tonight?'

'Thought we might dine out, treat ourselves to a night at the Criterion. Reserved a table for six sharp.'

'The Criterion!' exclaims Mrs. Woodrow. 'Woodrow, how clever of you! But that only gives us an hour.'

'You best hurry. And I've booked the theatre at eight. Comedy. Hope you like the theatre, Miss Krout?'

'Well, of course,' replies Annabel.

'The Criterion, Piccadilly, my dear,' says Mrs. Woodrow, as if not quite satisfied her cousin has grasped the full significance of her husband's offer. 'It's the newest, most luxurious place in London. A restaurant and theatre together – and the theatre is underground, though you'd never know it – can you believe it? Quite the latest thing. It is just too perfect! Why, Woodrow, you might look a little more cheerful?'

'Yes, my dear,' replies her husband, forcing a smile and taking another sip.

❧

The cab that Mr. Woodrow acquires for the journey to the Criterion is more comfortable than the rented family brougham, not least in possessing seats for four passengers, rather than merely two. Annabel Krout, once more, tries to capture glimpses of the city as it passes by. Peculiar lights abound, from the dots of white-yellow gas that illuminate distant streets, to the tarpaulin tent that shelters a nocturnal coffee-stall outside King's Cross station, and the brazier that burns beside it. She marvels at the coal-red glow warming the faces of the handful of figures clustered around.

'A cold night, eh?' says Jasper Woodrow, following Annabel's gaze. 'You know, I shouldn't be surprised if a fog isn't setting in.'

'Really? How can you tell?' replies Annabel.

'Melissa will tell you I have a nose for it.'

'He does, my dear,' agrees Mrs. Woodrow. 'Quite uncanny.'

Woodrow shakes his head. 'One merely has to look into the distance. Muddy-looking, eh?'

'I can't tell,' replies Annabel, peering down side-streets as the cab trundles along.

Woodrow nods. 'Well, you don't know the city, Miss Krout – but I expect it all looks quite wretched compared to Boston. I expect Boston's a tidy little place, eh?'

'I couldn't say.'

'Quite right, my dear, a diplomatic answer,' interjects Mrs. Woodrow. 'Stop tormenting the poor girl, Woodrow!'

'I intended no such thing,' protests Jasper Woodrow. 'I merely wondered what Miss Krout made of the metropolis.'

'You are an awful ill-mannered brute,' says Mrs. Woodrow, affectionately, 'and you know it.'

Woodrow merely shakes his head.

'And,' continues Mrs. Woodrow, 'you have not told

us what is the play.'

'A surprise, my dear,' replies Woodrow.

'Well! I hope it is a pleasant one,' says Mrs. Woodrow, though her tone of voice suggests she is quite excited by the mystery.

Annabel, on the other hand, returns to placidly watching the streets go by, as the carriage turns and hastens along Gower Street, then along New Oxford Street. After a few minutes, it swings abruptly down a narrow lane.

'Where are we now?' asks Annabel.

'Soho,' replies Mr. Woodrow. 'Awful area – wretched foreigners everywhere – Frenchies, Italians, all sorts.'

Annabel Krout blushes, perhaps waiting for the list to include another particular nationality, but Mr. Woodrow does not notice her slight discomfort.

Mrs. Woodrow, meanwhile, returns to talking amiably of her favourite theatrical experiences, and the best theatres in London, and the famous theatrical personages she has seen in a variety of interesting circumstances. Her cousin stares out of the window. Soho, it seems to Annabel, grows darker and darker as the clarence penetrates further into its labyrinthine arteries.

'Damned fog,' mutters Woodrow. 'I knew it.'

Indeed, a fog is undoubtedly brewing: the gas-lights seem to flare in an increasingly brown-ish hue; the faces of the district's foreign exiles, leaving the coffee-shops and cheap lodgings, loitering outside cramped terraces, begin to take on a dull, shifting mutability; the very air seems to grow thick and smudged. But just as Annabel fears the cab cannot safely escape the warren of streets, they pull out into a wider, open boulevard, well-illuminated on both sides, and, within a few moments, draw to a halt by the Criterion.

'Ah, here at last!'

The two women wait for Mr. Woodrow to open the door, exit the cab and pay the driver. Annabel, in turn, then insists her cousin goes first after her husband. But as Annabel steps out of the carriage, taking Woodrow's hand, she is struck by the sound of her cousin's amused laughter. It is so distinct that Annabel worries she herself, through some peculiar breach of English etiquette, is the cause of it.

'My dear – look – how delightful – it couldn't be more apt.'

Annabel looks at the theatre. Even in the lowering fog, the grand white stone-work of the Criterion's classical façade is quite visible, though its smaller detailing – the chiselled cornucopias, cheery-faced cherubs and draped statuary, sunk in various alcoves beneath the entablature – is a little indistinct. But it is the iron-canopied entrance, and the sign beneath to which Mrs. Woodrow draws her attention, the sign announcing the evening's comedy: *An American Lady*.

'*An American Lady* – Woodrow, how clever of you!'

'Come then, let's go in,' says Woodrow. 'I hope the grill room suits you? I don't have much time for French muck, I'm afraid, Miss Krout. Still – I expect you Yankees are much the same – prefer a nice bit of well-cooked meat, eh?'

Annabel smiles politely; she decides she might enjoy a comedy after her dinner.

———

Harold: Marry an American lady? An impossibility.
Greville: Why on earth do you say that?
Harold: Oh, the American gentleman exists, for are

you not an American, Greville? But when you talk of
the opposite sex, well . . .

❧

'What do you make of it, Miss Krout? Not too bad,
eh?'

Annabel Krout bites her tongue.

❧

Harold: She's so unlike any woman I ever met; so
honest, so appreciative; by Jove she might almost have
been an Englishwoman!

❧

With the play long since finished, Annabel inches her
way forward through the Criterion's foyer, together
with Mr. and Mrs. Woodrow, having finally acquired
her coat and hat from the cloak-room. Unfortunately,
the queue to leave the narrow lobby, and acquire one of
the cabs that queue around the circumference of
Piccadilly Circus, is even greater than that for coats.
Moreover, the fog has developed into the treacly brown
variety that obscured Annabel's first night in the capital.
Thus, with the cabs themselves only dim outlines, best
located by the gleaming twin lamps at the front of each
vehicle, the progress of the outgoing theatre audience is
a slow one. Annabel watches the stop-start movement
of the crowd in the foyer's gilded mirrors: the men in
evening dress, restraining their steps to half-paces; the
woman shifting by inches, nervously wrapping their
skirts close to their legs, lest the footfall of a muddy boot
should tear the hem of a prized silk.

'Well, I do think it was awfully funny,' says Mrs.
Woodrow, as they approach the doors. 'Mr. Byron is
such a clever writer. Did you not warm to it, Annabel
dear?'

Annabel merely smiles and nods as the crowd trickles forward. Fortunately, any further discussion of the play's merits is curtailed as they push through the doors on to the pavement.

'Ah, thank goodness,' exclaims Mrs. Woodrow. 'Woodrow – where are you? Woodrow!'

'Here, my dear.'

'Go and find a cab, for pity's sake. Why on earth you did not reserve the carriage for our return, I do not know.'

'I was not sure of the hour.'

'I hardly see how that matters, my dear.'

Woodrow says no more and hurries off, but within a couple of minutes a dozen or two dozen more parties come out of the Criterion with precisely the same intention. Jasper Woodrow, at length, returns with the news that only a hansom can be found.

'I suppose it best the pair of you take that, and I'll find another,' says Woodrow.

'But my dear—' exclaims Mrs. Woodrow.

'The blasted fellow will take someone else, if you are not careful, Melissa. I've already given him two bob – come now.'

To Annabel's relief, Mrs. Woodrow consents, doubtless contemplating the merits of a hansom against standing in the cold, fog-soaked air.

Jasper Woodrow, meanwhile, watches the cab turn off the main road and disappear into the swirling mist. Without a glance to the remaining carriages, he sets off at a brisk walking pace, in the direction of Holborn.

CHAPTER TWELVE

OUTSIDE WOODROW'S GENERAL MOURNING Warehouse, beneath the shop's glowing advertisement for 'Every Article of the Very Best Description', stands a solitary man, wearing the heavy woollen great-coat that is obligatory for anyone spending November in London. In the darkness, illuminated only by the residual glow of the gas-lit sign, he appears and disappears with the movement of the fog, with every gust of wind. Indeed, it is only a handful of passengers in passing cabs and carriages that even notice the figure waiting by the kerb, peering into the road. Nonetheless, the man in question is no nocturnal phantom, but the new partner-to-be in Woodrow's General Mourning, Richard Langley.

Langley takes out his pocket-watch, finds that the dial is impossible to make out, and snaps the case shut in annoyance. He walks a few nervous paces back and forth. In fact, he gives every impression of being about to leave his self-imposed sentry-duty. He is only stopped by the approach of a second party, indistinct in the nocturnal gloom, who, by the booming sound of his voice, reveals himself to be Jasper Woodrow.

'Langley! My apologies!' exclaims Woodrow, shaking his new partner firmly by the hand. There is a hint of alcohol on his breath.

'Sir, you said half-past ten.'

'My dear fellow,' says Woodrow, 'I know, forgive me. I had another small matter to dispose of. Didn't anticipate the fog – should have said we'd meet in a decent public. Still, no harm in taking a look at the old place. Part yours now, of course – well, from tomorrow.'

'I still do not quite see why we could not have waited?'

'Wait? I thought you were keen? Wet the baby's head and all that? Just a little tipple. Thought you enjoyed a drink?'

'Yes, but—'

'Well then. Come, what do you say to the Casino – just round the corner?'

'Well, I have never . . . I mean to say, I don't normally keep such late hours.'

'Didn't think you did, old chap – precisely why I suggested it. You look like you need a bit of gaiety. We all do, eh? Best place in London for—'

Langley interrupts. 'I know, you have mentioned it before.'

'What do you say, then?'

Woodrow looks steadily at his companion.

'I suppose so.'

'No harm in a little drink, a little dance with a young gal, eh? Good for the spirits. Are you courting, Langley?'

'No,' replies Langley.

'Well, all the better. I'll see you right, my boy – come, this way. Haven't been there for years myself, of course. Not much call for old dogs like me in such places. Not at all.'

Jasper Woodrow gestures towards the east and, without waiting for a reply, strides purposefully into the fog, forcing Langley to follow.

Duncan Terrace.

'Jacobs, are you there?'

'Sorry, ma'am. Yes, ma'am.'

'Take these coats and do your best to clean them; the fog is terribly bad and we are both quite covered in smut. And I might take a bath before I retire.'

'Yes, ma'am. Is the master not home?'

'No, he is delayed; we had difficulties finding a cab for all three of us.'

'You have some post, ma'am.'

'Thank you, I'll look at it later.'

In a corner of the Holborn Casino's great hall, Jasper Woodrow leans back upon his chair, tilting the legs, surveying the couples dancing a lively *schottische* upon the dance-floor. Langley, on the other hand, seems to sit rather nervously on his seat.

'Lively little saloon, ain't it?' says Woodrow.

'The music is a little too loud for my taste,' replies Langley.

'They do bang it out,' replies Woodrow. 'Here, grab that chap there . . . never mind, I've got him . . . here, boy, over here!'

Woodrow grabs the arm of a waiter, who bends solicitously over the table.

'Two brandy and waters, and make them large ones, eh?'

The waiter nods and heads in the direction of the nearest bar, one of several alcoves beneath the hall's gallery that distribute liquid sustenance, beneath signs reading 'Refreshments'. He soon returns, bearing two brandies, Jasper Woodrow raises his glass in the air.

'To partnership, Langley!'

Langley smiles. 'To partnership.'

'That's better,' says Woodrow, as Langley takes a gulp of the liquor. 'Now, tell me, what do you make of that filly over there, eh?'

'Which?'

'The dark-haired one, with the silver round her neck.'

'The girl with the necklace?'

'Fascinating little thing, isn't she? Why don't you ask her to dance?'

'She has a partner, I think.'

'That boy? No match for a full-grown fellow like you, Langley. Go to it – ask her, if you've a mind to.'

'I don't really.'

'Here, finish your drink – I'll get us another. Boy!'

———

Melissa Woodrow sits naked in the hot tin bath before her bedroom hearth, her hair tied back loosely. She washes her face clean with soap and water, wiping it with a flannel, which instantly acquires streaks of grey-black dirt. Then, once she is done, she takes a bar of transparent soap from the nearby wash-stand, and carefully applies it to her skin, to her arms and legs, stretching her hands out towards the flames. Before long, the clear water in the bath has itself turned into a stagnant murky pond around her body. Melissa Woodrow frowns, staring at the water, lost in thought.

As the water grows colder, she climbs out of the bath, towelling herself dry in front of the fire-place, before she puts on her chemise and silk dressing-gown. She walks over to her bed, pulling the brass ring of the needlework bell-pull that hangs from the picture-rail.

The servants' bell rings in the distance. Mrs. Woodrow first unties then begins to brush her hair.

The sound of rapid footfalls upon the stairs echo on the landing, until there is a knock at the door.

'Come in.'

Jacobs enters. 'Ma'am?'

'No sign of the master?'

'No, ma'am.'

———

Jasper Woodrow walks from the dance-floor and falls on to his seat, exhausted, as the orchestra in the gallery strikes up a new dance. Richard Langley sits down beside him, his face rather pallid, his eyes slightly bloodshot. They are followed by two young women, in breathless, giddy conversation.

'Ladies,' says Woodrow, pulling out two chairs, 'come join us. My dears, my friend and I've never had the pleasure of such exquisite partners. You must both be thirsty – let me buy you a bottle of pop, eh?'

The older of the two, though no more than twenty-one years, smiles in agreement, and sits down. Her friend, though giving Woodrow a rather nervous look, follows suit as he orders a bottle of the house's champagne.

'What's your name?' asks Woodrow.

'Susan,' says the older girl. 'And this is Jemima.'

'Sweet names,' says Woodrow, 'although they are a little plain for two such fascinating ladies.'

The younger girl giggles at the word 'ladies'.

'I'd call you Bella,' he continues, addressing the older, reaching to touch her cheek with his finger.

The girl smiles but lightly brushes his hand aside. 'And what about my friend?'

'Well, I don't know. What would you say, Langley?'

'I'm sorry,' says Langley, looking blearily at his companion, speaking with a distinct slur, 'I'm sorry – that dance – I feel a little off-colour.'

The two young women look less than impressed by this announcement; the younger whispers something to the older, at which both laugh.

'My dear fellow,' says Woodrow, 'I hope you haven't over-indulged? And I thought you'd hardly touched a drop!'

'If I have I . . .'

Langley trails off in mid sentence as he attempts to stand, leaning unsteadily against his chair. Woodrow glances apologetically at the two young women.

'I'd best find my friend a cab, eh?'

———

Melissa Woodrow finishes brushing her hair, putting her comb down upon her lace-covered dressing-table. Beside the comb lies an envelope she brought up earlier from the hall, merely addressed to 'Mrs. Woodrow'. She takes it gingerly in her hand; there is no postmark, nor any other sign of its origin. She looks at it for several minutes before finally she tears it open and reads the sheet of paper inside:

YOUR HUSBAND KEEPS SECRETS
A friend

She bites her lip, then hurriedly opens the drawer in her dresser that contains her petticoats, shoving the letter to the back.

———

'There you go, old man,' says Woodrow, easing Richard Langley into the hansom and shutting its twin folding doors.

'Thank you . . . I'm not normally . . .'

'Of course not. Say no more, my boy,' says Woodrow, looking up at the driver, perched at the rear of the cab. 'St. John's Wood, my man – drive slow. Poor fellow's feeling a bit queer.'

The driver nods and the hansom rattles off in the direction of Oxford Street. As the vehicle disappears from view, the fog still all-encompassing, Woodrow's smile disappears. He turns and, with a nod to the doorman, walks briskly back into the Casino. Once inside, however, he finds the bottle of champagne at his table is all but finished, and the two young women in conversation with two young men.

He is about to interrupt them, when another woman catches his eye as she walks past. He turns and catches up with her.

'Miss, one moment. Haven't we met once before . . . ?'

Chapter Thirteen

A LITTLE AFTER MIDNIGHT.

Opposite the locked gates of Abney Park, two figures stand together in a shop doorway, watching the cemetery's entrance. The night still possesses a vaporous hint of fog, such that the glow of the nearby tall gas-lights, which line the High Street, seem to glow a muted brown, as if filtered through the medium of a dirty beer bottle. Nonetheless, for all that, the two men can still make out the opposite side of the road from their hiding place, and observe the twin lodges that guard the cemetery gates and courtyard. For, despite its many defects, the suburb of Stoke Newington lies a good four miles north of the Thames, and is not, therefore, subject to the same soot-heavy atmosphere that suffocates the heart of the metropolis.

Sergeant Bartleby shuffles uncomfortably, flapping his arms against the sides of his great-coat.

'We could be over there, sir, enjoying a shot of something,' says the sergeant, nodding in the direction of the Three Crowns public house. It is an old-fashioned coaching inn of middling size, its illuminated sign visible in the darkness, not a hundred yards or so distant from where the two men stand.

'They'll be closed soon. And, besides, that would hardly serve our purpose, would it, Sergeant?'

Bartleby gives Webb a rather plaintive look, which the latter does not notice.

'But did we have to come tonight, sir?'

'No-one waiting for you at home, is there, Sergeant?'

'No, sir,' replies Bartleby. 'You?'

Webb raises his eyebrows at the sergeant's question.

'Sorry, sir,' replies Bartleby, hurriedly. 'None of my business.'

Webb peers at the gates.

'We are here tonight, Sergeant, because your news from Mr. Siddons rather intrigued me. And because it brought me back to thinking about this whole business with the body. I wanted to have a walk round the outside by night, to see what opportunities there were for a fellow minded to break in.'

'And a pleasant walk it was, too, sir,' says Bartleby, with only the slightest hint of sarcasm.

'I'm glad you thought so. And what have we learnt thus far, Sergeant?'

'Sir?'

Webb sighs. 'We are agreed it must have been done by night, yes?'

'Yes, sir.'

'Why?'

'I suppose the chap could hardly have excavated a grave in daylight, not unnoticed. Mr. Pellegrin keeps a sharp eye on things.'

'It seems so. Unless it was one of the grave-diggers,' says Webb, albeit hesitantly, like a lecturer offering a wholly erroneous thesis, in preparation for demolishing it.

'But then they'd know how to cover it up properly. Easily done with a bit of turf, I'd have thought. And Pellegrin would have spotted it.'

Webb nods. 'Quite. That is a fair assumption.

Therefore, we suspect it was an intruder, at night. But we've been round the cemetery wall, and it seems unlikely.'

'You'd need a ladder, at least,' suggests the sergeant.

'Or a degree of agility – of course, it is not that high. But it is behind the gardens of the local houses, or in plain sight of them. Smart little houses too, with decent tenants, I should imagine. I saw a couple of curtains twitch when I tried that gate. You recall?'

'Yes, sir,' replies Bartleby. If he is weary of being addressed in the manner of a schoolboy, he succeeds in concealing it.

'So our thief would have to be something of a talented burglar.'

'Unless he lives in one of the houses?'

Webb smiles. 'Sergeant, you are inspired. Although I'd think in most cases one would run the risk of being seen by one's neighbours. Still it is a possibility. Nonetheless, I think we are rather obliged to make trial of the night-watchman. Ask any professional thief, Sergeant, and they'll tell you the swiftest way to "break a drum" is through the servants. The same applies here.'

'You aren't proposing we stand here all night, sir?'

Webb shakes his head. 'I don't think so. Now, be a good man and pop over to the pub and get a bottle of brandy, will you, Sergeant? Large.'

Bartleby smiles with surprised delight at the thought of a warming glass of liquor. A sharp look from the inspector, however, returns his features to their previous composure.

'It isn't for us, is it?' says Bartleby.

Webb shakes his head.

'Won't be a moment, sir,' says the sergeant ruefully. He begins to cross the street but, putting his hands in his pockets, he turns around and addresses Webb once more.

'You might want to lend us a couple of bob, sir.'

⸺

'You took your time, Sergeant,' says Webb, as Bartleby returns to the doorway, some ten minutes later, a bottle in hand.

'They're calling last orders in there, sir. Damn busy.'

'I hope you didn't indulge yourself, Sergeant?'

'Never on duty, sir.'

'Hmm.'

Bartleby looks expectantly at the inspector.

'What is it, man?' asks Webb.

'Aren't we going across then, sir?'

'We'll wait until the pub's closed.'

Bartleby looks dejectedly back at the Three Crowns, and, to keep warm, stamps his feet.

It is gone half-past midnight when the regulars of the Three Crowns exit on to the street. Most exhibit a degree of inebriation either in their gait or in the raucous shouts they address to departing companions, as they disappear into the mist. There is one man, however, who shouts something in the direction of the cemetery's lodge, where the night-watchman's lamp is visible through the square little building's small windows.

'All right, Jem?'

There is no reply.

'All right?' repeats the man. It is not a pleasant greeting, and sounds more like a taunt. A figure appears at the door to the lodge; an old man wrapped in a coat that looks far too large for him.

'Keeping warm?' says the man outside the gates.

From the policemen's position upon the opposite side of the road, the watchman's reply is inaudible.

'Well, you'll be the only one there what is, won't you, eh?' shouts the drunken man, waving at the watchman and bidding him goodbye. The watchman does not so much wave back as dismiss his interlocutor with a swiping movement, perhaps indicative of the manner in which he would prefer to say farewell – were he upon the other side of the gate, and thirty years younger. At length, however, peering through the gate to ensure his tormentor has departed, he returns to his post.

Webb looks back at the pub.

'I think that's the last of them. Come on then, Sergeant, give me that bottle and follow my lead.'

Bartleby nods, and the two men cross the street and walk along to the cemetery gates, where Webb motions for them to stop.

'Where was it, again, Bill?' says Webb, loudly, apropos of nothing, in an accent not entirely his own.

Bartleby looks startled at this familiar form of address, but does his best to reply. 'Err, where was what?'

'The house. Where did you say it was? Ellis Road, was it? Or was it Eltham?'

Sergeant Bartleby widens his eyes, as if struck by a sudden understanding. 'Ah, err, Elton, wasn't it, Charlie?'

Webb, in turn, raises his eyebrows, mouthing the word 'Charlie' with a rather interrogative expression. Bartleby shrugs.

'No,' continues Webb, with feeling, 'that weren't it, not at all. Blow me, if we ain't been walking round here an hour or more.'

Before the sergeant can expand upon this theme, the sound of the lodge door opening, on the other side of the gates, causes the two men to turn about. The watchman, a man about sixty years old, steps into the courtyard with his lantern.

'You there, what are you rowing about? Off with you!'

'We'd go, mate, if we knew where we were going,' says Webb, in a decent impression of inebriated bonhomie. 'A pal of ours lives round here. Do you know, what's it called now, Eltham Road?'

'Ellis?' suggests Bartleby.

'No,' says the old man.

'Elton then?'

'Never heard of it. New road, is it?'

'Oh yes,' replies Webb, 'he said it were a beauty of a place, nice new house, didn't he, Bill? We were s'posed to be seeing Fred and the Missus for supper, see, but we had a couple in that house just down there, the Crowns or something, and then . . . well, it's a queer thing, ain't it, Bill?'

Bartleby nods. 'Can't recall the name. You sure you don't know it?'

'How should I know it if you don't?' asks the old man.

'Best we head home, Billy boy,' says Webb. 'Do you reckon we'll find a cab to the Borough, mate?'

The old man shrugs his shoulders. 'You might have to walk it.'

'Walk!' Webb exclaims. 'In this weather? I'll be frozen solid. And I'll cop it when I get home.'

Bartleby notices the bottle of brandy, which Webb dangles rather ostentatiously in his hand. 'Bloody waste of that brandy, too.'

'We best have a taste of it on the way, I suppose,' says Webb. 'Damned shame – I was looking forward to taking a drop, civil like.'

The old man eyes the bottle. 'Brandy, you say?'

'Best bottle they had – waste of good money.'

'Well,' says the old man thoughtfully, 'if you're cold, I've got a fire going in here.'

'Fire? Oh, but we couldn't possibly take advantage, could we, Charlie?' says Bartleby. Webb, however, gives him a brief, threatening glance.

'You've a Christian spirit, sir,' says Webb. 'Here, now what say we share a drop of this liquor between us?'

'Oh, I don't know, when I'm on duty . . .' says the old man.

'No harm in it,' suggests Bartleby.

'Well, I suppose I've a couple of glasses knocking about somewhere,' says the old man, as he walks to the gate, and undoes the padlock. 'Here, come through.'

'Very kind of you, mate, very kind,' mutters Webb.

⬥

Decimus Webb pours another glass of brandy, as the old man reclines in his chair, in front of the small hearth in the cemetery lodge.

'Are you here every night?' asks the inspector, allowing himself a sip of liquor.

'Aye,' says the watchman, following Webb's example, and downing a gulp of brandy, 'twenty years I've been here, never missed a night, except when the Missus died.'

'Well, I'm sorry to hear that,' says Webb.

'No need; seventeen year ago that were.'

'Is she buried here?'

The old man nods. 'Aye. Bless her. 17606. F07.'

'Beg your pardon?' says Bartleby.

'Her number. That's her number in the register – I memorialised it in my head.'

Webb nods. 'I expects the work ain't much trouble, in a place like this?'

The old man snorts, gesturing towards the cemetery

proper. 'No, they don't give me much trouble, they don't.'

Webb smiles. 'No, I'd hope not. Still, I think it'd give me the creeps.'

'What's your trade?' asks the old man.

'Horses,' suggests Bartleby. Webb looks askance at his colleague.

The old man shakes his head. 'Never liked horses myself.'

'It ain't haunted then?' says Webb, with a grin.

'Nah,' says the old man. 'Or if it is, they keep clear of me. I tell you, though, I did have a scare, not a few weeks back.'

'What was that?'

'A gentleman, as was locked in at night. Found him wandering around, all lost, by the chapel – now, I thought he was a bloody ghost! Said he'd lost track of time, looking at the graves. In the dark – I ask you! So I said to him, "You'll lose track of your bloody neck, sir, if you fall into an open hole!"'

'You're right,' says Webb. 'A gentleman, you say? Still, I expect that happens a lot.'

'That were the queer thing; I always walk round twice, to check, afore we locks the gates at nightfall. But I'd missed him, see? A right scare. A fellow could lose his place over a thing like that, too. Here,' continues the old man, suddenly confidential, 'keep that dark, eh?'

'Don't you worry, mate – we won't blab. Here, have another glass. Steady your nerves. Was he alone, then, this man? I expect you marched him straight out, eh?'

'That's what I said, didn't I?'

'I don't suppose he had a bag or some such?'

'That's a queer question,' says the old man, frowning.

'Did he though?'

'Not that I saw.'

'How old was he? Do you remember what he looked like? Well dressed?'

'Smart enough. I don't recollect; it were dark. Middling sort of fellow. Here, now, what is all this?'

'Nothing at all,' says Webb, soothingly, 'just curious. Billy, I reckon we should be off. It's a long walk home, eh?'

—

The watchman lets Webb and Bartleby through the cemetery gates, and then locks them. If he has a suspicion in his mind as to the authenticity of his visitors, it is secondary to his desire to continue sipping brandy in front of a warm fire. Webb, meanwhile, walks briskly along the pavement, a look of satisfaction on his face.

'What did you make of that, then?' asks the sergeant.

'Well, I'd say it's a good chance that "gentleman" was our man, Sergeant, even though our friend can't tell us much about him. Can't be certain, of course. Let's say he hides until the place is shut, digs up the grave, then . . . well, I suppose there's still a problem, isn't there?'

'He left without the body?' says Bartleby.

'Quite. It looks like it, unless of course he had an accomplice. But then, this is what puzzles me: if it was something in the grave he wanted, where did he put the bones? Why not bury them again? But if he wanted the body, why not take it?'

'Maybe he stashed them somewhere, and came back for them.'

'Charming thought, isn't it?' says Webb. 'Very well – tomorrow, come back and interview the fellow – see if you can get a better description when he's sober; see if he remembers you for a start; he may not be particularly reliable, if tonight is any guide. And take a thorough look around the grounds – take a couple of men with you, plain clothes – and make sure there's nothing we've missed.'

'Like what?'

'The remains. I suppose a cemetery might be the best place to hide them.'

Bartleby nods. 'Are we really walking back into town, sir?'

'Unless you know a means of summoning a cab, Sergeant, I'd say we are. Why?'

'Just a shame you left the rest of that brandy behind, sir.'

CHAPTER FOURTEEN

IT IS TWO A.M. as Melissa Woodrow walks into the darkened hall of her home, a candle-stick in her hand. Her dressing-gown trails over the parquet floor as the sound of a key being jabbed inexpertly into the front door echoes through the house. Finally, after what seems an age, there is a distinct click. The key slots into the lock, and the door opens. A man's hand slowly pulls back the heavy curtain that all but conceals the entrance.

'Woodrow, is that you?' she says in an urgent whisper.

'Course it's me, damn it,' replies Jasper Woodrow, stepping a little unsteadily inside. His cheeks are flushed red with drink, his eyes decidedly bloodshot. 'You think I'm likely to be burglarising my own house, eh?'

'I didn't know what to think,' she says, her voice a peculiar mixture of anger and anxiety. 'Where have you been all night? You said you would get a cab.'

'Just for a little drink, my dear. Met up with your man Langley – thought we'd have a drop of something to celebrate.'

'Langley? What, had you arranged it?'

'After a fashion, my darling, after a fashion. Useless little milksop, mind you. Can't take his liquor –

wouldn't think it to look at him. Or, come to think of it, perhaps you would. But,' says Woodrow with a rather lopsided smile, tapping his nose with his finger, 'his money's good.'

'You didn't say anything,' says Mrs. Woodrow, indignantly.

'I needed a drink,' says Woodrow with a rather angry emphasis.

'But we thought you were coming home directly. Annabel and I were worried.'

'Ah, the delightful Miss Krout,' says Woodrow, rather slurring his words. 'Where is she, my dear? Must kiss her good night, eh? Must be civil to Miss Krout. Her old man might lend us some money, eh? No need now, mind you. Good old Langley. Lucky I found him.'

'Woodrow, hush! I have never said anything about money – Annabel is in bed. Don't you know what time it is?'

'It is,' says Woodrow, pulling out the chain to his pocket-watch, and fumbling with the case, 'it is . . . time for bed, eh? Don't suppose you'd care to join me, Melissa?'

'I really can't talk to you in this state, Woodrow,' she replies, 'really, I can't.'

'Don't have to talk, my dear,' says Woodrow. He looks at his wife, but she deliberately avoids his gaze. 'Damn you, then,' he says. 'I'll just go and kiss Miss Krout good night, eh?'

With that, Woodrow walks purposefully towards the hall stairs, though almost tripping on the rug that lies before them. Melissa darts after him, a look of horror on her face.

'Woodrow! You'll do no such thing!'

'Just a quick peck, my dear.'

'Please,' she says, grabbing hold of his arm.

He shakes her hand roughly free, with such force that he knocks it against the banister. Melissa, in turn, leans back against the woodwork, her mouth wide with surprise at the sudden blow; tears well up in her eyes.

'Here now, enough of that,' says Woodrow. 'I was only chaffing you, woman. It's your own damn fault, you know.'

Melissa Woodrow shakes her head, but offers no words.

'I'm going to bed,' says Woodrow, in a sullen tone.

—

Annabel Krout stands by the door to her room in her night-gown, listening to the raised voices downstairs. She can make out little more than the passing mention of her own name, and the distressed sound of Mrs. Woodrow's voice. Then there is the sound of Mr. Woodrow's heavy footsteps upon the stairs. Unconsciously, she holds her breath as he passes her room, and enters his dressing-room upon the opposite side of the landing. A minute or so later comes the lighter step of Mrs. Woodrow, the rustle of her dressing-gown. Annabel ponders for a moment whether she should open the door and talk to her; but she cannot quite muster the confidence to do so. Nor can she imagine what she might say that would not merely embarrass her cousin. In consequence, though she waits a minute or two more, to see if either party ventures forth from their respective bedrooms, she eventually returns quietly to her bed.

Pulling up the covers around her body, Annabel lies back and closes her eyes.

It is not long before she falls into fitful sleep.

—

Annabel wakes.

At first she is conscious only of a cold sweat, soaked through her night-gown, the fabric sticking to her arms. It takes her a moment to recollect her surroundings. But then she notices, from the corner of her eye, a peculiar movement in the darkness; something quite out of place. Her stomach suddenly turns over inside her, as she moves her head to see a small figure in white, walking noiselessly past her bed.

For a moment, she is quite paralysed by the strange sight, the slow processional movement of what, for all the world, looks like a little ghost. She wonders if she is still dreaming. Memories of childish night terrors, tales told by nurses to scare their infant charges, rush unbidden into her half-waking mind. She watches in silence, struggling to reassure herself that she is quite awake, as the figure walks towards the window of her room, gently pulls aside the curtain, and taps its fingers on the glass.

Annabel reaches for the match-box beside her bed, and strikes a light, nearly setting fire to the entire box in her fumbling fingers. But then even the faint glow of the match, let alone the candle for which it is intended, is quite sufficient to dispel any mystery surrounding the figure by the window.

'Lucy!' exclaims Annabel.

The little girl says nothing. In truth, she gives no indication of having heard her name. Rather, she stands staring through the window, her hand still tapping insistently upon the pane.

Annabel calls her name again, but still elicits no reply. Taking the lit candle, she gets out of bed and walks over to the window. The child stands quite still, her feet bare, her eyes fixed upon the street below.

'Lucy, what is it?'

Lucy gives no answer. Annabel reaches to touch her arm but she is interrupted by the sound of footsteps upon the landing, and the breathless appearance of Mrs. Woodrow at the door to her room.

'Oh, Lord! I thought I heard her on the stairs. Don't wake her,' exclaims Mrs. Woodrow.

'Wake her?'

'My dear, I am so sorry, I should have said something – oh, I blame myself,' says Mrs. Woodrow in a stage whisper, walking briskly over to her daughter. 'Lucy has, well, a nervous condition . . . she is given to sleep-walking. I would have said, but she has been quite good of late.'

Annabel glances anxiously at the little girl. 'I suppose there's no harm done.'

'No? Why, I expect she scared you to death. She can't even hear us, you know. It's such an awful trial – the doctors say she will grow out of it, but really, I don't know.'

'What should we do? What do you suppose she is looking at?'

'Nothing, I am sure – it's akin to a trance; she doesn't actually see anything, I think, or at least nothing she remembers. One merely has to lead her back to bed and keep an eye on her. I suppose there is nothing for it. Jacobs will have to share her room again. And she won't thank me for that.'

'To watch over her?'

'Yes, she might harm herself, or fall or anything, you see – they have no proper sense where they are, my dear, not in this condition.' Mrs. Woodrow sighs, and bends down to address her daughter. 'Lucy? Come on now, darling, this is cousin Annabel's room, not yours. I'm taking you back to bed.'

Lucy gives no indication of hearing her mother, but when Mrs. Woodrow takes her hand, she silently consents to be led away from the window, and out on to the landing.

'I'm so sorry, dear,' continues Mrs. Woodrow as she walks, her voice low, 'please, do go back to bed and get some sleep.'

'There's really no need to apologise, cousin . . .'

Annabel's voice trails off, as Jasper Woodrow opens his bedroom door abruptly, dressed in his shirt and trousers. His balance appears unsteady, and he leans against the door-frame. He peers out on to the landing, which is lit only by the flickering light of Mrs. Woodrow's candle.

'What's all this?'

'Nothing, Woodrow. Go back to bed, dear.'

'Don't give me orders, woman. Damn me, not again?' he says, gesturing towards Lucy, who stands quite oblivious by her mother.

'It's nothing, dear, really.'

'Don't tell me it's nothing, when the child's not in her right mind. Look at her. Give her to me.'

'Woodrow, no, please don't—'

'Give her here, I said.'

Mrs. Woodrow's protests go unheeded, as her husband grabs the little girl and shakes her. He is relatively gentle at first, but then takes her more violently by the shoulders. And if waking his daughter is the object, then Jasper Woodrow's methods have the desired effect. Indeed, Annabel watches as the girl's face changes from its peculiar blank serenity to consciousness, albeit a wakeful state of confusion and fear and, finally, choking sobs.

'Woodrow, stop it! You're hurting her!'

Woodrow looks down at his daughter, who stands limp in his grip, her cheeks burning red and wet with tears. He lets go of one arm, pulling her up with the other.

'Lucinda, can you hear me?'

The little girl nods, though her face is still fearful.

'That was for your own good. You must learn to control yourself. Do you hear?'

Lucy nods again.

'If you do not, I do not want to but I will punish you. Do you understand me? Speak up.'

'Yes, Papa,' says the little girl.

'Good. Now take her back to bed, Melissa, for God's sake – let us have a night's peace.'

Melissa Woodrow darts a glance at her husband, but says nothing, shepherding her daughter up the stairs. Woodrow himself is about to return to bed, when Annabel, having stood silently in the doorway to her room, steps out on to the landing.

'I am sorry you had to see such a display, Miss Krout,' says Woodrow. 'I hope you can still get some sleep.'

Annabel takes a deep breath. 'Sir, I doubt I can, unless I speak my mind.'

Woodrow frowns. 'What do you mean by that?'

'I think,' she says, trying to keep a measured tone, 'you were very harsh with your daughter.'

'Do you, indeed?'

'Surely she cannot help herself. I mean, though I do not know much about the condition . . .'

'No,' says Woodrow, firmly, 'you do not. And, although it would not surprise me, Miss Krout, if the Yankees were to start breeding lady doctors, until that time, I'd be grateful if you'd keep your ill-informed opinions to yourself. I bid you good night.'

Jasper Woodrow steps back into his bedroom and slams the door behind him.

Annabel, for her part, takes a deep breath, trying to calm her nerves. She turns around and goes back into her room, where her candle still burns by the bed. It does not take her long to discover that she cannot sleep. She contemplates lighting the lamp and writing a letter home, but instead goes back to the window where Lucy stood a few minutes previously, and looks out on to the street.

But there is nothing to be seen.

PART TWO

CHAPTER FIFTEEN

THE FOG OF the previous night has finally cleared, but a dense pall of black cloud hangs over the streets of the metropolis, threatening rain. Outside Woodrow's General Mourning Warehouse, a pair of young men undo various padlocks and grapple with the panelled wooden shutters that protect Woodrow's plate-glass windows. They exchange a few friendly words, then the screens are raised up from the polished brass sills into which they are slotted during the hours of darkness. In a matter of minutes, the shutters are stacked against the exterior of the building, then despatched with expedition to some secret location at the rear of the shop. Indeed, it is the hour when shop-keepers throughout the capital stir into action, and so the same delicate exercise is carried out all along High Holborn, uncovering the displays of several stationers, a gentleman's outfitter, Henekey's Imperial Wine and a dozen other redoubtable retail establishments.

But the young men of Woodrow's notice something different about their daily task. For such early-morning activity, no matter how mundane it may be, generally attracts the satiric attention of some ragged street-child, lolling by the nearest lamp-post, or the rather more pleasant scrutiny of a maid-servant, bound upon an errand, who finds something peculiarly admirable about one or the other of the winged-collared young shopmen. Today, however, there are no curious passers-by, no-one intrigued by the secret life of the London shop. Such idle individuals are, instead, gathered a few hundred yards to the south and east, crowding the road and pavement around the steps of the Holborn Casino.

This crowd, in itself, is quite unusual. For the Casino is normally quite shut up during the day, when there is little call for drink and dancing, and respectable folk might catch an unwelcome glimpse of its sinfully gilded interior. In consequence, the peculiar gathering soon attracts its own peripheral hangers-on, who merely stop to make the simple inquiry 'What is the matter here?' Then they too are swiftly absorbed into the milling group. For the answer to their question, in one word, whispered between man, woman and child, complete strangers who exchange the news with an odd familiarity, is 'murder'; and it is an answer that encourages most of them to linger and crane their necks towards the entrance to the infamous dance-hall.

It is the presence of this self-same crowd that leaves Decimus Webb in no doubt of his destination, as his cab pulls up on the opposite side of the street; but this is, perhaps, the only positive aspect of such unchecked public enthusiasm. In fact, it takes Webb a good couple of minutes to edge his way through the mob to the burly pair of constables who guard the doors, despite proclaiming the word 'police' at the top of his lungs, and he acquires at least one bruised rib and a stubbed toe in the process. Once inside the Casino's lobby, however, he finds that he is on his own. Walking down the entrance stairs, past the cloakroom and sundry ante-rooms, he pulls open the glass-panelled doors that lead into the great marble hall. It is quite empty, with only the odd relic of the previous night's revelry, whether an empty wine bottle or a broken glass, lying beneath one or two of the tables. It strikes him that there is almost something eerie in the absence of noise.

'Bartleby?' shouts Webb, puncturing the silence.

There is no reply but his voice echoes around the empty chamber. Then the sound of rapid, muffled footsteps echo in the gallery above.

'Is that you, Sergeant?' continues Webb.

'Yes sir, I'm coming,' replies the sergeant. Webb waits patiently, until Bartleby appears, trotting down the carpeted stairs that lead up to the gallery.

'Thought I'd just have a look around, sir.'

'Did you?' says Webb.

'I knew we'd end up busy this week, sir. What did I tell you?'

'I expect you said just that, Sergeant. In any case, before we begin this conversation, I should like to make you aware of two facts. First, your telegram, or rather the wretched youth that delivered it, woke me from a profound and deeply satisfying sleep. Second, I came here directly without so much as a sip of coffee touching my lips.'

'Sir?'

'I merely suggest you tell me the details directly, Sergeant, and, in particular, why this could not wait at least until I had had breakfast?'

'Sorry, sir. I thought you'd be keen, that's all, given the circumstances.'

'Sergeant . . .' says Webb, lending the word a heavy tone of admonition.

'Sorry, sir. Well, I got in early myself – didn't get much sleep as it happens – and no sooner had I sat down than we got word down the line to come here, double quick. I came myself, first off, and well, all things considered—'

'What things, Sergeant, for pity's sake? Do you think I enjoy mysteries?'

'It's the same one, sir. That did for those two girls in Knight's Hotel. He's done it again.'

Webb follows the sergeant through a narrow corridor at the rear of the Casino, behind the musicians' portion of the gallery above. The décor becomes increasingly plain as they progress and it is not long before the red and gold wall-paper above the wainscoting gives way to flaking white paint and bare plaster. At last, they come to a battered-looking door, that leads outside into an small open courtyard, surrounded on all sides by tall window-less walls, with an alley, round the side of the building, the only other obvious method of egress.

'Here?' says Webb.

'Just round the corner, sir,' says the sergeant, leading the way. Webb follows him, towards a trio of large dust-bins and several wooden crates, full to the brim with empty wine bottles. The atmosphere of the alley is unpleasantly acrid and Webb cannot help but cough.

'Foul, isn't it, sir?' says Bartleby. 'I'm told the gentlemen generally use it for a privy, if the WC back there is occupied.'

'Yes, I rather gathered that, Sergeant.'

'Just behind the bin, sir,' replies Bartleby. 'I haven't moved her.'

Webb steps past the sergeant, and looks behind the over-size tin dust-bin. On the ground, curled up into a ball, lies the body of a young dark-haired woman, her hair loose, her burgundy dress torn along her arm.

'I see. Throat, you said? Have you examined the wound thoroughly, Sergeant?'

'No, ah, not in any detail, sir,' says Bartleby.

Webb reaches down and gently pulls back the dead woman's locks, revealing a dark gash across her throat. He scowls, and deliberately tilts the head slightly back, exposing the blood-encrusted wound.

'There, Sergeant. Can you see it? He cut through her windpipe.'

'I'll take your word for it, sir.'

'Sergeant,' says Webb, annoyance in his voice, 'I do not expect you to possess a degree in medicine, but you must familiarise yourself with basic anatomy.'

Bartleby reluctantly leans over the body. 'Yes, I see it, sir.'

'Good,' says Webb. 'And the paper was where?'

'Just by her hand, sir. I reckon he put it in her hand again. Probably fell out.'

'Show it to me.'

Bartleby reaches into his pocket, revealing a small piece of paper, with writing in scrawled block capitals.

'"There is no darkness, nor shadow of death, where the workers of iniquity may hide themselves."'

'Job again, I believe, sir,' interjects Bartleby.

Webb looks at him quizzically.

'Lot of Dissenters in the family, sir. Given to studying the Good Book.'

Webb sighs. 'Well, at least you're good for something, Sergeant. And this alley, where does it lead?'

'Along the side of the building. Out to High Holborn. But it's barred and gated. You wouldn't get past it. They open it only for the dustmen on a Monday.'

'And the person that found her?'

'Young woman, sir. Comes in early to clean the place out, every morning – there's a few of them that does it – she just found her lying there when she was tipping out the ashes. Quite distraught – I've got her in one of the rooms out front. You won't get much sense out of her though.'

'No, I don't expect I will,' says the inspector wearily, looking back at the body. 'Has the manager of the place been contacted?'

'Sent out a constable to do just that, sir.'

'Very well, Sergeant, I think you'd best also send for Inspector Hanson; it's only fair we notify him. He was rather prescient, wasn't he?'

'Yes, sir. Very good, sir.'

'And not a word about this piece of paper to anyone except Hanson, eh?'

'Sir?'

'Whoever is doing this, Sergeant, wants to be recognised in some way. He is enjoying sending out these little messages. I do not know why – but I do not intend to give him the satisfaction of seeing it in the press.'

'No, sir. But they'll put two and two together soon enough, won't they? I mean, three girls in one week?'

Webb frowns.

'Three girls? Yes, I suppose they may well. Let us just hope, Sergeant, that is the limit of the wretch's ambition.'

'Yes, sir.'

'Wait a moment, Sergeant,' says Webb, 'what's this?'

The inspector bends down beside the dust-bin, and peers into the dirt, flicking it away with his fingers, revealing a small red-beaded purse, half-hidden by spilt ash. Webb picks it up and shakes it.

'Look, Sergeant. Now that hasn't been there long, I should think. Tell me, did you not notice it, or were you trying to test my powers of observation?'

'No, sir.'

'Well, in any case, let us look inside. What have we here? Three of four shillings in change; a silk handkerchief; and, ah, this is better, a folded receipt for nine yards of muslin, at one shilling and one pence a yard. A black-bordered receipt at that, on printed paper, with the word "Deduct". stamped upon it.'

'Does it have the name of the shop, sir?'

'Woodrow's General Mourning Warehouse.'

'Woodrow's? That's just round the corner,' says Bartleby. 'Do you think it belonged to the girl?'

'I do not know,' replies the inspector, 'but I think we had best pay them a visit.'

CHAPTER SIXTEEN

ANNABEL KROUT TURNS over in her sleep and wakes
with a start; her blankets are loose, pulled awkwardly
to one side of the bed, and she can feel a chill down her
arm, exposed to the cold air. She tucks herself back
under the covers, wondering what hour it might be.
The room is in semi-darkness, although she fancies she
can make out the barest hint of daylight, visible behind
the heavy curtains that conceal the twin sash windows
opposite. Then there is a noise outside; the bedroom
door creaks, and opens an inch or two.

'Who is it?' she asks tentatively.

'Only me, Miss,' comes the reply. 'Beg pardon,
Miss, I didn't want to wake you.'

'No, no, I was awake, please come in.'

Jacobs steps into the room, bearing the familiar
pitcher of steaming water, which she deposits on the
wash-stand. Her appearance, scheduled for eight
o'clock on previous mornings, suffices to give Annabel
an indication of the time; she raises herself up.

'Can you open the curtains please, Jacobs?'

'Yes, Miss.'

Jacobs walks over and pulls on the draw-string that
opens the curtains. The room brightens a little, but if
there is daylight outside, it seems to Annabel a
distinctly gloomy, metropolitan variety.

'What's it like out there?' asks Annabel.

'Outside, Miss? Well, the fog's gone.'

Annabel smiles. 'That's something, I suppose.'

'Oh, it can settle for days on end, Miss – something awful. You can go without seeing the sun for a fortnight.'

'Is that right?' says Annabel.

'Yes, Miss. Will there be anything else?'

'No,' says Annabel, then, reflecting for a moment, 'no, wait. May I ask you something, Jacobs?'

The servant frowns, a rather anxious expression creasing her brow. 'As you like, Miss.'

'Did you hear any, well, any trouble last night?'

'Trouble?' says the maid-servant, uncomprehending.

'I found little Lucy in my room. Mrs. Woodrow tells me she walks in her sleep.'

'Oh lor!' exclaims Jacobs, then immediately puts her hand to her mouth. 'Oh, beg your pardon, Miss. I just thought that she was getting better, that's all.'

'Why, does she do it often?'

'Now and again, Miss,' replies Jacobs. 'It's a shame, poor little thing.'

'Mr. Woodrow was most . . . well, upset about it.'

'Was he, Miss?' says Jacobs, looking away from her interlocutor and rearranging the items upon the wash-stand.

'I'm sorry – it's not your place to say, I know. I should not have mentioned it.'

'No, Miss, it's just . . .'

'Just what?'

'Don't think too badly of the master. It may seem he comes down hard, but he means well.'

Annabel smiles politely. 'I am sure you're right.'

'I only mean to say,' continues Jacobs, as if determined to make her point, 'it's a bad business for both of them.'

'Both of them?' says Annabel. 'I don't quite understand.'

Jacob blushes and her frown returns. 'Oh, I shouldn't have said anything, Miss. Please don't tell the Missus.'

'Tell her what?'

'Well,' says Jacobs, leaning forward, her voice a low, nervous whisper, 'the master, he suffers from it too.'

'You mean he walks in his sleep?'

Jacobs nods, then stares at her feet.

'I haven't heard anything,' says Annabel. 'Surely Mrs. Woodrow would have told me, if there was any chance of him . . . she would have spoken to me about it.'

'Oh, he don't do it now so much, Miss. Says he's willed himself to stop. But, between you and me, he takes something for it, to help him sleep sound.'

'I see,' says Annabel. She observes a rather anxious look upon the maid-servant's face. 'I'm sorry – I did not mean to keep you from your work. And I swear I won't speak a word about it, not even to Mrs. Woodrow.'

Jacobs smiles in gratitude. 'May I go now, Miss?'

'Of course.'

———

The table in the Woodrows' dining-room is laid out for breakfast, but Annabel finds that she is quite alone. The only noise is the ticking of the clock upon the mantelpiece, and the slight creak of the floorboards, as Annabel seats herself. She looks at the clock – telling ten minutes past nine – and notices, for the first time, a photograph of the family which sits near by: Mrs. Woodrow sitting down, demure, if a little uncomfortable; Lucy cross-legged and serious in front of her parents; Mr. Woodrow standing bolt upright in his dress-coat, a severe paterfamilial gaze into the camera.

Jacobs appears silently by the door.

'Bacon and eggs, or porridge, Miss?'

Annabel turns.

'Jacobs, you made me jump.'

'Sorry, Miss.'

'I'll have the bacon. Am I the only one down for breakfast this morning?'

'Yes, Miss – the master's gone out already, and the Missus says to beg your pardon, but she's feeling a little tired.'

'I see,' says Annabel. 'Thank you.'

'And will you have tea and toast, Miss?'

'Yes, please.'

'Thank you, Miss,' says Jacobs, and retreats.

Annabel, in turn, gets up from her place and walks around the room. Mr. Woodrow's copy of the *Islington Weekly Chronicle* lies upon the sideboard, folded and open at an inside page. Annabel picks it up, takes it back to the table and sits down once more, casually running her eye over the close-packed type. Her eye catches a particular item at the bottom of a column:

THE HOTEL MURDERS

Three days have passed since the discovery of the bodies of the two young women, Elizabeth Violet Carter, aged 18, and Annie Finch, aged 17, brutally murdered in Knight's Hotel, Ludgate Hill. Both victims were what are called 'unfortunates' and the hotel was frequented by females of that class. Nonetheless, it is impossible to imagine a crueller and more dastardly assault upon two defenceless women, and the City of London force are making every conceivable inquiry into the matter. The circumstances of the case, not least a singular epistolary communication found in Annie Finch's room, incline the police to believe a lunatic is responsible for the crime. As yet, however, they do not possess any clue to the person or persons who committed the outrage.

Jacobs appears, standing by Annabel's side with a pot of tea, looking over her shoulder.

'How awful,' says Annabel, putting down the newspaper.

'Miss?' says Jacobs, peering at the paper. 'Oh, that hotel business? Yes, poor devils. Here's the toast, Miss.'

⁓

Annabel Krout, with her breakfast finished, returns upstairs to the second floor. She does not, however, go directly to her room, but pauses outside that of Mrs. Woodrow. After a moment or two's hesitation, she knocks upon the door.

'Who is it?' comes back as a muffled response from within.

'Annabel, cousin. May I come in?'

There is a short interval. Then, finally, 'Yes, my dear, come in.'

Annabel enters the bedroom and finds Mrs. Woodrow sitting up in bed in her dressing-gown, her hair loose, a needle and thread and a pair of stockings by her side. She does, indeed, appear tired, or at least a little pale.

'My dear,' she says immediately, 'you must forgive me for being so rude. I really ought to have come and spoken to you myself; I am just a little fatigued. Tell me, did Jacobs not say anything?'

'She did,' says Annabel, 'but I thought I might come and see how you are? I didn't mean to intrude, cousin.'

'No, no. You're a dear girl, Annabel. It's just my nerves, I am sure. Lucinda was so unruly last night; it took me a good half-hour to quiet her after . . . well, after that little incident. Now, did you have a decent breakfast?'

'Yes, I did,' replies Annabel. 'Is Lucy all right?'

'Well, I believe so. Jacobs will keep an eye on her. But I am afraid we must cancel our plans for today, my dear. I could not possibly step out of the house in my condition. I'd positively die.'

'Of course,' says Annabel, though unable to disguise a note of disappointment in her voice, as the prospect of finally visiting St. Paul's or the fabled Crystal Palace recedes further from her horizon. 'Well, perhaps I could go out myself, just for a little stroll? I might take Lucy for a walk?'

'Oh no, dear. She's far too sensitive after one of her turns; it might bring on another. It's best not to over-stimulate her, not today.'

'Well, what if Jacobs were to come with us?'

'Oh, Annabel dear, she is far too busy around the house. Now, really, I fear I must rest. I was going to do a little darning, just to distract myself, but I am quite exhausted. I might take a little nap. Can you find something to occupy yourself, my dear? I have a couple of books on loan from Mudie's, I think they are downstairs. Or do you like Walter Scott, my dear? Woodrow has a beautiful bound set in the study. I don't think he's opened them once – such a shame.'

'May I play the piano?'

'Oh, I am not sure. The noise travels awfully . . .'

'Then I would not think of it, cousin. I am sure I can find something to amuse myself.'

'Good,' replies Mrs. Woodrow. 'I promise you, my

dear, once I feel better, we shall go out and enjoy ourselves.'

'Please, don't worry,' says Annabel. 'Shall I have Jacobs bring you anything?'

'Perhaps some more toast, my dear. I might eat some toast.'

'I'll see to it,' replies Annabel. 'And shall I come back later, to see how you are?'

'Yes, in an hour or two, my dear,' says Mrs. Woodrow graciously.

Annabel departs the room with a polite smile; it vanishes from her lips, however, the moment she closes the bedroom door. She returns to her room with a long face, and, sweeping up her skirts, sits heavily upon the bed, the prospect of a long house-bound day stretching before her. At last, however, she remembers to ring the bell-pull, with a view to ordering Mrs. Woodrow's toast. As she pulls it, there is the concomitant high-pitched metallic trill in the basement, faint and distant. But, strangely, there is no sound upon the stairs, no hurrying footsteps.

Annabel waits a minute or so, then tries the bell once more. Again, there is no reply. She gets up and walks out on to the landing; but there is still no sound. Furrowing her brow, more in perplexity than irritation, she proceeds downstairs to the first floor, where she encounters Jacobs running hastily up.

'Miss, I'm terrible sorry. I was just ticking off the butcher's boy – our meat today was something awful – I didn't hear the bell.'

Annabel smiles. 'It's only that Mrs. Woodrow wants some toast.'

'I'll go tell Cook, Miss,' replies Jacobs.

Annabel nods, and Jacobs returns downstairs with equal celerity. Annabel herself walks idly into the drawing-room, bestowing a rather longing look towards the piano. She looks through the window, on to Duncan Terrace. There is no sign of the butcher's boy with his basket, nor any other passing tradesman; but her thoughts are more occupied with the tedious day ahead.

She leans over the piano and runs her fingers along the highest, quietest octave, performing a tentative arpeggio. She half expects to hear Mrs. Woodrow thumping upon the floorboards above. But there is no sound.

Annabel sighs to herself, and closes the piano lid.

CHAPTER SEVENTEEN

INSPECTOR WEBB WALKS briskly into the elegant entrance-hall of Woodrow's General Mourning Warehouse, accompanied by Sergeant Bartleby. He ignores the bow given by the doorman, liveried in black and gold, who acts as guardian of the establishment. Instead, he walks directly to the nearest counter, that of the stationery department, where a lone shopman stands ready to receive customers. Beneath the glass-topped counter are the various grades of black-trimmed envelope and writing paper available to the more fashionably bereaved, but Webb ignores the display and beckons the man forward, whispering in his ear. It is only a few discreet words, and they are not distinct enough to be heard by the sergeant. Still, doubtless they encompass the phrase 'an urgent police matter', for the young man in question hastens toward the rear of the building, and returns with a more senior member of staff. In turn, the second man, grey-bearded and solemn as the stationery, leads the two policemen upstairs, and through the door marked '*Employés*', which leads to the back offices.

'We may talk here, sir,' says the gentleman in question, leading Webb and Bartleby into the small private room which constitutes his workplace. 'I would offer you a seat . . .'

Webb looks around: the office is a rather barren affair with only a single desk and chair. There are a few ledgers and the implements of a book-keeper, a pen, inkstand, blotting pad, balanced upon the desk; but nothing else except a series of shelves, stacked with files.

'Don't trouble yourself, Mr. . . . .'

'Prentice, sir. I am the senior clerk and floor-manager. I am afraid my superior, Mr. Woodrow himself, is not yet on the premises; we do not expect him for a half-hour or so.'

'I am sure you will suffice, Mr. Prentice. Tell me,' says Webb, retrieving the receipt from his pocket, 'what do you make of this? A customer of yours, perhaps?'

Prentice retrieves a pair of gold-rimmed spectacles from his jacket, puts them on, and casts his eyes over the receipt. 'No, sir. I should say not.'

'Not?' says Bartleby.

'No, sir,' replies Prentice, quite firmly, 'it is not. This stamp, you see, "Deduct". It means it is a receipt given to one of our staff, one of our girls, though I cannot say which one in particular. A deduction from their salary.'

'Ah, I see,' replies Webb.

'You mean for material they have bought for themselves?' asks Bartleby.

'Or family. It is a common arrangement; nothing underhand, I assure you,' replies Prentice hurriedly. 'We find the girls like to make themselves up a new dress, now and then, to wear of a Sunday; if we have any old stock, then we allow them to purchase at a discount.'

'For regular dresses, not mourning?' asks Bartleby.

'Of course. I am told a dark colour, such as we suggest for half mourning, can be quite fashionable, if made up to the latest taste. Of course, a young woman will squander much of her remuneration upon whatever might be the fashion, if given the opportunity – we only allow it once per annum.'

'Indeed?' says Webb. 'And, tell me, do you know the girls well yourself? They live on the premises, I assume?'

'Certainly; we have twenty females and eight young men; and a lady superintendent.'

'To care for their morals?'

'Indeed.'

'Admirable. Now, Mr. Prentice, do you encourage the girls to go out at night? Do you give them much in the way of liberty?'

'Liberty, sir? Why, the usual amount, though we are not early closers here at Woodrow's. We say one evening per week between seven and ten, and Sundays, of course.'

'But you expect them back by ten, of an evening?'

'Of course. This is a decent, well-conducted establishment, Inspector. Forgive me, sir, I do not follow any of this – where did you find this receipt?'

'I regret it was a short distance from the body of a murdered girl, Mr. Prentice. Not far from here.'

The gentleman in question stands back in astonishment. 'Good Lord.'

'Tell me, are all your girls at work this morning?'

'Yes, of course,' replies Prentice, then checks himself. 'Well, all except one. But she is due her notice, the moment I set eyes upon her.'

'A trouble-maker?'

'Quite. A Miss Price – she has been with us a year or more but the girl is nothing but a source of vexation, Inspector. And she hasn't been seen all—'

'Is she a dark-haired girl, about five feet three inches tall?'

'Good Lord, you don't mean to say . . .'

'I mean to say nothing, my dear fellow. But if you can spare us a few minutes, I am afraid I must ask you to go with the sergeant.'

'Now? Go where?'

'The Holborn Casino. That's where we found the girl – your Miss Price, I fear it is quite likely – but we won't know until you take a look at her?'

Mr. Prentice takes a step back. 'Surely not? I am not the man to do it. I mean to say, Mr. Woodrow will be here shortly. I mean, I should not leave my post.'

'Come, Mr. Prentice, it is only a few minutes. It is a matter of some importance, as you can imagine. Besides, I should think it nothing to a man like yourself, in your line of work.'

Mr. Prentice pales visibly. 'We dress the living, Inspector. I have very little acquaintance with . . .'

'Bodies?' suggests Bartleby.

'It's just that there's no time like the present, in our line of work, sir,' says Webb, amiably. 'And you would be helping Her Majesty's Police. Think of that.'

'Well, I suppose . . .' stammers Prentice.

'Good man,' says Webb.

CHAPTER EIGHTEEN

JASPER WOODROW APPROACHES the General Mourning Warehouse at his regular time of half-past nine. As is his custom, he first applies his muddy boots to the iron scraper situated by the entrance. He is interrupted, however, by the sudden appearance of one of his chief clerks upon the doorstep.

'Prentice, for God's sake, man,' exclaims Woodrow, 'let me get through the door, won't you?'

'I'm sorry, sir, but a rather urgent matter has arisen. I thought it prudent to speak to you at the earliest opportunity.'

'There,' says Woodrow, looking down at his boots, 'that must do, I suppose. Well, might we step inside?'

Mr. Prentice nods and retreats back into the shop, followed by his employer. Woodrow strides upstairs, and Prentice follows.

'I don't wish to alarm you, sir, but there has been, well, an unfortunate incident.'

'Go on,' says Woodrow, as he ascends the steps.

'One of our girls, sir, Miss Price . . . an awful business . . . I don't quite know how to put it . . . she has been found dead.'

Woodrow stops upon the stairs, resting his hand upon the mahogany banister.

'Found dead?' echoes Woodrow.

'Murdered, sir, to be more accurate,' says another voice, unknown to Woodrow, as a slightly stout man in his fifties, dressed in a tweed suit, descends the stairs to meet them.

'Please, Inspector,' says Prentice in an urgent hushed tone. 'Not so loud, if you please. Think of our reputation. Mr. Woodrow, this is Inspector Webb, of Scotland Yard, sir.'

For a moment, Jasper Woodrow looks nonplussed by this information; but it is only a moment.

'I think,' says Woodrow, 'we had best retire to my office, gentlemen.'

Webb bows his head. 'Of course, sir. You'll forgive me, I hope, if I spoke too plainly. I fear we policemen easily forget the social graces. Point the way.'

'It is not far,' says Woodrow.

———

'A terrible business,' says Decimus Webb, seated in Woodrow's office, though he does not say the words with any great feeling.

'Terrible,' reiterates Jasper Woodrow, seated behind his desk. 'And I am sorry for the poor girl's family, naturally, Inspector. But, really, I must think of my livelihood and that of my employees. I do not suppose it can be kept out of the papers?'

'Do you know the Casino, sir?' asks Webb.

'Yes,' says Woodrow, hesitating. 'I know its reputation, yes.'

'An unenviable reputation, I think you'll agree. Then you know what the papers will make of it, sir.'

'We are certain it is Miss Price?'

'Couldn't be more certain, sir,' says Prentice, who stands at the back of the room. 'I'm afraid . . . I have seen her for myself, sir.'

'I don't suppose you know if the girl had any enemies?' asks Webb.

'Enemies, Inspector?' asks Prentice.

'Well, we must consider the usual possibilities . . . rivals in love, or jealous suitors, that sort of thing?'

'Not to my knowledge, sir,' replies the clerk.

Woodrow looks grimly at his employee. His finger taps noisily on the desk. 'Not to your knowledge, Prentice?'

'No, sir.'

'I suppose,' continues Woodrow, an undercurrent of anger in his voice, 'it was not to your knowledge, either, that she was out disporting herself at the bloody Casino at all hours of the night?'

'No, sir,' replies the clerk meekly, looking at the floor. 'I was about to dismiss her, in any case.'

'Why?' asks Webb.

'In truth, Inspector,' says Prentice, 'she was attracting the wrong sort of gentlemen to the premises.'

'Gentlemen? But all your girls are well turned out, surely,' says Webb. 'What sort of gentlemen?'

'Loungers, Inspector,' says Prentice. 'You know the sort.'

Woodrow sighs with exasperation. 'Well, now we know where she met them, eh? And why in God's name was she out at such an hour?'

'It seems,' says Prentice, rather nervously, 'that our superintendent has not been as scrupulous on these matters as I might have hoped.'

'As you might have hoped?' exclaims Woodrow. 'Damn you, man, you're no good to me here. You may as well go back to work.'

Prentice readily agrees and shuffles hurriedly from the room.

'This could spell ruin for us, you know, Inspector,' he says at last. 'Ruin.'

'Nobody likes a scandal, sir,' replies Webb. 'But we must catch the wretch who did this. We can't keep it quiet.'

'I suppose you must.' Woodrow takes a deep breath. 'I don't believe I can help you any further. You said your sergeant will talk to the other girls – must he speak to all of them?'

'I think that's best, sir. The word will get round, mark you, however many persons we talk to. You did not know Miss Price yourself, sir?'

'I have seen her about the place, no doubt. But I deputise Prentice and a couple of others to deal with the counter staff. I have very little to do with them.'

'Naturally. Long-standing business this, isn't it?' inquires Webb. 'I seem to recall it being here on Holborn a good while, albeit perhaps a little smaller in size. A different name, though, if I recollect correctly.'

'It was my wife's father's, Inspector, and his before that. But I fail to see how that pertains to the matter in hand.'

'Forgive me, Mr. Woodrow, professional curiosity, that is all,' says Webb, getting up. 'One feels an obligation to constantly ask questions; a terrible habit. Still, I will not detain you any further, eh? I'd best be going.'

'You have no idea who killed the wretched girl, then, Inspector?' says Woodrow as the two men get up.

'I wish I did. But you know, sir, it occurs to me, being in the trade, you might be able to help me with another unrelated matter.'

'Really?'

'Yes, you well might. By any chance, have you heard of a gentleman by the name of Munday, Jeremy Sayers Munday?'

Woodrow pauses, and speaks rather nervously. 'I . . . I can't say as I have, Inspector. Why do you ask?'

Webb shakes his head, as Jasper Woodrow reaches over and opens his office door. 'Just someone in your line of work, sir. Another case entirely. Don't trouble yourself.'

'I'll show you out, Inspector,' continues Woodrow.

'No need, sir. No need. I know the way,' says Webb, walking through and taking his billycock hat from the stand outside Woodrow's room. 'We will let you know of any progress, sir, rest assured.'

'Thank you, Inspector,' says Woodrow.

Webb smiles politely and nods goodbye.

The two clerks who sit in the ante-chamber glance briefly at the policeman, then return to their work.

___

Jasper Woodrow, closing the door behind Webb, suddenly looks peculiarly pale, the blood drained from his naturally ruddy complexion. He walks over to face the hearth, stretching his hands out towards the fire. But the warmth of the blaze does not have the desired effect and so he returns to his desk where, at the back of a drawer, sits a silver flask of brandy. Woodrow takes it out, unscrews the lid and downs the liquor in a single swig. He sits down and, for several minutes, seems to gaze vacantly into space, as if considering some insoluble problem.

'Jones!' he shouts, at last.

In a second, one of the clerks who dwell outside the office opens the door and stands on the threshold.

'Send a message to Mr. Siddons, Salisbury Square. Have one of the boys take it – tell him that I need to meet with him, as a matter of utmost urgency.'

'Nothing more, sir?'

'Did I not make myself plain?'

'Yes, sir. Right away.'

The clerk exits, leaving Woodrow once more alone with his thoughts.

———

'Ah, there you are, Sergeant,' says Webb, descending the stairs to the ground floor of the Warehouse.

'Just arranging a quiet room to interview these girls, sir.'

'Good, good. Although I don't suppose you will find out anything.'

'You think the fellow picked her at random, sir?'

'More than likely. Still, one never knows. Perhaps she knew him, or they had met before at the Casino. It is worth investigating. See if she kept company with any particular men; apparently she was rather a magnet for a certain type.'

'I'll do my best, sir. Oh, and a telegram from Inspector Hanson. He'll be here directly – asked if you might wait for him at the Casino.'

'I'll do no such thing, Sergeant. I expect it has escaped your notice, but I still have not eaten. I require, at least, a cup of strong coffee and a rasher of bacon, if that is not too much to ask?'

'Shall I send back to Inspector Hanson, sir? Should I mention the bacon?'

'Attempts at wit don't suit you, Sergeant. Let him have a look around, show him the girl before you move her. Then ask him to come to the Yard – I'll see him there, one o'clock, if he can spare the time.'

The sergeant assents, and Webb makes to leave Woodrow's Warehouse, but then turns back abruptly, beckoning the sergeant to his side, speaking quietly.

'Another thing, Sergeant – find out what you can about Mr. Woodrow. I should particularly like to know how long he's been engaged in the mourning business.'

'May I ask why, sir?'

'Just idle curiosity, Sergeant.'

Bartleby looks back at Webb with an expression of perplexity that his superior finds infinitely annoying.

'Well, get on with it, Sergeant,' says Webb.

Bartleby nods, as Webb turns once more on to the street, and strolls out into High Holborn, in search of a cab.

'"I do not suppose it can be kept out of the papers,"' mutters Webb to himself, taking out his pipe and tobacco as he stands by the side of the road. 'I shouldn't think so, sir. Not by a long chalk.'

CHAPTER NINETEEN

ANNABEL KROUT SITS at her writing desk. A steel-nibbed pen is poised in her right hand, but the white page before her is quite blank, devoid of ink except for a title of 'London's Theatreland', twice underlined. Five minutes pass, then ten. As church bells in nearby streets begin to toll noon, she returns the pen to its place in the ink-stand. She gets up and walks once more to the window, looking down on Duncan Terrace, with its narrow strip of quiet pavement and railinged garden. But there is nothing to see. Indeed, the scene, which she fears may become her principal memory of the metropolis, is quite unchanged, and does nothing to stimulate her imagination. She frowns, and reluctantly puts the idea of writing to one side.

She walks downstairs and finds Jacobs upon the landing, applying polish to the banisters, with a rigorous determination that thwarts any possible attempt at conversation. In fact, the only intelligence that Annabel receives is that 'the Missus' is not to be disturbed on account of 'fixing her mind on sleeping till four', which does nothing to raise her spirits.

Recalling Mrs. Woodrow's advice, Annabel, therefore, decides to turn her steps to the Woodrows' study, located at the rear of the first-floor landing. She walks over and carefully turns the brass door-knob, almost tempted to knock, although she knows there can be no-one within. As she opens the door ajar, there is a scent, which strikes her as strangely evocative of something she cannot quite place. At first she fancies it is the smell of books; bound leather and paper. Then it comes to her. It is an intimate, lingering aroma of tobacco and brandy, which, in diluted form, is a fragrance she rather associates with her host.

'I am just going to borrow a book,' she says, turning to Jacobs, then immediately regretting it – for she has no need to ask for permission. The latter, however, merely nods and returns her attention to her work more briskly than might be considered entirely polite, as if to say 'What does it matter to me?'

Annabel swings open the door and enters the room. On first impression, although there is a tall sash window looking out on to the Woodrows' garden, it seems to be the smallest room in the house and rather gloomy; not half as grand as she imagined. The study's principal contents are a modest fireplace and single comfortable chair placed directly in front of the hearth. The alcoves upon either side of the fire are taken up entirely with shelves, containing an array of books and large red volumes, which, upon closer perusal, reveal themselves to be bound copies of *Punch*. Annabel runs her finger along the spines of the books, finding the collection of Scott, quite pristine, just as Mrs. Woodrow described. She stops at random at *The Bride of Lammermoor*, pulling the book from the tight grasp of its confederates upon the shelf. And, though the room is a little cold, she sits down upon the edge of the arm-chair, turning the pages, ignoring the introduction:

Few have been in my secret while I was compiling these narratives, nor is it probable that they will

ever become public during the life of their author.
Even were that event . . .

Annabel stops reading, however, as her foot touches upon something under the arm-chair, a small, torn piece of paper that rustles as her shoe crushes it. Bending down to pick it up, she discovers it is a ticket of some kind, with half the print smudged by some unknown stain:

TICKET OF ADMISSION
for 13th November 1874
to an Evening of Unmatched Entertainment
in Song and Dance at the
HOLBORN CASINO, High Holborn

CAUTION! *It is necessary to retain this part of the ticket to serve as a pass between the Hall and Salon and prevent improper intrusion; its production may be respectfully requested.*

With no particular knowledge of the reputation or location of the Holborn Casino, Annabel nonetheless cannot help but wonder why such a ticket should be found in the Woodrows' home. She concludes, with a frown, that it offers some explanation of Mr. Woodrow's tardy and drunken appearance on the previous evening.

At length, she places the ticket in her book, with half a mind to show it to her cousin, and recommences her reading.

———

It is with barely a chapter completed that Annabel quits the small study. For, without the warmth of a few burning coals, she finds the room is a little too cold, and the walls a little oppressive. She contemplates calling back Jacobs, long since disappeared from the landing, with a view to lighting a fire in the small room. But she wonders whether Mr. Woodrow might consider such an action a little presumptuous in his private retreat. Thus, finally, eschewing the other more formal rooms of the house, she returns to her bed-room, where she settles herself upon the bed in an upright pose. With the fire burning brightly in the hearth, she is quite determined to devote herself to *The Bride of Lammermoor* when there is the sound of footsteps, and a rather quiet knock at the door.

'Come in?'

Lucy Woodrow lets herself in, turning the brass door-knob with both hands. Annabel smiles, puts down her book and beckons her in.

'Hello, my dear,' says Annabel.

'Hello,' replies the little girl. 'Are you ill too?'

'Why, who is ill?'

'Mama. She's in bed.'

'No, dear,' says Annabel, 'I was just reading. And I think your Momma is just a little out of sorts, that is all.'

Lucy shrugs. 'Jacobs said I could come down and see you, if I was good.'

'And have you been good?' asks Annabel.

Lucy nods.

'And what have you been doing this morning?' continues Annabel, sitting on the edge of the bed.

'Reading. Mama said I should read; but they're the same silly books,' says Lucy, 'and reading is an awful bore.'

It sounds like the latter phrase is parroted second-hand, perhaps copied from her mother or father, but the girl says it with great sincerity, nonetheless. Annabel looks down at her novel, and puts it to one side. 'It is, isn't it? Tell me, Lucy, have you been outdoors since we went to the Zoological Gardens?'

Lucy emphatically shakes her head.

'And I have not been outdoors all day. Tell me, Miss Lucinda Woodrow,' says Annabel, a rather mischievous glint in her eye, 'would you like to go for a stroll?'

'Yes please,' replies the little girl.

~

'Miss,' says Jacobs, appearing in the hall, 'where are you going?'

'I'm just taking Lucinda for a stroll,' says Annabel, straightening the little girl's coat and scarf. 'We both need some air.'

'It's cold outside, Miss, and the Missus—'

'Is asleep. We won't be five minutes, will we, dear?'

'No,' says Lucy, as if shocked by the very idea.

'But where will you go, Miss? You don't know your way.'

'Five minutes, Jacobs,' says Annabel, allowing a note of frustration into her voice. 'We can hardly get lost in five minutes.'

'I don't know, Miss,' says Jacobs.

'You don't have to know,' says Annabel, exasperated, pulling back the curtain and opening the front door. 'Come, Lucy.'

Lucy smiles and obliges; and if she does not actually thumb her nose at the maid-servant, she looks at her with precisely the expression of satisfaction and triumph she might have worn if she had.

Outside the air is somewhat colder than Annabel had expected. She looks down at Lucy but, rather than shivering, her little cousin looks positively invigorated – or at least more cheerful than a few moments before.

'Shall we go and look at the canal?' says Annabel.

Lucy nods. It is a brief walk, around the perimeter of the gardens, and on to the adjoining street, before they stand in the road above the entrance to the Islington tunnel, with little to indicate the presence of the channel buried beneath their feet. Lucy stares at the visible easterly portion of the canal through the railings that protect its raised banks. A solitary barge makes leisurely progress through the dirty water towards the next lock, but this does not seem to hold her interest. In fact, the little girl tugs rather impulsively at Annabel's fingers and Annabel allows herself be led to the iron gate that conceals a narrow sloping track going down to the canal itself. There is another boat, moored by the tow-path, with two young men busying themselves about the roped tarpaulins that conceal its cargo. One of the men, dressed in brown fustian, a battered-looking cloth cap on his head, looks up from his work.

'Can I oblige you with anything, Miss?' he says, grinning.

'Enough of that, Jim,' says the other.

Annabel pulls her reluctant charge away. 'We'll, just go along the road here,' she says, looking pointedly at the young man.

Lucy frowns at the sudden movement, her face presenting the disappointment of which only children of a certain age are capable.

'Or shall we go back home?' muses Annabel. 'I suppose we should not be too long, or Jacobs will worry.'

Lucy shakes her head.

'I did promise,' says Annabel. 'Five minutes. Very well – just to the end of the road and back. Come on now, and I will tell your Momma that you were especially good today.'

The little girl pouts, but, perhaps weighing up the

advantages of a creditable report, eventually accedes
to the request. And it can be no more than a few
minutes' walk, for they proceed to the end of
Colebrooke Row and back again, before walking once
more round the gardens, into Duncan Terrace.

'Lucy,' says Annabel, as they walk back, 'tell me, do
you remember anything odd about last night?'

'No,' says the little girl emphatically.

'Do you remember,' says Annabel, trying not to
sound overly inquisitorial, 'coming into my room?'

'No,' says the girl, confused.

'Do you remember if you woke up at all?'

'Yes,' says Lucy, at length.

'Where was that?'

'In the hall.'

'And what was going on?'

'Papa was angry.'

'Do you know why?'

Lucy shrugs. Annabel, in turn, smiles in sympathy.

'I think,' continues Annabel, stopping and bending
down to be nearer her cousin's height, 'that your
Poppa can be very angry sometimes, even though I am
sure he loves you very much.'

Lucy shakes her head.

'I don't think he does.'

Annabel frowns. 'Well, if you're feeling bad, if your
Poppa's been mean to you, you'll come and talk to me,
won't you?'

Lucy nods.

CHAPTER TWENTY

DECIMUS WEBB SITS in one of the three private bars of the Clarence public house, Scotland Yard. It is a secluded enclave, segregated from the rest of the establishment by a pair of dividing partitions, carved mahogany panels, topped with etched glass, and with its own door on to the street. This must be the principal attraction for the policeman. For the pint of beer that sits before him upon the table is virtually untouched, and the only smoke he enjoys is that lingering effervescence of beer and old tobacco that hangs in the air. At length, however, the street-door opens and a familiar face pokes inside.

'Inspector Hanson,' says Webb, 'I had given you up for lost.'

Hanson nods and walks in. Webb gestures at him to take a seat.

'The men at the Yard said I might find you here,' says Hanson.

'Yes, well, have you seen my office? I find this more congenial when I have something on my mind. We have an agreement, the landlord and I. He turns a blind eye to my sitting here with a solitary pint of ale for an occasional afternoon.'

'What do you do in return?'

'I ignore the fact that he gives poor odds on the two-thirty at Epsom Downs.'

'Gambling? Surely he cannot get away with that, so near to the Yard?'

'My dear fellow, who do you think places the bets? In any case, I leave such things to the Assistant Commissioner.'

'The City force would not tolerate it.'

'I dare say, Inspector. Would you care for something?'

'No, thank you,' replies Hanson.

'Then I suppose we should address the matter in hand. You've spoken to Bartleby and seen the girl, then?'

Hanson nods. 'I have. May I please see the note? You have it with you?'

'Same scrawl as the last one, if I recall,' says Webb, retrieving the paper from inside his wallet, and placing it upon the table.

'Identical,' replies the City policeman, glumly staring at the missive. 'We are investigating the same case, Inspector. I knew he'd do it again. I simply knew it.'

'Quite. Not a pleasing prospect, is it,' says Webb, 'this fellow gaily carving up some young female every couple of days?'

'Hardly,' replies Hanson. 'I confess, if that is his idea, I find it difficult to see how we are to stop him.'

'I take it my indomitable sergeant had discovered nothing of great interest regarding Miss Price's habits or acquaintances?'

'Not that he told me.'

'Then you may be assured that he has not. Discretion is not one of Bartleby's strengths. You see, I had wondered if she went to the Casino alone or with another girl; or perhaps someone helped her evade the superintendent at Woodrow's? But then they are

169

hardly likely to come forward, even if such an individual exists.'

'The Casino has a certain reputation.'

'Well-deserved. Ask anyone in E Division. No girl with any pretence to decency will admit to having accompanied her to such a place – much less having seen anything untoward. Not if she wishes to keep her place, at least.'

'Not even to prevent another murder?'

'Well, perhaps. One might hope that would be incentive enough,' says Webb.

'Other witnesses, then?' asks Hanson.

'We will send men around the local publics; talk to the girls and the flash sorts who frequent the place. But I would not hold you breath, Inspector,' says Webb. 'He picked his spot well – I don't suppose it was very odd to see a man sneaking down that alley with a girl, or coming back alone. You know, forgive me, but you look rather disheartened.'

'In all honesty, I had hoped you might provide me with a little inspiration,' says Hanson, rather dejectedly.

'Tell me something of your own progress, then.'

'That progress, or rather the lack of it,' replies Hanson, 'is precisely why I had entertained hopes . . . well, never mind. Let me acquaint you with the details. Our doctor performed an autopsy on both women at Knight's.'

'Anything out of the ordinary?' asks Webb.

'There was quite a potent dose of laudanum in Betsy Carter's stomach; I can have the report despatched to you, if you like.'

'No, there is no need. Was there anything else?'

'A good deal of brandy.'

'The brandy. So the brandy was dosed. But why?' Webb muses aloud. 'The girl was pretty much at the fellow's mercy, after all – why drug her then stab her?'

'I have no explanation,' says Hanson. 'Unless it was some morbid interest in having the girl completely in his power. I am afraid it is rather difficult to know when he . . .'

'Made free with her person?' suggests Webb.

Hanson coughs. 'Or perhaps the man is something of a coward when it comes to the kill; he likes to be sure of success.'

'And the second girl – Finch, was it not?'

'A hint of liquor but nothing like so much; and certainly nothing soporific in nature. She was smothered – I was right about that much, Inspector.'

'I am sure. I would not berate yourself overly much, Hanson – I can see no logic to this wretched business. And did you find the missing decanter?'

'Smashed to bits in a nearby yard, but yes. We can only infer the contents.'

'And what of your Mr. Brown?'

'He rather slipped the net, as you know.'

'Well, I will not ask how that occurred.'

'Drink. I have disciplined the man in question.'

Webb allows himself a slight smile. 'I see – do you think Brown knows something? Or does he merely not take to being watched?'

'I can't say as to that,' says Hanson, 'but I'd rather we knew where he was, all the same.'

'Yes, well, he is our only witness to this whole mess,' says Webb. He leans forward and takes up his pint glass, taking a sip. 'Now, I am curious, do you still think our man is a maniac? That is where the problem lies, is it not? I've been giving it some thought. If he is acting upon a whim, then we are quite sunk – how does one prevent it? To act, we must anticipate him.'

'Very well,' says Hanson, 'let us imagine he has some purpose, however obtuse or lunatic. There is no connection between the women, as far as I can make out.'

'None at all?' asks Webb.

'Miss Finch and Miss Carter did not frequent the Casino – I am almost sure of that; I would have heard about it by now.'

'What about vice versa? Miss Price, I mean to say.'

'From what I gathered from your sergeant, Miss Price lived with her father in Enfield before coming to Woodrow's. I suppose she might have been to Knight's Hotel, but, really, how will we ever find out such a thing? The only connection is in the mind of the fellow who killed them.'

'True. But there is, at the very least, a twisted purpose to it, Hanson. He took the trouble to drug the first one; he leaves us these wretched little billets-douxs. He has given the whole business a good deal of thought, I should say.'

Hanson sighs. 'I take your point, Inspector. But that still leaves us very much in the dark.'

'Hmm,' says Webb. 'Have you exhausted every inquiry? Was there not some sweetheart, some chap the two girls had argued over?'

'I hardly think that's relevant, Inspector, though I've been to every public house and gambling den round St. Paul's, every possible haunt, talked to anyone claiming acquaintance with either girl. From what I can make out, it was some fast sort they met in a gin palace. Took them both out on the town then went for the Finch girl, made the other a little jealous. Quite routine for that sort of girl. They enjoy the occasional spat.'

'What about this man – what do we know about him?'

'Allegedly something of a gentleman – but I'd say you may take that with a pinch of salt, the types I've been talking to. Although I'm told the girls at Knight's are quite sought after by a certain class of young swell; they can do quite well for themselves. I'm reliably informed there's a Baroness in the West Country who traces her beginnings to room twenty-nine.'

Webb smiles. 'You would not believe how many times I have heard that story, or something similar Hanson. I suppose it provides a rather necessary crumb of comfort for the worst off.'

Hanson shrugs. 'In any case, I confess I am struggling as to how to proceed.'

'I wish I could advise you. Finding your Mr. Brown may be a start. For my own part, I can only say I will keep you informed of any progress, and I hope we may expect likewise?'

'Of course,' replies Hanson.

'Good. In the meantime, I am afraid I have another case to attend to – I had hoped to leave it to Bartleby but he is doubtless preoccupied with practicalities at the Casino, for today, at least.'

'Another murder?'

Webb shakes his head. 'A missing person. Well, in a manner of speaking.'

'How so?'

'Would you believe a case of body-snatching? I will not reveal the cemetery in question; the manager is rather nervous as to the effect on trade.'

Hanson raises his eyebrows. 'I thought we'd put paid to Burkers forty years ago.'

'You know,' says Webb, as he gets up, 'I was labouring under the same misapprehension myself. Remarkable, is it not?'

CHAPTER TWENTY-ONE

RAIN HAS SET in for the night, as Jasper Woodrow returns home, gone six o'clock. It does not, however, bear down directly upon Woodrow's head, but patters noisily upon the roof of the hansom that conveys him up Pentonville Hill, and, likewise, upon the unfortunate cab-man who directs the speeding carriage. Indeed, the latter, his broad-brimmed hat and oilskin cape streaming rivulets of dark water, drives his horse at a frenetic pace, as if hoping to out-distance the weather, charging at full speed past Amwell Street, past the Angel, and, finally, swinging into Duncan Terrace. The rain, however, is not to be beaten – but at least the journey is a swift one, which is agreeable to his passenger who swings open the twin doors and alights on to the pavement almost before the vehicle has pulled to a stop. Once the cab-man has been paid, Jasper Woodrow hurriedly ascends the steps to his front door, fumbling for his house key.

Inside, he is met by his manservant, Jervis, who promptly removes his master's hat and coat.

'Where is my wife?' asks Woodrow as he takes off his gloves.

'She retired to her room this morning, sir.'

'Not seen since?'

'No, sir.'

Woodrow takes a deep breath. 'Get me a brandy, for God's sake, man.'

'Yes, sir.'

Jervis departs, leaving Woodrow alone in the hall. Some trifling sound catches his attention, the rustle of a page being turned, and he walks to the doorway of the morning room, where Annabel Krout sits before the fireplace, a few chapters into *The Bride of Lammermoor*. She turns and raises herself up in her seat as she hears Woodrow's footsteps. Woodrow coughs.

'Ah, Miss Krout, please do not get up on my account.'

'Sir.'

There is a pause.

'I trust you have had a good day.'

'A quiet one, thank you.'

'What is that you're reading?'

'Walter Scott. Melissa said I might borrow it.'

'Of course.'

Another pause.

'Miss Krout, this is not perhaps the time to touch upon it, but I feel I may have spoken too plainly last night. If I gave any offence, in relation to that business with Lucinda, I had no intention of doing so. I was, I can only say, rather tired.'

If Annabel Krout considers this a fulsome apology, she does not reveal it in her expression. 'Of course,' she replies.

'Good. I would not want us upon an awkward footing. Now I must really go and see my wife.'

'She has been in bed all day; give her my best.'

'I will,' replies Woodrow, with the hint of a bow, quitting the room.

Jasper Woodrow enters his wife's bedroom without so much as a knock upon the door. His wife is sitting upright in bed, still in her dressing-gown, her eyes closed. She is not, however, asleep, and opens her eyes, turning to look at her husband.

'Oh, good,' she says in a quiet voice, 'I am glad you are back. My dear, I have had such a head all day.'

'I am sorry to hear that; I do not like to see you in low spirits.'

'Have you seen Annabel? I fear she is quite weary of us already. She looked rather dejected when I said we could not go out today.'

'Did she? I spoke to her downstairs. She was reading some wretched thing by Scott.'

'Oh, yes, I said she might borrow it – you do not mind?'

'No,' says Woodrow, though he sounds rather preoccupied. 'I can't stand the fellow.' He sits down upon the bed, then places his hands upon his thighs, as if bracing himself for some sudden shock. It is sufficiently out of character to unnerve his wife, who reaches out her hand to his shoulder.

'My dear, is there something wrong? Is it Lucy? I have told Jacobs that she must sleep in her room for now.'

'No, it is not Lucinda,' says Woodrow, although the mention of her name seems to cause him to frown. He wordlessly moves his lips, as if struggling to find the right words. 'Melissa, you know I would normally not trouble you with such matters, but I must be frank; I have need of your help.'

'Whatever do you mean, Woodrow?'

'There has been a . . . well, I do not know what is the word. An unfortunate circumstance. One of the shop-girls was found dead, this morning.'

'Dead? Why, how awful.'

'No, you do not understand me. The girl was murdered; it is a terrible business; they found her at the Casino. Her throat was . . . well, I am told it was unpleasant. The work of some madman; they have not caught him yet.'

Mrs. Woodrow sits back. 'Good Lord.'

'Quite.'

'The Holborn Casino? But what was she doing there?'

'What is any girl doing in such a place?'

'Lord. The poor creature. What was her name?'

'Good God, woman, damn her name, what about ours? Don't you see what this means? Bad enough it should be one of our girls, but at the Casino? The whole thing will be in every paper in London by Monday. It could spell the ruin of the business.'

'Woodrow, please. Do not shout. The servants will hear you.'

Woodrow takes a deliberate, deep breath. 'Forgive me. I did not mean to be so . . . intemperate. But you do not understand the gravity of the situation.'

Mrs. Woodrow looks puzzled. 'My dear? Of course, it is quite terrible, I mean to say I cannot imagine, and people will talk. But we have such a good reputation. We will just have to wait it out.'

Woodrow shakes his head. 'People have long memories. But that is not the worst of it. Langley has backed out. I have spent two hours with him this afternoon; I went to see him. I explained the situation, so he at least might hear it from me, and not read it in the *Daily News*. He says he is not certain he can "commit myself under the circumstances".'

Mrs. Woodrow shrugs. 'Well, then, if that is all, the new premises will have to wait. I know you have cherished the idea, my dear, but surely you can bear that?'

Again, Woodrow shakes his head. 'You do not understand. We need his money; we need it now.'

'Why?'

'There are things I have not told you. Business matters that do not normally . . . there are debts.'

'But surely you can pay them from—'

'No,' says Woodrow, emphatically. 'Bad debts. There are certain transactions I have made, perhaps unwisely. Well, I shall spare you the details. They would mean nothing to you, in any case. We need Langley's money; we need it rather badly.'

Mrs. Woodrow puts her hand to her brow. 'My dear, how bad is it?'

'I can pay the wages in the New Year; we should have enough, too, for the gas and coal.'

'But then?'

'That is it. Unless things change, we are done for.'

Mrs. Woodrow stares at her husband in shock. Neither of them speaks for a good minute. 'Good Lord, what would Papa say?'

Woodrow gets up from the bed.

'Melissa, your blessed father is dead, rest his soul,' he replies, a suggestion of anger in his tone. 'He left the business in my hands.'

'And this is what you have done with it. I cannot believe it.'

Woodrow looks sharply at his wife but bites his lip. 'It still might be saved if we can find sufficient money; an investment in the future.'

'We?'

'If you were to speak to your cousin. Perhaps her father might consider a loan. Even five hundred might be sufficient; just enough to square some of the creditors.'

'Woodrow, good Lord, how many are there?'

'That does not matter. After a point, one robs Peter

to pay Paul; it is the amount that is the thing. Will you speak to her?'

Mrs. Woodrow wipes her eyes and looks down into her lap. When she finally speaks, it is almost in a whisper.

'I cannot.'

'You cannot? What the blazes do you mean by that?'

'Woodrow, you know full well – what would the family say?'

'Damn the family. Would they prefer us bankrupt? On the streets?'

Mrs. Woodrow sighs. 'Now you are being ridiculous.'

'I wish I were.'

'What about Mr. Langley? He is such a decent man – perhaps if you outlined some of the circumstances; explained yourself fully.'

'He may be rich but he is not a fool, Melissa.'

Melissa Woodrow looks up at her husband, who stands dejectedly by the window.

'I wish,' says Woodrow at last, 'I wish I had not told you.'

Mrs. Woodrow pulls back the covers and gets out of bed; she opens the drawer to her dresser, rummaging underneath her silk petticoats.

'Well, at least now,' she says, 'I know the meaning of these. That is something.'

Woodrow turns and looks at her, confused. She holds a handful of paper.

'Here,' she says, offering them to him. 'I should have shown you. I know I should. But, Woodrow, I didn't know what to think.'

Her husband takes the notes and reads them; a peculiar litany of accusations.

YOUR HUSBAND IS A FRAUD

YOUR HUSBAND KEEPS SECRETS

DO NOT TRUST YOUR HUSBAND

'Where did you find these?' asks Woodrow.

'Someone has been sending them here, in the post. It started a couple of weeks ago. I was going to tell you, I swear, but there has not been a time when I felt I could say something. Do you know who it is?'

Woodrow shakes his head.

'Although,' continues Mrs. Woodrow, 'I cannot conceive why anyone should be so spiteful, even if you owe them money.'

'No,' replies her husband, rather mechanically, 'nor can I.'

'What is it?'

'Nothing,' he says, crushing the notes in his hands. 'You're right. These things are quite foul. Malicious. I shall burn them. You must tell me if you get any more.'

Mrs. Woodrow sighs and takes hold of her husband's arm. 'We can weather any storm together, my dear, we can truly.'

Woodrow nods, still looking at the crumpled paper.

'Woodrow, look at me. Did Mr. Langley say he would definitely not take up the partnership?'

'He was vague,' replies Woodrow. 'Doubtless I embarrassed him, pleading with him.'

'But if you had the money, you think the Warehouse could prosper? You could pay these people what you owe?'

'I should not make the same mistakes twice.'

'Then I shall invite him to dinner, in a day or two.'

'What good will that do?'

'It might put him in a good mood; make him more open to persuasion. Show him that you are not daunted by what has happened.'

'He may not come.'

'Perhaps, but I shall make a point of saying Annabel would be glad of his company. He rather likes her, I am sure of it. I've seen him look at her.'

'Well, she is a fine-looking young woman.'

'Woodrow!'

'Not finer than you, my dear.'

'I should think not.' Mrs. Woodrow smiles at her husband. She rests her head against his shoulder. 'Woodrow, we shall come through this, I promise you.'

Jasper Woodrow looks down at his wife and tries to smile back.

'You have told me everything, haven't you, dear?'

Woodrow nods.

'Then I shall tell Mrs. Figgis to make a start on dinner.'

INTERLUDE

The Bible?

Why, yes, I take a good deal of comfort from it. And yourself, Miss Krout? Are you familiar with the Good Book? I am glad to hear it. This wretched city would be much improved if there were more young women like yourself and less . . . well, I will not say the words.

No, you must believe me. You have been protected from the worst of it, Miss Krout, as is proper. If, God forbid, you were to walk the streets of the metropolis at night, you would soon see such disgusting exhibitions of vice, scenes that would provoke utter repugnance in the heart of any true Christian. I confess, I have even passed through a City churchyard, and seen half a dozen young women, mere girls, openly plying their abominable trade amidst the graves. There is no place on earth so degraded as London by night, I am sure of it.

I am sorry, I did not mean to raise my voice.

Of course, yes, Eloi Chapel. Indeed, that is where it began; that is the rotten, cancerous core of this whole business. Tell me, Miss Krout, have you read about our fair city during the forties? We had outgrown our quaint English churches you see, the ancient medieval sort that so please your countrymen. The City grave-yards were the worst; more akin to swamps, overflowing with bodies, packed twelve deep in narrow shafts, from paupers to princes. In some, they topped up the earth, until it almost spilt over the church walls; in others they merely burnt the coffins and buried the corpses one atop the other. In the poorer parts of the metropolis, you could see men jumping into the graves to push them down, to break the bones if they needed; it was a regular occurrence.

You think I exaggerate?

No, I am not angry. I simply try to be accurate. Let us merely say such arrangements were rather too intimate for our English taste. So we built our new cemeteries; parks and gardens for the dead, instead of swamps. I gather we rather borrowed the idea from the French, but it was a good notion, all the same. You are not so crowded in Boston, I dare say?

Mount Auburn? No, I have not heard of it. Is it picturesque?

Well, in any case, it became clear there was money to be made by those providing homes for the dead; new burial grounds, stocks and shares in burials companies – a good deal of money. Now, you know as well as I, every type of commerce attracts scoundrels, Miss Krout. It is a universal law; some men are always less scrupulous than others. The burial business was no exception.

I believe the Eloi Chapel Company opened in 1846 or thereabouts; you must find the date for yourself. It was cheap, I know that much, and so much more convenient, for the working man, than some distant plot at Kensal Green or Highgate. They cleared the vaults thoroughly before they began; took out all the old rubbish. Indeed, it was a large church off Fetter Lane; close to Fleet Street. And I should think it was pleasant enough, to begin with; until it filled up. But they kept filling it, you see; to the very brim, floor to ceiling with cheap wooden boxes. And when it was full, they simply opened the boxes and emptied them out, rather like one tips ashes into a dust-bin. Except the refuse in this case was, shall we say, rather more troublesome, and so they were obliged to be a little secretive. He saw to that – Mr. J.S. Munday, Esq. – he formed the company, sold the shares. A clever young man; ambitious.

But in the summer of forty-eight, they'd left the tipping-out a little too long, and the place was over-ripe. I expect urgent measures were required; perhaps they were careless. Then someone saw their cart one night, full of . . . well, let us merely say *disiecta membra*.

Mr. Munday was ruined, poor fellow killed himself before the trial; and the stock was worthless.

A moral little tale, really. At least, that is what I thought until a couple of months ago. It is peculiar how a chance meeting can turn one's life topsy-turvy, is it not?

Forgive me, Miss Krout. In my present circumstances, one is obliged to play the philosopher.

'Our Lord's forgiveness'? My! Do you intend to effect my reformation?

No, no. I await His judgment, that is all.

CHAPTER TWENTY-TWO

ANNABEL KROUT WAKES. She can hear the now familiar early-morning progress of Jacobs about her room. The maid is quiet but there is noise all the same: the installation of the morning's hot water, with the porcelain being placed upon the wash-stand; the pattering of the girl's feet across to the hearth; then the striking of a single match to kindle the fire.

'Good morning, Miss.'

'Ah, good morning, Jacobs. Thank you.'

'Shall I do the curtains, Miss? It's cleared up a bit outside.'

'Yes, if you would.'

Jacobs obliges. There are, Annabel notices, several patches of blue sky. She sits up, rubbing her shoulder.

'Thank you.'

'Didn't you sleep too well, Miss?'

'It's just a little ache, that's all. How was Miss Lucy?'

'Quiet as a little lamb, Miss. More than I can say for myself.'

'You watched over her then?'

'Yes, Miss. Moved my bed into her room.'

'That must be a nuisance for you, Jacobs.'

'It's no trouble, Miss,' says Jacobs, without much conviction. 'I've done it before. Is there anything else?'

'No. Thank you.'

'Oh, and Mrs. Woodrow says she'd like a word before breakfast, Miss. In her room, if you please.'

'Thank you, Jacobs. Is Mrs. Woodrow feeling better?'

'She seems a bit more herself, Miss.'

———

Annabel, having dressed and finished her morning toilette, proceeds to her cousin's room, where she indeed finds her considerably improved, in comparison to the previous day. Mrs. Woodrow sits fully dressed before her mirror, teasing the small ringlets of hair that grace her forehead.

'Annabel, my dear. Do come in and sit down for a moment. Did you sleep well?'

Annabel does as instructed, taking a seat beside her cousin's dressing table. Before she can answer, however, Mrs. Woodrow turns to face her and begins speaking once more.

'My dear,' begins Mrs. Woodrow, rather hurriedly, 'I'm afraid there is something I must tell you; something unpleasant. I should have spoken to you last night, but I was not myself, and Woodrow was hardly any better. It was all I could do to eat something. I expect you thought us very rude at dinner.'

'No, not at all,' replies Annabel politely; then a thought crosses her mind, an anxious look clouding her face. 'Cousin, it's not about Momma or Poppa?'

'Annabel – what an idea! Heaven forbid! No, nothing like that. Well, I would not mention it at all, but it will be in the papers, and doubtless the servants will gossip; that is why I thought we might talk in private.'

'Excuse me, I don't follow you, cousin.'

'No, I am not being clear,' replies Mrs. Woodrow,

sighing. 'There has been an awful tragedy; a shop-girl, one of our girls, well, there is no nice way of putting it, she was found dead yesterday; the police have told Woodrow she was attacked by some madman.'

'Attacked? You mean she was murdered?'

'Yes, my dear, awful, isn't it? Worse, I fear, she was found in a place with a very bad reputation, a dance-hall, near the Warehouse; it seems likely there was some element of, well, impropriety on her part.'

'How terrible.'

'Yes, it is rather bad,' replies Mrs. Woodrow. 'It will not reflect well on the business, not at all; Woodrow is quite desolate about it. I just thought you ought to know, my dear, in case . . . Well, I have not said anything to the servants as yet, my dear, but it will come out. I am not quite sure what to do for the best.'

'No, of course.'

'One almost feels one should wear some token of mourning; I mean to say, I did not know the wretched girl, but really it is such a bad business. Still, I will say no more about it. I have probably said more than is decent – are you quite shocked, Annabel?'

'No, not shocked. I mean, Melissa, I am but I don't know what to say.'

'My dear, you need say nothing. I discussed it with Woodrow and it just seemed best we did not keep it from you; you are not a child, after all. Now, I suppose we must just put it behind us and dwell on something more pleasant. It need not interfere with your stay. What about today? I think we shall go to church for the eleven o'clock service, if you care to come.'

'Of course.'

'Good. Oh, and Woodrow says we might go for a little drive afterwards. Some fresh air might do us all a world of good, don't you think? You were only saying as much yesterday.'

Breakfast passes without incident and with little conversation. Mr. Woodrow himself seems distant and a little tired, his eyes possessing the same bleary character that Annabel noted upon her first morning at the breakfast table. Once the food is cleared away, Woodrow retires to his study, and his wife to her boudoir, to ponder the precise choice of jewellery for the day, and of a hat appropriate for Christian worship. Annabel, upon the other hand, her literary imagination fired by Mrs. Woodrow's news, goes to her room and begins to contemplate writing an article entitled 'The London Tragedy', to reveal some telling contrasts between British and American criminality for the readers of the *New England Monthly Bazaar*. In truth, she finds herself quite disappointed that Mr. Woodrow did not choose to wax lyrical about the circumstances of the incident over his poached eggs.

At length, however, Annabel is roused from her daydreaming by her cousin's appearance at her bedroom door; and, after sundry comments upon her dress and hair, which she does her best to amend to Melissa Woodrow's exacting standards, the family gather in the hall. Lucy, in particular, is arrayed in her Sunday best, though she does not appear best pleased at the prospect of going to church and wears a particularly sullen expression.

'You look pretty, Lucy,' suggests Annabel. The little girl merely scowls. Any further discussion, however, is forestalled by the ringing of the Woodrow's door-bell.

'Now, who would call at this hour on a Sunday?' asks Mrs. Woodrow.

Jasper Woodrow does not wait for the arrival of his maid-servant, but swiftly resolves the question by unceremoniously opening the front door himself. He reveals Joshua Siddons standing upon the front steps.

'Ah, forgive me, Woodrow, and you, ma'am,' says Siddons. 'I see this is an inconvenient time.'

'Mr. Siddons, why, how pleasant to see you!' exclaims Melissa Woodrow. 'But we are all off to church.'

'Indeed, ma'am,' he replies, 'my apologies.'

'There is no need to apologise, sir,' replies Mrs. Woodrow. 'Now, what am I thinking of? I don't believe you have met my cousin, Miss Krout?'

'I am charmed, Miss Krout,' says Siddons, with a small bow.

'Now, would you care to come with us?' asks Mrs. Woodrow.

'Why, my dear lady,' replies Joshua Siddons, 'I should be delighted.'

'But I expect Siddons wants a word with me, Melissa,' says Jasper Woodrow, hurriedly interposing in the conversation. 'Just a small matter we need to discuss.'

'On a Sunday morning, Woodrow? Really!'

'All the same, my dear. A quick word. We shall follow on.'

'I will not detain him long, my dear lady,' says Siddons.

Mrs. Woodrow acquiesces and the last thing she and Annabel Krout see of the two men is when they climb into the waiting carriage on Duncan Terrace.

———

'Well,' says Joshua Siddons, seated in the Woodrows' drawing-room, 'so that is the cousin? Delightful little creature, eh? But you never said a word, my dear chap! When did she arrive?'

'Never mind that. Why did you not come last night?'

'A burial in Woking, if you must know, Woodrow. I did not get back until late. Now, what is so pressing?'

'I had some bad news yesterday,' replies his host, standing before the fireplace.

'Ah,' replies Siddons, with a slight smile, 'yes, that awful business at the Casino. I confess, I have already heard. I saw something at the station last night; some piece of gutter journalism. Can't be good for the firm, eh? I wish I could help. Still, rise above it; that is my motto. Always has been.'

Woodrow, still dressed in his coat, clenches his hands tightly around the brim of his hat, which he holds in front of him. 'That is not all. Langley has pulled out of the partnership.'

'Oh, well, that is a shame, certainly. But, come, my good fellow, I fail to see what I can do about it.'

'There is much you could do, if you chose,' says Woodrow emphatically, 'as well you know.'

'My dear Woodrow,' exclaims Siddons, as if having been offered some awful insult, 'an arrangement is an arrangement. What is the matter? Are you in some difficulty?'

'Your payments are a burden at the moment; this will only make it worse. I swear, any decent man would consider our account long since settled.'

'Nonetheless,' says Siddons, waving his hand as if to swat away any awkwardness.

'Moreover, I now find that you have not kept your part of the bargain,' says Woodrow, glowering at the undertaker.

Siddons raises his eyebrows. 'I hardly think one might say that.'

'You're a liar. The policeman who came to see me, about the wretched girl, he also asked me if I knew a "Jeremy Munday".'

'Munday?' says Siddons, again smiling, as if trying to recall the name.

'Don't toy with me, sir. I am not to be trifled with. Why should he ask me that?'

'Why, indeed?'

'Do not provoke me, I swear, by Almighty God, if you—'

'I have done nothing,' replies Siddons with a theatrical sigh. 'However, the police came to me as well, I confess.'

'Why?'

'Well, it is quite remarkable – it was to inform me some mysterious Burker had been at work at Abney Park, digging around. Can you believe it?'

'Good God,' replies Woodrow, his mouth open in astonishment, 'you do not mean—'

'That Jeremy Munday has been disturbed in his eternal rest? That is precisely it. Nothing but an empty coffin left behind. Queer, is it not?'

'Why did you not come to me at once?'

'Why, indeed! Why did I not simply bring the police sergeant directly to your door?'

'I said,' says Woodrow, raising his voice, 'do not play these games of yours. Why, in heaven's name, should this happen? Why now? Have you told anyone?'

'My dear fellow, do contain yourself. I have said nothing. The police only came to me because of the coffin; Mr. Pellegrin informed them of the manufacturer.'

Woodrow shakes his head. 'It is impossible. It has been twenty-five years. More.'

'Come now, you have nothing to fear. Perhaps it was a joke; a wager amongst students of anatomy. Yes, that might well be it. You know the sort. "We'll find old Munday's corpse; dig him up, see how he likes it." That would explain it, eh?'

'A joke? No – at the time, perhaps. But not now – who would go to such lengths?'

'I have no idea.'

'Besides, you mean "we" need not fear, do you not?'

'Of course,' replies Siddons, in a soothing undertone. 'Come, we shall be late for the service.'

'No. It makes no sense, don't you see? Why should this happen now?'

Siddons sighs. 'My dear fellow, what do you want of me? Your wife and her pretty young cousin will be waiting.'

'Who have you spoken to?' says Woodrow, persisting, his voice now rather desperate and frantic. 'You must have told someone. That is the only explanation.'

'I have spoken to precisely no-one. However, if you carry on in this manner, well, I fear you will give everything away, without my assistance.'

'And we are in this together?'

'Of course.'

'Very well,' says Woodrow, taking a deep breath, 'listen to me. At least postpone this month's payment. I swear, on my mother's life, the business cannot bear it. Nor can I.'

Siddons frowns. 'Must we return to this?'

'A month's grace is all I ask,' says Woodrow.

'One might say I have done you enough favours.'

'I will pay it back, with interest.'

Siddons sighs. 'Oh, very well. You know, Woodrow, you do not look quite well. I thought as much last time we met.'

Woodrow looks away. 'There are other . . . delicate matters.'

'Really? What?'

Woodrow shakes his head.

'You will not tell your oldest friend?'

Woodrow snorts in derision. 'Friend?'

'Truly,' says the undertaker, looking at him quizzically. 'What is it? What is troubling you?'

Woodrow looks him in the eye. 'I would not tell you if my very life depended upon it.'

CHAPTER TWENTY-THREE

ST. MARK'S CHURCH in Myddleton Square is a rather imposing Gothic affair, set like an island in the square's very centre, flanked on all sides by tall four-storey Islington terraces. Indeed, the ornate tracery of its windows and high, pinnacled bell-tower are rather incongruous amidst the plain Georgian houses that surround it and there is almost something of the panopticon in its peculiar central location. Nonetheless, it is a popular location for Sunday worship amongst the residents of the parish, and, at the end of the service, it takes some time for the Woodrow family, accompanied by Joshua Siddons, to make their way to their waiting carriage.

'Did you enjoy the sermon, Mr. Siddons?' asks Mrs. Woodrow, as they reach the vehicle.

'Not bad, ma'am. In truth, I prefer a little stronger meat.'

'I've never heard a fellow sound so wet,' adds Jasper Woodrow. 'Wouldn't know the Lamb of God from his Sunday lunch.'

'Woodrow! He will hear you. The poor man merely has a lisp.'

'If you say so, my dear.'

'In any case, I must be going, ma'am,' adds Siddons. 'A pleasure, as always.'

'You must come for dinner,' replies Mrs. Woodrow, 'I will write an invitation tonight, I promise you.'

'I would be honoured, ma'am. A great pleasure to meet you too, Miss Krout,' continues the undertaker, taking Annabel's hand and pressing it between his palms. 'A great pleasure indeed.'

Annabel responds politely in kind and it is not long before Mr. Siddons strolls off across the square. Jasper Woodrow, in turn, motions his family inside the coach.

'Come on, Lucinda,' says Woodrow, hurrying his daughter along.

The little girl clambers inside the coach, ignoring her father's proffered hand.

'Where are we going?' asks Mrs. Woodrow, as the driver shuts the carriage door. 'Not another surprise?'

'Thought we might have a stroll round Abney Park, my dear, that's all, as the weather has improved.'

'I don't think I've heard of that one,' says Annabel. 'Is it similar to The Regent's Park?'

'What an idea!' exclaims Mrs. Woodrow. 'No, it is a little more appropriate for a Sunday. It is a cemetery; a very fine one.'

'Ah, I see. Do you go there often?'

'More so in the summer, dear. Woodrow, you don't suppose it is a little cold for Lucinda?'

'Are you cold, child?' asks Mr. Woodrow.

The little girl shakes her head.

'There, she is quite all right. Besides, a chap must keep a professional interest, eh? One likes to see what the prettiest widows are wearing. Where they go, the others follow.'

Mrs. Woodrow smiles. 'My wag of a husband is joking, Annabel. As always, I counsel you to ignore him.'

Mr. Woodrow bows his head in mock penitence.

The journey to Stoke Newington takes little more than twenty minutes. Annabel observes the public buildings and theatres of Islington disappear, replaced by the white stucco of suburban terraces, interrupted only by the occasional church or chapel. At length, the Woodrows' carriage turns down Stoke Newington Church Street, a narrow road, whose houses largely eschew the organised dimensions of the architect's pattern book. Instead they seem an idiosyncratic mix of old cottages, ivy-clad red-brick mansions and quaint villas, made to proportions entirely in accordance to their owners' whim. Finally, the vehicle draws to a stop by an iron-work gate and railinged wall.

'Here we are,' announces Mr. Woodrow.

'Did you not prefer the main entrance, my dear?'

'I think Miss Krout will find this gives a better view of the chapel.'

Melissa Woodrow agrees. Once they are settled upon the pavement Annabel notices a man sitting just inside the gates, upon the grass, by a solitary white tomb-stone, sheets of paper in his hand. Dressed in a cheap checked jacket, he gets up as they approach, doffing his rather battered-looking hat.

'Plan of the park, sir? Shows all the walks and famous personages. All the best tombs. Just a penny? How about you, ma'am?'

'No thank you,' says Jasper Woodrow, shepherding his group along, 'I know the way.'

'Really,' says Mrs. Woodrow, 'as if we needed such a thing.'

Abney Park is a popular destination upon a Sunday. Small groups, men, women and children, clad mostly in black, move quietly along the gravel paths, admiring the manicured lawns, the multiplicity of carefully arranged shrubs, noting the embossed cards testifying to each plant's Latin name, placed for the education of the passer-by. Others stop to read the inscriptions upon tomb-stones, memorials testifying to affectionate husbands and indulgent fathers.

Annabel Krout walks slowly with the Woodrows along the central path. The park itself is laid out around its ancient trees: a circular walk around a great cedar of Lebanon, graves radiating outwards; an avenue between twin rows of yews. But the focus is the chapel in the very heart of the cemetery; its steeple a lofty Gothic needle atop twin turrets, the stained glass of its rose window shining deep red and purple in the fleeting winter sunlight.

'Don't you think it a beautiful location, my dear?' asks Mrs. Woodrow. 'So very peaceful. Much nicer in the spring, of course.'

'It's not,' says Lucinda Woodrow.

'It is a very pretty park, though, Lucy,' says Annabel.

The little girl shrugs. 'Apart from all the stones,' she says at last.

'Lucy, my dear, look at this,' says Mrs. Woodrow with a sigh, gesturing to the tall pillar by her side, topped with a draped urn. '"If thou should'st call me to resign what most I prize; it ne'er was mine; I only yield thee what was thine; thy will be done." What do you think that means?'

If Lucy Woodrow is about to answer, she is interrupted by an exclamation from her mother.

'Why, look who it is!'

Annabel Krout follows Mrs. Woodrow's glance to see the approaching form of a familiar figure, Richard Langley.

'Sir. Ma'am. Miss Krout,' says Langley, as he draws near, doffing his hat.

'Why Mr. Langley,' says Mrs. Woodrow, 'what a coincidence! Whatever brings you here?'

'My parents are at rest here, ma'am, just along the way. They passed away last year. I make a point of visiting them once a month or so.'

'Oh, I am so sorry to hear of your loss, sir,' says Mrs. Woodrow.

'Thank you,' replies Langley. 'Ah, perhaps you might care to see the plot? I am just on my way. There is a fine monument.'

'In truth, sir,' says Mrs. Woodrow, hurriedly, 'I confess I suddenly feel a little faint. Woodrow – there is a bench by the Watts Memorial, is there not? Could we sit down there for a moment? Mr. Langley, forgive me. But I am sure Annabel would be delighted, though, would you not, my dear?'

Annabel Krout smiles a little nervously. 'Why, I suppose so.'

'Very well,' says Langley. 'If you do not object, sir?'

'No, of course not,' replies Jasper Woodrow.

'Shall we come back to the Memorial?'

'Yes, we will wait there,' says Mrs. Woodrow, her voice sounding almost confidential, as if conspiring in a secret assignation.

Langley nods and, with a few pleasantries, leads Annabel along the path. Jasper Woodrow waits until they are both out of earshot before he addresses his wife.'

'Melissa, are you quite all right?'

'Woodrow, must you be quite so dense? That young man is smitten with Annabel, I swear it. I told you that we saw him at the park?'

'Yes, indeed.'

'Well, do you think this is a coincidence? He is positively pursuing her. These "chance" encounters!'

198

'I hardly think it right the fellow should be following us about,' says Woodrow.

'You were much the same with me, I recall, my dear.'

'That was different. I am sure your dear cousin has no need of a match-maker.'

Melissa Woodrow looks coquettishly at her husband. 'If you say so. Oh, Lucinda – please don't wander off.'

Lucinda Woodrow, in truth, seems stubbornly inert and not at all inclined to do anything of the sort. She returns to her mother's side without complaint, and the family then walk in silence, until they approach the Watts Memorial, where the famous hymn-writer stands immortalised in stone.

'You know,' says Mrs. Woodrow, 'when Mr. Langley returns, I shall invite him to dinner tomorrow night.'

'Must you?' asks Woodrow, rather distractedly.

'Of course! Woodrow, you must put some faith—'

'My dear, forgive me, but I won't be a moment. A call of nature.'

Melissa Woodrow sighs, as her husband hurries off in the direction of the chapel.

'Whatever shall we do with your father, my dear?'

Lucinda does not reply.

❦

Jasper Woodrow glances over his shoulder, then walks as quickly as he can, past the chapel, towards the rear wall of Abney Park.

He is not surprised to find that the small section of ground he is looking for is unattended by mourners and quite deserted by those engaged upon a casual perambulation of the park's avenues. Indeed, as he draws closer, the monuments become less grand; the monoliths, angels and urns give way to merely a collection of wooden crosses. And in one plot the earth around is freshly turned, a series of wooden boards placed neatly across the grave of one Jeremy Sayers Munday.

'Damn me,' says Woodrow to himself, his face losing all its colour.

CHAPTER TWENTY-FOUR

DECIMUS WEBB SITS in his back-parlour, reading the previous day's *Times*, indulging in his pipe. His modest home in Sekforde Street, Clerkenwell, is peaceful upon a Sunday, since it lies upon a small residential side street, hidden away amongst the warehouses, workshops and manufactories that dominate the district but lie dormant upon the Sabbath. Indeed, if truth be told, Webb rented the property, upon joining Scotland Yard, precisely for its peculiar seclusion amidst the busy streets; at the time, it seemed to him an agreeable combination. And yet, today, day of rest or not, Decimus Webb cannot quite seem to focus upon his paper; he puts it down and looks instead into the fire that crackles in the grate.

At length, he places his pipe upon the tiles of the hearth, and walks over to his desk, retrieving his notebook, open at the page he left it the previous evening. It contains sundry notes from official documents transcribed at the Office of the Registrar-General, including a note of the death certificate of Jeremy Sayers Munday: 'Asphyxiation caused by compression of the neck due to the hanging'; 'Suicide when of unsound mind; Tho. Melkin, Coroner for East Middlesex'. Webb pauses, then flicks over another page, where a series of names and addresses are listed, drawn from the last census of the metropolis. Most are crossed out but his eyes fix on the last entry, headed 'St. Luke's' – 'Eliza Munday – Fallen'.

He thinks for a moment, then picks it up, taking his jacket from the chair, and walking through into the hallway, where his coat and hat hang from a wooden stand.

─━━─

The parish of St. Luke's lies a half-mile to the east of Webb's home in Sekforde Street. Whitecross Street market is at its heart, and it is into this bustling thoroughfare, at its busiest upon a Sunday, that Webb turns his steps.

The goods on show in Whitecross Street would tempt few in the wealthier west of the capital, upon any day of the week. For the items on show are principally of the second-hand variety: clothing, pots, pans, sundry staples of daily life. Almost every yard of pavement is covered in brightly painted trestle-tables and show boards, upon which these every-day things are displayed. What little space remains is taken up with food. Edibles and inedibles of every kind compete for attention, the wares of grocer, butcher and baker mixed together. Roving boys with 'eight whelks a penny' wander between the costers' carts. Full-grown men bear trays of muffins and crumpets 'all full hot'. Webb, although having breakfasted, cannot help but feel particularly hungry as he passes by the baker's. For the scent of roasting meat, two dozen Sunday lunches, bought and paid for, each one in its own deep earthen-ware dish, wafts along the road. It is almost, he thinks to himself, worth walking the length of Whitecross Street for the privilege of its olfactory sensations. And, as if to prove him right, as he proceeds down the road, on the western side, the great Golden Lane brewery, its chimney looming above the roof-tops, mixes its aroma with the lingering scents, leaving the air full of an exhalation of spirits and the malt tang of 'heavy wet'.

At last, however, Webb comes to his destination, a narrow lane leading directly into an old courtyard, just off the market street. The yard itself is a rather muddy quadrangle of decrepit-looking houses. All are three storeys high, topped by slates at various jaunty angles, their bricks dull and blackened, as if magnets for all the soot of the neighbourhood. In several, panes of glass are broken and replaced by wood. The only colour is a small brass bird-cage. a miniature palace in smutted gold, that sits upon a third-floor window-ledge. Webb refers to his note-book and tries the nearest door, marked by its scratched black paint-work, but not any indication of a number. His rap on the door elicits an almost immediate response, in the form of an old woman, sixty years of age, wrapped in a thin red shawl, who swings the door open and greets him with less than enthusiasm.

'It ain't rent day.'

'I am not collecting,' replies Webb.

'We ain't buying, then.'

'I am not selling. Tell me, ma'am, do you by any chance know a woman by the name of Munday who lives hereabouts?'

'Who are you then?'

'Police, ma'am.'

'Don't ma'am me,' says the old woman. She turns and shouts down the hallway of the house. 'It's only some bloody peeler, Bill.'

'As I say,' persists Webb, 'a woman by the name of Munday.'

'How should I know? And what if I do?'

'I would be indebted to you.'

The old woman ponders a little. 'There was a Liza Munday; that's going back a ways. But she ain't here no more.'

'Did she move?'

'After a fashion. Died, I heard.'

'How?'

'How should I know? Same as how I'll go, catching my death standing here, I shouldn't wonder.'

'Well, what did she do for a living? Do you know that much?'

'You're precious keen, ain't you? She did anything to make ends meet, like the rest of us.'

'Seeing gentlemen?'

'Maybe, when she were younger. She was bone-picking, Mogg's dust-yard, before they took her away.'

'Away to where?'

'The workhouse. Now that's what did for her, I'll warrant you it was.'

'Ah, I see. I expect that would be St. Luke's, by the canal?'

The old woman nods agreement. 'What's it worth, then?'

Decimus Webb smiles. 'As I say, I am indebted to you, ma'am.'

The old woman closes her door in disgust. 'Blow that,' she mutters to herself.

⌒

Webb, retracing his route through the market to Old Street, finds his way past St. Luke's church, up Ironmonger Row, and through the narrow back streets that lead to the City Road. It is no more than ten minutes' walk and he soon stands before the gates of the St. Luke's Workhouse. In fact, it is not quite a regular metropolitan workhouse, being solely devoted to the hospital care of female paupers within the

Holborn Poor Law Union. Nonetheless, the grey, prison-like, rectangular block that forms the main body of the building looks as grim as any of its namesakes in the capital. It also rather suffers in comparison with its immediate neighbour, the Eagle Tavern. For the latter, a music hall and public house combined, boasts a large walled garden covered with colourful notices for its famous Grecian Theatre's current extravaganza, *Cupid's Holiday: A Musical Miscellany*. St Luke's, upon the other hand, featureless and remorselessly practical in every aspect, gives the outward impression of complete hostility to any form of gaiety. Indeed, it only possesses a single painted black-and-white notice by the gate – a gloved hand, which directs all new-comers to the Relieving Office.

Webb finds the clerk on duty a stickler for form, to the extent that he must produce the warrant that testifies to his authority before he can proceed inside. Nonetheless, once this is accomplished, and having made inquiries of the records held by the office, he is eventually directed up a stone staircase to a particular ward within the monolithic building.

Webb tentatively opens the door. If he hesitates, it is because the ward sounds peculiarly silent. Inside he finds a long barn-like room, its roof supported by large iron beams. Against each wall are simple beds, arranged in precise intervals, perhaps forty or more upon each side; and from the ceiling dangle not only gas-pipes, though it is too early in the day for the taps to be lit, but also painted sign-boards bearing improving legends, testifying to the greatness of the Creator. There are windows, too, at regular intervals, large sash windows that shed light upon the patients: women of all ages, dressed in a uniform of striped grogram gowns, either recumbent upon the beds or sat upright, reading or engaged in solitary needlework or some similar domestic occupation. The only noticeable sound is the click of knitting needles, the work of a half-dozen or so of the more active patients; it carries through the air like the chatter of insects.

Webb approaches the ward's nurse, a middle-aged woman in a uniform mob cap and pinny, who sits at a desk by the entrance, watching her charges.

'Ma'am,' says Webb, in a whisper, 'forgive me, my name is Webb. I am a police inspector. Might I have a word with you?'

The nurse nods. It strikes Webb that she shows no sign of surprise at his appearance; but doubtless the employees of the Union are used to such official interruptions. The nurse beckons him outside, back into the adjoining stairwell.

'You have arrived during a quiet hour, Inspector. I did not wish to disturb the girls more than necessary. Whom have you come for?'

Webb smiles. 'Ah, no, ma'am, you misconstrue me, although I am, rather, trying to find the relatives of a particular individual, in relation to a particular case of mine. You will forgive me if I spare you the details? Suffice to say it is not a current patient but one of your former charges, deceased, as I understand it.'

'Who was it, Inspector?'

'The woman's name was Eliza Munday. Your records suggest she died here last year; April sixteenth.'

The nurse looks thoughtful, then a look of recognition passes over her face. 'Munday? Yes, why yes, I do recollect her. It was her heart, I think, Inspector. But it was not a police matter.'

'No, I did not think it was. You arranged for her interment, I take it? The City and Tower Hamlets cemetery, according to your books?'

'All our interments are with that company, Inspector. They are very reasonably priced.'

'Ah, I see. Was her family notified?'

'There was no family, if I recollect. No, wait, one moment – of course, that is why I know the name. There was someone.'

'Who?'

'A lawyer visited the ward, I believe, shortly before she died. I am afraid it was not on my shift; I recall one of my colleagues, Miss Barton, telling me about it. He represented a cousin, or uncle or some such. There was talk of a legacy. She thought it all very exciting.'

'I see. Might I arrange to speak to your colleague, do you think?'

'I am afraid not, Inspector. Miss Barton has since passed on.'

'Ah. My profound sympathies, ma'am,' says Webb with a sigh. 'This lawyer – you said there was talk of a legacy – did anything come of it?'

'Not that I know of, Inspector. But I do not know the details.'

'And I don't suppose the woman ever spoke about her family? Her husband perhaps?'

'Not that I recall.'

'Tell me, do you have this lawyer's address? I rather need to contact the family myself.'

'Let me check my book, Inspector. One moment.'

Webb waits until the nurse returns.

'Here we are,' she says, reading from the page, 'Mr. Cardew. Cardew and Sons; 214 Newgate Street.'

Webb frowns. 'Really? Are you sure?'

'Whatever do you mean, Inspector?'

'You have the right road and number?'

'Of course. The gentleman himself wrote it down for us. It is in a man's hand.'

Webb sighs once more.

'I knew this would prove complicated,' he mutters under his breath.

'Inspector?'

'Tell me, you did not see this man yourself, the lawyer? Would anyone else recollect him?'

'I doubt it, Inspector. It is almost a year ago now.'

'I am sorry, ma'am, my apologies. It is just that I am afraid you were duped. The numbers upon Newgate Street, to the best of my recollection, do not extend much beyond number one hundred and twenty. I doubt this firm exists.'

'Well, then it was an odd pretence, Inspector. Who was he, do you think?'

'In truth, ma'am, I do not know.'

INTERLUDE

HAVE YOU VISITED one of our Union workhouses, Miss Krout? I would recommend it before you return to your native land. You might find it instructive. They are veritable seed-beds of vice, the most fertile ground for all our social ills. I assure you, half the women that are upon the streets are workhouse foundlings, orphans or the like; and half the villains in Newgate, too. And, you know, when they are done with this life, they invariably go back to the House to depart from it; where else would take them? From the cradle to the grave. A capital system, is it not?

Pity? Yes, of course. I was raised a God-fearing Christian, Miss Krout. I had pity when I saw her lying there – who would not? But she was so degraded, so corrupted by her condition, I could barely bring myself to speak to her. I could see that the life to which she had been reduced had utterly consumed her. Indeed, it was like some terrible cancer had attacked all that was womanly or decent in her body and spirit. The sight of it positively repulsed me.

I am sorry. I speak too freely. But that is the nature of the social evil, Miss Krout. It is produced by immorality, it begets immorality.

No, every unchaste woman is not a whore; but she becomes one by force of necessity. I am sorry, but what else is a creature who gives for money what she should only give for love? She can hardly be a woman at all; she loses everything that elevates her nature above the beasts. It is a mercy that she died when she did.

Yes, I pitied her greatly. And I was angry, Miss Krout. It burnt deep inside me, like a furnace.

CHAPTER TWENTY-FIVE

DECIMUS WEBB ARRIVES at his office in Scotland Yard at precisely eight o'clock in the morning. There is a presentiment of daylight in the streets outside, but nothing more. Consequently, he is obliged to light the gas and read the morning paper in the glow of the pale flame. It is not five minutes, however, before there is a knock upon the door. Webb raises his head from the paper to see the face of Sergeant Bartleby.

'Late again, Sergeant?' asks Webb.

'Sorry, sir.'

'Have you seen the papers, Sergeant?'

'Any good notices, sir?'

'Don't be flippant, man. I read the *Telegraph* simply because it is this sheet, and its ilk, that seem to provide the Assistant Commissioner with the solitary benchmark against which he judges our progress. You'd be wise to do the same, if you want to keep your job. Here, listen:

CASINO MURDER

Another cold-blooded killing of a young woman, a murder of a similar character to those recently committed in Knight's Hotel, was perpetrated in the early hours of Saturday morning at the

Holborn Casino. There is every reason to suppose that the same monster is responsible for both atrocities. Moreover, the creature's brutality is only equalled by his audacity in repeating this wanton slaughter, his victim another hapless unfortunate. As yet, there have been no arrests, and it seems our police and detective agencies are, once more, quite powerless. That such foul crimes can be committed is itself a rebuke to our civilisation; that they should remain unpunished is a scandal which only serves to bring the once noble institutions of our state into utter disrepute. We understand that Inspector Webb of Scotland Yard is superintending the police investigation; let us hope he is determined to bring this woman-killer to justice.

One unintended consequence of the criminal's actions may be to precipitate the closure of the Holborn Casino, long known as a place of evil resort. There can be no true economy of suffering and misery but if the Casino should shut its doors for good then, at least, we may hope to see some improvement in the nocturnal morals of the metropolis. For it is these self-same dance-halls and saloons that serve to foster the manifold social ills that beset our great metropolis. Is it surprising, when we permit such places to flourish, that we are repaid in kind? How long must the spectre of death stalk our streets before we admit that we are rewarded tenfold by the wages of sin?'

'Well,' says Bartleby, 'it could be worse.'

'"Once more quite powerless"? "Wages of Sin"?'

'I wouldn't pay it much heed, sir,' suggests the sergeant.

'Hmm. Well, let us hope the Assistant Commissioner agrees with you. What progress did you make upon Saturday?'

'Autopsy of Miss Price done at Bow Street, sir, in the evening. The doctor was very accommodating but he found nothing much in her, ah, gut; a bit of an oyster and a touch of spirits.'

'Is that all? How very frugal. Nothing else?'

'Not that he could find, sir. Said the throat was unusual, though.'

'Apart from being cut?'

'I mean, sir, he said it was most likely done from the front, facing her,' says Bartleby, taking a breath. 'He said it looked like it'd been chopped at more than sliced. Could have been she struggled. He said probably a right-handed man, too.'

'Well, that tells us little except the fellow is willing to kill without compunction. But we knew that already. Has anyone reported anything more?'

'No. No-one saw nothing, sir. That's how it seems anyway. Oh, and I spoke to the manager and the staff at the Casino, like you said. Not one of them remembers the young lady in particular; or whom she was speaking to.'

'For heaven's sake, man, there must have been four or five hundred people there that night; one must have seen something. What about Miss Price's colleagues at the Mourning Warehouse?'

'Nothing worth knowing, sir. She kept company with young gentlemen a little too freely; but no names – well, no surnames, anyhow, that they recalled.'

'Good Lord,' says Webb. 'I had hoped for a little more to work with.'

'You have my word, sir,' says Bartleby hastily. 'There wasn't anything else to speak of. Oh, I asked about Mr. Woodrow, too – apparently he's run the place for about five years, since his wife's father died.'

'Really?' says Webb. 'Do we know what was his line of work before?'

'No, sir.'

'Hmm. Well, look into it, will you?'

'Any particular reason, sir?'

'If you must know, Sergeant, I thought he seemed a little unnerved when I was speaking to him and happened to mention Jeremy Munday's name. But he claimed never to have heard of him. It struck me as curious, that is all. Is that good enough for you?'

'You think he knows something about it, sir? Or the business at the Casino?'

Webb sighs. 'Perhaps, Sergeant, if you were to make some inquiries, we might actually find out.'

Bartleby, resolving not to debate the matter further, diligently draws his note-book from his jacket and scribbles something in pencil. 'I spent all morning interviewing the girls, sir. I promise you.'

'I am sure, Sergeant, I do not blame you. Let us put it to one side for a moment, and return to Mr. Munday. Have you organised the search of Abney Park?'

'Ah, no, sir. I've been tied up enough as it is.'

'Well, have it done today. I confess that there is something even odder about that affair than I thought.'

'Sir?'

'I went to Somerset House and found Munday's wife in the census; she died in St. Luke's Workhouse last year.'

'No other relatives, sir?'

'Not that I could find, although that is no guarantee. But a man visited her before she died; he claimed to be a lawyer, talked to her about a legacy.'

'Claimed?'

214

'The fellow gave a false name and address. How does that strike you, Sergeant?'

'It's the same party that was at Abney Park, sir. Must be. Perhaps he was looking for the same thing as he was looking for in the grave?'

'Precisely what I thought. But she was in the workhouse, Sergeant. What could she have had left that was of such value?'

'Maybe not an object, sir,' suggests the sergeant. 'What if it were some kind of clue or information? Ah, here's a thought, what if it were something that led this man to her husband's grave?'

'Well done, Sergeant,' says Webb. 'But the question is what was it? What could be so important after twenty-five years?'

Bartleby pauses.

'I haven't a clue, sir,' confesses the sergeant.

Webb shakes his head. 'Someone does, though, Sergeant. I just wonder if we can find him?'

❦

Joshua Siddons opens the midday post in his office in Salisbury Square. He recognises the handwriting of one letter, dated that morning, and opens it immediately.

My Dear Mr. Siddons,

It was a pleasure to see you yesterday, and it brought to mind that it has been an age since we had the pleasure of your company for an evening. Will you excuse this very short notice, and favour us with your presence at dinner tomorrow? The dinner hour is half-past seven. It will be a small gathering with our cousin Annabel, whom you met today, and Woodrow's acquaintance Mr. Langley, a delightful young man with whom I believe you are also already acquainted? I should not consider our little party complete without you. Do not trouble yourself to send with an answer; we will send to you for it in the course of the day.

 Yours ever sincerely,
  Melissa Woodrow
Duncan Terrace, November 16th.

Siddons takes the letter and folds it neatly in two, placing it inside his coat pocket, smiling to himself.

CHAPTER TWENTY-SIX

'WHAT TIME IS it, my dear?' asks Melissa Woodrow, as she applies the finishing cosmetic touches to her face, admiring her complexion in the mirror of her dresser.

'Nearly half-past seven,' replies Annabel Krout who sits patiently upon her cousin's bed.

'Oh, Lord,' replies Mrs. Woodrow. 'That will have to do. What a fright!'

'Hardly, cousin,' says Annabel.

'You are too sweet, my dear. Are you sure you do not want some cream, just for your cheeks? The heat in the dining-room so dries out one's skin.'

Mrs. Woodrow selects a small pot labelled 'Princess of Wales Oil of Cacao', and turns to her cousin, who shakes her head.

'No, really, I am fine.'

'Well, you have the advantage of youth, my dear. No, do not blush, you look a picture. Come, let us go and wait in the drawing-room. I am sure Mr. Siddons will be punctual; he always says it is a necessity in his profession.'

'I should think so,' says Annabel, uncertain quite how to respond. As they quit Mrs. Woodrow's bed-room and descend the stairs, however, the door-bell rings.

'What did I tell you, my dear? To the very minute.'

'Is Mr. Siddons a business acquaintance, like Mr. Langley?' asks Annabel.

'Oh heavens, no. I mean to say, he is in the undertaking trade, my dear, but he is an old friend of Woodrow's and also knew my father. In fact, do you know, he introduced us.'

'Really?'

'Yes,' replies Melissa Woodrow, though with little concentration as they enter the drawing-room, her mind more focused upon the sounds from the hall below. 'Oh dear. Did I ask Jacobs to check the salt? It will cake in the cellars; I have told her time and again. I'll wager she has forgotten. Ah, that is Mr. Siddons – I'd know his voice anywhere. I believe there is someone with him.'

Indeed, the sound of footsteps up the stairs is followed by the entrance not only of Joshua Siddons but Richard Langley, both of whom are ushered in by Jervis. Both men wear black dress suits and white neckerchiefs, but the former, for all his professional familiarity with formal dress, does not somehow appear as dapper as his younger companion.

'Mrs. Woodrow, how delightful to see you,' exclaims Siddons, bowing slightly. 'And you, Miss Krout.'

'We were just talking about you, sir,' replies Mrs. Woodrow.

'Nothing bad, I hope, ma'am,' replies Siddons, repeating his bow.

'Please, don't tease me, sir,' exclaims Mrs. Woodrow with a rather girlish laugh. 'You know I cannot defend myself. And how are you, Mr. Langley?'

'Very well, thank you,' says Langley. 'I trust you are well?'

'Yes, thank you, sir.'

'Did you come together?' asks Mrs. Woodrow of her two guests.

'A lucky chance, ma'am,' replies Siddons. 'We met on the step. Now, where is your husband, dear lady?'

Melissa Woodrow shakes her head, affecting, at least, indulgence towards her husband's shortcomings. 'That man! I expect he has not heard the bell. He is still in the study.'

'I'll go and fetch him, ma'am,' interjects Siddons. 'Save the maid's shoe-leather, eh?'

'Really, there is no need . . .'

'Ma'am,' says the undertaker, 'it is already done. I am sure Mr. Langley can entertain you.'

Langley smiles, as graciously as possible, under the circumstances.

'I'll do my best, ma'am.'

———

Once the errant host is found, after a decent interval, Mrs. Woodrow musters her small party downstairs to dine. The Woodrows' dining-table, despite Mrs. Woodrow's fears for the salt, seems to Annabel Krout almost perfect. A vase of fresh flowers forms a meticulously placed centre-piece, illuminated by a small pair of silver candelabras, three candles in each, one on each side of the floral tribute. Twin silver salt cellars and cruets are marshalled around it with a similar military precision, as well as two open decanters of sherry. Then the knives, forks and spoons, resting on the damask slip that protects the table-cloth, all perfectly polished, reflecting the candle light; then pristine white napkins folded to one side. Jervis, meanwhile, stands in attendance, only moving to seat Mrs. Woodrow at the head of the table. Jasper Woodrow himself seats his American cousin, then takes his place opposite his wife. Finally the two remaining guests are guided to their seats, the undertaker besides Annabel Krout and Richard Langley facing.

'Tell Jacobs she can begin, will you, Jervis?' says Woodrow, at which the butler discreetly disappears in the direction of the kitchen stairs.

'Mr. Langley,' says Joshua Siddons, 'have you had the pleasure of dining at home with Mrs. Woodrow before?'

'No, sir, I have not,' replies Langley, amiably, as he places his napkin upon his lap.

'Then you are in for a treat, sir. Mrs. Woodrow's kitchen is a model of efficiency and artistry. You will return home singing her cook's praises. Every dish, sir, fit for the Kensington School.'

Langley smiles. 'I should not be surprised,' he replies, directing an agreeable nod to his hostess.

'In fact,' continues Siddons, 'too good for them. I do Mrs. Woodrow a disservice. Would spoil them for anything else. They would taste it and not make another dish.'

'There is a school of cooking, in Kensington?' asks Annabel.

'Part of the Exhibition last year, my dear,' replies her cousin. 'I believe they have kept it open. Though why any decent young woman would need instruction in such matters, I don't pretend to know.'

'It sounds very practical,' suggests Annabel.

'Do you have a good cook at home in Boston, Miss Krout?' asks Richard Langley.

'I've never really thought about it, sir. But, yes, I would say so.'

'I don't know about Boston, dear,' interrupts Melissa Woodrow, 'but a good cook is like gold dust in London. In fact, Annabel, these days it is more common for a good cook to ask for the character of a family, than vice versa.'

'Now you're teasing me, cousin.'

'Only a little,' suggests Jasper Woodrow, gruffly. 'You wouldn't believe what Figgis expects per annum.'

'Jasper!' exclaims Mrs. Woodrow. 'Don't be so vulgar.'

'Worth every penny, though,' affirms Siddons. 'Ah, and here is the first *bonne bouche* if I am not mistaken.'

The room falls silent as Jacobs approaches bearing a bulbous-looking silver tureen on a tray of the same metal, polished to an almost mirror-like sheen, which she deposits upon the sideboard. Her arrival provokes something of a lull in the conversation, as she opens the tureen lid and the aroma of the steaming oyster soup fills the room.

'Exquisite, my dear lady,' says Siddons, as Jacobs serves him his soup. 'It is more than cream and oysters, though? Or do my olfactory nerves deceive me?'

'Champagne, mushrooms and scallops.'

'Delicious,' says Siddons, though not yet having tasted a drop. 'Ah, now who is this, come to see us?'

The undertaker's gaze is directed not to his hostess, but to the doorway behind her. Mrs. Woodrow turns round to see her daughter, dressed in her white night-gown, standing upon the threshold between the dining-room and the hall.

'Lucinda – what are you doing downstairs?'

'Can I have some soup?' says the little girl.

'No, my dear, you cannot. Go back to your room this instant.'

'I'll see to her, ma'am,' says Jacobs, returning the soup ladle to the tureen, and making towards the door. She is, however, interrupted by her master's voice.

'You will do nothing of the kind,' says Woodrow in

his sternest tone, hurriedly pulling his napkin from his lap and standing up so abruptly that his knife and fork rattle upon the table. 'Lucinda – you will go to bed.'

'I don't want to go to bed,' she replies.

'You will do as I say,' replies Woodrow, at which he walks over to his daughter and grabs her arm. 'Forgive me, gentlemen, Miss Krout, I am afraid my daughter can be too easily excited. I will not be a moment.'

'Of course,' says Siddons, as Woodrow leads his daughter in the direction of the stairs, at a pace not quite suited to her stature.

Mrs. Woodrow looks apologetically towards her guests, a nervous smile fleeting across her face. 'You must forgive Lucinda, gentlemen. She is just a little sensitive. Woodrow says she lacks discipline, but I think it is just her nature.'

'You can't put a price on discipline, ma'am,' says Siddons, sipping his soup, 'not in my experience. It's a father's duty as a Christian. If you spoil them, ma'am, they're spoiled for good.'

'But she is only a small child,' suggests Langley.

'Can tell you're a bachelor, Mr. Langley,' replies the undertaker, slurping.

'Are you married, sir?' asks Langley.

'Widowed sir, twice. Fine women, both of them. Buried them myself. No expense spared.'

'Ah, I am sorry to hear of your loss,' replies Langley.

'Thank you,' says Siddons, taking another sip of soup. 'Still, they say three times for luck, do they not?'

'Mr. Siddons!' exclaims Mrs. Woodrow, laughing. 'Really, you are the limit.'

'Forgive me, ma'am, Miss Krout,' continues the undertaker, with a hint of drollery in his voice. 'I only meant to say that, even in an old man like myself, hope springs eternal.'

'You are hardly that, sir,' replies Mrs. Woodrow.

Annabel Krout adds nothing to the discussion but cannot help but think that, for the briefest moment as he talks of marriage, the undertaker looks at her rather pointedly, then winks.

———

'So, Miss Krout,' says Richard Langley, 'have you seen all the sights in London?'

Langley's question serves to fill another gap in the conversation, as Jasper Woodrow begins to carve Mrs. Figgis's *pièce de résistance*, a sucking-pig. The smell of the succulent roast meat is enough to cause the whole party to pause in admiration. With the pig's head already separate from the body, its back split in half, Woodrow deftly cuts the shoulder and hind leg on each side.

'Not yet, sir,' replies Annabel. 'We have been to Regent Street, though. And the Criterion Theatre.'

'I expect you have more adventures planned for this week?'

Woodrow begins to cut away at the ribs, whilst Jacobs serves the accompanying tray of parsnips and suet dumplings.

'Well, not as yet,' replies Annabel.

'We have been,' says Mrs. Woodrow, 'I confess, sir, quite remiss in our duty to dear Annabel. I myself was a little under the weather on Saturday, and she has barely been out of the house.'

'Nothing serious, I hope, ma'am?' says Siddons.

'No, not at all. It is a shame, though, that we do not have an acquaintance who might come with us. I fear I am not quite at my best, and rather hold Annabel back.'

'Cousin, not at all!' protests Annabel.

'Well,' says the undertaker, 'what do you think of that, Mr. Langley? Terrible shame for Miss Krout.'

'Really, it isn't,' says Annabel.

Langley blushes. 'I am sure, if I am not being too forward, if Mr. Woodrow does not object, I would be happy to accompany you both, ma'am, one day this week, if you have need of an escort.'

'Mr. Langley,' exclaims Mrs. Woodrow, 'really, I could not dream of such an imposition.'

'It would be a pleasure,' he replies. 'Sir?'

'Good of you, Langley,' replies Woodrow. 'I'm always too busy.'

'Well, that would be delightful, would it not, Annabel?' replies Mrs. Woodrow.

'Of course,' replies Annabel.

'Well, glad that's settled, eh?' says Woodrow, finishing the last cut into the meat. 'Rib?'

———

It is gone ten o'clock when the Woodrows' dinner party enters its final stage, after a dessert of meringues and cabinet pudding, and liberal consumption of sherry. Mrs. Woodrow and her cousin retire to the drawing-room, leaving the three men to brandy and cigars. Once all three have a glass in their hands, Jasper Woodrow gives his manservant leave to retire from the room.

Joshua Siddons sips his drink, and then his face adopts a rather puckish expression.

'Did you know, Mr. Langley, that Woodrow here used to be in my employ?'

'No, sir, I did not,' replies Langley.

'Worked his way up, as they say. A protégé of mine.'

'Yes,' says Woodrow, giving Joshua Siddons a rather dark glance, 'we all have to start somewhere in life.'

'And now, with your interest in the business, sir, who knows how well things may turn out, eh?'

Langley smiles rather awkwardly. 'Well, who knows, indeed?'

'Don't let this awful affair at the Casino worry you, sir,' continues Siddons, lowering his voice. 'It will make no difference to the prospects of the Warehouse, I am sure. Rich rewards in the trade, sir, you have my word. Forty years, man and boy; I know a thing or two, rest assured.'

'You speak very frankly, sir,' says Langley, taking a sip of brandy. Jasper Woodrow bites his lip.

'Think nothing of it, my dear fellow,' says Siddons, ignoring Woodrow's admonitory stare.

'Perhaps,' says Jasper Woodrow, 'we might talk of something more pleasant.'

'Yes, of course,' says Siddons. 'Tell me, Woodrow, about your American cousin. I have never met such a delightful young woman.'

'There is nothing much to tell. Her mother is Melissa's aunt. Told her she wanted to see – what is it the Yankees call it? – "The Old World". Melissa said we'd look after her.'

'I expect she's on the look-out for a husband, eh?' says Siddons. 'A girl of that age with a bit of money behind her.'

'Indeed,' replies Woodrow. 'What do you think, Langley?'

'I have very little experience of such things,' says Richard Langley, visibly blushing.

'Well,' says Woodrow, turning back to Siddons, 'then it seems the field is all yours, sir.'

'Hah!' exclaims Siddons. 'If I were but twenty years younger, perhaps, I might plough that particular furrow. Still, the thought of it stirs the blood, eh?'

'Gentlemen, please,' says Langley.

'Quite,' says Siddons, with a distinct drunken nod of his head, 'quite right. I meant no offence to the young lady. And I expect she'd much prefer a younger fellow, eh?'

Langley blushes once more.

❦

A half-hour late, with their cigars extinguished, the trio of men adjourn to the Woodrows' drawing-room. There, Joshua Siddons is the first to beg leave of his hostess, in a rather lavish manner, giving a lengthy panegyric upon the merits of Mrs. Figgis's cooking, and the wisdom of her employer. Richard Langley lingers a little longer, during which time a week-day visit to St. Paul's Cathedral and Westminster Abbey, in the company of Mrs. Woodrow and her cousin, is settled upon. Nonetheless, he leaves the house no more than five minutes after his fellow guest. Finally, Annabel Krout excuses herself and makes her way upstairs to bed.

Jasper Woodrow sits down heavily upon an armchair. Mrs. Woodrow waits until Annabel is out of earshot before she says a word.

'Did he say anything?' she asks her husband.

'Langley? Said he liked the pork.'

'You did not talk about the business?'

'Siddons did. The old fool was drunk, I swear. Practically had to gag him to shut him up. I should never had told him Langley had pulled out. I swear, he does everything to provoke me; it seems to amuse him.'

'Nonsense!' exclaims Mrs. Woodrow. 'What a thing to say! Why should he? He is our oldest friend.'

'No reason. None at all,' says Woodrow, though he does not look his wife in the eye.

'He was just trying to help, my dear. But Mr. Langley . . . well, he seemed quite cheerful, did he not?'

'Affable enough, I suppose. Once I'd shut Siddons up, at least.'

'Mr. Langley has such good manners,' says Mrs. Woodrow. 'I swear, he would be so right for Annabel.'

Woodrow scowls. 'I don't care about his damn manners.'

Mrs. Woodrow sighs. 'Never mind. We shall think of something, Woodrow, I promise you.'

CHAPTER TWENTY-SEVEN

T HE HALL CLOCK strikes eleven as Annabel Krout removes the pin from her chignon, letting her hair fall down over her shoulders, concealing the lace trim of her night-gown. Sitting in front of her writing desk, she can hear footsteps upon the adjoining landing, Mrs. Woodrow and her husband, retiring to their bedrooms. She turns up the oil-lamp, so that its orange glow extends further over the sheet of paper before her, and takes up her pen, dipping it in the nearby ink-well, writing 'An English Dinner Party' at the head of the page. She ponders a first sentence for some minutes, but her thoughts are suddenly interrupted by an urgent knock at the bedroom door.

'Come in?'

The Woodrows' maid-servant swings the door open, and walks breathlessly into the room, looking anxiously around her.

'Jacobs? What is it?' asks Annabel.

'Lor, Miss, I thought she might be here.' She pauses for a moment, red-faced, almost tearful. She seems to struggle to speak, as if she cannot quite bring herself to say the words. But, at last, she bursts out, 'Oh, please, help us.'

'If I can,' says Annabel, 'but what is it?'

'Miss Lucy. I can't find her.'

'I'm sorry, I don't understand. Is she missing?'

'Yes, Miss. I mean, I don't know. I should have been keeping an eye on her. I was only downstairs for a moment, just to get some water. I thought she was sound asleep.'

'And now she is not in her room?'

The maid shakes her head. 'No, Miss. What if she's had one of her turns again? I was supposed to be watching her.'

'Perhaps she is with her mother,' suggests Annabel.

'Oh no,' says Jacobs, anxiety in her voice, 'I'd hear about that quick enough.'

'You have looked upstairs?'

'Every room, Miss.'

'Downstairs?'

'Not yet.'

'Then,' says Annabel, hurriedly tying her dressing-gown tight around her waist, and picking up the lamp upon her desk, 'don't worry, we shall look for her together. She can't have gone far. She is just playing a trick on you.'

'Thank you, Miss,' says Jacobs. 'You're so good.'

'I just do not want her to get into more trouble with her father,' says Annabel quietly, as they go out on to the landing and descend the stairs. 'You look in the study, Jacobs, I will check the drawing-room.'

Jacobs obeys, but before Annabel can reach the drawing-room door, she feels an intense cold draught of air. Stopping short of her destination, the sensation causes her to look down into the hall below, where she notices the heavy curtain that conceals the front-door lies partially pulled back, and the door itself slightly ajar. A shiver runs down her spine.

'Jacobs,' she exclaims in an urgent whisper.

'Yes, Miss?'

229

'Look,' says Annabel, pointing at the open door. 'Why is the door open?'

The maid-servant stares open-mouthed at the open door. 'Oh, Miss, you don't think? Don't say it. The master'll have my guts.'

'Go and wake Mr. and Mrs. Woodrow,' says Annabel firmly. 'If she has gone out, we must all go and look.'

'Miss, I can't . . .'

But before Jacobs can say another word, Annabel Krout has ran down the stairs, her dressing-gown flapping about her legs, and out into the street.

———

Annabel almost despairs as she steps out into the night air. For the fog of previous days, though only thin wisps of vapour, seems to have begun maliciously to re-form. Moreover, her lamp, though adequate for reading in bed, seems barely to penetrate the darkness; likewise, her house-slippers suddenly seem rather inadequate upon the hard stone, so that she half trips as she descend the steps from the front door to the street.

'Lucy!' she shouts.

There is no reply.

'Lucinda!'

She waits but again hears no response. Then she sees a movement, a hint of something white, just like the little ghost she saw in her room, moving past the gas-light upon the other side of the gardens, then abruptly disappearing from view. She cannot fathom it for a moment, how the figure vanishes so suddenly; but then it comes to her: the gate down to the canal.

Annabel does not hesitate but sprints across Duncan Terrace, and around the iron-railed gardens, the weight of the heavy lamp making her run in ungainly leaps and bounds. Mud splashes her velvet slippers, soaks into the soles of her feet. Losing her balance, she bangs her arm against the corner of the railings. But she does not fall and keeps running until she reaches the gate. She can hardly see down the slope that runs down to the tow-path, for the only light by the canal itself is the one she carries. Nonetheless she levers open the barrier.

'Lucy!'

Again, no reply. The slope is rather wet and slippery and, in the darkness, the surface of the still, black water below looks somehow strangely solid, a smooth, dark trench. She cannot help but think that it would be tempting to reach out with her foot and try to walk across to the other side; and then, thinking of Lucy, the idea rather chills her. She extends her arm, holding the lamp as far from her body as she can, as if swinging it will somehow generate some additional radiance that will reveal the little girl. But nothing comes of it, except that she abruptly feels terribly cold and tired. Worse, the fog seems to grow even denser with each passing moment.

But then there is something that makes her spin around; not a sign of Lucy but a rumbling, heavy moan, which sounds like it comes from within the very bowels of the earth. First one terrible resounding, reverberating thud, then another, growing louder each time. Then a small ball of yellow light hovering in the air, appearing as if from nowhere; the low roar of a churning engine, the splash of water. Annabel stands transfixed, as the light grows bigger and more lurid, the machine noise louder; then comes an almighty hiss as clouds of billowing smoke issue from the Islington tunnel, mixing with the fog, like the breath of some ancient river-dragon. The sight seems weirdly Tartarean, fantastical. Indeed, it takes her a moment to catch her breath, to make out the true character of the beast: a steam-tug coming through the tunnel, making its way free of the arched entry, dragging its quota of clattering barges behind, each one banging against the stone walls. But the captain of the vessel is quicker to respond.

'Who's there? On the path? You there!'

'Please, stop for a moment,' shouts Annabel.

'Hold there,' shouts the man in question. But Annabel barely hears him. For, in the lamp-light that shines from the rear of the tug, she can just make out a small white figure, standing silently by the edge of the tow-path, a couple of feet before it terminates, back by the entrance to the tunnel. Annabel stumbles along the path, driven by a mixture of excitement and fear, until she can make out Lucinda Woodrow standing quite still.

'Lucy! Can you hear me?'

Lucy does not reply. The captain of the boat, however, now drawn to a halt, shines his lamp back along the path, illuminating Annabel and the little girl. Annabel holds up her light, and finds Lucy's eyes as vacant as when she stood in her bedroom, staring into the street.

'What's happening there?' shouts the man, his voice a mixture of irritation and curiosity. 'Who's that?'

Annabel does not reply. For she realises that her little cousin is not simply standing still, but pointing her finger down into the water. Annabel bends down, holding her lamp by the very side of the path.

And though it is dim, it is quite sufficient to reveal the body of a man, floating in the canal, his head submerged in the dark water.

PART THREE

CHAPTER TWENTY-EIGHT

DECIMUS WEBB CLOSES the iron gate behind him, and walks hesitantly down the mossy track that leads to the tow-path of the Regent's Canal, a few steps behind the rather more agile Sergeant Bartleby. It is a chill morning, with a hint of mist hanging above the water, and the ground under foot is muddy enough to warrant caution. Ahead of them, by the bank itself, stands a uniformed policemen, wearing the stripes of a sergeant. He looks up and waves.

'Inspector Webb?'

Webb nods, although he does not quicken his pace.

'Hope we haven't got you both here under false pretences, sir,' continues the sergeant. He steps forward to offer Webb and Bartleby a firm handshake. 'My name's Trent.'

'False pretences, Sergeant Trent? I should hope not too,' replies Webb. 'Where is your inspector?'

'Gone back to the station house, sir. The damp is bad for his rheumatics. He said you may as well talk personal-like, to myself, seeing as I was here first.'

'Hmm. Well, send him my compliments,' says Webb, looking along the canal. 'So where is your little find?'

'Just here, sir, though he ain't so little,' replies the sergeant, motioning Webb and Bartleby a few yards back along the tow-path. There, along by the side of the sloping track that they came down, lies a dirty-looking blanket, not too distinct from the muddy earth around it, barely covering the outline of a body.

'We haven't moved him since we got him out of the water. Big fellow, though, took three of us to shift him.'

'Yes, well, that would be right,' murmurs Webb. 'For heaven's sake, man, let me see him.'

'Right you are, sir,' says Sergeant Trent, stepping to one side, as Webb leans down and pulls back the cloth concealing the dead man's face.

'That him, sir?'

Webb looks down at the features of the corpse. Though his jowls are a little devoid of colour, his hair bedraggled, his eyes glazed and vacant, it is unmistakably the face of Vasilis Brown.

'Yes, it is,' replies Webb. 'You did well to let me know, Sergeant.'

'In fairness, sir, it was one of my men, Constable Hicks, what recognised the description you circulated, when we swapped shifts. We've sent word to the City force too. Inspector Hanson, wasn't it?'

'Indeed, Inspector Hanson. Still I think we must begin here without him; my apologies if you are later obliged to repeat yourself, Trent. Now, when did you find the body?'

'Well, sir,' replies the sergeant, 'it was about half-past eleven last night when I got here. Can't say how long the chap had been in the water.'

'Not too long, I should think,' says Webb, bending down, looking at the dead man's face and hands, examining the skin.

'No, sir. Can't have been, in fact. The boats come here pretty regular, every couple of hours even during the night. He'd have taken more of a battering, if he had been in there that long. Although there's a nasty wound on the back of his head, if you lift him up a bit, sir. Unfortunate business, eh?'

Webb tilts the dead man's head, gently parting Brown's thick locks of black hair, revealing bruised, torn skin and, with the blood washed away in the dirty water, a pale white hint of bone at the back of his skull.

'Unfortunate for him,' says Webb. 'Now, what do you make of that, Bartleby? What caused it?'

'It might have been a boat, of course,' suggests the sergeant. 'Or do you think it was foul play, sir?'

'Does it really look like he went under a boat, Sergeant?'

'I'd say not, sir. You'd expect more damage to the rest of him. The neck at least.'

'Good. Now—'

'Wait a moment,' says Bartleby, observing a particular spot upon the brick wall behind them, by the mouth of the tunnel. 'There you go, sir.'

'What?'

'It looks like blood,' replies the sergeant, pointing.

Webb gets up and peers closely at the coarse brick; it is, indeed, stained with a splash of dark colour, and several wiry black hairs, like those of the dead man, appear to be snagged in the rough stone. Webb smiles.

'I'll have you know, Sergeant Trent,' says Webb, sardonically, 'Bartleby is one of our best men. Nothing escapes him. Well done, Sergeant.'

Sergeant Bartleby does not rise to the bait, but merely nods.

'So, gentlemen,' continues Webb, looking at the dead man, then back to the wall, 'there was a struggle here; the mark is at the right height, is it not? Bash! The fellow's brains are crashed against this wall, with some force, mind you, then his body despatched into

237

the water. Did you find any other clues, Sergeant? No footprints? Nothing on the man's person?'

'Footprints, sir? Well, I should think there was, only it was impossible to say who belonged to them, seeing as how such a crowd was rushing up and down.'

'A crowd? Why was there a crowd here? You have a man on the gate,' says Webb, looking up towards the road above. 'Has he been charging a penny a look?'

'Sir!' says Trent.

Webb sighs. 'You must forgive my flippancy, Sergeant; I have no wish to impugn your integrity. But I fail to see why there was a "crowd"?'

'I think,' says Trent, frowning, 'you must have misunderstood, sir. I was the first officer here, but it weren't me that found him.'

'Then who was it?'

'It seems, sir, it was a little girl that wandered out of a nearby property.'

'Correct me if I am wrong, Sergeant, but these,' says Webb, gesturing towards the backs of the homes that overlook the canal, 'are respectable households, are they not? What was a little girl doing out at such an hour?'

'Apparently she walks in her sleep, sir.'

'Really?'

'So I was told, sir. Her mother and father were out here looking for her,' continues Trent, retrieving his notebook, 'and another female, a cousin, and a female servant—'

'That will suffice, Sergeant. Where are they now?'

'We told them to wait on us calling this morning, sir. I actually popped in earlier, said you might be wanting a word. The master of the house weren't too happy, between you and me, sir. Said he didn't have time for such things; "a business to run".'

'Did he now?' says Webb. 'Well, at all events, tell

238

your man to let no-one else down here, until Inspector Hanson should arrive at least.'

'I will do, sir.'

'Now, where might I find this gentleman who is too busy for such trifles?'

'I'll show you, sir. Just across the way on Duncan Terrace. Woodrow's the fellow's name. He's in the—'

'Not the mourning trade?' suggests Webb.

'Eh? Do you know the man, sir?'

'It seems likely,' says the inspector, casting a quizzical glance at Bartleby, 'that we do.'

━━

Webb rings the door-bell at Duncan Terrace. It is a matter of seconds before the door is answered by the Woodrows' manservant, and both the inspector and sergeant are ushered swiftly inside. Thus, if the Woodrows' neighbours must observe the attendance of Her Majesty's Police upon the household, they are at least given the shortest possible time in which to do so. Jervis leads the two policemen expeditiously up to the drawing-room upon the first floor, where Jasper Woodrow stands by the window, turning to face his guests as they enter the room.

'Inspector Webb. Sergeant,' he says, nodding.

'Mr. Woodrow. I believe you are not surprised to see us.'

'I saw you from the window, Inspector. I was told to wait for the police. But I confess, I was surprised to see you. Do you deal with every tragedy in London?'

'Of course not, sir. Just the awkward ones.'

'No more than you're involved in them all, I should expect, sir,' adds Bartleby. Webb gives the sergeant a minatory glance.

'I mean to say,' continues Bartleby, 'it's just one of those queer coincidences, eh, sir?'

'I am not "involved" in anything, Inspector,' says Woodrow, indignantly. 'What does your man mean to imply?'

'I am sure nothing was meant, sir,' says Webb, soothingly.

'I am glad to hear it. It is bad enough this wretched fellow should do away with himself upon our door-step—'

'I beg your pardon,' interjects Webb. 'You're of the opinion it was suicide?'

'Of course. Happens every few months. Some poor wretch throws themself in. They dragged a girl out of the lock only last month.'

Webb tilts his head in a non-committal manner.

'If you don't believe me, Inspector, talk to your local chaps. They'll tell you as much. I guarantee it.'

Webb smiles. 'Well, perhaps you're right, sir. Too early to say. Now, we'll need to interview whoever was there when or immediately after the body was discovered. That makes most of your household, I understand? In particular, it was your daughter who found him?'

Woodrow raises his eyes to the heavens. 'Is this really necessary? I thought the sergeant might have explained it. The girl sleep-walks, Inspector. Our wretched maid left the door open and she wandered out. I don't know how much you know about the condition, but she will not recall a thing.'

'Must be a terrible affliction, sir. Still, I would like to speak to her. And the rest of the house; I understand you were all there?'

'We thought we had lost Lucinda, my daughter, Inspector. Naturally we formed a search party.'

'And you found her. One tragedy averted, at least. Still, I should like to talk to her, and the rest of your family, separately if I may.'

'Good Lord, Inspector, are we under some kind of suspicion?'

'I merely wish to hear from each in turn. It will help with our inquiry; the chain of events. I am sure you understand, sir.'

'Well, I'll arrange it, if I must, Inspector. It is far from convenient. And my wife has had no rest all night.'

'Still, thank you. Tell me, how old is your girl?'

'She is only six,' says Woodrow.

'Well, perhaps I might see the little girl and her mother together then.'

'This really is the limit, Inspector,' replies Woodrow, his annoyance audible in every syllable.

'We'll do our best to be brief, sir. I take it, from what you've said, you don't know the man in question, sir, the dead man?'

'How could I?' says Jasper Woodrow.

'Never seen him before?'

Woodrow blinks. 'Never. Do you know who he was, Inspector?'

'Oh yes, sir. But I won't burden you with the unsavoury particulars.'

CHAPTER TWENTY-NINE

'Is THIS ALL REALLY necessary?' asks Sergeant Bartleby, in a whisper, as Susan Jacobs, having ended her account of the previous evening, departs the Woodrows' drawing-room. Bartleby looks down at his note-book, almost full with the household's accumulated memories of the incident upon the canal. 'I mean to say, we already know what they saw, don't we?'

'I was hoping the little girl might be more forthcoming,' says Webb.

'If she doesn't remember anything, sir, then she doesn't.'

'But why did she wander out there, in particular?' asks Webb. 'And do you imagine it is merely a coincidence she found Brown's corpse there?'

'Well, sir – of course there's a connection—'

'Hush, Sergeant. The American cousin is next, and we are nearly done. You can speculate later.'

Annabel Krout knocks and enters the room. The two policemen stand; she offers them a rather nervous smile.

'Miss Krout, do take a seat,' says Webb, guiding her to a chair at the drawing-room table. 'Now, my name is Webb and this is Sergeant Bartleby. You understand we are obliged to ask a few questions? I gather you are Mrs. Woodrow's cousin, visiting from Boston?'

Annabel Krout sits down. 'Yes, sir, I am.'

'Well,' says Webb, 'I will not ask you what you make of London. I suspect last night would have been rather an ordeal for any young woman.'

'Well, I am a little tired, sir. I did not sleep too well.'

'I am sorry to hear it. I will not keep you long, Miss. Susan Jacobs tells us she alerted you first to young Miss Lucinda's absence. Can you tell me what happened then?'

'Of course. I told Jacobs I would help look for her. But then the front door was open, and I could see Lucy had got outside.'

'You knew all about the little girl's condition?'

'She had wandered into my room a couple of nights before, Inspector. So, yes, I knew she had these attacks.'

'And what did you do, when you saw the door was open?'

'Naturally I went to look for her. And I told Jacobs to wake up the family.'

'You went out on your own? That was rather foolish, Miss, going out alone at night,' says Bartleby, 'for a young lady, such as yourself.'

'I expect it was, Officer,' says Annabel. 'But I did not think there was any time to waste.'

'And how did you find her?'

'I saw her go down to the canal, or at least I caught a glimpse of her.'

'And what was she doing there?'

Annabel Krout frowns. 'I don't know. But when I found her she was just standing there, pointing at the . . .'

'Body, Miss?'

Annabel nods. 'But she was quite in a trance, Inspector. I can't explain it.'

Webb smiles sympathetically. 'No need, Miss. And,

I'm sorry to mention it, but, tell me, did you by any chance see the man when they pulled him clear of the water?'

'Well yes, I did. I insisted upon it, I am afraid. I should have gone back inside, but I had to make sure.'

'Make sure?' asks Webb.

Annabel Krout looks puzzled. 'Did my cousin not say anything, Inspector?'

'No, Miss,' says Webb. 'I am a little lost, I confess. What do you mean?'

'I'd seen the man before, Inspector. Twice. Even, well, in those circumstances, I knew I recognised him.'

'Twice?'

'Once outside the house, and once he spoke to me, in a café on Regent Street.'

Webb frowns. 'The same man, you are quite sure?'

'I'd know him anywhere, Inspector.'

———

Jasper Woodrow paces around the morning-room. His wife sits in the window-seat, overlooking the garden at the back of Duncan Terrace.

'What is keeping the man? We might as well be prisoners. It's damned impertinence.'

'Woodrow, please. I am sure he means nothing by it. They have to make their inquiries.'

'I cannot imagine what he hopes to learn,' says Woodrow.

'Annabel said she was sure she knew him; the fellow who accosted her in Regent Street. She thinks she saw him loitering outside the house last week.'

'We can hardly be blamed if she attracts such followers.'

'Woodrow!'

'Well, damn it, Melissa, is it my fault?'

Mrs. Woodrow bites her lip, and turns to stare into

244

the garden, gazing at the old elm that marks the end of the family's plot.

'Woodrow – tell me the truth. This man was not one of our creditors? Was it him who sent those awful notes?'

Woodrow turns round abruptly, walking up to his wife, kneeling down beside her. 'Good Lord! You did not tell them about our affairs?'

'Of course not. But was it him?'

Woodrow shakes his head. 'No, of course not. You do not imagine that I could . . .'

Mrs. Woodrow smiles weakly, taking her husband's hand in hers.

'No, of course not.'

⟡

Decimus Webb enters the Woodrows' morning-room some five minutes later, accompanied by his sergeant and Annabel Krout.

'Well, sir, I believe we are done for the moment. Miss Krout, I hope we did not try your patience over much.'

'No, Inspector. I was glad to help,' replies Annabel.

'I trust we will hear no more of this awful business, Inspector,' says Woodrow. 'My family have been put to enough trouble.'

'Yes, well you see, sir,' says Webb slowly, as if choosing his words with some deliberation, 'it rather appears the dead man had some interest in your family. Apparently he spoke to Miss Krout here, only a few days ago. It might rather aid our investigation to determine what that interest was, don't you think?'

'I don't care a whit about your investigation, Inspector. I do not expect to be harassed in my own home.'

'Woodrow,' says Mrs. Woodrow, a chiding note of caution in her voice.

'Well, really, Melissa. It is a bit much.'

'I'm sorry if we've caused any difficulty, sir. But a murder is a murder. It demands close attention.'

'Murder? I've never heard such nonsense. The fellow drowned. Most likely drunk.'

'No, sir. I fear I must speak plainly, since you raise the matter. He was killed; someone propelled his head into a wall, I think. Quite deliberately.'

Mrs. Woodrow blanches a little. 'Garotters?'

'No, not robbers, ma'am. I'm afraid it probably was someone who knew the man. Who took him down to the canal, for whatever reason. Probably thought it was a nice quiet spot.'

'Well,' interjects Woodrow, 'I think we have heard enough.'

'Oh, I expect so, sir,' says Webb. 'You must forgive me. Well, we can see ourselves out, no need to call your man. Ah, no wait, there is one thing. I understand there was a dinner party last night, earlier in the evening?'

'Not a grand affair, Inspector. Just a couple of acquaintances,' says Mrs. Woodrow.

'Perhaps you might give me their names and addresses, ma'am, all the same. I would like a quick word with them too.'

'What good can that do?' asks Woodrow.

Webb shrugs. 'It is possible they saw the fellow outside; one never knows.'

'Very well,' says Woodrow. 'I can tell you now, if you like. Mr. Joshua Siddons, of Salisbury Square, Fleet Street, and Mr. Richard Langley, 4 Alpha Road, St. John's Wood.'

'Ah, really?'

'Yes, Inspector, really. Is something the matter?'

'No, sir. Just another curious coincidence. We happen to have had some dealings with Mr. Siddons recently. Bartleby, did you get the other gentleman's name?'

'Yes, sir.'

'Well, then we are finished here. Again, I thank you for your time. Good day.'

'Good day, Inspector,' says Woodrow.

———

As Webb and Bartleby depart from Duncan Terrace, their attention is caught by a shout from the canal.

'Inspector!'

'Ah, Hanson,' says Webb, walking briskly over to the City policeman. 'It rather seems we have found your Mr. Brown. A little the worse for wear, though.'

'So I see. You've just been speaking to the people that found him. An odd business?'

'More than you know, Hanson,' says Webb, briskly ushering Hanson to one side. 'Come, walk with us a while.'

'You seem in a hurry, sir?'

'I would rather you were not observed, Inspector,' says Webb, 'by certain parties. Certain parties whom we may need to keep an eye upon presently.'

'I had hoped to speak with the family, Inspector,' says Hanson, sounding a little aggrieved.

Webb shakes his head. 'We have already been quite thorough in that regard. Now, I trust you are better at shadowing a man than the fellow you employed to watch Brown?'

'I should hope so.'

'Then, whilst we make further inquiries, I have a suggestion.'

CHAPTER THIRTY

'Do you think Hanson and his lot are up to it, sir?' asks Sergeant Bartleby, as the clarence cab in which they travel rattles along the Euston Road, then past Portland Place and the southern boundary of Regent's Park. 'If I didn't know better, I'd say you were just keeping him busy.'

'Sergeant, really,' says Webb. 'He has an interest in the case and, if truth be told, his is the prior claim – assuming we are looking for the same man, of course.'

'That must be odds on, sir. The girls and Brown: I'd say the same fellow's done for them all. If he has something against the girls, not surprising he should go after him too.'

'Or simply silence the only witness? Regardless, I am not convinced of his supposed religious mania, Sergeant, not by a long chalk. Our Mr. Woodrow is the key; I am sure of that much.'

'You think he knew Brown, sir? He was awful nervous, I thought, when you spoke to him.'

Webb pauses, looking out of the cab window at the entrance to Baker Street railway station, as they pass by. 'I thought so too. He knows something, but what? You must find me a little more about his background.'

'I will do, sir, when there's a spare moment.'

Webb looks sharply at the sergeant.

'I'll do it today, sir,' says Bartleby.

Webb does not reply. Bartleby, however, cannot resist a further query.

'You don't think Woodrow's the guilty party, sir? He acts rather too high and mighty, don't you think, as if he's something to hide?'

'You will find most people have something to hide, Bartleby. Mr. Woodrow is concealing something; a fool could see that. The question is whether that something is actually what we are trying to uncover.'

'I don't quite follow, sir.'

'For example, he might simply know Brown because he has paid a visit in the past to Knight's Hotel. He is hardly likely to admit to such a thing, with his wife sitting downstairs. That does not make him our murderer; not yet, at least.'

'Well, I hope Hanson can keep an eye on him, sir.'

'So do I. Ah, at last, we are here.'

Richard Langley's home in St. John's Wood, whilst not a mansion, is a slightly grander affair than the Woodrows' home in Duncan Terrace. For, though part of a row of substantial houses, it is situated upon a corner plot, surrounded by a whitewashed stone wall and neatly tended shrubbery upon all sides. The house itself stands three storeys high, a large, square suburban temple of white stucco, Grecian in style, with little exterior decoration, save for an imposing Doric porch. The two policeman quit their cab and proceed through the gate to the front door, where Bartleby rings the bell. The formalities of announcing themselves completed, the two men are led inside by a maid-servant whose face betrays a degree of anxiety at the arrival of Scotland Yard detectives. Nonetheless, she promptly directs them to her master's library, where Richard Langley sits at a desk, with large sheets of paper, bearing pencilled designs and hastily written notes, scattered about him.

'Ah,' says Langley, getting up to greet his guests. 'Inspector . . .'

'Webb, sir. This is my sergeant, name of Bartleby. Sorry to trouble you, sir, but we're making inquiries relating to an unfortunate incident last night; well, a murder to be precise.'

'Murder? Good heavens. I confess, I am quite at a loss.'

'A gentleman was found dead, sir. Not far from the residence of your acquaintance, Mr. Jasper Woodrow – I gather you had dinner with the family last night?'

'Oh, good heavens. Well, how unfortunate. Yes, of course, I did indeed. But how does any of this pertain to me?'

'Well, you were in Duncan Terrace, sir. Did you see anything suspicious?'

'I can't say as I did, Inspector,' replies Langley. 'I took a cab directly there, and hailed one on the City Road on my way back.'

'No foreign-looking gentlemen in the vicinity of the house?' suggests Bartleby.

'Not to my recollection, Sergeant. Was the man foreign?'

'The dead man was a Greek, sir,' says Webb. 'Swarthy-looking type; a big man.'

'I don't recall seeing anyone of that description.'

'Well, if you think of anything, be sure to contact the Yard, sir, if you please. May I ask, do you know the family well, the Woodrows?'

'I confess, it is more a matter of commercial rather than social ties, Inspector, though Mrs. Woodrow was good enough to invite me to dine,' says Langley. He gestures at the plans upon his desk. 'I have been designing Mr. Woodrow's new Warehouse. I even had a mind to invest in the business, before . . . well, recent events. The poor girl who was . . . well, I am sure you have heard about it.'

'Ah,' says Webb, nodding, 'I see you are appraised of the unfortunate incident at the Casino on Saturday. Another investigation of mine, I am afraid, Mr. Langley. I have all the luck.'

'It is bound to affect the business, Inspector. I was obliged to withdraw. It has rather soured my relations with Mr. Woodrow, I fear. Still, he shall have his plans complete, if nothing else.'

'If you don't mind me asking, sir,' says Webb, 'how long have you known Mr. Woodrow?'

'A couple of months, Inspector. Why?'

'Oh, I just wondered, sir.'

'Inspector – forgive me – these two incidents, the poor girl and now this man, are they connected in some way?'

'Why do you ask that, sir?'

'Surely it seems an odd coincidence, to say the least?'

'We are much of the same opinion, sir.'

'Well, but this is terrible. I should not wish to think Mrs. Woodrow or her cousin were in any danger.'

Webb smiles. 'Ah, I see. Well, your concern for, ah, Mrs. Woodrow is admirable, sir. We will keep an eye upon them, rest assured.'

'I am glad to hear it.'

'We'll bid you good day, Mr, Langley. Remember, be sure to let us know if anything comes to mind about yesterday evening, anything remotely unusual may be of interest.'

'I am sure I cannot think of anything.'

'Still, if it does.'

Annabel Krout sits listlessly before the fire-place in the morning-room of Duncan Terrace, idly staring at *The Bride of Lammermoor* but hardly reading a word. As she turns a page, Jasper Woodrow appears at the door, dressed for the office, his great-coat slung over his arm. His face appears rather flushed and aggravated.

'Miss Krout, a word if you please.'

'Sir?' replies Annabel, looking up.

'I wonder if you might, in future, be a little more circumspect.'

'I'm sorry, I don't understand,' replies Annabel.

'Your remarks to the inspector concerning this fellow who drowned. Implying that the fellow had some connection with this family. It won't do, Miss Krout. I suppose the damage is done now; but I would rather you said nothing further on the matter, particularly not to Lucinda; she is quite disturbed enough.'

'I only told him the truth, sir,' says Annabel.

'Miss Krout,' says Woodrow, raising his voice, 'you may imagine yourself pursued all over London by strange men, but I will not have such fancies passed off as plain fact to the police. They have better things to do with their time, I am sure, than chase the phantoms of your imagination.'

'The man was dead, sir. I did not imagine that.'

'Nonetheless,' says Woodrow, his voice far from authoritative; there is almost a hint of hysteria in it, 'I have had my say.'

'Sir,' says Annabel Krout, 'I disagree—'

'Miss Krout,' says Woodrow, 'do not defy me. You will come off the worse.'

'Sir?'

'You heard me, Miss Krout.'

———

'Ah, Sergeant,' says Joshua Siddons, ushering the two policemen into his rooms. 'Come, take a seat. And your colleague is . . .'

'Webb, sir. Inspector Webb.'

'Well, an honour to meet you, sir. A positive honour. Pray, have a seat.'

'Thank you,' says Webb as the two men sit down.

'Is this more about the Munday business, Inspector? I am afraid I have not been able to locate our ledger. Shabby of us, I must confess. I suspect it was lost back in fifty-four. There was a fire, you see; almost ruined the firm. Lost a lot of stock too. In any case, I don't believe there is much more I can tell you.'

'No, it's a different matter, sir,' says Webb. 'I understand you dined last night with Mr. Jasper Woodrow?'

'Woodrow? Yes, of course. Mrs. Woodrow invited me to dinner. Marvellous woman. And their cook – no words to describe it, Inspector. I hope there is nothing wrong, sir? Good heavens, I hope nothing has happened?'

'Not to the family, Mr. Siddons. But a man was found dead in the Regent's Canal, late last night, murdered. We understand he had been pestering Mr. Woodrow's cousin; he may have even been watching the house. We wondered if you saw anything or anyone acting suspiciously.'

'Miss Krout? Poor girl! Lovely creature; charming. I'm afraid I caught a cab pretty sharp, Inspector. Saw no-one, far as I recall. How awful, though, eh?'

'The man was a Greek, sir. Large build, dark hair,' adds Bartleby.

'A Greek? Good Lord. No, Sergeant, I don't think I saw anyone. You must forgive me. At my age, the eyes are not quite what once they were, you know.'

'Have you been a friend of the family long, sir?' asks Webb.

'Many years, Inspector. Knew Mrs. Woodrow's pater; capital fellow. And Woodrow, of course, used to work for me; did you know that? Managed our Manchester office before he was married.'

'I see. Did he work there long?'

'In Manchester? What an inquiring mind you have, Inspector. Well I should say it must be a good twenty years or so. Worked his way up; always been a determined sort of fellow.'

'You found him reliable too?'

'That's why I asked him to London, sir. Head clerk, before he married and came into the wife's property. Always said, sir, anywhere money changes hands, one needs a man one can trust, eh?'

⁓

'We are no further on, sir,' suggests Sergeant Bartleby as the two men depart Salisbury Square.

'Oh, I'm not sure I'd say that, Sergeant. We know a little more about Mr. Woodrow, at least.'

Bartleby says nothing, but a look of skepticism clouds his face.

'You'd best be off to Abney Park this afternoon, Sergeant,' continues Webb. 'I want the place thoroughly searched. We have left it too long already.'

'But with everything else, sir—' protests Bartleby. Webb, however, interrupts.

'We have Hanson watching Woodrow; and I fear there is little else to do today. Besides, it may prove just as important, Sergeant. It worries me that the same names keep re-occurring. There may even be a connection between the Abney Park business and the rest of this affair.'

'Like what, sir?'

'If I knew that,' says Webb, exasperated, 'you would not need to search the place.'

'I'll leave no stone unturned, sir,' says the sergeant, keeping his face entirely straight.

Webb shakes his head. 'You have far too much of the music-hall about you, Sergeant.'

CHAPTER THIRTY-ONE

As THE HALL CLOCK strikes six p.m., Annabel Krout sits opposite her cousin, in front of the warm hearth of the Woodrows' morning-room. Mrs. Woodrow, for her part, leans over a wooden tray upon her lap, engaged in the delicate process of embroidering a monograph upon one of her husband's pocket-handkerchiefs. But there is something lacking in her concentration, and despite the curlicued 'J.W.' clearly drawn upon the tracing-paper, the progress of Mrs. Woodrow's needle does not quite seem to match the pattern. Annabel, meanwhile, having abandoned Walter Scott, the book sitting open upon a nearby table, takes up the *Ladies Home Journal*, and idly reads the correspondence page, which principally is devoted to a debate upon the proper management of the home aquarium. It does not hold her attention for long, however, and she slumps back in the plum-coloured leather of the armchair, and gazes around the room, from one corner to another, from the gaselier to the grate. The china statuettes upon the over-mantel, however, seem to stare back at her in silent rebuke at her inattention to the wisdom of the *Ladies Home Journal*, and she returns to its pages once more. But she cannot bear to read it for long and soon glances back at Mrs.

Woodrow. Her cousin seems strangely silent, even when she pricks her finger upon her needle, and flinches in pain.

'Do you think Mr. Langley will still come tomorrow?' says Annabel at last. 'I do not suppose anyone would mind if we still went out?'

Mrs. Woodrow looks up from her work, a rather forlorn expression on her face. 'Oh, my dear,' she says, 'I do hope so. You deserve a pleasant outing. This awful business with the police – what must you think of us?'

'It is not your fault, cousin.'

'But, my dear,' says Mrs. Woodrow, as if about to protest, but then breaking suddenly into tears. She takes a fresh handkerchief from her sleeve and dabs her eyes.

'Melissa, please, not on my account.'

'You don't know the worst of it, my dear,' says Mrs. Woodrow, choking back a small sob. 'Jervis gave me his notice this morning.'

'Oh, I see.'

'I cannot blame him. He said he "hoped he had given satisfaction, but would prefer a quieter establishment". Can you believe it? I expect we are the talk of the street by now. And how long before we lose Mrs. Figgis and Jacobs?'

'Melissa—'

But Annabel's words of comfort are cut short by the appearance of Jacobs at the door, as if conjured by the mention of her name.

'Ma'am, beg your pardon . . .'

'What is it?' asks Mrs. Woodrow, straightening in her chair.

'It's Miss Lucy, ma'am. She won't touch her dinner. I wouldn't trouble you, ma'am, but she hasn't eaten all day.'

Mrs. Woodrow sighs. 'She'll be the death of me, I swear it.'

'I expect it is all the excitement of this morning,' suggests Annabel.

'No doubt,' replies Mrs. Woodrow. 'But what am I to do with her, my dear? She has such a delicate constitution at the best of times. And, I confess, I am not at all myself.'

'Shall I go up and speak to her, cousin?' suggests Annabel. 'Perhaps I can help.'

'Annabel, are you sure? You are an angel.'

'It is no trouble,' says Annabel. She gets up and, with a nod to the maid, follows Jacobs out of the room.

'Thank you, Miss,' says Jacobs, once they are on the stairs, out of hearing distance of her mistress. 'I've tried my best, Miss, Lord knows.'

'I'm sure you have,' replies Annabel. 'Is she ill, do you think? Or just unsettled by this morning?'

'Stubborn is what she is, begging your pardon, Miss.'

Inside the nursery, Annabel finds Lucinda at her little desk, much as upon the first day they met, poring over her alphabet. Her food sits untouched upon a small table on the other side of the room, a vacant chair beside it.

'Lucy?' says Annabel. 'Are you all right, dear?'

It seems an age before the girl answers. 'Yes,' says Lucy, at last, not looking up.

'You haven't eaten your dinner,' says Annabel.

'I don't want it.'

'Well, I expect it's cold now. Shall I have Jacobs heat it up for you?'

'I don't want it,' says Lucy emphatically.

Annabel bends down next to the little girl. 'What's

wrong, dear? You can tell me. Is it something about last night?'

Lucy shakes her head, but her eyes look fixedly down at the nursery floor, as if trying to avoid Annabel's gaze.

'It is, isn't it?' says Annabel, gently touching her arm. Lucy scowls, and nods.

'What is it, dear?'

'I told a lie,' she says, hesitating, 'to the policeman.'

'Go on,' says Annabel, puzzled.

'I did see him.'

'Who?'

'The big man. I saw him lots of times.'

'You mean you saw the man who . . . well, you saw him here, outside?'

'Lots.'

'But why didn't you say so?' asks Annabel.

'Because he was fighting with . . .'

But then Lucy shakes her head and puts a finger to her lips. For, at the same moment, there is a sudden pounding of feet upon the stairs. Annabel turns around to see Jasper Woodrow stride into the room. Even though he is a couple of feet distant, she can smell liquor on his breath. Annabel stands up.

'I would talk to my daughter, Miss Krout, if you please,' says Woodrow. There is already a suggestion of anger in his voice.

'Well, of course,' says Annabel, 'but she was just telling me—'

Before Annabel can continue, however, Lucy tugs sharply at Annabel's skirts, in an apparent effort to stop her. The little girl's face has a peculiar look of terror upon it.

'I don't care what she was telling you, Miss Krout, just please step aside. Lucinda – stand up straight and come here.'

Lucinda dutifully stands up and walks over to her father.

'I have just come home and your mother tells me you have not eaten your dinner.'

The little girl looks at the food and nods.

'Why do you persist in disobeying us? Do you not think your mother has enough to contend with?'

The little girl says nothing, though her eyes look tearful.

'Sir,' interjects Annabel Krout, 'I hardly think you can blame her. She has been through a terrible trial herself.'

'Miss Krout, please,' says Woodrow, though his tone is far from conciliatory. 'It is not your place to apologise for my daughter. She must learn the consequences of her actions. She has been told many times before. Lucinda, hold out your hand.'

Lucinda mechanically holds out her arm, palm upwards, without being bidden any further. Woodrow, in turn, unbuckles his belt, tugging it violently from his waist, doubles it over, and leans down over his daughter.

'I am sorry I must punish you, Lucinda,' he says. 'I am your father and it gives me no joy, I assure you. But you leave me no choice. You must learn to obey your mother and father. That is your duty.'

And with that, he swings the strap of the belt sharply down upon her outstretched palm. The child's face crumples in pain.

'Now, Lucinda, think hard before you answer, will you finish your dinner?' says Woodrow, gesturing at the cold plate of beef and potatoes. Lucy, still wincing, her face bright red, angrily shakes her head, tears streaming down her cheeks.

'Very well,' says Woodrow. He brings the belt down again. The little girl cries out.

'Now,' he continues, 'will you eat your dinner?'

Lucy makes no response, but Annabel steps forward, interposing herself between father and daughter. 'Sir!' she exclaims indignantly. 'For pity's sake – she is only a little girl!'

'Miss Krout,' says Woodrow, drawing a deep breath, 'you have no right to be here.'

'I cannot stand by and watch this . . . barbarity, sir. There is no other word.'

'By heavens, Miss Krout,' says Woodrow, raising his arm theatrically, his face as red and flushed as that of his daughter, 'if you do not stand aside, I shall whip you both.'

Annabel does not flinch, at least to all outward appearance. But she cannot help involuntarily closing her eyes as Woodrow, seeing that she will not move, brings the belt crashing down. It is only at the last moment, the strap swinging inches from her face, that he turns and slams it upon the table, sending the plate of food flying on to the floor with a resounding crash.

Woodrow takes a step backwards, looking at the mess. 'Very well,' he says at last, 'Lucinda, you will go hungry until you apologise to your mother.'

The little girl again remains silent. Jasper Woodrow takes a deep breath and, with a fierce glance at his wife's cousin, stalks from the room.

Annabel Krout visibly sags as Woodrow departs. When she has recovered herself, she bends down to Lucy Woodrow, gently taking hold of her hand. The little girl remains stolidly silent.

'We'll put something on that to make it better,' says Annabel.

Lucy nods, her cheeks still awash with tears.

'Lucy,' says Annabel, hesitantly, 'I am so sorry your Poppa did that.'

Again, silence.

'Before, though, when we were talking, about the man outside? You said you saw him fighting? There's no need to be frightened. He's gone now. Can you tell me, who was he fighting with?'

Lucy Woodrow shakes her head, very firmly indeed.

'Tell me, just nod if this is true, was it with your Poppa? Did he fight with him?'

Lucy Woodrow neither nods nor shakes her head, but looks glumly at the floor. It strikes Annabel Krout, however, that Lucy does not disagree with the proposition.

And, suddenly, she herself feels quite frightened.

CHAPTER THIRTY-TWO

ANNABEL KROUT SPENDS several minutes comforting her young cousin and, in truth, regaining her own composure, before she quits the nursery and walks out on to the landing. She finds Jacobs waiting on the stairs, making a rather unconvincing feint at dusting the banister.

'Can you get Miss Lucy some ice, please, Jacobs?' asks Annabel, looking back towards the nursery door, and wondering how much explanation is appropriate. 'She needs it for her hand.'

'Of course, Miss,' replies Jacobs.

'Where is your master, do you know?'

'I think in the study, Miss.'

'And Mrs. Woodrow is still downstairs?'

'Yes, Miss.'

'Good. Thank you,' replies Annabel, hurrying past the maid and down the staircase. She does not stop until she reaches the ground floor. Indeed, she is slightly out of breath when she returns to the morning-room, where she finds her cousin still engaged in her desultory attempt at needlework.

'Annabel, my dear,' says Mrs. Woodrow, 'are you quite all right?'

'I'm fine, Melissa,' replies Annabel, carefully closing the door behind her. 'May I speak to you for a moment?'

'Why, of course. Will Lucy eat her food now, do you think? Oh, Woodrow is home – did you see him? He said he was going up.'

'I did,' replies Annabel, sitting down opposite her cousin, leaning towards her. 'Cousin, I . . .'

'What, my dear? Why, you look so pale all of a sudden!'

'Forgive me, there is no pleasant way to put this – Melissa, I am not sure that I can stay here any longer. I do not feel I am, well, quite safe.'

'Not safe? Oh, Annabel, first Jervis, now you too!' exclaims Mrs. Woodrow. 'This morning was too awful, I know, but, really, it is done with now. And where would you go?'

'It is not a question of what happened this morning,' says Annabel, shaking her head. 'Not entirely.'

'Whatever do you mean, dear?'

'Your husband . . . well, just now, I am sorry, Melissa, but I am afraid he nearly struck me.'

'Woodrow? Surely not.'

'He was punishing Lucy for not eating her food,' replies Annabel, rushing through her words. 'He would not listen to me and he began whipping her with his belt. Cousin, she was in a terrible state, and I stepped between them and—'

'Oh, Annabel, my dear child,' says Melissa Woodrow, with a slight hint of condescension in her voice, 'I know you have a good heart, my dear, but you should not interfere. I mean to say, I don't know the Boston way of doing such things, but Woodrow must discipline Lucinda at times – why, it is his duty, more than anything. You know he has a temper. He cannot help that. And he did not actually strike you, I take it?'

'No. But it is not just that – I was talking to Lucy and, well, she did not come right out and say it, but I am sure she saw them fighting.'

'Who?'

'Her father and the . . . and Brown. But she is too scared to say anything. She said she lied to the police.'

'Fighting? Annabel, whatever are you implying? Besides, I was with Lucinda all morning; I am sure I would know if she was lying. I am her mother.'

'And I must show you this,' continues Annabel, reaching down and picking up her book, her movements as hurried and anxious as her speech. She flicks through the pages until she finds the paper ticket of admission to the Holborn Casino. Mrs. Woodrow takes the ticket from her and looks at it with some perplexity.

'I found it,' continues Annabel, 'in the study on Saturday. I did not know if I should say anything, but now I feel I must.'

'Annabel, I'm sorry. Are you claiming this item belongs to Jasper?'

'Melissa, I found it, I swear. He must have dropped it there. Don't you see? He was there that night. When that poor girl was killed.'

'You do not mean to suggest that he had anything to do with it?'

Annabel looks down at the rug, not meeting her cousin's stare. 'I do not know.'

'I know you have an active imagination, my dear, but this is too much. Do I understand you right? You think Jasper is somehow involved with . . . well, what happened at the Casino and this wretch in the canal?'

'I think he knows something about it, at least. Otherwise, why did the same man follow us on Regent Street?'

'My dear, we have discussed this already. It is just an awful coincidence. Or he took some peculiar liking to you. You must learn to curb your fancies.'

Annabel shakes her head. 'Melissa, I am sorry to say

such a thing, really, but I am just not sure it is safe for me to stay here.'

'My dear, you forget yourself. The man you are talking about is my husband. I dare say I know him a little better than you. You must give up this nonsense – if I did not know better, I would say this whole sorry affair has disturbed your mind.'

Annabel looks away. 'I must tell the police, what Lucy said.'

'You are being ridiculous, my dear. Let me go and fetch Woodrow, and we can discuss it. I am sure he can bring you to your senses.'

'No,' says Annabel emphatically. 'I am sorry, cousin. I think it best if I go and find a hotel. What is the big one called, on the main road, by the station? You said it was very respectable?'

'Yes, yes, the Midland Grand,' replies Mrs. Woodrow. 'It is – but at least stay here tonight. Good Lord, your Mama said you were headstrong, but I would never have believed this of you, Annabel. You are over-excited; a moment's sober reflection and you will see this is simply nonsensical. You cannot imagine Jasper would harm you in any way?'

'I hope not,' she replies.

'Where has this come from? I cannot believe it,' continues Mrs. Woodrow, her features now betraying an increasing annoyance, 'after all we have done to make you welcome.'

'I'm sorry, Melissa. I'd better go and pack my things.'

Mrs. Woodrow, for the first time, looks harshly at her young cousin.

'Yes,' she says with a sigh, 'I rather think you better. Things are difficult enough. Perhaps when you have calmed down, you will realise you are being quite unreasonable. I'd best tell Woodrow myself – whatever will he think?'

'I think he will be happy to be rid of me.'

———

A short time later, a cab is directed to the front door of Duncan Terrace, where Annabel Krout stands waiting with her belongings. Her cousin stands beside her, ensuring the cab-man has proper instructions for the loading of each item of luggage, but there are few words exchanged between Mrs. Woodrow and her American guest. At last, when everything is stowed inside, with half a dozen items upon the rack on the roof, Annabel Krout gets in, and the vehicle rattles off towards Pentonville.

As it turns on to the City Road, a solitary man makes a note of the cab's number in his pocket-book, and signals to another cab, parked near by, which immediately follows Miss Krout's carriage.

Inspector Hanson, meanwhile, returns his pocket-book to his jacket, and looks back along Duncan Terrace.

———

Mrs. Woodrow returns to the morning-room where her husband stands warming his hands before the fire.

'Is she gone then?' he asks.

'Yes.'

'Well, I'm sorry for it, Melissa, but really, a man can only put up with so much in his own home, eh? If that's a sample of the average Yankee female, well, thank heavens for the English variety.'

'Woodrow, please.'

'I hope you do not think I ought to have asked her to stay? The girl's practically determined to give me in charge; and what's all this nonsense about Lucinda?'

Mrs. Woodrow shakes her head.

'I need a stiff brandy,' says Woodrow.

Mrs. Woodrow nods as her husband leaves the room. She lifts up her hand, and opens the piece of crumpled paper in her palm. Again, she reads the decorous language of the Holborn Casino's injunctions to its customers; then she squeezes it into a ball for a second time, and throws it into the fire.

INTERLUDE

Mr. Brown? Yes, I saw him lurking in the road, outside the house. It was rather comical, a large man like that skulking about behind the shrubbery. It is a miracle the whole street did not remark on it. Well, you saw the fellow yourself – it would take more than a couple of twigs to conceal a man of his size, eh? He recognised me too, of course – he was not the sort to forget a face, I should think – but I do not think he knew what to make of it.

Did I intend to kill him?

I should hope so, Miss Krout. One would not want to leave such things to chance.

It was not so difficult as all that. I could see what had happened. It was Brown who had been through the rooms at the hotel and hid the evidence; though I suppose I was a little naïve to imagine that a procurer should behave with integrity under such circumstances. I should count myself lucky he did not dispose of the girls entirely; I would have had to begin from scratch.

I am sorry, Miss Krout. You ask these questions, after all. If you do not wish to—

No? Very well. I could see what he was about. It was simply a matter of money. In any case, I made the appropriate noises; said that I might act as agent for a certain party, and so on. I said I was going home along the canal, that we might talk along the way. He was a little shy, but I expect he was curious to know more, to see where I lived, if nothing else. Doubtless he set me down as one of his future marks; the man was nothing if not a thorough rogue. We went down the path together, and then I stepped to one side and pretended to see something in the water. He was not so strong as you might expect. Besides, my limited experience in these matters suggests that surprise more than compensates for muscle. And he did not think that I was dangerous, I am sure of that. He certainly did not expect me to dash his brains against the wall. Indeed, I recall, he did look rather surprised. But, then, I suppose anyone would.

Remorse? I do not think so. The fellow was a parasite; a leech. What else do you call a man who makes his living in such a manner, off the backs of profligates? And then to add blackmail to his crimes! God's judgment awaits all the whoremongers and adulterers, Miss Krout, you may mark my words. It is a terrible thing to defile the marriage bed, you see?

Of course. Again, forgive me. I did not mean to sermonise; it is too late for all that. Yes, I made quite sure that he was dead, then toppled him into the water; I intended to hide him, at least until I might make my escape. I had an idea that he might sink, but he was too full of wind for that. And I was foolish to go along the canal, of course; I might have been seen by the lock-keeper. I ought to have gone directly back to the road.

In any case, it did not matter. It served my purpose well enough.

CHAPTER THIRTY-THREE

Having finished her breakfast, Annabel Krout wanders through her new suite at the Midland Grand Hotel. It consists of two substantial rooms, bedroom and sitting-room, upon the second floor of the great building. Both are lavishly decorated, walls panelled with perfect oak wainscoting, and each possessing a fire-place with a surround of blue-green marble supporting the mantel. A great gilt mirror hangs above the hearth, confidently reflecting the entire room back at the occupant. Above the carved, floreted wood of the wainscot is a stencilled wall-paper of spectacular colour, coruscating patterns of flowers in deepest red and green, the like of which Annabel has never quite seen before. And yet, once alone in the sitting-room, Annabel pays little attention to her surroundings; certainly there is no outward impression that they gladden her in the least. Rather, she merely stands, staring out of the room's tall windows, looking over the smoky rooftops of Bloomsbury, at the spires of distant metropolitan churches that penetrate the haze, then she lowers her gaze to watch the parade of morning traffic on the Euston Road below.

She is interrupted, however, by a delicate knock at the door.

'Come in,' says Annabel.

A maid-servant, dressed in the uniform cap and apron of the hotel, opens the door.

'Yes?' says Annabel.

'There's a gentleman, Miss, sends his card.'

'A gentleman? Let me see.'

The maid passes over a small *carte de visite*, which bears the name of Richard Langley, and a brief hand-written note that begs the pleasure of her company.

'Where is he? Downstairs?'

'In the lounge, Miss.'

'The lounge?'

'Beg pardon, Miss. At the bottom of the main stairs, and then right, round to the entrance hall. You'd have passed it on your way in. May I tell him to expect you, Miss?'

Annabel falls silent for a moment. 'Yes,' she replies at last, 'you may.'

━━

Annabel leaves her room and makes her way along the corridor, and down the grand serpentine staircase that winds in elegant twin coils from top to bottom of the building. The public spaces of the hotel are no less sumptuous than its rooms and, like the exterior, are in the manner of a great medieval cathedral, albeit one devoted to comfort and ease of visitors, rather than worship. A single Axminster carpet covers the floor, a seemingly unending train of royal red cloth; the walls around the staircase are likewise papered in a deep red with a pattern of golden fleurs-de-lis; moreover, every window, corridor and door is framed by a Gothic arch, supported by dark green marble columns, tipped with carved stone capitals, which on close inspection prove to be sculptures of pygmy dragons that cast a wary eye over the steady procession of guests who saunter past. What most strikes Annabel Krout, however, is the muffled sound of the adjoining St. Pancras station, the muted snort of steam engines, the shouts of porters, the clatter of carts full of luggage. For the Midland Grand Hotel sits directly in front of the station, rising high above it, elegantly masking the arrivals and departures facilitated by the Midland railway company, and it is impossible to conceal thoroughly the noise from guests. For some guests it is a minor irritation; for Annabel Krout, if anything, it calls to mind her journey from Liverpool, and, in turn, makes her think of quitting London as soon as possible and returning home.

She finds the coffee-lounge with little difficulty, for the chimes of the hotel's silver and china being fetched and carried echo along the ground-floor corridor. Indeed, the lounge rather belies its name in being larger than any great dining-room Annabel has ever visited, and thus proves impossible to miss. It extends some hundred feet in length, in a great bow-shaped curve, following the distinctive arc of the building, and it is only with the assistance of the maître d'hôtel that she finally locates Richard Langley, seated at a table for two, by one of the green pillars of polished limestone that ornament the interior wall. As she approaches, escorted by a waiter, he rises to greet her.

'Miss Krout, how good of you to see me.'

Annabel Krout takes the seat opposite him. 'Not at all.'

'Can I bring you anything, Miss?' asks the waiter.

'Not for the moment, thank you.'

The waiter departs with a bow, leaving Annabel and her visitor alone.

'I am afraid we are not good for their business,' says Langley, looking at the empty table. 'Are you sure I cannot order some tea?'

'Not for me, sir,' replies Annabel.

'No?' says Langley, a little nervously. 'Well, Miss Krout, as you may have gathered, I visited Mrs. Woodrow this morning. But it appears you have broken our arrangement.'

'Sir?'

'I had thought we planned a tour of the cathedrals,' says Langley, in a mock aggrieved tone. 'I wondered if I might tempt you?'

'No, not today.'

'Forgive me, Miss Krout,' says Langley, blushing, 'I can see my levity is not appropriate.'

Annabel shakes her head. 'There is no need to apologise. What did my cousin tell you, Mr. Langley?'

'Well, simply that you have had a falling out with Mr. Woodrow. That you were rather upset by this awful business at the canal.'

'You have heard about it?'

'The police came and spoke to me. They thought I might have seen something,' says Langley, 'but, of course, I could tell them nothing.'

'I was not "upset" by that so much, sir, though it was far from pleasant. I . . . well, you'll forgive me, but I am not sure if I should confide in you.'

'Miss Krout,' says Langley, rather hesitantly, as if plucking up courage as he speaks, 'I confess, I did not come here in anticipation of acting as tour guide. It is probably not my place, given our brief acquaintance, but I was concerned for your welfare. You may tell me anything you wish; you have my word.'

'Even if it relates to Mr. Woodrow?'

'Mr. Woodrow, Miss Krout, is . . . well, an acquaintance, nothing more. I have no intimate connection to him. I would be honoured to be taken into your confidence, I assure you.'

'You honestly mean that?' asks Annabel.

274

'Of course, upon my word, as a gentleman,' says Langley.

'Very well,' she replies, steeling herself to speak out. 'I believe he had something to do with the death of that man. I even have reason to think that he was at the Holborn Casino the night that poor girl was murdered.'

Richard Langley raises his eyebrows. 'Are you quite sure?'

Annabel frowns. 'I am not sure, sir. I am not a detective. But Lucinda saw him fighting with the man who was killed in the canal. She as good as admitted it to me. She kept it from the police; I do not know why – loyalty or fear perhaps. Her father is a complete tyrant.'

'He has something of a temper, I know,' replies Langley.

'I fear it is much worse than that, sir. What should I do? Should I go to the police?'

Langley looks down, not speaking for a good few seconds.

'I suppose,' he says at last, 'perhaps you must.'

Annabel sighs. 'I do not know even where to begin. The whole business is so awful. What if I am wrong?'

'Miss Krout,' says Langley, 'if I may, would it help if you told me the facts?'

'It might,' she replies.

'Very well, begin from the beginning. And then, if necessary, perhaps we shall speak to the police together?'

Annabel smiles. 'Thank you, sir. You have been very kind.'

'I assure you, Miss Krout, I will do whatever I can to help.'

CHAPTER THIRTY-FOUR

It is gone ten o'clock in the morning, as two men approach the stone lodge and the gates of the City of London Cemetery, Little Ilford. The cemetery itself is a little larger than Abney Park, and considerably further from the heart of the capital, built not for commercial gain, but by the City authorities. None-theless, looking through the gates, it bears a similar likeness to a well-kept arboretum, with its landscaped vista of kempt gravel lanes, further delineated by carefully planted trees, rhododendrons and azaleas.

'We're too late,' suggests Sergeant Bartleby to Webb, peering down the central avenue. 'We should have caught the earlier train.'

'My dear sergeant,' says Webb, 'please. I strongly suspect that the Eastern Counties Railway is still considerably quicker than any carriage obliged to travel the length of the Romford Road. Have some patience.'

Sergeant Bartleby says nothing for a few moments, but then adds, 'Well, call me a heathen, sir, but I'm getting heartily sick of cemeteries.'

'It is not my fault that you found nothing at Abney Park yesterday,' replies Webb, looking reproachfully at his companion.

'There was nothing to find, if you don't mind me

saying so, sir,' replies Bartleby. 'Except, maybe, that the grave-diggers are a little partial to drink.'

'I am sure,' says Webb dismissively. 'Well, nonetheless, this little excursion is the least we can do, given Hanson's efforts on our behalf.'

'You think it will help, sir?'

'It is not a bad idea of Hanson's, Sergeant. Funerals attract all sorts, in my experience. Let us see who turns out for Miss Carter and Miss Finch. Ah, hush, here they are, if I am not mistaken.'

Webb nods in the direction of the rural road that leads west back into the City of London. Coming round the bend that leads to the cemetery's gates can be seen three distinctive vehicles. The first is a regular hearse of painted black wood and cast iron. It is, however, of a rather second-hand appearance, with the etching on any one of its glass panels bearing no resemblance to that upon any of the others, and the iron scroll-work upon its roof, a black tiara of roses and thorns, marred by a number of missing blooms. Following the hearse are two machines of the funeral-omnibus variety. Half funeral carriage and half mourning coach, each bears five or six mourners, visible through the coach windows, sitting in some discomfort on the narrow unpadded benches within.

'I've never seen a more miserable-looking crowd,' suggests Bartleby.

'It was never going to be a grand affair, upon parish money, Sergeant,' replies Webb. 'They are probably burying a few together, I should think.'

And, indeed, as the carriages pass by the two policemen, who swiftly remove their hats, it becomes clear that at least seven or eight coffins are contained within the procession, under loose black cloths; seven or eight bodies with only a dozen souls to mourn their passing, paupers destined for a common interment.

'They'll stop at the chapel,' says the sergeant. Webb nods, and the two men follow behind the slow progress of the three carriages, to the cemetery chapel. But only the mourners are unloaded, swiftly shepherded by the waiting parson into the church; the dead are left behind. Whether this haste reflects a degree of social embarrassment at the prospect of officiating over the grief of such a poor collection of individuals, it is hard to say. Nor is it perhaps fair to suggest that it may coincide with a comparative dearth of gratuities at funerals of the collective parish variety. But, for whatever reason, the progress of the living indoors is quick enough, and the deceased are not provided for.

As the mourners disappear, a quartet of men in working clothes, their trousers and jackets stained with grey streaks of clay, appear from behind the building, and join the carriages as they move off again, each jumping on the rear board like a conductor upon a regular omnibus.

'Shall we go to the service?' asks Bartleby.

Webb shakes his head, gesturing at the sergeant to proceed. 'No, let us follow the diggers. I'll have a quick word with the driver once they are stopped.'

Bartleby nods and they follow the carriages for a good five minutes until they come towards the boundary of the cemetery, marked by a row of young yew trees. An open pit lies waiting, six feet in diameter, perhaps twelve feet in width. And there, the coffins, of various shapes and sizes, made of rough elm that looks to have hardly seen the edge of a plane, are unloaded and placed upon the ground by the grave-diggers. As this process is completed, a fifth man appears, strolling across the grass, dressed in a smarter unsullied suit, with a rather official-looking appearance, bearing a note-book. Then all five enter into conference, the result of which is that the tallest of the diggers jumps down between the wooden buttresses that shore up the pit. From the grave, he throws up a pair of thick ropes, which the remaining men string over the opening, hooking the ends round pegs already driven into the earth, to form a makeshift hammock for the lowering of the coffins.

'Always room for a few more, eh?' says Webb, strolling over to the cemetery official. Certainly, as he looks down into the pit, there are already half a dozen coffins inside, left from a previous parish funeral. He cannot help but wonder for how many days they have been resting there.

'Can I assist you, gentlemen?' says the man.

'Scotland Yard,' says Webb amiably. The man is suitably surprised.

'Oh dear,' he replies. 'I trust nothing is amiss?'

'Not at all. Tell me,' says Webb, nodding towards the coffins, 'do you have a list there of names?'

'Yes, of course,' he replies, holding up his note-book.

'Finch and Carter?'

'Ah,' says the man. 'Yes, indeed. Tragic.'

'Well,' says Webb, 'do carry on. We won't get in your way.'

The official nods, nervously taking leave of the policeman and proceeding to the coffins.

'Drop us the first box, Arthur,' comes the voice from the pit. The cemetery official nods; the first coffin is slid into position upon the ropes.

'Fidyck, William,' says one of the diggers, peering at the tin plate upon the lid.

The official scans his list and says, 'Away,' much in the manner of someone launching a ship.

———

The drivers of the funeral omnibuses are both taciturn men, and it takes all of Webb's powers of persuasion to wrestle a few simple facts from them. Nonetheless, it becomes clear, from a combination of overheard conversations and the men's own register of passengers, that the passing of Betsy Carter has, at least, attracted one mourner – an elderly woman by the name of Brookes. In consequence, the two policemen resolve to wait with the drivers for the mourners to return. As they stand by the pit, they observe the slow descent of each coffin into the earth, listening to the various cries of 'only a short'un here' or 'to the left' or 'to the right' that issue from below the ground.

The mourners, in fact, arrive early from the chapel. But the clergyman's haste in conveying them to the grave proves counter-productive. For the bereaved are obliged to watch the descent of the last two 'boxes', a consequence that seems to inspire the grave-diggers with such a degree of anxiety that the process is, if not botched, then mishandled, with the sound of clattering wood, and subdued curses from within the pit. Thus it is only when the final coffin is laid to rest, and the diggers have departed, pulled up by the ropes, that the clergyman can begin his few words upon the subject of mortality. It occurs to Webb, however, as he watches the scene, that the priest, with his thick winter great-coat, collar turned up at the neck, and comforter wrapped tight around his throat, looks far less an expert upon the subject than the ragged mourners, at least one of whom looks ready to tumble directly into the earth.

'Which is Mrs. Brookes?' whispers Webb to the nearby driver.

'There,' says the man in question, pointing out a woman in her sixties of a strong-looking build, with a ruddy complexion and a tartan shawl covering her head and shoulders.

Webb nods. Then after a moment, he speaks to the driver once more.

'Where are you bound after this? Straight back to the City?'

'Aye, maybe.'

'Not stopping at a public on the way?'

'Aye, maybe.'

'And where's the nearest place, from here?'

'The Bull and Gate, just down the road, quarter mile or so,' replies the driver, a little wary.

Webb smiles, taking a half-sovereign from his pocket and pushing the coin into the man's hand. 'Make sure you stop at the Bull then, and stand a drink for all concerned, eh? But take your time getting there. Then you may keep the change.'

The man nods, seemingly not quite believing his luck. Webb, in turn, motions to Bartleby to come away.

'Where we going, sir?'

'The Bull and Gate. Apparently it is a charming little hostelry, a brisk walk. Now do hurry.'

—

The Bull and Gate is, it turns out, a decent public house of the tavern variety, in a prominent position upon the Romford Road. It is more ancient and roomy than the common ginnery that can be found in the centre of the metropolis, and still possesses a multiplicity of nooks and corners, hinting back to days when it was more of a private house, and when a landlord of the old type held court in his own small parlour, and when drinks were ferried from cellar to patron by honest potmen, without need for a bar or counter.

But those days have long passed, and the present-day landlord is used to trade from the City of London Cemetery. Consequently, the appearance of Webb and Bartleby, followed in short order by the mourners arriving by coach, causes him no great consternation, nor much disturbs his regular clientele. If he is surprised by the peculiar generosity of one Jack Bludgen, a coachman he has known for some years, in standing the whole party a drink, he has the grace not to show it. And, if he notices how the first two men soon separate off from the group, entering into conversation with a particular woman, then it matters little to him.

'Who did you say you was, again?' says Mrs. Eliza Brookes, downing a second glass of stout donated by her new companions.

'Commercial travellers,' says Webb, hurriedly. 'Just buried a pal of ours. Terrible business.'

'Comes to us all,' says the woman, grimly. 'I'm a widow myself.'

'Was it close family today, ma'am?' says Bartleby.

The old woman shakes her head. 'Knew her mother. Thought she deserved someone 'spectable to see her off. Poor creature.'

Bartleby raises his eyebrows at the word 'respectable'.

'Long illness, was it?' says Webb.

The old woman looks about her, then whispers, 'Murdered in cold blood.'

Webb struggles to look suitably shocked. 'Good heavens.'

'That's what I said,' replies the old woman, warming to her theme. 'I tell you something, sir, awful business. I used to do her laundry, you know.'

'Really?'

'Course, I don't wish to speak ill of the dead, sir. Between you and me, she had gone wrong; some young girls will, however you learn 'em. But she didn't deserve what she got. Poor little thing.'

'I expect the police were involved. Murder and all.'

'Oh, I steer clear of them bluebottles, sir. Never done me no good.'

Webb smiles. 'She had no family then? Sad state of affairs.'

'No,' says the old woman, draining her glass. 'Long gone.'

'Here,' says Bartleby, 'let me get you another.'

'Kind of you,' says the old woman.

'No sweetheart either?' continues Webb.

'Didn't I say, sir? She'd gone wrong, I told you, didn't I?'

'Of course.'

'Now, there was one fellow she had hopes of . . . well, that's all done with now, anyhow.'

'You can tell me, ma'am,' says Webb, leaning towards her, tapping his nose, 'man of the world, I am.'

'Well, he said he'd leave his missus. I said to her, "Betsy, that's all moonshine. Means nothing." But she wouldn't have it.'

'Criminal, ma'am,' says Webb, as Bartleby returns with more stout. 'Tell me, you know the chap's name?'

She shakes her head. 'She kept that dark. Saw him a couple of times. Here, you're a queer sort of salesman, you are. I thought you was going to try and flog me something.'

Webb smiles. 'You have me. I give in.'

'What are you, then?' asks the old woman suspiciously.

'A bluebottle, as you put it, ma'am. But, we'll let that lie,' says Webb, taking a sip of ale, 'because we may need your help. Now describe this man who kept company with Miss Carter.'

———

The two policemen stand outside the Bull and Gate some half an hour later, waiting for a passing cab.

'That woman can't half drink,' says Bartleby

looking back at the pub, where Mrs. Brookes still sits comfortably ensconced.

'She's a washerwoman, Sergeant; they're used to sweating it out; probably takes her a couple of pints just to get up in the morning. But she still has her wits about her. That is all we need to make sure of. We must take good care of her, mind; she is our only witness.'

'But to what, sir? I mean, what if the Carter girl had some fellow sweet on her? It doesn't necessarily mean a thing.'

'But what if it is our Mr. Woodrow, Sergeant?' says Webb. 'The description matches well enough. What if it's him, eh? That would put an interesting complexion on matters.'

'So what's your plan, sir?'

'We'll get a cab, and give her over to Hanson. He'll have a better idea about her story; and, remember, it is still his investigation. I do not wish to tread on his toes. Though I will suggest he allows her to get a good look at our man, surreptitiously, as soon as he can.'

'And if she identifies him?'

'Then we must have a quiet word with Mr. Jasper Woodrow.'

CHAPTER THIRTY-FIVE

I̤ₜ TAKES SOME TIME for Webb and Bartleby to return
to the heart of the capital, with Mrs. Eliza Brookes in
tow, and it is the afternoon before they reach the City.
It takes longer still to locate Inspector Hanson. In the
end, however, they find the latter, in combination with
two other detectives of the City police, maintaining
an unobtrusive vigil upon High Holborn, watching
Woodrow's General Mourning Warehouse, waiting for
the eventual exodus of its owner. After some discussion,
a plain-looking cab is hired for the day, parked opposite
the warehouse with Mrs. Brookes settled inside, with a
view to following Jasper Woodrow upon his departure
from his office. If Mrs. Brookes' confession that her eyes
are 'not what they were' does little to induce great faith
in her powers of recognition, her powers of consumption are undimmed and several bottles of stout are
laid by to see her through the afternoon.

Once Mrs. Brookes is comfortably settled, there is
nothing more to be done until Woodrow's departure.
Webb, moreover, learns little of interest from Inspector Hanson concerning Jasper Woodrow's movements. He is, at least, appraised of the sudden
nocturnal departure of Annabel Krout from Duncan
Terrace. At length, with their exchange of information
finished, a second cab is hailed at a discreet distance

from the Warehouse, taking Webb and Bartleby in the direction of Scotland Yard. The former takes the opportunity of smoking his pipe; the latter, perhaps having learnt from previous journeys, says very little. But as the cab turns from Whitehall under the low arch that leads into the Yard and comes to a halt, Bartleby feels obliged to speak out.

'I think we have a visitor, sir. I wonder what he wants?'

Webb peers out of the window, to see the figure of Richard Langley, standing rather nervously by the doorway that leads up to the inspector's office, fidgeting with a pair of gloves.

'Mr. Langley,' says Webb, as he steps out on to the cobbles. 'An unexpected pleasure. Have you recalled some incident from Monday night?'

Langley frowns. 'Not quite, Inspector. Can we speak somewhere, well, more in private?'

'Naturally. Come up to my office,' replies Webb, indicating the way. 'You must forgive the state of the place.'

'Of course,' replies Langley as they ascend the stairs. 'I hope this is not an awkward time.'

'Not at all,' replies Webb, leading him into the room, brushing aside a small heap of papers from the chair. 'Have a seat.'

Langley sits down but looks nervously back at the sergeant.

'Anything you say may be said in front of Bartleby, Mr. Langley,' says Webb.

'Very well,' says Langley, taking a breath. 'I have come from Miss Annabel Krout, whom I understand you met yesterday. She has asked me to convey some of her concerns to you about a certain matter . . .'

'Yes, yes,' says Webb, a hint of impatience in his manner, 'do speak freely, sir. I gather she has quit the

Woodrows' home entirely, and set herself up in a hotel.'

Langley looks startled. 'But how on earth did you know that?'

'Never mind, sir. We have our sources. Carry on, please.'

'Well, Inspector, to put it bluntly, Miss Krout has reason to believe that Mr. Woodrow may have quarrelled with the man you found drowned.'

'Quarrelled?'

'She believes his daughter, Lucinda, saw them fighting, although she was too fearful to mention it to you.'

'The little girl?' says Webb. 'She said nothing at all, Mr. Langley. Not a hint. But she has confessed all this to Miss Krout? Is that what you are saying?'

'So I gather. Miss Krout . . . well, she also has reason to believe that Mr. Woodrow was at the Holborn Casino the night the poor girl from his establishment was killed.'

'Does she now? But she has sent you, Mr. Langley, to speak to us on her behalf – why, precisely? I would be quite happy to speak to her in person. She knows that, I should think.'

Langley hangs his head, looking at his glove, now rather twisted between his clasped fingers. 'She is in something of a state, Inspector. But, in truth, I persuaded her that I should act as a go-between.'

'Go on,' says Webb.

'I know nothing about the man in the canal, but I can vouch that Mr. Woodrow was at the Casino that night. You see, to be frank, sir, I was there with him myself, in the beginning at least.'

'Were you, Mr. Langley?' says Webb, raising his eyebrows in surprise. 'Mr. Woodrow did not mention any of this.'

Langley looks nervously at the policeman. 'I must confess, Inspector, Mr. Woodrow spoke to me the next day; I believe it was after you visited his establishment. He asked me not to say anything about it, if asked, and not to admit that we were there; to consider his reputation, and mine. But after what I have heard today from Miss Krout, well, I rather felt obligated to come forward. I would be grateful, however, if you would say nothing about it to her.'

'That rather depends. Why were you there?' asks Webb.

'Mr. Woodrow suggested it, Inspector. To celebrate our prospective business partnership. It was not my choice at all but I went with him; rather weak-willed of me. I have no liking for such haunts, honestly. Nor would any man of principle. In fact, I fell ill soon after we arrived – I expect it was the cheap champagne the wretched placed serves – and I caught a cab home.'

'And Woodrow stayed on?'

'Well, I cannot say with absolute certainty, but I believe so, yes.'

Webb looks down at the papers on his desk. 'Let me get this straight, Mr. Langley. I will put it bluntly to you; I hope you do not object. Does Miss Krout believe Jasper Woodrow is a murderer? That, for some unknown reason, he killed these two persons?'

'I fear so, Inspector.'

'How about you, Mr. Langley. You know the man – what do you think? Is Miss Krout correct?'

'I am no judge, Inspector. But she is not hysterical, I will say that much. She has her reasons, at least.'

'All the same. It is a grave charge.'

Langley frowns. 'I only know Mr. Woodrow has something of a temper, Inspector. But as to anything else, I cannot say one way or another. Should I not have told you all this? Do you think it is mere idle speculation?'

'Oh, no, not speculation, sir,' says Webb. 'Valuable information. You did the right thing in coming to me.'

'Then what will you do, Inspector? Arrest him?'

Webb smiles thinly. 'I think, under the circumstances, Mr. Langley, it is quite likely. But I should like to hear directly from Miss Krout, first. She is staying at the Midland, I gather?'

'Yes. I can take you there now – I said you might wish to speak with her in person. I hope you do not mind my interference. I just thought it best we speak in private – about the Casino. You understand?'

'Of course,' replies Webb.

❧

It is just gone five o'clock when Jasper Woodrow quits his business premises. He follows his normal route across the shop floor, past the glass counters displaying rolls of bombazine and crape, past the young women in black who decorously drop a brief curtsey as he passes by. He does not tarry on the staircase, quite the opposite, and ignores the salutation of the doorman, striding briskly into the gas-lit street. Rather, he puts on his hat, and walks purposefully north, hurrying across the road in the direction of the British Museum. There is perhaps something a little too headlong about his progress, something suggestive of a degree of unhealthy nervous energy; but, whatever it may be, it does not slow him down.

He does not notice the cab that rolls patiently behind him, a good hundred yards or more distant.

❧

'Inspector,' says Annabel Krout, motioning rather nervously for the two policemen to take a seat.

'I thought it might be best if we met in your room, Miss,' says Webb. 'This is rather a delicate matter, after all.'

'Of course,' replies Annabel. 'Mr. Langley has spoken to you? You know why I am here?'

'Indeed. I gather some argument with Mr. Woodrow, Miss?'

'Not just an argument, Inspector. He all but threatened me with violence.'

'When was this, Miss?' asks Bartleby.

'Yesterday. It was Lucinda, you see . . . she saw him fighting with that man, I'd swear.'

'With Brown?'

'Yes . . . I'm sorry, Inspector. I am not putting this clearly. I am still not quite myself.'

'Perhaps you had better tell us everything from the beginning, Miss?'

Annabel Krout takes a deep breath. 'Yes, I will. I just . . . well, if I am right, Inspector, what will happen?'

'One step at a time, Miss,' says Webb.

⁓

Jasper Woodrow's route home is his normal trajectory through the stuccoed terraces of Bloomsbury, and then towards Myddleton Square and the City Road. But then he turns, instead, along the Gray's Inn Road, north towards King's Cross and Pentonville. It is, undoubtedly, an insufficient diversion to arouse any suspicion in the mind of Inspector Hanson, as he waits to choose a moment when the cab may draw up beside his quarry in the evening traffic, without causing suspicion, and close enough for Eliza Brookes' eyesight. But as Woodrow exchanges a few words with the newsvendors at the bottom of Pentonville Hill, he glances back at the cab and then abruptly vanishes from view, just as a crowd of travellers spills onto the pavement, surging from the underground station of the Metropolitan Railway. So sudden is Woodrow's disappearance that it takes Hanson a moment to realise what has happened; namely that his man has dashed towards the stone stairs down to the station platform.

Even as the police inspector urges the cab to stop, fighting to get out amidst the bustle of the street corner, he is restrained by a firm hand upon his shoulder.

'That was him,' says Eliza Brookes. 'I'll swear an oath on it.'

CHAPTER THIRTY-SIX

'LOST HIM? How did you manage that?'

The voice is that of Sergeant Bartleby, standing in the semi-darkness, upon the corner of the City Road and Duncan Terrace. Beside him stands Decimus Webb, and facing him, the object of his incredulous interrogation, Inspector Hanson.

'Forgive my sergeant, Hanson. He is prone to such outbursts. But you must admit this rather places us in an unfortunate position. You are quite certain that he saw you?'

Hanson sighs rather defeated. 'I am. It was the old woman's fault, Inspector, or at least her eyesight. It was quite a palaver getting close enough to him for her to see him. We should have waited until morning. Or took her to meet him in person.'

'Well, perhaps,' says Webb. 'I had hoped to be more circumspect. At least she says she recognised him. How long ago was it you lost him?'

'About three-quarters of an hour. I left Mrs. Brookes at the local station house; then I came here, as we arranged.'

'I see. Just as we finished our chat with Miss Krout. The question is whether he has flown the coop entirely, is it not? The Underground is hardly going to get him far, after all.'

'I have notified the principal stations, of course,' says Hanson.

'That's something,' says Bartleby, rather bitterly.

Webb gives the sergeant a rather crushing stare. 'You may have panicked him. He might return home, when he has calmed down.'

'Or we may never see him again,' suggests Bartleby.

Webb ignores the comment. 'If we do find him, I think we must seek his immediate arrest, Hanson. Agreed?'

'Agreed,' says Hanson. 'Though the evidence is still rather thin.'

'Yes,' says Webb. 'I know that, Inspector. Bartleby, give the necessary notice, all divisions – I believe the London District Company has a telegraph office at the Angel; don't let them charge you for it. Hanson, may I suggest we pay a call upon Mrs. Woodrow? Someone should be at the house, I think.'

'Agreed,' says Hanson. 'Lead the way.'

———

Webb and Hanson find Mrs. Woodrow at home in the first-floor drawing-room at Duncan Terrace. Webb takes some exception to the manservant's announcement of simply, 'The police, ma'am,' but it does not take much to discern that the relationship between Jervis and his employer is a little strained; thus he ignores the slight sneer upon the butler's face, and instead directs his energies towards Mrs. Woodrow.

'Forgive the intrusion, ma'am. I think you have not met my colleague, Inspector Hanson?'

'No, I have not had the pleasure, Inspector,' replies Melissa Woodrow. 'Have you come with some news?'

'Of a sort, ma'am. What hour do you expect your husband?'

'Why, at any time, I suppose.'

'I am sorry to say it, ma'am,' says Webb, 'but we have good reason to think he may have fled. Possibly he may be attempting to leave London; I cannot say for sure. Of course, he may return home, but it is hard to be confident about it.'

'No, I am sorry, Inspector, you have the better of me. Fled?'

'I think he is aware of the fact that we wish to speak with him, ma'am. Let me be frank. We suspect Mr. Woodrow knows more about this canal business, and certain other matters, than he has admitted. And we rather suspect he doesn't wish to discuss it with us. He was last seen catching a train on the Metropolitan Railway, at King's Cross, in something of a hurry.'

Mrs. Woodrow laughs. 'Why, Inspector, surely this is some mistake. Just because my husband chooses to catch a train, you think he is some kind of common criminal?'

'There's more to it, ma'am. I don't want to distress you.'

'I think, Inspector,' says Mrs. Woodrow, putting her hand to her heart, 'that you are rather doing a good job of that already.'

'Forgive me, ma'am. Not my intention, I assure you. May I take a seat?'

'Of course.'

'We might settle certain points, ma'am,' says Webb, sitting slightly uncomfortably on the nearest chair, 'if we were perhaps allowed to look over the premises?'

'Good Lord, are you suggesting you search the house?'

'I should think you have nothing to hide, ma'am?' says Webb.

'Of course, but really . . .'

'Then perhaps Inspector Hanson might at least have

a word with your staff, say? I know we have spoken to them already, but it might assist our inquiry.'

'Very well, if that is all. I'll ring for Jacobs.'

'No need, ma'am, I'll find my own way downstairs,' says Hanson, as if on cue, and, before Mrs. Woodrow can object, he leaves the room.

'What is this all about, Inspector?' asks Mrs. Woodrow, pleadingly. 'Have we fallen under some kind of suspicion? I swear, your sudden interest in my husband seems, well, words fail me, positively malicious.'

'Miss Krout, ma'am, whom I spoke to not half an hour ago, has made certain statements to us. They cast your husband in a rather unflattering light.'

'Annabel? Inspector, she is only a girl. Her mother told me she was fanciful. She writes little stories, for ladies' journals, did you know that? She has probably seized on some misunderstanding; or misunderstood something Jasper said.'

'You do not deny that she has broken off staying with you, though, surely?' asks Webb.

'She had some sort of tiff with Woodrow last night, Inspector, something to do with him punishing Lucy. I thought it best to let her cool down.'

'An expensive way to go about it. Or was it your husband who needed to "cool down", ma'am? I gather he is known for his quick temper?'

'What are you implying, Inspector?'

'Nothing, ma'am.'

Mrs. Woodrow sighs. 'I do not think Annabel is naturally spiteful, Inspector, but I can only assume this argument has rather coloured some peculiar impression she has formed of my husband.'

'It is not her impression, so much as that of your daughter.'

'Lucinda? What has she to do with it?'

'I gather from Miss Krout that your daughter saw Mr. Woodrow quarrelling with Mr. Brown.'

'Nonsense,' replies Mrs. Woodrow. 'She would have said so yesterday. You spoke to her, if you recall.'

'I would like another word with her, all the same.'

'She will be asleep.'

'Ah. Will she? Tell me, ma'am, I gather your husband suffers from the same condition as your daughter?'

'Who told you that?'

'Miss Krout.'

'Well, she had no right. My husband is in full command of himself, if that is what you mean, Inspector. He takes a draught to help him sleep, but that is all.'

'I see,' replies Webb.

Mrs. Woodrow opens her mouth to speak, but before she can say anything, the Woodrows' maid-servant bursts breathlessly into the room.

'Beg pardon, ma'am, but it's more than a person can bear,' exclaims Jacobs, looking over her shoulder.

'Jacobs, what on earth is the matter?' exclaims her mistress.

'This policeman, ma'am. He's looking through all our things downstairs, opening every cupboard; and now he's in the scullery. Mrs. Figgis says it's too much for any respectable creature. She'll strike him, ma'am, I know she will.'

Mrs. Woodrow gets up, striding towards the door, followed by Webb. 'What is the meaning of this, Inspector? He is searching the house – you promised me.'

'I can't imagine what has got into him, ma'am,' says Webb, as he notices Hanson appear in the hall, and turn up the stairs to the first-floor landing.

'Hanson,' continues Webb, calling down to the

approaching policeman with a rather conspiratorial wink that goes unseen by Mrs. Woodrow and Jacobs, 'what were you thinking?'

'Forgive me,' says Hanson, addressing the lady of the house, 'but do these belong to your husband? I found them in your scullery.'

'He was in the laundry, ma'am,' says Jacobs, indignantly.

'Inspector, this is a gross intrusion . . .' exclaims Mrs. Woodrow, but her attention is diverted by what he holds out towards her: a pair of worn shirt cuffs, once doubtless pristine white, but now stained a dark rusty brown, virtually from top to bottom.

'I'm sorry, I don't understand,' says Mrs. Woodrow, hesitantly. 'What is this?'

'Blood, ma'am,' says Webb, taking one of the cuffs and turning it over in his hands. 'I don't suppose Mr. Woodrow has cut himself, rather badly, in the last day or two?'

Mrs. Woodrow shakes her head. 'I want you out of my house, both of you,' she says emphatically, although there is almost a hint of hysteria in her voice.

'I am afraid one of us must wait, ma'am,' says Webb. 'In case Mr. Woodrow comes back.'

Mrs. Woodrow turns to face Webb, looking him squarely in the eye. 'He will come back, Inspector. And when he does, we shall both go directly and speak to my cousin, and sort this wretched nonsense out, once and for all.'

'It is not Miss Krout's fault, ma'am,' says Webb, looking down at the piece of cloth in his hand.

Mrs. Woodrow shakes her head. 'Woodrow said she was determined to ruin him. I did not believe it, Inspector. Not until tonight. How can she tell such lies? Does she not see the consequences?'

Decimus Webb is about to respond when his face,

his rather inexpressive, jowly visage, decidedly drops. He throws down the shirt cuff, and turns to run down the stairs.

'What is it?' shouts Hanson, calling after him.

'Miss Krout!' is the reply, as Webb swings open the Woodrows' front door, and hurries breathlessly into the night.

───

Annabel Krout sits in her bedroom at the Midland Grand; she is still in her day-dress, although an evening gown lies before her on the bed. On her dresser is a copy of *The Bride of Lammermoor*, negligently packed in her hurry to depart Duncan Terrace.

A knock upon the door.

'Come in,' replies Annabel. 'What is it? I did not send for—'

'No, you did not send for me, Miss Krout,' replies Jasper Woodrow, entering the room. 'And I rather wish we had never sent for you.'

CHAPTER THIRTY-SEVEN

ANNABEL KROUT STANDS up, facing Jasper Woodrow. 'Sir!' she exclaims, 'what do you mean by this?'

Woodrow takes a step forward; there is, once more, the familiar aroma of brandy about him. In turn, Annabel takes a hasty step back, scraping her ankle against the wooden leg of the dresser. Woodrow throws his hat and gloves down upon the bed.

'My apologies,' he replies, 'if I do not observe the social niceties. It is only because, Miss Krout, I do not know how much time I have left me.'

'I do not understand you, nor do I wish to. Please, sir, leave at once, or I shall ring for the maid, and have you thrown out.'

Woodrow looks over his shoulder at the bell-pull behind him, by the door.

'I think not,' says Woodrow. 'And I am not sure I ought to give much consideration to your feelings, Miss Krout. You have certainly not taken those of myself or my family into much account.'

Annabel looks at the door and the bell, then back at Jasper Woodrow. His rather breathless speech and flushed complexion, his features locked and rigid, all combine to give the impression of barely suppressed rage.

'You are drunk, sir.'

Woodrow shakes his head. 'You mistake indignation for intoxication, Miss Krout.'

Annabel says nothing. Woodrow breathes a weary sigh, as if attempting to compose himself. 'Come, there is no need to make a scene. I am simply here to ask you to cease your spiteful campaign against my family.'

'Sir, you are drunk.'

'Hardly surprising, Miss Krout,' says Woodrow, 'if a man seeks a little Dutch courage before confronting a . . . well, I will not say the word. But, then, I confess, I can hardly credit what you have done.'

'And what do you suppose I have done?'

'Concocted some perverse tale for the benefit of the police. Perhaps even poisoned my own daughter against me. Is that not sufficient grievance for any man?'

'Sir, as to the latter, well, I should think you have done a fine job by yourself. As to the rest, yes, I have spoken to the police, but only to confirm what I know to be truth.'

'More insults. I come here, only to receive more insults! They are pursuing me through the streets, Miss Krout,' says Woodrow, his voice far from measured, reaching forward and suddenly grabbing Annabel's arm. 'Did you know that? Like some common criminal from the gutter.'

Annabel squirms in Woodrow's firm grip. 'You are hurting me! For pity's sake, let me go. The police shall hear of this, I promise you.'

Woodrow grabs Annabel's free arm, holding her at arm's length in front of him.

'The police have heard enough from you already,' says Woodrow. 'You must retract whatever you have said, every word. Confess it is all a fiction.'

'It is not,' she replies, though her eyes brim with tears, 'I will not.'

'Damn me,' exclaims Woodrow, 'if you were a man,

I would strike you down, I swear it, and give you the beating of your life.'

'I do not doubt it,' says another male voice at the door. Woodrow looks over his shoulder to see Decimus Webb standing behind him. 'But, under the circumstances, sir, I strongly suggest you release Miss Krout immediately.'

Woodrow stares at the policeman, then throws Annabel Krout roughly down on to the bed, turning to face Webb.

'You believe this girl's charges?' says Woodrow. His voice trembles with emotion.

Webb shrugs. 'I merely would like to discuss things a little further, sir. We don't need to make it any more unpleasant than it already is, eh?'

Woodrow stares at Webb for a moment, and nods. But his acquiescence is somewhat artificial; for, as he steps towards the door, following the policeman's guiding hand, he makes a dash past Webb into the sitting-room. And Decimus Webb, for all his merits, has neither the strength nor the speed to prevent Jasper Woodrow shrugging him off, as he sprints back into the corridor, leaving the inspector slumped upon the carpet, lying against an armchair.

'Are you all right, Inspector?' asks Annabel Krout, her voice stammering, standing in the door between the two rooms.

'Don't concern yourself, Miss,' says Webb, levering himself up from the floor. 'Did he hurt you?'

'No,' replies Annabel, unconsciously rubbing her arms.

'Good,' says Webb, 'then please wait here and lock the door until I come back.'

Annabel Krout nods, as the inspector runs into the gas-lit corridor. Webb is far from athletic in physique, however, and, in truth, does not harbour high hopes of catching up. Nonetheless, he makes his best effort at pursuit, following Woodrow's trail by the highly audible complaints of several discomforted guests of the Midland Grand, pushed to one side by Jasper Woodrow's headlong progress down the grand staircase. As he himself comes to the steps, which seem to extend in an endless fatiguing arc, he can hear a greater commotion below. And when he finally reaches the ground floor and follows the curving corridor towards the entrance hall, he finds a small crowd of guests has gathered around the source of all the noise. Webb pushes his way through, to find Sergeant Bartleby and a constable grappling Jasper Woodrow to the ground. Woodrow's protests echo round the hall, his feet scuffing the mosaic floor, as Bartleby cuffs his hands behind his back.

'This what you were looking for, Inspector?' says Bartleby. 'I thought you might need some assistance.'

Webb nods, taking a handkerchief from his coat pocket and wiping his brow. 'Well done, Sergeant.'

'You are making a terrible mistake, Inspector,' growls Woodrow, straining at the handcuffs, to little effect. 'It is some sort of vile conspiracy, I swear it.'

'Get him out of here, Sergeant,' says Webb.

'Inspector!' protests Woodrow.

'You'll get your say, sir, I promise you that.'

CHAPTER THIRTY-EIGHT

DECIMUS WEBB SITS in his office in Scotland Yard, pondering various pieces of paper laid out upon his desk. He leans forward and adjusts the gas, though it does not quite dispel the rather dismal character of the room. As he does so, there is a knock at the door and Inspector Hanson enters.

'Ah, Hanson,' says Webb.

'Sir,' replies the City policeman, rather cheerfully. 'I understand you caught up with our man, at the Midland Grand?'

'Well, that particular honour rather belongs to Bartleby, but yes, we have him.'

'Have you spoken to him?'

'No, I thought I would wait for you, Inspector, and let him contemplate his situation,' replies Webb. 'He assaulted the American girl, Miss Krout, for one thing.'

'So your sergeant told me,' says Hanson. 'I have some more good news. We found Brown's lodgings; a constable in G Division recognised his face when we moved the body – he'd seen him a few days previously in a lodging-house in Shoreditch.'

'Go on,' says Webb.

'We found this, tucked away in his baggage,' replies Hanson, taking a small note-book, bound in black leather, and passing it to Webb. Upon inspection, it proves to be a long list of names and addresses, with sums of money against each name, plus various ticks, crosses and annotations.

'It appears to be some list of accounts,' says Webb, pensively, 'but the sums involved are too great for Brown's regular business, I should think; or perhaps I am behind the times?'

'No, indeed,' replies Hanson. 'And if you find Mr. Woodrow's name at the end, you'll see it's the largest sum of all.'

'Five hundred pounds. Good Lord,' exclaims Webb.

'I think it's blackmail,' says Hanson. 'I suspect they were all guests at Knight's Hotel. The dates and amounts; there's a clear monthly pattern to it. What better place for a blackmailer to work?'

'And you think Woodrow would not stand for it?'

'There is no tick in the book against his name. Perhaps he began with the two girls, and worked his way up to Brown.'

'Possibly,' says Webb. 'Although I can conceive of another possibility, if Brown was as venal as this suggests. What if he was simply blackmailing Woodrow about the murder of Miss Carter and Miss Finch?'

'You think Brown knew Woodrow killed them, from the off – for whatever reason – and tried to gain by it?'

Webb gets up. 'It is quite possible. Would that merit five hundred pounds, concealing the deaths of two women? In any case, he has stewed long enough. Let us go and have a word with the wretched fellow.'

Hanson assents and the two policemen descend the stairs, exchanging a few words as they walk across the muddy cobbles to the squat two-storey Whitehall police station that forms part of the Yard. The building itself is rather unprepossessing in appearance, distinctive only in being illuminated by a single gas-light encased in blue glass, the sign of the Metropolitan Police. Webb briskly leads the way inside, through the outer office and along a narrow corridor. He directs Hanson to follow him, and opens the last door on the left.

Inside, the small room contains a solitary constable, who snaps to attention as the two men enter, a desk and four chairs. Upon one of the chairs sits Jasper Woodrow.

'Inspector,' he says, standing up as he recognises his visitor. 'At last. This has all been a ridiculous mistake.'

'This is Inspector Hanson of the City force,' says Webb. 'Please, sir, take a seat. Inspector Hanson here has agreed to take notes of our interview. I hope you don't object?'

Woodrow hesitates, but sits down facing the two policemen. 'Interview? Look, Inspector, whatever you have been told is a lie. Miss Krout is determined to ruin me. I have no idea why, mind you. In fact, I have no idea what goes on in her Yankee head, I assure you.'

'It is not so simple as that, sir,' says Webb. 'In fact, it is hard to know where to begin. Let me put it to you as simply as I can. On Tuesday last, two young women were murdered in Knight's Hotel, St. Paul's. One, at least, Betsy Carter, was known to you.'

Woodrow begins to disagree, but Webb raises his hand. 'Allow me to continue, sir. Then a young girl in your employ was killed at the Holborn Casino. Then one Vasilis Brown, proprietor of Knight's Hotel, killed outside your door-step. Are you telling me this is all a coincidence?'

'Of course.'

'Miss Krout tells us you were seen brawling with Brown.'

'It is ridiculous. She could have seen no such thing.'

'Your daughter saw it. She told Miss Krout.'

Woodrow shakes his head. 'Fabrication.'

'We have a witness who will testify to your friendship with Betsy Carter, sir.'

Woodrow avoids the inspector's gaze. 'Do you, indeed? What of it?'

'So you do not deny that you knew her?'

Woodrow looks a little more thoughtful for a moment. 'No, I do not. Is that a crime?'

'That rather depends. In turn, this means you knew Vasilis Brown.'

'It depends what you mean by "knew",' says Woodrow.

'You said nothing about Mr. Brown to me, sir,' says Webb. 'You denied knowing him at all.'

'Do you really think I would claim acquaintance with such a man?' asks Woodrow.

Webb shrugs. Hanson looks up from his writing. 'Where were you when Betsy Carter was killed, sir?'

'When was that?'

'Four o'clock on Tuesday last, sir.'

'Tuesday of last week? I seem to recall I was out walking. I often go for a stroll to clear my head.'

'Anyone who can vouch for that, sir?'

'No, only to say that I left the Warehouse. I find walking the streets soothes the nerves.'

'Now, I find the opposite, most times,' says Webb, 'at least in London. I seem to recall, in fact, there was a fog. Did anyone else see you "walking"?'

'I could not say.'

'Did you visit Knight's Hotel that day?'

Woodrow pauses. 'No.'

'What about the Casino on the Friday night, when Miss Price was there?'

'No.'

306

'Richard Langley says otherwise, sir.'

'Langley? Ah. Well, it was only for his sake I was keeping it quiet – yes, we both did.'

Webb sighs, putting his palm to his forehead. 'Sir, the more you change your story, the worse it looks for you. You must realise that?'

Woodrow says nothing.

Hanson reaches into his coat pocket, and brings out a folded silk scarf, which he opens up upon the table, to reveal the two bloodied shirt cuffs stored within.

'Recognise these, sir?' asks Hanson.

'Never seen them in my life,' replies Woodrow.

'They were found in your laundry, sir.'

'Don't be absurd,' exclaims Woodrow.

'You deny they are yours?' asks Hanson.

'Of course, I do,' says Woodrow, pausing for a moment, a look of peculiar realisation passing over his countenance. 'By God, I see it now. You are party to it!'

'To what, sir?' says Hanson patiently.

'Not you too, I hope, Inspector?' says Woodrow, looking at Webb, who merely replies with raised eyebrows. 'This wretched conspiracy – all of you, to make me out as some kind of homicidal lunatic. I have done nothing wrong, I swear it. Webb – you seem a decent sort of fellow, you must believe me.'

'I am having all sorts of difficulties in that department, sir,' replies Webb.

'Why did you kill Betsy Carter?' says Hanson, ignoring Woodrow's pleading.

'I did nothing of the sort.'

'And what about Annie Finch?'

'I never even saw her. The whole thing is madness.'

'But you saw Betsy Carter?' says Hanson, with a knowing glance at Webb. 'You saw her, didn't you?'

'You are twisting my words.'

'I do not think so,' says Hanson. 'Tell me, sir, why did you drug her drink? Did you think she'd struggle too much without the laudanum? Or weren't you man enough to do it when she could still look you in the eye?'

Woodrow raises himself from his chair at this insult, as if about to lean forward and grab Hanson, but the constable beside him places a restraining hand on his shoulder. Woodrow looks up at the policeman with the same angry expression but, nonetheless, reluctantly sits back down, brushing the constable's hand aside. As his anger subsides, however, he frowns in thought.

'Laudanum?'

'Don't play the innocent, sir,' says Hanson. 'You know full well.'

'In the brandy,' says Webb, watching Woodrow's expression closely. He is surprised to find that Jasper Woodrow suddenly laughs, a strange exclamation of relief that momentarily brightens his troubled face.

'What is it?' asks Webb.

'It is a conspiracy!' says Woodrow, almost gleefully. 'If I am honest, Inspector, I almost doubted myself, thought I had lost my senses, but now it is quite clear. You say the brandy was drugged?'

Webb nods.

'Then I am quite innocent. Good Lord, the whole thing is one monstrous plot.'

Webb frowns. 'I think you had better explain yourself a little more clearly, sir.'

'I was there, Inspector. I admit it, when the poor girl was killed. The whole thing is grotesque and I cannot explain it. But I tell you, I am quite innocent.'

'And how is that?' asks Hanson.

'I drank the same liquor, you see. I must have slept through the whole thing.'

'You are joking?' says Hanson, exasperation in his voice. Webb, however, waves his hand for silence.

'Tell us exactly what happened,' says Webb. 'The truth, please, if you can.'

Woodrow sighs. 'Very well. I suppose it must all come out. I went to see Betsy that day, Inspector. We had a regular arrangement, she and I. She was a lovely creature.'

'I am sure,' says Webb.

'There was nothing out of the ordinary – I paid off Brown, went up to see her and, well, you can imagine the rest.'

'You had carnal knowledge of her?' says Hanson.

'Well, I rather suppose I did,' says Woodrow, allowing himself a slight sardonic smile. 'A fellow doesn't pay good money for nothing. But that was it, you see – the brandy. We always had a couple of glasses, before and after our . . . well, dalliance. The next thing I knew . . .'

'What?' says Webb.

'I woke up, Inspector. She was lying next to me, still warm. I saw the wound of course; she was cut open like some wretched piece of meat, and the blood, all down the side of my shirt. You cannot imagine what it was like, to see that.'

'I saw it,' replies Webb.

'No, no, you do not understand. For a moment, I truly thought it was me.'

'Did you now?' says Hanson.

'Please. I suffer from a condition, Inspector – somnambulism. I regret my daughter inherited the disease. I walk about in my sleep, or at least I used to, until I conquered the habit. Not only walking, either. I used to get dressed, stoke the fire, all sorts, never knowing what I was doing.'

'Ah,' says Webb, 'I see what you are getting at, sir.'

'But I do not,' says Hanson, sourly. 'Perhaps you could elaborate?'

'Don't you see? I feared that somehow I had killed her in my sleep. One hears of men who strangle their wives in bed, or some such, does one not? But I knew I had not done it, in my heart, I knew it. For a start, I do not carry a blade.'

'Still,' says Hanson, skeptically, 'just so we have this on record, sir, you feared the worst, and fled the scene?'

'I am not a fool, Inspector. I confess I panicked, I was terrified. But I knew what would happen if someone called the police. I had her blood on my shirt. It was a common bawdy house. No sane man would do otherwise.'

'Via the window?' asks Webb.

'It was not too far to jump down, holding on to the ledge.'

'And what did you do next?'

'I walked . . . I cannot say quite where. I lost my way in the fog. You must understand, Inspector, I was not myself. It was a good couple of hours or more before I could even bring myself to go home.'

'I see. And why did you swap the bottles of brandy?' asks Webb.

'Swap? I do not understand. There was only one.'

Hanson takes a wallet from his pocket and places a folded piece of paper upon the table. 'I suppose you never saw this in your life before either?'

'"He uncovers deep things out of darkness, And brings the shadow of death to light,"' says Woodrow, picking up the paper and reading it aloud.

'Book of Job,' says Webb.

'Is it? Well, I've never seen it, Inspector.'

'It was left by the bodies.'

'Really? Well, you must see it – this whole business

310

is some awful attempt to make me a scapegoat. Some lunatic has a grudge against me.'

Hanson shakes his head.

'Are these your shirt cuffs?' asks Webb, nodding to the items on the table.

'They can't be, Inspector. I burnt my shirt, you see, as soon as I got home.'

'And you are suggesting these are the actions of an innocent man?' asks Hanson, incredulously.

'You do yourself no favours, sir,' says Webb, 'my colleague is quite right. Tell me, how did you conquer your sleep-walking, if you don't mind me asking?'

'Will-power.'

'Nothing else?'

'Well, I do take a patent remedy to assist me.'

'Does it contain laudanum?' asks Webb.

'It may do,' says Woodrow. 'Look here, Inspector, that is neither here nor there.'

'So,' says Hanson, 'you are familiar with the properties of that particular drug, though?'

'Damn you!' exclaims Woodrow, abruptly thumping his fist upon the table. 'Cannot you see the truth? There is some lunatic out there laughing at you, whilst I stew in this wretched room.'

Hanson looks wearily at his notes. 'Let's discuss another matter, then. When did you last see Mr. Brown?'

'Brown? Wait, of course – it was him who wrote my wife the letters – he must have been part of it.'

'Letters, sir?' says Hanson wearily.

'Blackmail – he meant to blackmail me, Inspector. He sent my wife threatening notes.'

'That is why you killed him?'

'I tell you I killed no-one!'

—◆—

It is a full two hours before Hanson and Webb quit the room, leaving Jasper Woodrow no calmer than when they found him. The two policemen walk back in the direction of Webb's office.

'I've never heard such a string of lies,' says Hanson, as they step outside into the cold night air.

'You do not believe his story?'

'Heavens! Do you?' exclaims Hanson. 'He has changed it half a dozen times already.'

'He seems settled now,' says Webb. 'The problem is, Hanson, even if he killed the women, there is still much unexplained. The brandy, the notes – why he should even attack Catherine Price in the first place.'

'As to the notes – well, it is some perverse joke, that is all. And perhaps Catherine Price knew too much about his habits.'

'Two blackmailers? Even I find that a little far-fetched, Hanson.'

'It need not be that – perhaps she merely saw him in a compromising situation. He would not have expected one of his shop-girls to be at the Casino, after all. He'd already found out how easy it was to do away with these women. Who knows? Perhaps she threatened to tell his wife? Or perhaps he just had got a taste for it.'

Webb shakes his head. 'But why did he kill Finch and Carter?'

'The blackmail – he knew what Brown was up to, got himself into a rage, and took it out on them. But Brown thought he could make one last attempt – threatened to tell the police what he knew.'

'It's an awful hodge-podge of an explanation, Inspector.'

Hanson looks at Webb in disbelief. 'You do not think he is innocent? Or that he killed them in his sleep?'

Webb sighs. 'No, I doubt it. It is just an awful mess

of a case. Too few witnesses and too many suppositions. There is something missing.'

'I still say we charge him with murder, Inspector. We must. Do you agree? I would not care to bring a prosecution without the support of the Yard.'

'Yes,' says Webb, thoughtfully, 'I suppose so.'

'He may plead insanity, of course,' says Hanson.

'I don't think he is mad, Inspector,' says Webb. 'I am just not sure—'

'What?'

Webb shakes his head. 'Yes, charge him. You are quite right. It must go to trial.'

'In any case,' says Hanson, dismissively, 'if there is some master-mind behind this affair, as he claims, it will come out in court.'

'One would hope so,' says Webb.

———

'Mr. Siddons!' exclaims Melissa Woodrow. 'Oh, thank heavens! I did not know where to turn.'

'My dear Mrs. Woodrow,' replies Siddons, taking off his coat, 'what on earth is the matter? I came immediately, of course, but it is rather late, you know.'

'Woodrow . . . well, he has been arrested. I fear the police intend to charge him with the death of that poor man from the canal. And there are other things too . . . it is all quite impossible. I swear, I can hardly breathe.'

'Oh, my dear lady,' replies Joshua Siddons, 'this is terrible. Calm yourself. You must take some brandy.'

'But . . .'

'Come, calm yourself, my dear. First you must tell me every detail. Leave nothing out.'

'Mr. Siddons, I do not know what to do. I mean, if it should go to court . . . he will need a barrister . . .'

'Then I will arrange everything.'

PART FOUR

CHAPTER THIRTY-NINE

'Not looking at the Woodrow case again, sir? I thought you'd left it all to Hanson now,' says Sergeant Bartleby, poking his head around the door of Decimus Webb's office. Webb looks up at the sergeant and puts down the papers on his desk.

'It troubles me, Sergeant.'

'Weren't you there yesterday, sir, in court?'

'I spent an hour, listening to the summing-up. Mr. Woodrow looked quite ground down by the whole business.'

'I expect a stay in Newgate is pretty good for that, sir. What do you make of his chances?'

Webb frowns. 'If he had pleaded insanity, perhaps he might have found a place in a county asylum; his claims of a conspiracy are outlandish enough to border on mania.'

'Ah, he's stuck to his guns on that, leastways. Shame about the rest, though. He never should have admitted that he fought with Brown – and halfway through the proceedings too. Can't imagine what his brief made of that.'

'I think, Bartleby, he only did that to spare his daughter the dock,' says Webb, looking down at the papers on his desk. 'You know, Sergeant, I do not know what, but I had rather expected something else to surface. As it is, I am fairly sure of the outcome, if such a thing is possible with an English jury.'

'Guilty, you think, sir?'

Webb nods. 'I shall have a word with the ushers this afternoon; they generally know which way the wind blows.'

'Very good, sir,' says Bartleby, about to leave.

'Hold on a moment. I have something else for you,' says Webb, picking up a particular sheet of paper. 'A complaint.'

'Complaint?'

'From Mr. Pellegrin, Abney Park. It appears he is rather aggrieved that we still have not found his corpse.'

'Hardly my fault, sir.'

'He lists a range of charges against us, not least that you and your men "trampled all over the grounds like a herd of stampeding bull elephants". For good measure, he says he will write to the Assistant Commissioner.'

'Only following your orders, sir.'

'I only wish you had found something to appease the fellow.'

'There was nothing to find, sir. I told you at the time.'

'No, I suppose not,' says Webb.

'What time did you say you were going to court, sir?' says Bartleby, changing the subject.

Webb takes out his pocket-watch. 'I suppose I might go now. One never knows.'

Sergeant Bartleby breathes a sigh of relief.

⟡

Decimus Webb's journey to Ludgate Hill and the Central Criminal Court proves uneventful. His consultation with the chief usher of the Old Court, however, suggests that, in fact, a decision in the matter of R. v. Woodrow is rather imminent, by four o'clock at the latest. Thus, with the high-ceilinged room already packed full, not least in the gallery, Webb finds himself a place in the reporters' box, together with the gentlemen of the press.

It is, indeed, about four o'clock when the machinery of justice cranks into action. A silence falls over the plain wooden benches of the court, as the jurymen appear, filing into the jury-box, having completed their final deliberations. Then come the court officials and, ultimately, the presiding judge, his robes positively regal in their splendour. Indeed, the judge is the centre of the court, seated beneath a rather extravagant wooden canopy topped with a carving of the royal coat of arms, a haughty lion and a unicorn beneath a crown. Behind him, mounted upon the wall, is a polished sword of justice. It is, of course, ornamental in character and perhaps more aesthetic than the true instrument of the law, the hangman's noose. Jasper Woodrow is last to appear, led to stand in the dock by a pair of Newgate gaolers. He appears rather gaunt, his posture slumped, his eyes lowered; a change effected by the hospitality of Newgate Prison in a matter of a few weeks.

The judge, Earnshaw by name, peers about the room; it is a hot and stuffy place, even in winter. In part it is the gas-lamps; in part the over-heated excitement of the waiting crowd, packed into the narrow benches of the gallery. He looks pointedly at the jury bench, and intones the familiar ritual words of the criminal court.

'Gentlemen of the jury, have you reached a verdict?'

'Yes, your honour,' replies the foreman, rising to his feet.

'And how do you find the defendant regarding the wilful murder of Elizabeth Carter?'

'Guilty.'

'And that of Annie Finch?'

'Guilty.'

'And Catherine Margaret Price?'

'Guilty.'

('Never thought they'd fix him for that,' whispers the journalist seated by Webb.)

'And Vasilis Patroclus Ionnidou?'

'Guilty.'

Webb studies Woodrow's face as the foreman delivers the verdict. It seems quite unchanged, virtually immobile, certainly devoid of anything resembling hope.

'Very well,' says the judge, silencing excited chatter from the gallery. 'Jasper Woodrow, do you have anything to say why the sentence of law should not be passed upon you?'

Woodrow looks up, but the judge does not truly wait for an answer; for any answer would be, after all, an irrelevance. Instead, he unfolds a piece of black cloth from beside him on the bench and places it atop the heavy powdered wig upon his head.

'Jasper Woodrow, you have been convicted, by a most attentive and thoughtful jury of your peers, of wilful murder, one of the worst, most terrible crimes that human nature can perpetrate. Not once, but four times have you robbed your fellow creatures of life, including three helpless women who, although vicious in their habits, were, at least, thoroughly deserving of our pity and compassion. Instead they fell victim to your perverse and brutal character, the like of which I have rarely encountered in this court. I should add that your complete lack of remorse, and stubborn adherence to all manner of lies and falsehoods, speaks of a deep moral corruption. When you return to your cell, I would urge you to consider not only the

320

judgment of this court, but the judgment that is to come, and, if you are able, to make your peace before Almighty God.

'It now only remains to pass the sentence of the law. You will be taken from here to a lawful prison. Thence, on Monday next, to a place of execution, there to be hung by the neck till you are dead. May God have mercy on your soul.'

There is a cheer from the gallery. Jasper Woodrow slumps forward in the dock, leaning against the brass rail, but offering little resistance as the two prison warders turn him round and lead him away.

'I knew it'd go that way,' says the man beside Webb.

⁓

Decimus Webb finds the lobby of the Old Bailey full of journalists on their way to file their copy, sundry officials of the court, and former inhabitants of the public gallery, descending from their lofty perch, engaged in ardent discussions upon the Woodrow case. Amongst them, however, rather more sombre than many around him, he spots the black-suited figure of Joshua Siddons, shepherding Annabel Krout through the crowd. The lobby is so busy that he can only catch their attention when they are upon the street outside.

'Miss Krout!' calls out Webb.

'Ah, Inspector,' says Annabel Krout, turning and catching sight of the policeman.

'How are you, Miss?'

'I'm well enough, Inspector, thank you. I suppose I should be glad to see justice done, but under the circumstances . . . well, I have to think of my poor cousin.'

'She has not attended the trial?'

'She could not bear it, Inspector. At least, now, she and I are reconciled, thanks to Mr. Siddons here.'

'Hardly my doing, Inspector,' replies the undertaker, 'not after Woodrow admitted quarrelling with the Greek. I was merely Mrs. Woodrow's agent in the matter. A terrible business, though. But, as I always say, blood is thicker than water, eh?'

'In any case,' says Annabel, bestowing a smile upon Siddons, 'I am back at Duncan Terrace.'

'I expect Mrs. Woodrow has need of her family around her now, Miss Krout. How is the little girl?'

'I think she is too young to understand it all, Inspector. Thankfully, I suppose. I can't imagine how anyone could put their wife and daughter through this, Inspector. Is he insane? His story is so unlikely.'

Webb shrugs. 'They found him guilty, Miss. That is all that matters now. He'll be lucky to get an appeal.'

'Then you think he will be hanged, Inspector?' asks Siddons. Annabel Krout frowns.

'I should think so, sir, yes,' replies Webb.

Annabel looks nervously at Joshua Siddons. 'How will I tell Melissa?'

The undertaker takes her gloved hand and squeezes it between his. 'I have faith in you, Miss Krout.'

Miss Krout is about to reply when her concentration is disturbed by the appearance of Richard Langley, walking briskly from the court building towards them.

'Miss Krout,' says Langley, 'gentlemen. Forgive me. I saw you in the gallery but I was not sure . . . how is Mrs. Woodrow?'

'Not good, sir.'

322

'And yourself?'

'Well, Mr. Siddons has been very kind,' says Annabel, 'looking after us both.'

'It is my duty, Miss Krout,' continues the undertaker, 'and my privilege. I am content to do it. Rest assured, Miss Krout, you and your cousin may rely upon Joshua Siddons; you shall want for nothing during this ordeal.'

'Thank you, sir.'

'No need for thanks, my dear. Now, I really must return to Salisbury Court, but tell Mrs. Woodrow that things will take a turn for the better, I am sure of it. She must only wait for the truth to come out.'

Langley gives the undertaker a surprised look. 'You still think him innocent?'

'Don't you, sir?' says the undertaker.

Langley glances a little nervously at Annabel Krout. 'No, sir.'

'Well,' says Annabel to Siddons, 'you are a good friend to Mr. Woodrow, sir, though he does not deserve it. But I had best be going; the coachman will be waiting.'

'I too have a busy evening,' says Siddons. 'Two young men. American caskets: polished oak and electroplate. Won't attend to itself. Good day to you both. May I walk you to your carriage,' Miss Krout?'

'Thank you, sir,' replies Annabel Krout, as Siddons offers her his arm.

Decimus Webb watches as the pair depart, leaving him with Richard Langley. The latter shakes his head.

'Something wrong, sir?' asks Webb.

'I'm sorry, Inspector. I do not have a high opinion of Mr. Siddons. When we had dinner that night at the Woodrows', well, let us just say, when the ladies were not present, he had a very loose tongue. Quite foul, in fact. I cannot help but wonder . . .'

'What?'
'If his motives towards Miss Krout are entirely honourable.'

CHAPTER FORTY

Decimus Webb, having made his way back to Scotland Yard, spends the remainder of his day, and much of the night, at his desk, writing a report upon the Woodrow affair for the benefit of the Assistant Commissioner. He writes fitfully, however, reflected in the numerous blots of ink upon the paper, and, even when finished, he reads through the document with a sense of deep dissatisfaction. In the end, he merely places it in a drawer within his desk, safely out of sight, and extinguishes his lamp, making his way downstairs in the semi-darkness, illuminated only by the gas-lamp in the courtyard below, shining through the staircase window. There he finds Sergeant Bartleby, chatting to a couple of fellow sergeants.

'You off home, sir?'

'I am, Sergeant.'

'Sorry, sir. Forgot to say earlier – message from Inspector Hanson. Said that he was sorry to miss you in court, but he'll call tomorrow morning, compare notes, if you're agreeable.'

'Thank you, Sergeant,' says Webb, distractedly, and continues walking, through the arched gatehouse and past the Clarence public house, out on to Whitehall. As is his wont, Webb resolves to make his way home on foot. It is gone ten o'clock at night, and he takes his regular route past Charing Cross station and along the Strand, though his face retains a rather pensive expression.

It is a quiet hour for the streets of the capital; for the hotels and public houses have not yet called 'time' and evicted their merry clients on to the streets; likewise the theatres and music-halls still contain all their dramatic devotees. Upon the other hand, the day-time workers of the metropolis have all, by and large, long since headed homewards. In consequence, as Webb progresses down the road, past the ancient church of St. Mary's, which looms in the centre of the thoroughfare, rather like a ship marooned in the asphalt, the inspector barely notices a soul: a baked-potato man by St. Clement Danes, warming up his nightly call of 'All hot'; a solitary girl, no more than thirteen years, doubtless turned out upon the streets, loitering under the arch of Temple Bar. Webb is quite alone with his thoughts. It is only when he comes to Fetter Lane, however, that his musings prompt him to a definite action and, instead of proceeding north towards Smithfield and Clerkenwell, his normal course, he carries on down Fleet Street, until he reaches the alley that leads into Salisbury Square.

In truth, it is unlikely he expects much to come of the expedition; and if he is initially inclined to ring the bell to summon Joshua Siddons forth from his rest, he wavers when he sees no sign of gas-light within. But as he approaches the door to Siddons' establishment, still uncertain, he notices that it is slightly ajar. And, inside, he can hear the noise of someone stumbling around in the darkness, and see the occasional flash of light.

Webb pushes the door cautiously open, and peers into the undertaker's. In turn, he is abruptly met with the beam of a lamp shone directly in his face.

He sees enough, however, to make out the garb of its owner.

'Who's that?' inquires a stern voice.

'Put that blasted thing down, constable,' says Webb with considerable gravitas.

'Lord! Sorry, sir,' exclaims the blue-uniformed constable. 'It's Inspector Webb, ain't it?'

'I suppose it is pleasant to be recognised,' says Webb, 'although you almost blinded me, man. E Division, I see.'

'Yes, sir,' replies the constable, fingering the 'E' marked on his collar rather nervously, 'this is my regular beat. But I ain't called the Yard, sir, not yet anyhow.'

'Never mind that,' says Webb, impatiently, 'what brings you here, Constable?'

'Well, I normally say good night to the old party that lives here, sir, just to keep an eye on him. He owns the shop; lives above it.'

'But?'

'Found the place left open, sir. Thought it was burglars but I can't see nothing taken.'

'And Mr. Siddons?'

'You know the gentleman, sir?'

Webb sighs. 'Why else would I be here?'

'Well, there's no sign of him. It's not like him, sir. Man of regular habits is Mr. Siddons – known him for years; never known him to quit the shop, much less leave it open like that.'

'I suggest, Constable, you go back inside and light the gas. Then we can have a proper look and not break our necks, eh?'

Constable E59 accedes to the suggestion and, once the gas is lit, Webb enters the shop. A tour of the upstairs living quarters, however, reveals nothing. The two show-rooms downstairs likewise appear empty, though they contain the impedimenta of the trade: palls and shrouds, principally in white, black or purple, laid out in delicate folds; coffin fabrics, from cambric to silk; handles, name-plates, lid ornaments and crosses, in copper, silver and bronze. All are carefully laid out in cabinets and glass-topped sliding drawers. The second room, however, also holds a row of substantial shelves, upon which are laid a dozen or more display-caskets of varying sizes and designs. The room is deliberately reminiscent of a church vault, with an architecturally redundant arch of bricks above the shelves to emphasise the point.

'He's not here, sir,' says the constable.

'Wait a moment,' says Webb, pondering the shelves. 'Tell me, Constable, have you been in here before?'

'On occasion, sir. The old gent has showed me round once or twice, as it were. Proud of his work.'

'Do you recall if he normally stacks his boxes quite like that,' says Webb, gesturing towards the bottom shelf, where two substantial-looking oak caskets are laid, one atop the other.

'Can't say I do, sir – maybe they're running out of space.'

'The room is for display, constable. They do not need to pack them in. Besides, there is space. Here,' says Webb, bending down, 'help me lift this one clear.'

The constable offers Webb a rather puzzled expression, but does not disobey, and the two men lift the top casket and place it on the floor.

'Weighs a ton,' exclaims Webb, breathlessly.

'The best ones are lead-lined, so he tells me, sir. I'm sorry, sir, but what do you think is wrong?'

Webb motions for the policeman to be silent, as he tentatively crouches down over the shelf, and pulls at the lid of the coffin that rests there, tilting it up and back, so he can see inside.

As he does so, the constable audibly gasps. For inside, lying curled to one side in the ruched cambric layers, is the body of Joshua Siddons.

CHAPTER FORTY-ONE

'I THOUGHT YOU'D GONE home, sir,' says Sergeant Bartleby, as he enters the undertaker's in Salisbury Square. 'I sometimes wonder if you ever sleep.'

'Sergeant – well, I am glad the constable found you. I should have gone back to the Yard myself but I wanted a few moments alone here, to think.'

'I was playing a nice game of whist with the night-watch, sir.'

'Whist?'

'Well, a game of skill more than chance, anyhow, sir.'

'How much did you lose, Sergeant?'

'I brought you the notes you asked for, sir,' says Bartleby, ignoring the question, and proffering Webb several sheets of paper. Webb, in turn, takes them eagerly and scans each sheet until he finds something of particular interest.

'I knew it,' exclaims the inspector.

'Knew what, sir?' asks Bartleby, patiently.

'Come here, Sergeant,' says Webb, beckoning Bartleby towards the back of the shop.

'Have a look at this,' says Webb, pointing to the open coffin.

'Siddons.'

'Quite. I had realised that much, Sergeant. What else?'

Bartleby bends down over the body; it is peculiarly curled up on one side, the eyes open, the mouth almost contorted.

'Hardly serene, is he, sir?'

'No. Have a good look at his hands.'

Reluctantly, Hanson reaches down and holds each one of the dead man's hands up to the light. His nails are scratched and, in several cases, almost torn from the flesh; and two fingers hang at odd angles, apparently broken. He hurriedly puts them down.

'Someone left him in here alive, didn't they?' says Bartleby.

'Well done, Sergeant. He tried to push his way out; failed and suffocated. The coffins are lead-lined and quite air-tight. Now anything else?'

Bartleby looks up and down the wooden box. 'That's the only queer thing, sir. A penny. By his hand there.'

'Good. Now, come here,' says Webb, directing Bartleby to where the coffin lid lies on the floor. 'See how the fabric is shredded?'

'Where he tore at it.'

'Yes, but when he realised he could not escape, he did more than that, Sergeant,' says Webb, peeling back the torn cloth. 'Look. He got through to the lead; he knew he would.'

Bartleby crouches down besides the lid. Underneath the torn cloth, the metal is scored with a series of minute scratches. But they are far from random, since they form a sequence of rough characters.

<del>11201</del>

'Scratched in a hurry, with that coin. And I knew I recalled it from somewhere,' says Webb, brandishing the paper in his hand.

'Sir?'

'Jeremy Munday's plot. It is the number of Munday's plot at Abney Park. 11201 B12. "B12" is the grid location, but that is the number. Now tell me, Sergeant, why should this man expend his last moments on this earth, barely conscious, etching that number into his own . . . well, let us say resting place.'

'He meant to tell us something. But there's a line through it, too, like it's crossed out? Did he change his mind?'

'Don't be ridiculous, Sergeant. What does it mean, crossing it out? To negate it. What negates a burial? Though, I suppose I must admit, you gave me the clue yourself. You said there was nothing to be found at Abney Park. I think you were right. Because Jeremy Munday was never buried there at all.'

'Somewhere else?' say Bartleby, hesitantly, trying to follow Webb's reasoning.

'Read through the newspapers again, Sergeant. Munday was bankrupt; he knew he would be tried for fraud and Lord knows what else. It is the one possibility we have ignored, when we wondered what happened to his body. What if he found a unique way to rid himself of the problem? What if he convinced the world he had died by his own hand?'

'Sir?'

'A mock funeral, with Siddons' connivance. It would not take much more – a certificate was easy enough to come by in those days – why, it still is. The coroner would do little more than hear the word of some doctor, suitably corrupt, and the family. I wonder if the wife was in on their little game, or did they trick her too? A resurrection of sorts. It explains a good deal, I think.'

'Fanciful, sir. And you have no evidence. So you think Munday is still alive? That he did this?'

'I do not think that. Not quite. But with Siddons dead, I think only one other man knows the truth. And there is only one way to be certain, Sergeant. Come.'

'Where, sir?'

'Oh, Sergeant. Please. Newgate, where else?'

'Newgate? They won't thank you for it at this hour, sir. Not on a whim.'

'It is more than that, Sergeant. I don't care if we have to kick the warden himself out of bed. I will tell you more on the way.'

———

Newgate Prison is at its most dismal by night. The great granite blocks, which form its windowless walls, give the gaol the appearance of some vast pagan monolith, black enough to absorb the light of a thousand street-lights, let alone the dozen or so clustered around it. The Lodge, at which visitors must seek admission, is equally grim, resembling a medieval prison in miniature set into the great walls, fronted by a small door, no more than four and a half feet in height, topped with metal bars, tipped with iron spikes. Bartleby's estimation of their welcome proves correct, for it takes some half an hour before the two policemen are admitted and various bolts and locks released, in groaning complaint at such nocturnal irregularity. But, at length, they are indeed led inside by lamp-light, through several small rooms into the principal cell-block. Its dark iron-railinged walkways and galleries, extending over several floors, form the heart of the male wing of the prison. On either side are the cells of more than two hundred men, most awaiting trial at the Criminal Court. But it is at one end of the block, upon the first floor, where two cells for condemned men are located.

333

Webb ignores their guide's comments upon 'keeping odd hours at Scotland Yard', and follows the light of the guard's lantern in stony silence, until it shines into the cell of Jasper Woodrow.

'Visitor for you,' says the guard, addressing not Woodrow, but another officer who maintains a solitary vigil outside his room, seated on a wooden stool. The latter gestures magnanimously towards the bars.

'Mr. Woodrow,' says Webb, 'I would rather like to speak to you.'

The man, lying recumbent upon the solitary wooden bed within, stirs a little, but does not look up.

'He ain't asleep, sir, I promise you,' says the seated guard. 'Been tossing and turning all night.'

'You,' says Webb to the first guard, 'give me that light and let me in.'

'But how should I get back then, sir, without it?'

'Wait or take your chance. I expect you know the way well enough. Or do I charge you with obstructing the police?'

The guard sullenly hands over his lantern and unlocks the cell door, letting Bartleby and Webb enter, and pointedly slamming it behind them. It sends an eerie metallic reverberation that echoes along the entire floor, and distant complaints, the shouts of prisoners woken from their rest, answer it in return.

'Woodrow, rouse yourself,' says Webb. 'I must speak with you.'

The man in grey prison uniform merely turns over upon the bed.

'You must hear me out, sir,' says Webb. 'Your friend Siddons is dead. Killed. I think you must know who did it.'

At this, Woodrow sits up and turns to look at his

visitors. His eyes are bloodshot and tired, his face somewhat thinner than is natural.

'Dead? You think I killed him, I suppose.'

Webb ignores Woodrow's sarcasm. 'No, sir. I don't think that. But I think you know who did. The same man who dug up your grave, I expect.'

'My grave?'

'Don't play the innocent, sir; although, I suppose, it seems possible now that you are innocent, in a sense. Come, you are Jeremy Sayers Munday, are you not?'

CHAPTER FORTY-TWO

'W HO?'

Webb shakes his finger at the prone man. 'It is too late for that lark, sir. Far too late. I have my man, do I not? I am sure we can find someone in this city who might identify you, even now; there will be plenty willing to come and have a look. How would you like that, sir, eh? You cannot have changed beyond all recognition. It is a miracle you weren't recognised at the trial.'

'Good God,' says Woodrow, his voice trembling, 'it has all been for nothing.'

'You said nothing throughout the trial,' says Webb. 'To spare your wife, yes? You thought, you hoped that you might be found innocent, despite it all? But surely you realised this was at the heart of it? If anyone has been hounding you, if anyone could go to such lengths, it is surely Jeremy Munday that they are after?'

'I was not sure,' says Woodrow wearily. 'At one time, I thought it was Siddons, toying with me, though I could not say why he should turn on me. I have been on the verge of madness, I swear it. Inspector, you believe me, don't you? That I did not kill them? Any of them?'

Bartleby gives Webb a discouraging glance, but it goes unnoticed.

'Sir, I have said it before, if you will only tell me the truth. The absolute truth is the only thing that can save you. Do you not wish to see your wife and child again?'

'I am doomed, whatever I tell you.'

'But a twenty-five-year-old fraud does not lead to the gallows, Mr. Woodrow. Or should I call you Munday?'

'Woodrow is my name. It was my mother's maiden name. Munday is dead.'

'Dead? After a fashion,' says Webb. 'But surely you do not wish to actually die, choking for breath, hearing you own neck snap, for something you have not done?'

Woodrow looks up and shakes his head.

'Then tell me everything, from the beginning.'

'It is a long time ago. Another life.'

'No, sir. It is the same one. Out with it.'

Woodrow sighs. 'It was my idea, Inspector, I confess that much. To feign my own death after the business fell apart. The chapel had fallen prey to its own success. I expect you know the story.'

'Well enough. You were disposing of the bodies a little too readily?'

'Good Lord, not me, Inspector. I had several men working for me. It was nothing that a thousand others had not done before me.'

'But not on such a scale?'

'No. They were discovered on Hackney Marsh. It was most unpleasant for all parties.'

'Not least the deceased and their families, I expect,' say Bartleby.

'Ignore my sergeant, sir. Carry on.'

'I knew there was a trial coming; I would be implicated; responsible. I could not face it; I could not face prison – ironic, sitting here, is it not? Siddons did not take much persuading – I took what money I had

337

left from the company and paid him off. He arranged
the whole thing.'

'And your wife?'

'Liza? Yes, I am still sorry for that.'

'She knew about your plan, though, surely?'

'No. Siddons found some excuse; told her it would
distress her too much to see the body, something of
that kind,' replies Woodrow. 'She was a good woman.
My only regret is that . . .'

'What?'

'I swore to myself that I would come back for her.'

'Ah, I see. And you never did.'

Woodrow hangs his head. 'No.'

'You abandoned your own wife?' asks Bartleby.

'I thought, when I was decent again, when I had
raised myself up. But there never was a right time.
Months went past so quickly – years—'

'Never mind your self-pity, man,' says Webb. 'Then
what?'

'Siddons arranged a position for me in Manchester.
Away from anyone who knew me. I did quite well for
him. I built up his firm there.'

'Until you returned to London.'

'Twenty years had passed, Inspector. As I say, it
seemed like another life. It seemed safe; the principal
investors in the chapel had all long since died. And I
had just met Melissa.'

'So you returned for love,' says Bartleby with deep
cynicism in his voice.

'Yes, Sergeant, I did,' says Woodrow, completely
serious.

'And you did quite well, too,' says Webb. 'A new
business, a fresh start, again.'

'Melissa's father died. There was an arrangement. It
was not wholly my doing.'

'Sir?'

338

Woodrow sighs. 'We knew he was ailing. Siddons brokered it; persuaded him that I was suitable for his daughter. That I might run the business after he died.'

'To what end? What was in it for Mr. Siddons?' asks Webb.

'That I paid him a share of the profits.'

'Charming.'

'It was just money, Inspector. But I have always loved Melissa, you must believe me.'

'And Betsy Carter?'

'A man's appetites are a different matter. Surely you are a man of the world, Webb? You must see the same thing every day, in your line of work.'

'Men and whores? Of course. But it is the dead ones that principally concern me, sir,' says Webb, dourly.

'I did not kill her, Inspector.'

'How much of what you said in court was true?'

'All of it, Inspector. Every detail.'

'You fought with Brown?'

Woodrow hesitates. 'No.'

'He's at it again, sir,' exclaims Bartleby. 'You surely aren't taken in by all this?'

'Quiet, Sergeant. No, you say? But your daughter saw you.'

'Miss Krout has persuaded her of it. Perhaps she saw somebody – it was not me, Inspector.'

'And you lied . . .'

'To spare her the court-room. The sight of me there. The last thing she ever saw of me.'

'How noble,' sneers Bartleby.

'Sergeant, you are not helping matters,' says Webb. 'Let us just suppose, sir, that you are right. A conspiracy against you. That a single guiding spirit is behind all of this – the same person who unearthed the grave – who killed Miss Carter and Miss Finch – Miss Price too – then Brown – all of it to implicate you. All of it calculated to see you hang. They might have exposed you – but no, it was all to make you suffer. Oh, and of course, we have Mr. Siddons for good measure. Who might it be?'

Woodrow clutches the side of the bed. 'Do you not think I have been racking my mind these past weeks?'

Webb throws his head back and sighs.

'If you want my opinion, sir,' says Bartleby in a low voice, 'he's stringing you along.'

Webb frowns. 'Wait a moment, sir. You said you did not come back for your wife. But you found her in the end, did you not? Just before she died; you visited the workhouse to see her?'

Woodrow shakes his head. 'The house? Good God. I thought she would not suffer so much. When did she die?'

'Wait a moment, sir. You claim you do not know anything of this? She died last year at St. Luke's infirmary.'

'Good God. No, I never . . . I could not bring myself to find her. What good would it have done?'

Webb looks startled. 'A man, claiming to be a lawyer on behalf of her family, visited her just before her death.'

'It was not me,' says Woodrow, catching Bartleby's disbelieving expression. 'Why on earth should I lie about it now?'

'Did she have much family?'

'Of course. There were two uncles, and a cousin . . . they would not have seen her go to ruin. I had thought they would support her – that was how I comforted myself, at least. They would not have let her go to the parish, unless . . .'

'They disowned her?' suggests Bartleby.

'But there were no brothers, sisters? And you had no children?'

340

'None, Inspector.'

'Then who would care so much, Woodrow, about your wife, to track her down? Or you, for that matter. Why should they give a false name? Why this sudden interest in Jeremy Munday? Why now?'

Woodrow looks blankly at Webb. 'It is all twenty-five years ago, Inspector. I have no idea.'

Webb, however, suddenly looks at the guard. 'Get us out of here.'

'In a hurry, sir?' asks the guard, getting slowly to his feet.

'What is it?' asks Woodrow, perplexed. Bartleby looks equally confused.

'I have another theory,' says Webb. 'And we had better hope I am wrong; for if I am right, I have no idea what the man will do next. Guard! What are you waiting for? Let us out! Sergeant – go and get a cab. We must end this tonight. There is no telling what risks we run, if we do not.'

'For heaven's sake, Inspector,' says Woodrow. 'What is it?'

'Later, sir,' says Webb, breathless, 'and only if I am proved right.'

And with that, the two policemen hurry through the open door. The guard steps in and slams it shut once again.

'Shame they've gone, ain't it, mate?' says he, as he turns the key in the lock. 'Better than a night at the Alhambra – I was just beginning to enjoy it.'

CHAPTER FORTY-THREE

'Mr. Langley, it is rather late to be calling,' says Annabel Krout, seated in the Woodrows' drawing-room.

'Yes, I rather suppose it is,' says Richard Langley, taking out his pocket-watch and looking at the time. 'I did not mean to startle you. You had not retired, I trust?'

'No, well, not quite. But Mrs. Woodrow is already asleep, so please be brief. What is it, sir?'

He takes a breath.

'There are certain things I must tell you, Miss Krout,' says Langley, a faint hint of perspiration upon his brow. 'Things of an intimate nature.'

'Sir,' replies Annabel, blushing, 'I do not think this is the time—'

'I have admired you since we became acquainted, Miss Krout. Your honesty, your obvious strength of character. I did not think that you or Lucinda would be in any danger. You must believe me. I did not see how far things had gone. I did not realise how he had insinuated himself into your affections.'

'Forgive me, sir,' says Annabel, frowning, 'I don't understand you at all. Who? What danger?'

'Moral danger, Miss Krout. It was quite plain to me when I saw him today, the manner in which he touched you. Come, did you not look into his eyes? Could you not see what was stirring there?'

'Mr. Langley, who do you—'

'Siddons, Miss Krout. If you had heard him speak, like I had, speak such filth about you and your sex, you would not have encouraged him, I am sure of that. But you should not have done it, all the same. It is a contagion, you see, Miss Krout. It spreads so easily, with men like that.'

'Mr. Langley,' replies Annabel, standing, 'I suppose you can only be drunk. I must ask you to leave.'

'No,' says Langley, grabbing Annabel's arm and pulling her roughly towards him. 'I cannot allow that. Not when I know that she can still be saved, at least.'

'What in . . . ?' exclaims Annabel Krout. But before she can protest any further, Richard Langley has twisted her arms behind her back and, holding her wrists firm with one hand, with the other forced his silk handkerchief into her open mouth, crushing it between her lips.

'Please,' says Langley, pulling loose his cravat, and roping it around Annabel Krout's wrists, 'don't struggle. It will be easier on all of us.'

Annabel Krout looks on in helpless disbelief as Langley tumbles her on to the Woodrows' sofa. 'Forgive the indignity, Miss Krout,' he continues, as he tears at her dress. 'No don't struggle. You make it worse.'

Annabel Krout, despite this admonition, kicks out. Langley, in turn, pulls an ivory-handled clasp knife from his pocket, flicking open the blade. He reaches forward, pushing down on Annabel's legs with one arm, bringing the knife close to her face with the other.

'Don't struggle, damn it,' mutters Langley, reaching out with the blade, so that it touches Annabel's neck, the metal pressing into her pale skin.

'Do you hear me?' says Langley, wrapping the torn material of Annabel Krout's skirt around her ankles, 'do not struggle and it will soon be over.'

━

Richard Langley tentatively opens the nursery door. Lucinda Woodrow stands in the shadows, dressed in her day-clothes.

'Are we playing a game?' she asks.

'I told you before, we are going on a holiday,' says Langley. 'A secret holiday.'

'Is Mama coming too?'

'No, she will come afterwards.'

'And Annabel?'

'No, I do not think so. Come.'

Lucinda Woodrow obeys, taking hold of Richard Langley's hand, and letting him lead her outside on to the landing and downstairs. They descend past the drawing-room, with Langley casting a furtive glance in the direction of the closed door, but nothing more. It is only when Lucinda Woodrow sets foot in the hall, that rapid footfalls can be heard, ascending the kitchen stairs. Langley instinctively pulls the little girl back towards him, clutching her in front of him. Lucinda squirms in discomfort, unhappy at the game's progress.

'Let the little girl go, sir,' says Decimus Webb, breathless and red-faced, appearing from downstairs, with Bartleby immediately behind him. Langley stares at the policemen in disbelief.

'Just let her go, sir. Then we can talk.'

'No,' says Langley. 'I have a blade.'

And, indeed, the glint of a knife suddenly shines in Langley's right hand, close to Lucinda Woodrow's neck. Webb steps back, making a placatory gesture.

'The game is up, sir. We know the whole story now,' says the sergeant.

'Have they won?' asks Lucinda, looking up at Langley, bemused.

Langley shakes his head. 'You must let us go. Both of us. I am the only one who can care for her.'

'Where is Miss Krout? Mrs. Woodrow?'

Langley says nothing.

'Melissa Woodrow knew nothing of his past,' says Webb. 'She had no part in anything that has befallen you.'

'Befallen me? Please. I have been extraordinarily lucky, Inspector. I have no complaints.'

'Then,' says Webb, 'what has all this been for? Some petty act of revenge?'

'Not petty, Inspector,' says Langley, glancing at Lucinda. 'Justice. For my mother's sake, if nothing else. For my sister.'

'Your mother was Eliza Munday? Your father, well, we must call him Jasper Woodrow now, I suppose.'

'I was born eight months after he "died", Inspector. An unlucky child to be born of a dead man; that's the superstition.'

'It does not sound a particularly fortuitous start.'

'I was given up and adopted, Inspector. I was raised by a decent Christian family. That was my good fortune. I had everything any boy might ask for.'

'You knew your own history?'

Langley shakes his head. 'I only found out after my parents died, last year.'

'Ah, of course. So you sought out your natural mother?'

'I found her too. Or, at least, what was left of her, in St. Luke's Workhouse.'

'She told you about your natural father?'

'She even gave me his picture. I wanted to know the truth but it was not a pleasant revelation, I admit. Except I was misinformed, even then.'

345

'Because your father was alive?'

Langley hesitates. 'I had some pity for him, when she told me about his death. For a man to take his own life – it is a sin – but I had pity. And when I looked at that wretched creature in the workhouse . . . Did you know, at the end, before they took her in, she had been digging for scraps in the dust-heaps by the canal, grubbing in the dirt for a living, if you can call it that? Did you know that?'

'Yes, I did.'

'I blamed him. I cursed my own father's name. But I consoled myself that the matter was in His hands; that he had long since been judged for his crime.'

'But you were proved wrong?'

'Quite by chance. Fate, I suppose. Or perhaps divine providence. I found myself working for him. I recognised the face, you see, from the photograph. But I was not sure of it, even then.'

'So you dug up the grave? You could have consulted the authorities; talked to the police.'

'I knew what would happen if I left it in your hands; he would not pay, but not half so much as he ought.'

Webb frowns. 'I confess, sir, I do not quite understand the rest. You planned it all?'

'I have no time for this, Inspector. You must let us pass. I warn you Inspector.'

'You will not harm your own sister.'

'You do not know what I am capable of, Inspector,' says Langley. He is about to say something more, when a noise behind him distracts his attention.

'I do,' says a dishevelled-looking Annabel Krout, as she swings a lead poker roundly into Richard Langley's arm, so forcefully that he instinctively releases Lucinda Woodrow.

'Quick, Sergeant!' exclaims Webb as he grabs the little girl to protect her. Bartleby obeys, jumping forward and tackling Langley, forcing him to the ground, holding him down with relative ease.

'I think you will have time now, sir,' says Webb.

—

'Is this to be my confession, then, Inspector?' asks Richard Langley, handcuffed, seated in the Woodrows' morning-room. 'In this parlour?'

'We have time until the van comes for you, sir. Miss Krout is trying to calm down Lucinda. My sergeant is keeping an eye on Mrs. Woodrow.'

'Miss Krout is a remarkable woman; my arm still aches. I fear she has broken something.'

'You should have worked on those knots a little more,' suggests Webb, with a distinct lack of sympathy. 'I am surprised, frankly, that you did not despatch her like the rest.'

Langley looks surprised at the suggestion. 'She is an innocent, Inspector. Misguided, but innocent. Shouldn't you be taking notes?'

'There will be enough time for that. Just tell me the facts, if you care to.'

'Very well. You may as well hear it, though you seem to have guessed a good deal. I took the commission for the new Mourning Warehouse on a friend's recommendation. But it was not long before I realised "Jasper Woodrow" was . . . forgive me, it sickens me to call him my father. At first, of course, it was merely an awful suspicion; there were a few clues, a few things he said when drunk – and he is often inebriated, I assure you – but nothing certain. I had to be sure, and so I went to Abney Park. When I found the grave was empty, I knew the truth.'

'That still explains very little.'

'I cannot describe my anger, Inspector. It blazed inside me. I doubt you can comprehend it. Had you seen my mother in that place, the state of her, perhaps you would understand. She was once a decent woman; I am sure of that. I have half-formed memories of . . . well, I determined to pay him back, for every indignity he heaped upon her, for every night she went without food, for every time she gave herself up to . . . for his cowardice. So I wormed my way into his good graces; I did not merely work for him but played up to him; I went drinking with him, I boasted of money, of investments. He, in turn, told me all about his little vices, his tame whore at Knight's, his favourite gambling dens. I learnt a good deal.'

'But you did not approve?'

'The man is the devil incarnate, Inspector. You must see that?'

'So you decided to punish him?'

'No, I was not that ambitious, not at first. I decided to do away with him. But I wanted to expose him, too. Then it came to me – Knight's Hotel. What better place for such a specimen to be displayed, eh? It could not be hushed up; the world would see his true character.'

'You even prepared an epitaph.'

'More a lesson, really. "He uncovers deep things out of darkness, And brings the shadow of death to light." Apt, was it not?'

'And did one of the girls help you?'

Langley nods. 'Annie Finch. I made "pals" with Annie. I even told her I was a detective; that I was working for Mrs. Woodrow. Wanted to catch the old man *in flagrante* for the divorce. She had had some spat with the other girl, Betsy, Woodrow's favourite. It was quite easy to accomplish.'

'You got her to drug their drinks?'

'Not quite. I knew Woodrow's routine. He told me, in glorious detail, when I got him drunk. Revolting; it made me quite sick to the stomach. Still. I made sure I was with Betsy Carter myself before he was due to see her. I knew they would share a drink together after he had done with her. A few drops of laudanum into the brandy. I had tested it on myself the previous night.'

'Ah, I see. Then you returned later?'

'Annie let me in, through the back door. She thought it was a marvellous adventure.'

'But then she became redundant, and so you simply killed her?'

'What kind of madman do you take me for, Inspector? She saw what I was up to; saw the knife. I had to silence her, quickly.'

'You smothered her?'

'I simply wished to keep her quiet. But she struggled, you see?'

'I see. Continue.'

'I had intended to kill him outright. I went into the room, saw him slumbering there. It was not pity that stayed my hand, I assure you. Merely the thought he would die in ignorance of being found out; that he would not suffer enough. I changed my mind; I had an idea.'

'So you killed Betsy Carter in cold blood?'

'She was a fool to love such a man.'

'But she was quite innocent of any crime.'

'Innocent? Hardly. She was soiled already, Inspector. She was never an innocent. She served her purpose. I merely brought her closer to the judgment we all must face. That is all.'

'Your "idea" was that Woodrow would wake up next to a corpse – that he would be charged with murder?'

'He had as good as condemned my mother to a slow death. I wanted to see his face when they pronounced him guilty. I did see it today – it was rather satisfying.'

'Did you know about his sleep-walking?'

'No. That was simply a fortunate coincidence. Tell me, did he actually believe he had done it himself?'

'Half-believed it, perhaps.'

Langley merely smiles.

'But Brown got in your way, in some fashion?'

'I left a clue for you at Knight's, Inspector. A business-card from the Warehouse. It puzzled me how you had not found it. But then I saw Brown by the canal, it fell into place. He had removed it himself; he hoped to gain by it, to blackmail Woodrow like his other victims – I had heard something of his character from Annie, you see. And, of course, the wretched man saw me too, that night. He did not quite understand the situation, mind you. I had to explain it to him.'

'I think you made yourself pretty clear. You like leaving clues, don't you, sir? What about the cuffs we found at the house? Whose blood is on them?'

'Why, the girl at the Casino, of course. Price.'

'And how did they get here?'

'Simple enough. I excused myself during our little dinner party.'

Webb sighs. 'I see. And what of Catherine Price? Why did you do it?'

'Another whore. I thought I should try again, Inspector. I thought I could not make it any plainer for you.'

Webb shakes his head. 'No, sir. I don't think so. Brown was a matter of necessity for you. But I think you took some perverted pleasure from despatching these poor women.'

'They were a means to serve an end, Inspector. In death as in life.'

'And Siddons? It was today, outside the court, wasn't it?'

350

'I knew what he had planned for Miss Krout, Inspector. And I feared for Lucinda. I knew precisely what sort of man he was.'

'You think so? Still, a cruel death for an old man.'

'If you say so.'

'And so we come to Lucinda Woodrow,' says Webb. 'Your sister.'

'I saw how her father treated her; and everyone else. I planned to give her a new start, away from all this filth and corruption. Surely you can understand that?'

'She belongs with her mother and father. In fact, I am rather surprised you let Mrs. Woodrow live. I suppose we must be grateful for small mercies.'

'I thought she had suffered enough. In truth, Inspector, she reminds me a good deal of my natural mother. I hoped to spare her my mother's fate.'

'And you are a good judge, sir, of who lives or dies?'

Langley shrugs. Then he looks up. 'Will they release him now?'

'There are other matters to settle; in time, yes, I should expect so.'

'At least everyone will know him for what he is; at least he will live with that over him.'

'And how do you think they will remember you, Langley?'

Any answer is interrupted by Bartleby knocking on the door.

'The van's here, sir.'

'Very good. Take him to the G Division station house, Sergeant. It will be convenient for Hanson in the morning. Doubtless he will want to have a little chat.'

Langley looks back at Webb as Bartleby moves him off his chair.

'Tell Miss Krout, will you, Inspector? Tell her that I am sorry for her part in all of this, and that, if she can forgive me, I should like to speak with her.'

CHAPTER FORTY-FOUR

'My mother? My real mother? Yes, I have some memories of her before she gave me up. When I was a child, growing up in St. John's Wood in that great house, I used to think they were only dreams. But I had them again and again. A woman sitting, dressed in black, always black, in the corner of a wretched cold room, a tiny closet of a room with a solitary bed, watching me, smiling at me, even as she shivered. It was her. I am sure of it.

'Do you know what else I would dream? That I was locked outside that little room whilst she took men inside. I used to have that dream a good deal, different faces, different men. I did not know what it meant; not at the time. What a fine widowhood, eh? You know, even now, I particularly recall the sound of the bolt being drawn.'

Langley looks away and smiles.

'Or perhaps it is just my current situation that calls it to mind?'

Annabel Krout puts down her note-book and looks at Richard Langley through the wire mesh that separates them.

'It is not too late to make your peace with God.'

Langley shakes his head, nodding at some movement in the distance. 'I made my peace long ago. The warder is coming down the corridor. I think this must be your last visit. I know what day it is tomorrow.'

Annabel pauses, about to say something more, when Langley signals for her to keep silent.

'No more. They will bury me in the yard with the others. I have already seen the spot – they show it to you on the way to the Bailey. Give Lucy my love; I rather fear for her, you know.'

'Mr. Langley. Richard, please . . .'

'I am in the same cell as my father was, do you know that? Put that in your article, Miss Krout. It seems quite apt, somehow, eh? I am sure you will find a publisher.'

Langley motions to the warder behind him. Before Annabel Krout can speak, he is taken back, through the iron-barred door, into the black corridor that leads to his cell.

EPILOGUE

ANNABEL KROUT STANDS in the Golden Gallery of St.
Paul's, helping Lucy Woodrow to look over the
balcony, and see the bird's-eye view of the capital,
spread before them without the obstruction of the
railings. Yet, athough it is free of fog, the sky is still
liberally smeared with dirty smudges of smoke, seep-
ing from countless chimneys. Only the metropolitan
churches are quite visible, however, dozens of steeples
and towers pointing to the heavens whilst, in the
distance, the royal parks resemble faint green islands,
set in a swirling sea of dust. The smoke is worst along
the river, the product of the factories that line the
southern bank of the Thames, generating a thick haze,
like dirty muslin, draped over the entire Surrey shore.
In some parts it is difficult to make out where the city
ends and the heavens begin.

Lucy Woodrow leans forward, peering down at the
minute carts, cabs and omnibuses streaming along
Ludgate Hill.

'Can I go round again?' she asks.

Annabel nods, lifts her down and lets the little girl
walk round the Gallery on her own for the third time.
She follows behind, keeping a watch on her young
charge, not noticing the gentleman coming up the
stairs.

'Miss Krout,' says a familiar voice.

'Gracious! Inspector, you startled me. What on earth are you doing here?'

'Your maid told me where to find you. I thought I would come and see how you were. I saw Mrs. Woodrow downstairs.'

'She says she does not much like heights. I thought I would bring Lucinda up here.'

'You can see Newgate from here, you know.'

'I have seen it.'

'I am sure he did not suffer. You did your best.'

'I hope he sought forgiveness at the end. Have you heard? Did he say anything?'

'Not a word, Miss. I'm sorry. How is the little girl?'

'She seems well enough. You know, I blame myself, Inspector.'

'For what?' asks Webb.

'If I had not persuaded her that she saw her father fighting with . . . well, things might have gone differently.'

'It is not your fault, Miss Krout. You had everyone's best interests at heart. There is little that we could have done.'

'Mr. Woodrow might have been hanged, Inspector. Lord knows his faults are legion . . .'

'You show considerable restraint in your choice of words, Miss. Still I don't think we can hold him much longer. I can't see the Commissioner deciding to charge him over the Eloi Chapel affair, not now; we don't have much in the way of evidence. And, to be frank, I don't think they want to see him in court again, if they can avoid it. The whole thing makes us look rather foolish. I've told Mrs. Woodrow she may expect him home in a week or two.'

'But, don't you see? I might have deprived Melissa of her husband, Lucy of her father.'

'That would have been as much his doing as yours. Neither you nor the little girl could have known the truth. In any case, I gather there is some talk of emigration, a fresh start?'

'I think there is no other hope for them, Inspector. Why, the marriage is not even legal. They must begin anew somewhere. I've asked my father if he might help.'

'Is, ah, Lucinda not with you?' asks Webb.

'Oh, now where has she got to?'

———

Lucinda Woodrow looks back to see her cousin engaged in conversation. Peering through the railings of the balcony, she takes a moment to look down at the granite walls of Newgate Prison, and the block-like buildings within.

'Lucinda!' calls Annabel Krout. 'Come back now.'

Lucinda Woodrow grudgingly walks back towards Annabel Krout and Webb. The latter kneels down in front of her.

'Your father may be home soon, Miss,' says Webb.

Lucinda Woodrow frowns.